Year's Best
Weird Fiction

VOLUME FIVE

Also by Robert Shearman

Also by Michael Kelly

Year's Best
Weird Fiction

VOLUME FIVE

Guest Editor

ROBERT SHEARMAN

Series Editor

MICHAEL KELLY

UNDERTOW PUBLICATIONS

CONTENTS

v

Michael Kelly

Foreword

Welcome to the fifth, and final, volume of *THE Year's Best Weird Fiction*!

Indeed, this will be the final volume of this anthology series. When I started the series, I told myself I would give it five volumes, then reassess. There are many underlying reasons as to why I am shuttering the series, but the main factor is simply the lack of sales. Not enough people are buying the books to keep it viable. In terms of time and money, it is an extremely costly book to assemble. And, as publisher and series editor, I bear all the costs myself.

It would be fair to say that I am sad and disappointed at this development. The series, to me, was unique in that each volume had a different guest editor, thus ensuring the book was fresh and distinctive each year. In my opinion, no other genre 'Year's Best' anthology was as broad and diverse in range and scope. The *Year's Best Weird Fiction* rarely had any overlap with the other anthologies. In fact, I felt it did an admirable job of filling in the gaps of the other 'Year's Best' anthologies with stories that fell between genre cracks. Which was part of our mandate. I did make numerous attempts at placing the series at another publishing house, and there was little to no interest. 'Best Of' fatigue, I suppose.

For the past five years the *Year's Best Weird Fiction* has unearthed a number of exceptionable and inimitable voices, redefining and broadening genre distinctions and labels, bringing a diverse new group to the forefront of speculative fiction. But what *exactly* is Weird Fiction? It's something I've addressed in the previous volumes, to be sure. And that's part of the problem. It's not easily defined, yet we still attempt to slot it into particular genre niches. Weird fiction, *in my opinion*, has a much broader scope than that. And, as with anything that is trending or is "hot," Weird Fiction (or weird fiction), has been co-opted. Ask any spec-fic writer what they write these days and they'll answer, 'weird fiction.' Unfortunately, the term is becoming redundant. Very few are strictly writing horror, or fantasy, or slipstream, or science fiction. And while *I* believe that weird fiction is a genre unto itself that can and does encompass other genres, a genre that does deserve its own standalone 'Year's Best' volume, the lines have become blurry and there does not appear to be a market for the continuation of the *Year's Best Weird Fiction*.

I am very proud of all 5 volumes. They were a lot of hard work, but they were worth it. Robert Shearman has done an exceptional job assembling this final volume, and it's a fitting coda to the series. I can think of no finer guest editor to helm this last volume in the series. Thank you Rob for your dedication, hard work, and friendship.

Thanks are due, as well, to all the previous guest editors—Laird Barron, Kathe Koja, Simon Strantzas, and Helen Marshall—for not only their tireless efforts, but also for their belief in the series, and the concept. You've each made an indelible mark on the field, and I thank you.

Thank you, the readers, for allowing us the privilege to sit on your bookshelves and to take up some of your precious, hard-earned time and money. I have appreciated all your notes, comments, and advice.

Lastly, thanks to the Undertow Publications staff and my family for trusting in me and the books.

It's been a fun ride. Time for a new adventure.

—Michael Kelly
Pickering, Canada
July 23, 2018

ROBERT SHEARMAN

Introduction

WHEN I WAS A LITTLE BOY, I READ A SHORT STORY that has haunted me to this day. I found it disconcerting on a level I had never really considered before, and it's no exaggeration to say that it helped determine my choice to be a writer, and the sort of stuff I'd choose to write. I found it in a magazine of my mother's, one of those old-fashioned things full of beauty tips and cookery suggestions and whatnot, and it wasn't very long, maybe only a couple of thousand words? And it came with pictures, just like the stories I read in books for my own age, and that's probably what drew me in.

This is, roughly, what it was about.

It is the story of a woman. I dare say she has a name, but I don't remember what it is, and the pictures take such pains to make her seem as blandly generic as possible, she is Everywoman. Everywoman has a dilemma. Her husband has called from work to tell her that he is bringing some of his colleagues home that night to dinner. Every-woman is in a panic, because she looks in the mirror, and her hair is a disgrace. She calls her local hairdresser to make an emergency

appointment, but they're all booked up. So she has to venture all
the way to the other side of town to entrust her locks to an entirely
unproven stylist. She's wary of the new stylist's methods, and at several
points during the operation she wants to call the whole thing to a
halt, but Everywoman is very brave and she toughs it out. And that
bravery pays off; it turns out well; the hairdo is spectacular. But here's
an obstacle. As she leaves the shop and begins her long journey back
home the clouds open and there's a downpour. Everywoman tries her
best to keep dry, but it's a disaster—her glorious new hair is ruined.
Her husband will be so disappointed in her; these people coming to
dinner are important!

Yet there's a twist. When the guests arrive, they all bring their wives.
And the wives have all been caught in the same downpour, and their
hair has been ruined too. Much hilarity ensues, and that breaks the
ice, and it ensures the success of the whole party. The end.

I'd love to pretend it was the gender politics that bothered me, but
to be fair, I was a kid. What troubled me was the lack of consequence.
I asked my mother, but what happens next? Are there any other stories
featuring this woman with the hairdo? No, of course not. It's just a
funny little story, what's the problem? It's just a funny little story, and
it's *her* funny little story, and it's the only funny little story she'll ever
get. This is a character that has been brought to life, and for this sole
purpose only—for needing to get her hair done. This is the only thing
that ever happened to her that was worth recording, this anecdote is
the single defining moment of her entire life.

I couldn't articulate it properly at the time, but to me that went
beyond unconscious satire. That bordered upon the genuinely surreal. And from that point on I became almost too aware that the
people I met, my teachers at school, the friends of my parents, my
parents themselves, may all one day be summed up in a couple of
thousand words doing something achingly trivial. (And years later,
as I sat through the funerals of both my parents, and I heard a vicar
who had never met either of them give inaccurate précis of their lives,
I felt much the same thing.) Other stories I read were so much more
normal in comparison. Yes, that whole episode with Jack and his
magic beans had odd things about it, but it was that very obvious

oddness that, paradoxically enough, made it seem strangely under-
standable and safe. I could easily see *why* someone had bothered to
write it down in the first place. If our Everywoman had ever had an
adventure with a giant up a beanstalk that's the tale of hers we'd be
reading—instead, that madcap day at the hairdresser's was the best it
would ever get.

I am not, of course, suggesting that 'The Mysterious Adventures of
Hairdo Woman' was a genuine tale of the Weird. But it opened up a
door to me to the uncanny power of fiction to distort reality—and
suggests also why I think the short story is Weird's natural voice. It
isn't necessarily the action of the tale that is off balance, it's the bizarre
emphasis placed upon that action. Because for all the characters in
this volume too, these tales are the limits of their existence. These are
the only moments of significance they will ever get, and it's a reader
even tacitly knowing this which gives their narratives such strange
dissonance. You feel that a lead character in a novel, no matter what
he or she is put through, is at least being granted the dignity of a full
length manuscript. The minutiae don't need to be examined in such
detail—there are more important incidents to attract the attention of
the reader.

But in the short story, the minutiae are often all we get. Every
hanging thread of conversation, every little movement—there has
to be a *reason* the writer bothered to include it. We stare at these
moments a little longer than we're used to, and they get stretched and
distorted. And it's within these minutiae that it seems to me the whole
world gets shuffled off its axis.

Put something familiar under the magnifying glass and watch
it become new and unrecognisable. And we turn up the resolution
tighter, then tighter still—until, at last, the lens cracks. The thousand and one images your brain takes in and discards in everyday life
suddenly have new meanings, subtle hints at other stories that are
fathomless and unknowable. There must be a reason why the writer
shines a light on the things we train ourselves to see as irrelevant. Why
does the woman alone on the beach dig so intently in the sand? Why
in the heatwave won't that old man take off his overcoat? And why,
dear God, why, in this huge crowd, is only the baby smiling?

There's always debate about why it is the short story is considered as so less commercial than the novel. But the answer, surely, is apparent: the novel is a reassuring form, and the short story is not. Even if the subject matter of a novel is designed to provoke unease, its structure isn't—the way that, by and large, it promises you a beginning, a middle and an end, and usually in that order, and will find the space in the luxury of its length to give definite clarity and meaning into the bargain. The short story, in contrast, never allows the reader to relax, never *wants* the reader to relax, and all the time you're reading one you're asking yourself at what point it might betray you. If a novel is a trustworthy tour guide, a short story is the unauthorised taxi driver who will take you into the darkness far from where you wanted to go and beat you up. Short stories are nasty, paranoid little things—and the best of them distort the minutiae of what you trust so acutely that you're left reeling at the implications outside their own confines.

I think it's why the Weird leans so often towards horror, although its eagerness to wrongfoot the reader is why it's such a great comic form as well. The stories gathered in this collection are the weirdest I could find. Some of them are deliberately written to be horror—and others feel like jokes that go profoundly, savagely, wrong. All of them made me feel just that little bit more paranoid, and less certain about the rules that pretend to govern our world, and they made me excited about the wild potential that the weird short story offers. (All of them, too, are stories that I wish I had the wit or insight to have written myself, but that's my own problem—I will say, though, I do not offer them to you with love but with seething jealousy.) I want to offer a huge thank you to all the authors who've let themselves be a movement in this paranoid symphony.

And I want to thank Michael Kelly too. For the past four years the annual edition of Year's Best Weird Fiction has been a highlight of my reading year, and his dedication to the form has inspired me and kept me writing whenever I was going adrift. One of the great joys of the Weird is that there is no single definition of what it is—you've just read mine, but it runs counter to four other wonderful guest editors who have come before me and whose own choices of story have challenged me and enthralled me. I can't tell you how genuinely bereft I felt to discover that this will be the last volume—our community will be so much poorer without the series—but also how honoured and lucky I feel that I was invited to contribute my own take on it. The Weird itself, of course, will go on, in all its fractured glory.

And thanks too, to the writer of Hairdo Woman, whomever he or she may have been.

Year's Best
Weird Fiction

VOLUME FIVE

KURT FAWVER

The Convexity of Our Youth

A DISCLAIMER

THE CHILDREN OF BURKE'S POINT ELEMENTARY can't be blamed. When the orange ball rolled onto their playground, they couldn't have known what it was. We didn't discuss the orange ball with them, didn't explain to them its importance, its danger. We didn't even tell them it existed, though some of them had undoubtedly heard vague rumors about it from sadistic older siblings and precocious cousins with little parental supervision. We wanted to turn a blind eye to the orange ball, hoping that what we didn't acknowledge couldn't touch our lives. If we didn't speak of it then surely it would have no reason to seek us out; it would roll past our town and work its horrors somewhere else, somewhere far away. Though it might bounce against the concavities of our skulls, tinting every thought orange, orange, orange, we feared to let its name roll off our tongues. We believed in the prophylactic power of ignorance, that if we provided no magnetic pole of recognition, the ball's compass would never point in our direction. So the children of Burke's Point Elementary—our children—couldn't have guessed that when the orange ball spun its way onto their blacktop and they began kicking it back and forth, shoes slapping rubber, rubber throwing up pebbles and dust, laughter spilling over the schoolyard as the ball seemed to zig and zag of its own volition, it would, for all intents and purposes, kill them all.

A BACKGROUND

Our town is, in many ways, like any other town. Imagine parallel lines of artisan boutiques running beside a brick-laden boulevard that sprawls outward, onto a few dozen crosshatched streets along which stand sentinel rows of townhomes and condos. Beyond the townhomes and condos, imagine that the streets gain curvature and turn to winding roads that slide by cozy one-story, two-story, and three-story homes replete with manicured yards and picket fences and two-car garages. And on the fringes of it all, where the roads meet the infinite progress and regress of the interstate highway, imagine the dense modern fortifications of commerce—the strip malls and chain stores and supermarkets and fast food parlors and gas stations and motels and casual family eateries all vying for patronage. Our town is, in this, like any other town: the fruition of some sort of dream and the image of some sort of beauty, though neither may be ours.

Just as is the case with our parents and grandparents, most of us have lived here our entire lives, with, perhaps, a brief four-year foray to a college or a university within driving distance during our early adulthood. Occasionally we venture outward, to other towns, other cities, other regions of the world where people speak with intonations different from ours and wear clothes designed more for function than for form, but, though we may be charmed or fascinated or surprised by those other places, we are, inevitably, neither drawn away from our town for long nor tempted to remain elsewhere. We are tethered to our town by a dull, soothing comfort and, with the lengths of our tethers, have woven complex webs of existence to further secure ourselves here.

Life is, you might say, easy for us. We have no great wealth but also no real poverty, no overwhelming love for our neighbors but also no outstanding hatreds. We are not a people who leave our doors unlocked throughout the night, but neither are we a people who suffer from any crimes worse than petty theft and vandalism. We have achieved a level of contentment and stasis in which our primary worry is losing our contentment and stasis. Thus it is that everything we do, every decision we make, every social, cultural, fiscal, philosophical, theological, and political step we take as adults, as citizens, and as parents is designed to uphold the most sacrosanct of our shared values: security.

A SYMPTOM

After the orange ball had been spotted on the elementary school playground by an astute second-grade teacher, the sixteen boys and girls involved with its play were rushed to a secure hospital facility where, mere hours later, the symptoms of contact began to manifest. We knew what to expect as we huddled by the side of our children's beds. First came the uncontrollable leg spasms that, had the children been upright, would have sent them sprinting into the blustery night at ten or fifteen or however many miles per hour their muscles and ligaments could carry them before completely shearing away from bone or snapping apart. Impervious to muscle relaxants, the spasms lasted for several grueling hours during which our children alternately laughed and cried, sang unfamiliar songs and shouted words we'd never taught them. As they sweated through their bedsheets, we sweated through our clothes, waiting for a resolution that we'd fooled ourselves into believing might arrive.

Once the spasms had run their full course, metabolic exhaustion set in and extreme cramping stole over our children's tender bodies from head to toe. Despite the best efforts of doctors and nurses to rehydrate our children and replenish their depleted electrolytes, chorales of anguish blared from the isolation ward, driving us to near madness with their fiery accusation of our universal impotence. If hell has an anthem, truly we believe it must be the ululation of one's children in hysterical, unending pain.

As our babies screamed and thrashed through a hurricane of tears, we wrung our hands and tore at our hair and prayed to our myriad deities for succor and mercy. We discovered, however, that succor and mercy were in short supply, even for us, even for our town, which we had always assumed must exist as a tiny sparkle in the corner of our gods' eyes. Indeed, only when the doctors pumped the children full of opiate pain killers—so many, in fact, that we feared coma must be near—did the cries subside and our beloved quietus regain temporary control of our lives. Then, only then, with our children in deep chemical slumber, did we again feel safe.

Of course, this was only the first symptom of the ball's infection and, as we understood it, the least severe. There would be two more symptoms yet to come, two more symptoms for which none of us could be properly prepared, unimaginable as they were.

Our peace was, in the end, a fragile lie.

A REALIZATION

We initially learned of the orange ball seven years ago. Rumors of the ball's existence had been spreading across the internet for months prior to our localized revelation, but this spotty information was relegated to fringe news sites, shared social media posts, and obscure discussion forums—none of which registered on our tightly focused radar. We didn't read to the margins of our world; we didn't feel that we needed to. The margins were for those people too unmotivated or too deviant to find their way to a more stable center. Surely, we believed, our town and our lives were near the center of whatever vast page reality had been impressed upon. Thirty minutes curled up with the local nightly news on television, an occasional foray across the main page of a cable news network's website, a glance at a nationally distributed magazine: these were the energies we deemed it necessary to expend in order to remain informed citizens of greater, polished society. So while the ball rolled on and families in other communities—dust-ridden rural locales and bullet-populated inner city neighborhoods, mostly—dealt with its aftermath and expressed their despondency, their fear, and their anger through peripheral channels, we went about our days in relative peace and naiveté.

It wasn't until the ball passed through a town much like ours, a town sealed tight in its onion-layers of self-satisfaction and supposed normalcy, a town with the anywhere name of "Vernonville," that the mainstream media followed its bounce. In Vernonville, cameras captured grim men in pressed, button-down shirts and sensible khaki pants, quavering women with tasteful makeup in smart, monochrome wrap dresses, and tearful children in all manner of character-emblazoned shirts, pants, and shoes. These were a safe people, an ordinary people, a people with enough time and money and respect for the prescribed social order to arrive for interviews entirely photogenic, even in the face of crisis. We worried over the people of Vernonville, because, in truth, what the cameras in that quaint suburban town captured was nothing less than ourselves, doubled at another point in space.

To the media, the people of Vernonville spoke of an inexplicable childhood illness run rampant in their town, of an orange ball with which the stricken youths had played. They spoke of their outrage, their sadness, their memories, their lack of understanding. They asked for prayers and protection and they insisted that the Centers for Disease Control and the World Health Organization investigate the disease, for, surely, disease it had to be that their children had contracted. To pacify the people of Vernonville, the CDC and WHO did, indeed, finally launch an investigation, but, ultimately, neither found evidence of a pathogen or a wicked foreign invader endlessly multiplying in the blood of the town's children. The lone key fact the doctors and scientists at the CDC and WHO discovered—or what they knew all along, more likely—was that a series of past incidents in other locations mirrored the situation in Vernonville. All the rural nowheres and the urban centers that had cried out for the selfsame recognition and investigation that Vernonville received were at last acknowledged, if only as fragments of a greater pattern and decimals in a ledger.

The situation in Vernonville, combined with the newly revealed information that the incident was not isolated and that the orange ball had spread a sickness to children elsewhere, sent us into a low-boiling panic. We began to discuss the ball at work, at PTA meetings, at the gym, in our bedrooms well after midnight—anywhere that our children wouldn't hear. We drove by our homes and our children's schools during our lunch breaks, just to spot check for orange balls that might be lolling about outside. We threw into the garbage any orange balls that our children or our pets possessed and bought them shiny new blue or green ones for their enjoyment. Even the recreational basketball league at our local YMCA switched from traditional orange and black balls to red, white, and blue Team USA balls.

As days passed, our fear did not abate, but, instead, settled into our routines. We formed a community watch group to buy all the orange balls in the all the stores in town and burn them in pre-selected dumpsters; we gathered up orange traffic cones and hurled them into gutters wherever we passed them; if we were sports fans, we stopped following the NBA and NCAA basketball altogether. We even purchased oranges at the grocery store with less frequency. And yet, despite all our activism, we spoke of the ball less and less, almost as if we didn't give it second thought, almost as if it was something we'd never heard of, almost as if it didn't even exist.

A SECOND SYMPTOM

After our children's cramps unknotted and melted away, the second symptom began to manifest. Its appearance could have been mistaken for an unusual rash or an off-color bout of jaundice, but we knew better. The circular, orange blotches that crept over our children's skin had no dermatological precedent except in the history of the towns the ball had visited.

For many of us, this was the most difficult stage of the illness. Though our sons and daughters remained firmly ensconced in cradles of opiates so as to not feel the flesh-peeling inflammation that the children of Vernonville had, we found the mere presence of their infected bodies intolerable. We sat by their beds with our faces turned away, unable to watch as the blotches spread and joined with one another, forming Rorschach patterns we feared to interpret for what they might reveal about ourselves. We were asked by doctors and nurses to comfort our children, to hold their hands and wipe their chins as saliva leaked from their lips, but we could not bring ourselves to touch them. With every new sore, with every new patch of smooth, glistening orange, they drifted from us, becoming less a part of us and more a part of the ball. Theirs was a future we could not countenance, let alone accept.

In the hallways and common areas of the secure facility, we pounded vending machines with our fists though we were not seeking refreshment and we stared into bathroom mirrors for hours though we were not preening. In the facility's lobby, we gave interviews to assembled reporters, our faces properly stoic, our words sufficiently labored. In the facility's parking lot, well-meaning friends and family lit bonfires and invited us to stoke the flames with balls of diverse size and color, balls that they had purchased for precisely that therapeutic kindling purpose. And all the while, as we sulked about the facility in our bubbles of distraction, our children lay in their rooms, alone, transmuting.

The bravest among us eventually worked up the courage to return to our ailing offspring. We pulled up chairs beside the hospital beds and, tears welling at the corners of our eyes, whispered unheard endearments to our sons and daughters while stroking their swollen pumpkin-hued foreheads. Even for those of us with iron resolve, however, the caresses did not last long. We pulled away our fingers and wiped them on our pants, our dresses. We ran to the nearest bathroom and scrubbed our hands under scalding water, so desperate were we to remove the sensation of our children's rashes against our flesh. For what we touched when we stroked their heads was not soft, pliable skin, but a hard, dense surface that barely yielded to the pressure of our fingertips. Where once had been ridges and divots and tiny, perfectly formed imperfections was now an expanse of smooth, featureless orange. Doctors who had biopsied the rashes of children in other towns had long ago determined the nature of this impossible flesh. It was a substance the world knew well, a substance that had no place in human biology, and we shuddered to witness it merging with our children, becoming our children, our children becoming it.

Brave or not, we fled into flasks, into puffs of cigarette smoke, into passionless sex in the hospital bathrooms. We spent our last remaining energies in pursuit of merciful distraction. We refused to contemplate the truth of the situation, and the truth was this: by the time the second symptom had run its course, our children would no longer be copies of ourselves, but products of forces far beyond our control. By the time the second symptom had run its course, our children would be, effectively, rubberized.

A REFERENDUM

When, a few months after Vernonville, the orange ball appeared in another town like ours and the death toll ticked higher in that small burgh than it had in any of the previous places the ball had infected, we experienced a surge in anxiety unlike any we'd known before. Every bounce of a kickball and spin of a bowling ball and hollow plink of a ping-pong ball against a table sent us into cold sweats and caused us to glance over our shoulders to make sure nothing was rolling up behind us. Accident rates in town doubled. 9-1-1 calls reporting suspicious incidents tripled. We became a study in paranoia. So, in conjunction with the PTA and several local religious groups, our mayor called a meeting to discuss "the ball dilemma" and invited all concerned adults from the community to attend. Minors—even teenagers who understood the issue at hand—were strictly prohibited from entering the town hall during the meeting due to the nature of the subject matter.

On the evening of the "ball dilemma" discussion, seating at the town hall was elbow to elbow and hip to hip. It seemed that every person in town over the age of eighteen had come to listen, if not participate. We all wanted resolution. We wanted the mayor or the president of the PTA or a local minister or rabbi or imam to give us instruction, to tell us that our town would be safe if we simply followed an enumerated plan with easily accomplished steps. Instead, we were faced with a coterie of leaders who, through PowerPoint slides and Excel spreadsheets, explained that no feasible protection was possible. We couldn't wall off the town from the rest of the world—though some of us would have surely felt more at ease behind medieval battlements—nor could we afford a video surveillance system for the town's perimeter. We couldn't track the ball's movements—not even the Department of Homeland Security had been able to manage that feat yet, or so it claimed—nor did we have the resources to set up an official ball patrol. We couldn't even print informational posters because we had no information to convey that might have been of use in case of the ball's appearance. For all intents and purposes, we lacked any meaningful choice of action.

It was, therefore, not surprising that when the presentations ended and the mayor opened the floor for questions, the town hall broke into a silence reserved for sepulchers. We dared not speak or move, as speaking and moving would imply that the meeting was truly nearing its conclusion, that our authorities had failed us and left us without plan or direction. The notion of confronting such a limbo we could not abide. So we sat and waited in the anticipation of one last key address or instructional video. Our leaders fidgeted, unsure of the silence's tenor. We held our breaths, unsure of the question to ask. And, somewhere, the ball kept bouncing, entirely sure we could not stop it.

Finally, after the tension had grown so sharp it could slice through the hall's concrete walls, one of us—Marcus Jefferson, the proprietor of our town's used bookstore—stood and asked the question that would govern our lives for years to come.

"If you don't have a plan to deal with it," he said, "and we can't prevent it from happening, then why are we even talking about it?"

The question provoked no answers from our leaders, but it did raise applause and echoes.

Other voices in the crowd, our voices, yelled at the stage, asking "Why? Why? Why do we need to discuss it? Why should we even bring it up?"

The mayor responded the only way she could. She asked us what we wanted to do about "the ball problem." She asked what our democratic solution might be.

Again we slid into silence. We'd never imagined the decision might fall to us. We had no idea how to prevent the ball's coming; we had no special information, no learned insight. We only knew that we were frightened. So when Jessica Cadiz—a manager at one of our town's three banks—stood and said, "Let's try to ignore it. Let's imagine it doesn't exist. Let's push it away as best we can. Let's strike it from our vocabularies and close the browser windows when we see stories about it online and turn off the tvs if newscasters start yammering on about it. And, for the love of God, let's never allow the kids to know what it is, to know that it's out there. At least not until they're older," we all understood why.

The applause for Cadiz's suggestion shook the floor and rattled the windows. A chant of "ignore it, ignore it, ignore it" erupted from the crowd. We, the people, had spoken. Shortly thereafter, our mayor called for a vote, a referendum, and what would become known as the Cadiz Proposition unanimously passed into our town charter and into our law.

A FINAL SYMPTOM

A child whose skin has remolded itself into a two-inch thick layer of orange rubber can barely be referred to as a parent's "flesh and blood," yet this is how, even after the second stage of the ball's impact, we still thought of our children. The doctors at the secure facility kept them under constant sedation, so it was impossible to know how much the transformation had affected their perception of the world. Did they still think like our children? Would our fumbling hugs still soothe them? Did they still feel the warmth of sunlight and cool breezes the way we did? Was a kitten's fur softer or harder under the stroke of their new skin? Would they still look at us and call us "father" or "mother" or would they now refer to us by words we couldn't understand? We didn't ask, and they couldn't tell.

The doctors claimed that the sedation was imperative, not because the rubberized flesh by itself would necessarily cause pain, but because the final stage of the ball's infection involved a horror for which there was no cognate in the annals of medical literature. Ushered from the treatment rooms due to what the medical staff called "the unpredictability of the final stage," we watched our children on monitors from areas within the facility labeled only as "safe zones." Vaguely scented like fresh carpet, these areas resembled bizarrely arranged discount furniture store show rooms, with disparate couches and loveseats and plush recliners and end tables encircling central banks of computer monitors and television sets. The walls of the "safe zones" were also entirely lined in mirrors, which both lent to the commercial effect and led many of us to believe that as we watched our children, so too were we being watched from behind those mirrors.

Over the course of the three days following our children's dermal mutation, we sat in these safe zones in relative silence. Occasionally, we would leave and find our way to the hospital's roof. There, six stories from the ground, we would consider leaping off the edge, into a more certain madness. However, none of us had the energy or the willpower to actually make the jump. Instead, we would simply stand on the rooftop ledge and wonder what revelations the air between the tips of our toes and the tarmac below might hold. Perhaps the wind whipping by our faces in that two or three second plunge might speak to us of death's mysteries. Perhaps the very ground below might whisper wisdom as it collapsed our forms. We would never know.

If we did not head to the rooftop, we would leave the safe zones and wander through the dark wards that sprawled under our children. We would pass skeletal figures hooked to spider webs of IV tubes, bodies suspended in vats of brightly hued gels, and other children stuffed inside windowed copper tubes, clearly suffering from a dread malady different from that of our own children. We would continue downward, downward, until we reached the basement of the facility, where we discovered the morgue and its seemingly infinite rows of tabled corpses, some of which were wrapped in thin, clear plastic sheets and others which were encased in silver mylar bags. To this room we would take our husbands, our wives, our boyfriends and girlfriends and secret lovers and there, amongst the plenitude of the dead, we would explode into a molten flow of volcanic sex, entwining with our partners in as many configurations as we could devise, often knocking bodies to the floor with the force of our writhing and tumbling naked after them. We didn't care that the dead watched us, were part of the act. Indeed, we wanted them to see. We wanted them to know. Why, we couldn't explain.

So, mostly, we remained in the safe zones, silent and unmoving, unless, of course, we didn't. All of which is to say that we knew not what to do with ourselves or how to act as our children, for all intents and purposes, died. While we sat in silence, every one of our children's bones and internal organs were evaporating. They did not liquefy or explode or turn putrescent and rot; they just evaporated, into air, leaving behind nothing but an expanding bubble of space and increased pressure. Brain and heart, spine and scapula: it all dissolved to nothing. As our children's brainwaves diminished and their heartbeats flatlined, the space within them grew larger and more rounded. Their tiny bodies expanded and inflated and gained contours no human shape was ever meant to contain. Their shoulders and torsos became one with their heads, with any trace of their necks disappearing; their legs and arms descended into the vastness of their abdomens. With every passing hour, they took on new convexities, new spheroid shapes. They were all Violet Beauregarde, eternally trapped in Wonka's chocolate factory.

Over the final symptom's three day reign, our children continued to expand, to inflate, until, when all was said and done, there were no more bones or organs left to dissolve. What lay in our children's beds then were no longer our children, but enormous orange rubber balls with the distorted and elongated faces of our individual sons and daughters imprinted upon one of their sides. Somehow, even after this, even after the final symptom had run its course, the worst had not yet arrived, for, when the life-giving machines were shuttled away and times of death were officially stamped on certificates, our children, whatever they now were, began to move once again. They began to bounce. They began to roll from side to side. They began to roll toward us. And we, more fearful than we'd ever been, more uncertain and filled with shame than we thought possible, clawed at our eyes and wished that we had never tried to hide the ball from our children or ourselves in the first place.

A SCIENTIFIC INQUIRY

Epidemiologists have studied the effects of the orange ball and have determined with certainty that the symptoms it causes cannot be traced to a viral, bacterial, fungal, or parasitic source. Despite extensive tests of our children's every conceivable tissue and bodily secretion, there is, they say, no detectable pathogen present in their bodies either pre-transformation or post-transformation. This conclusion has led numerous researchers to suggest that the vector for transmission may lie on the molecular or atomic level—a potentially provable proposition, but one that will require many more years of study.

Another faction of scientists—mostly biophysicists—have conjectured that what occurs to the infected children has little basis in any macrocosmic discipline. These experts have advanced a hypothesis that the wholesale restructuring of an organism can only find its catalyst in the quantum realm, amidst probabilities so infinitesimally small and possibilities so strange they might be thought impossible. Therefore, in their view, it is far better to approach the issue as a problem of fundamental forces and abstract equations than cellular division and genetic re-encoding. Intriguing though the concept may be, it is untestable with current medical technology.

Still another segment of the scientific community washes their hands of the entire matter, choosing to believe that the orange ball and its accompanying syndrome must be either grossly misreported or an outright hoax. To the myriad MDs and PhDs in this camp—none of whom have seen a ball-child in person—the situation is undeserving of serious attention and, in their assessment, a blemish upon those scientists willing to examine the phenomenon.

Needless to say, the underlying reason for the changes to our children remains unknown and we are forced to wonder not just "Why?" but also "How?"

A TREATMENT

The symptoms having finished their grotesque parade, we were left with their result—a roomful of huge rubber balls bouncing and rolling about the hospital ward under what appeared to be their own volition. We watched, fascinated and horrified, as the faces of our children, forever frozen in a dilated sleep, spun about the balls' surfaces. The doctors assured us that the balls were not our children, could not be our children, as our children had surely died when the dual hemispheres of their brains evaporated. Time and again they explained that, clinically, our children were gone. And yet, for all the explanation and entirely rational assurances, the movement of the balls—nonstop and just a degree under total chaos—reminded us of our daughters and our sons and their feverish orbits of play. When we gazed through the windows of the secure ward, we saw both our children cavorting in a schoolyard and utterly alien beings performing a dance we could not understand, and, in truth, we could not distinguish between the two despite our best efforts. We watched the balls for many weeks this way, our terror becoming familiar, our sense of certainty in the world further eroding.

Thus it was that by the time the doctors at the facility presented us with two options for the balls' futures—to leave them in the facility for continued study or to take them home with us—we chose to take them home. The doctors, the facility's administrators, and a panel of high-level bureaucrats from various government agencies all attempted to convince us that turning over guardianship of the balls to the facility would be in everyone's best interest. These things, they said, should not exist—by all rights, cannot exist—yet they do. These things, they reiterated, were not our children. These things, they warned, would be well beyond our control and may even pose a danger to others. Of course, we knew the doctors were right. We knew that we would never be able to touch our children again without shivering, that we would never be able to look at those child-sized orange balls without worrying that unknown intelligences might be looking back. We knew that we could never talk to them again without nervously contemplating all the unfathomable thoughts and incomprehensible plots that might be incubating beneath their surfaces. We understood that the balls were not our children anymore. Yet, by the same token, we could not shake the impression that the balls were not *not* our children, either. Somewhere within them still floated fragments of our DNA and, therefore, we believed that somewhere within them surely floated remnants of our children. However fleeting or memorial those remnants might be, we could not leave them to the emptiness of the facility and its doctors clinical probing. So, instead, we took them home with us. In this decision we were sorely unprepared.

Once in our houses, the balls went wild. Brimming with an unnatural energy, they slammed against our walls and bounced from our floors to our ceilings in rapid, machine gun succession, perhaps testing the boundaries of our homes. They cracked our windows and shattered our lighting fixtures, knocked over our tables and splintered our chairs. They rolled throughout our houses every minute of every day, always in motion, always progressing toward a destination we could seemingly not provide. Sometimes they even bounced against *us*—often with enough force to make us stumble or send us sprawling to the ground—and we, unsure of what else to do, fled from their advances, scraped and bruised as we were. Whether the bouncings were attacks or gestures of play or symbolic movements beyond our guessing, their violence caused us to worry for our lives, especially after several of us suffered concussions and broken bones. Therefore, in order to protect ourselves, we did what any reasonable community would do—we instituted a treatment plan for our ball-children's unchecked mania.

Our options to this end were admittedly limited. We owned no golden egg with which to bankroll a major project and we received no meaningful guidance in our planning. At secret meetings held in neutral locations, we brainstormed and we deliberated and, ultimately, we embarked upon a plan that we thought most effective under the circumstances. Laughable though it may seem, we bought high-end treadmills and, between their arms, rigged leather harnesses that would support the weight and girth of our transmuted children. Into these harnesses we wrestled the frenetic balls, locking them in place with a variety of straps and buckles while making sure that they could still spin freely within their binds. We provided a modicum of leeway in the harnesses' lengths so that the rubbery dynamos could also bounce a few inches into the air, off the treadmill track, if they needed to bounce at all.

Once we were certain that the ball-children had been firmly restrained and fully introduced to their new living arrangements, we turned on the treadmills and set them rolling at a sprinter's pace. There, in those harnesses, we'd planned that they would spend every moment of the rest of their strange existences, safe and secure, locked in place yet spinning ever forward, on a path we'd made for them, a path that could cause no damage or destruction. We would never unfasten their buckles or loosen their straps; we would never lift them out of their bindings or wash the residue of the treadmills' rubber belts from their orange sides. We would not even pause the treadmills' circulation unless their motors burned out. We were too frightened to do anything other than maintain the ball-children as surreal conversation pieces and monuments to our parental failure. We were not offering a cure to our children, but a palliative to ourselves. And, in this, we were relatively satisfied, at least for a time.

A DIVIDE

Other towns deal with the orange ball and their own infected offspring in other ways.

In Mercury, Ohio, the citizens have built a windowless, private gymnasium the size of an entire office complex for their ball-children. Within this gym the ball-children permanently reside, never allowed to exit the building's triple-locked steel doors, even with supervision. The people of Mercury reason that their ball-children should never want to leave the gym, given that it's equipped with a dizzying array of tubes and chutes and mazes and wheels in myriad sizes and shapes. It is, after all, designed to be a ball's veritable paradise. And yet, when questioned about the usual movements of the ball-children within their unique enclave, Mercury residents recite an odd fact: no matter how often the ball-children run their mazes or blast through their chutes, no matter how much exuberance they seem to emit as they slide and bounce and roll, they always end their day by congregating around the doors, rebounding against them lightly.

Elsewhere, in Sutter's Glen, Tennessee, every family of a ball-child owns an oversized, triple-reinforced bouncy castle which their individual ball-child inhabits. These bouncy castles are a significant source of revenue for the people of Sutter's Glen, as they allow the families of ball-children to offer wealthy curiosity-seekers the opportunity to purchase exclusive admissions to view their ball-children. It's rumored that, for the right price, the people of Sutter's Glen will even allow patrons to enter the bouncy castles and play with their ball-children.

Through this trade, the community has grown quite wealthy—so much so that Jaguars and Porsches and Ferraris are now common sights on the streets of Sutter's Glen. It should be little surprise then, that, privately, many of the town's citizens whisper a desire for the orange ball to return, to transform the rest of their children, to help them erect more bouncy castles in their backyards.

In yet another locale—Kylersburg, Wyoming—the ball-children are herded onto a ranch with absurdly high, electrified fences. There, after they have been stamped with a unique number and fitted with a tiny tracking device, they are given free reign of the open fields and sky. On the ranch, they are treated much as any other herd of livestock; they are frequently rounded up and counted, often driven from one area of the ranch to another so as to evenly wear on the land, and occasionally used in special rodeos during which ranch hands attempt to rope and tie them or ride them like angry steer. The people of Kylersburg contend that, as a whole, their treatment method is by far the most natural and humane of all known treatment methods. Perhaps surprisingly, few outsiders argue with the assertion.

Finally, in Vernonville, Texas, in the town that ignited our initial fears, the people have no ongoing treatment plan, as the treatment they eventually instituted was of a singular and final variety. "Shots from heaven," some of the citizens of Vernonville call their particular treatment. Others refer to it more modestly as "A mercy." No matter what moniker they choose, the people of Vernonville claim they feel no remorse or guilt over their actions. They say they simply copied the treatment from their traditional methods for handling lame horses and terminally ill pets. They say that the greatest kindness they could show to their children was to let the dead lie down. Whether or not this statement rings true, one thing is certain: the people of Vernonville no longer need to worry about their ball-children, because there are no longer any ball-children in Vernonville to worry about. Considering this outcome, some might argue that their treatment has been the most successful of all.

———

A REVELATION

After our treatment plan went into effect, we returned to lives of relative normalcy. We went to work and complained about paperwork and bosses rather than silently hunching at our desks, worrying over what the balls might be doing to our possessions and our loved ones while we were away. We attended movies and ate at fine dining establishments. We went out for drinks with our friends and argued politics and sports with our families. We walked about our homes with confidence, with surety, with the peace of mind that no weighty orange ball might be tracking us from behind, waiting to pounce upon us and send us careening down a flight of stairs or through a window to our certain dooms. Gradually, we returned to our blissful old routines and, in a sense, the sharp edges of our lives once again began to wear smooth.

Meanwhile, however, the treadmills kept running in the background.

The ambient thrum and whir of treads cycling around and around became as ubiquitous to us as the soft whistle of breath from our own nostrils. We avoided the rooms in which we'd placed the ball-children—often keeping the doors to those rooms closed, if not altogether locked—but no matter which room or closet or hidden alcove of our homes we might try to hide away inside, we could hear the treadmills spinning. Music, sound machines, televisions blared at painful volumes: nothing entirely muted the noise. It became clear that if we were in our homes, we could not escape the treadmills' flat song, and because we could not escape we were perpetually on the verge of remembering why they ran nonstop. Even when we were not at home, many of us heard the treadmills' rhythmic drone, as though it had somehow recorded a loop of itself upon the very drums in our ears. Animated luncheons with friends, meetings with important business clients, birthday parties for significant others: all of it played out with the soundtrack of the treadmills whispering in the background. Our lives may have been returning to a state of normalcy, but it was certainly not the normalcy we'd known before the ball.

It wasn't long before the noise from the treadmills took its toll. In small ways that would have been imperceptible to anyone unfamiliar with our community, we began to wear thin. Our laughter at even the best-told jokes faded faster. Our goodnight kisses took on an unexpected hardness. Our footsteps came faster, lighter, as though we were trying to outrun a looming danger without showing any appearance of panic. We began to suffer from insomnia and panic attacks, which would lead us to pace in our yards during the witching hours of the night and, trembling, stare at the starlit sky. We lost weight—small amounts at first, healthy amounts we should have lost anyway, but eventually enough to make strangers wonder which wasting disease we must have developed and how many months we had left to live. Worst of all, we began to let our thoughts float away from us. We began to consider the balls as our children. We began to imagine what they might do if they weren't on the treadmills, speeding to nowhere. We began to try to grasp their needs and intentions and desires, impossible though the task might be.

Through our unrelenting contemplation, we were slowly drawn back to the rooms in which we'd placed the treadmills. At first, we stole into the rooms for the briefest of seconds, barely glimpsing even a flash of orange. But seconds stretched to minutes and minutes stretched to hours. Soon, we were spending entire evenings in the treadmill rooms. We watched the ball-children roll in place, our thoughts rolling with them. We could not stop envisioning new scenarios for them, were we to set them free of their shackles. Some of us conjured wild fantasies about the ball-children forming utopian ball-societies that operated without prejudice or hatred or any of the plagues of our human society. Some of us sketched nightmares of ball invasions, with our spherical overlords inflating us to bursting in an effort to assimilate us to their ways of being. And some of us simply hoped that the ball-children might roll to the ends of the earth and back, collecting experiences and perceptions and loves and dreams along their journeys.

No matter their substance, beneath all our thoughts settled an abiding sense of guilt. When no one else was home, we curled up in the treadmill rooms and we wept. We cried for the children we'd lost and we cried for the things they'd become that we'd never let live. We knew we'd wronged the ball-children. We knew we'd trapped what was not ours to trap, held on too tightly to a control we never really had in the first place. If the balls were to save us, we knew it was right. If they were to destroy us, we knew that was right, too. And if they bounced off to distant futures not meant for us at all, we knew that would be best, for in those futures we would find a sanctuary that we'd been missing for quite some time.

So we conferred with one another and we decided to engage in a final treatment so shocking, so revelatory, that no other town had even considered it. We decided to unbuckle the ball-children, open wide the doors to our houses, and, with no small amount of commingled anxiety and excitement and regret, let them roll past us and out of our town. Our final treatment, the only treatment we could justify in the end, was to simply let them roll away.

A MYSTERY

There exists even less data on the nature of the orange ball itself than its terrible effects on our children. Its first documented appearance occurred in a rural farming community in the heartland of the nation—a place called Goldenrod, Nebraska—where, eight years before our own tragedy, it infected its first three children. Its trajectory since then has followed no discernible pattern or logical progression, thus making any prediction of its present or future movement an exercise in pure divination. Its origin is equally the province of speculation and often involves theories that touch on fantastical notions of extraterrestrial intervention, interdimensional slippage, demonic corruption, and clandestine military projects gone awry. Beyond firsthand accounts, visual evidence of the ball itself is also utterly nil, as every attempt to photograph it or record it to video has resulted in nothing but blurred or fuzzy images. Though numerous adults have seen the ball in person and can attest to its physical reality, it has, as far as we or anyone else knows, never been so much as grazed by an adult hand. Many people, ourselves included, wonder what might happen if such an interaction were to occur. Would we, too, be transformed into balls, dead in humanity but vibrant and alive in a new state of being? Is the transformation a curse exclusive to our children? Or have we adults already been cursed in a less tangible way? About any of this, we may never know.

BEN
LOORY

The

Rock

Eater

THERE ONCE WAS A MAN WHO ATE A ROCK. IT WAS a small rock, nothing big. The man found it in a field, and it was pretty—very pretty—and so he picked it up and he ate it. He wasn't in the habit of doing things like that—it surprised him as much as anyone—but there it was, on that day, just lying in the field, the rock—the pretty rock—and so he ate it.

The man felt great after he did it. It made him happy to have the rock inside him. And it wasn't just the physical sensation of the rock; it was also something else. Somehow, the man felt, the rock made him better. Somehow, he felt, it im- proved him. It gave him a lift, more self-confidence; some- how, it positively changed him.

And the man was very, very happy about it.

And then he told his wife.

You did what? said his wife. You ate a rock?

The man explained to her how it had happened.

That's insane, said his wife. You're lucky you're not dead.

It was just a rock, said the man. It was hardly going to kill me.

But after that, the man started to worry. He wandered around thinking about the rock. Should he not have eaten it? Could it really have done him harm? And, what's more, could it really do him harm?

He needed to talk to someone about it, but he was afraid all his friends would laugh.

So he went downtown and wandered around and knocked on the door of the doctor.

———

How big was this rock? the doctor said.

The man held up his hands to indicate the size. About this big, he said. Pretty small.

Hmm, said the doctor, and frowned.

What do you mean, Hmm? the man said. Is it dangerous? Well, I wouldn't say dangerous, the doctor said. It's just,

you know, rocks can grow.

Grow? the man said. He'd never heard of that.

Grow, said the doctor. When you eat them, that is. Why, I once saw a woman with an eighty-pound boulder in her gut.

He shook his head.

It wasn't pretty, he said.

The man stared at the doctor. So what do I do? he finally said.

It should probably come out, the doctor said.

Out? said the man. You mean, surgery?

Do you really think that's necessary? he said.

The decision is yours, of course, said the doctor. But personally, I would recommend it.

The man went home and thought about it. He told his wife what the doctor had said.

You should never have eaten that rock to begin with—what did you expect? she said.

That night, the man lay thinking about the rock. He could still feel it there, inside him. He could still feel its goodness radiating through him.

I don't want to lose the rock, he said.

Some time went by. The doctor called.

I think I will keep the rock, the man said. Are you sure? said the doctor.

Pretty sure, said the man.

Well, said the doctor, it's your decision. If you ever change your mind, though, let me know.

Okay, said the man.

And that was that.

More time went by. The man was happy. The rock felt good inside him.

But there was one thing that was bothering the man: The rock was definitely growing. The man's stomach was getting bigger and bigger. It was starting to stick out.

And the rock was getting heavier, too; the man was having a hard time standing up.

And finally, one day, it got to the point where the man couldn't get out of bed.

So what? said his wife. You're just gonna lie there? I can't move, said the man. What do you want?

This is all because of that dumb rock, his wife said. You should just get it cut out already.

I don't want it cut out, the man said. It's my rock. It's my rock; I ate it; it makes me happy.

Then the pain set in. The rock had grown so big it was crowding out the man's innards.

You have to do it now, the man's wife said. You understand—you'll die if this keeps up.

The man knew that his wife was right. He could feel the rock filling up his body. He could still feel the goodness of it in there somewhere—but it was buried now beneath the pain and fear.

All right, the man said. Go get the doctor.

Finally, his wife said.

And she did.

The surgery was hard. The doctor needed four men just to lift the rock out. They placed it on a scale, but the scale was crushed and the weight of the rock was never recorded.

Otherwise, everything went according to plan. They sewed the man's stomach back up. The doctor pronounced the procedure a success, and had a cigar on the porch.

Time went by as the man recuperated. Then one day he woke up feeling fine. He patted his stomach and got out of bed, took a breath, and headed toward the door.

Where are you going? the man's wife said.

For a walk, said the man. I feel great!

The man went out and walked and walked. It was a nice day and he felt the breeze and saw the clouds and heard the birds and everything was absolutely wonderful.

But after a while, the man started to feel different. He started to feel like something was wrong. He frowned and frowned, trying to figure it out, and then it hit him: It was the rock—the rock was gone! That was why he felt so hollow inside! There was a great big hole inside him!

And the man wiped his brow, and squinted, and squirmed.

And then the bad feeling got worse.

In a panic, the man turned and ran to the field where he'd found the rock on that day so long ago. He looked around, all around, on the ground, everywhere, staring down, walking round in circles.

Another rock will make me feel good again, he thought.

Another rock will be just what I need.

But he couldn't seem to find another rock like his. None of them looked right to him.

Oh, there were lots of other rocks, of course, but they were dull and brown and covered with dirt. None of them looked like the right one for him.

He ate some anyway, but they didn't work.

What am I going to do? the man said. How am I supposed to live like this?

And then it hit him, and he stopped and spun around. My rock! Where is my rock? he said.

The man ran frantically all the way home.

Where is the rock? he screamed. What rock? said his wife.

The rock! screamed the man. The rock, the rock! My rock!

Oh, said his wife. It's out back. It was too heavy to carry very far.

The man went out back. There it was—the rock!—over in the corner of the yard.

The man ran to it.

He knelt down beside it.

He wrapped his arms around the stone.

He ran his hands all over its surface. He rubbed his face against it. It was way too big for him to eat, of course, but he held it, pressed it to his chest.

Oh rock! he said. How could I have been so stupid? And how can I get this empty feeling out?

And then the man heard a noise, and the rock cracked open.

And he stared into its dark and hungry mouth.

BRENNA
GOMEZ

Corzo

ONE DAY WHEN I WAS IN THE SEVENTH GRADE, I came home to my father—Eduvigo Herrera III—cutting his heart out with a steak knife. He was sitting at the little kitchen table when I got home from school, his hand in a ragged chest wound the size of a plum.

"*Mija*, I need you to help me," he said. "I need you to take it out. Your hands are small. Just the right size."

"Take what out," I asked, though I knew.

"My heart."

"No," I said as I took off my backpack and sat down.

"Please do this for me. I never ask you for anything." We both knew this wasn't true. I was the one who took my brother on long walks on the weekends while my parents had their epic screaming matches. He expected me to get straight As, to never be in trouble. To be a good girl and he yelled at me when I didn't measure up.

"Stick your hand inside. It's okay. It'll be a little squishy, but you won't hurt me. I promise," he said.

My father's thick, long fingers were coated with blood. I slid my hand inside the hole and removed his heart. It was soft around the edges and firm in the center. Every so often it shuddered like it didn't know it wasn't being used anymore. It was a deep purple, so dark it looked black.

"Now cut it like you would meat when you and your mother make dinner."

I picked up the knife and slid it into his heart. I hacked big sections off and chopped those sections into bite-sized bits. That's when he passed me the empty tequila bottle. The label said *Corzo*.

"Put the pieces in there."

"Why?"

"I want it to look nice," he said.

I let each tiny piece plop to the bottom of the bottle. Over and over again, I slid the pieces through the bottle's neck, struggling with the bigger, uneven chunks.

My mother came home and by that time there were even bits of heart in my hair. Her heels clicked on the floor as she walked over to the table and picked up the *Corzo* bottle.

"You've done it then," she said.

"I told you I would," my father said.

"You shouldn't have made her do it." She grabbed me by the hand and led me to the shower. "Scrub until your skin turns red."

"It already is."

Every day my father would proudly point to the tequila bottle that held his heart as if it were a science experiment for which I'd received an A. My mother became strange. At night before dinner she'd light some incense and her Virgin Mary candle and put them beside my father's heart-bottle. Our dinner table would become a little altar for a time—I would cut the meat or the vegetables for dinner and my mother would kneel at the table, praying under her breath in Spanish. Sometimes my brother would come out to watch my mother pray. She refused to teach us Spanish, she said that people look at you different when you know it. I didn't tell her that I'd started a beginning Spanish class that semester or that all of my Hispanic friends made fun of me. "How can you be Mexican and not speak Spanish?" they'd ask and laugh when I told them my family had been American for a long time.

I could only make out one word in my mother's nightly prayers. She said it over and over: *muerte*. After a week of her mutterings, I was tempted to say something, but my brother beat me to it. I had helped my mother make ham and bean soup with little bits of fried bacon in it. We ate in silence for a while, just like we did every night, until my brother thought he had figured it all out.

"It's cow meat in the bottle," Freddie said.

"I told you, Eduvigo, that you shouldn't have taken the label off.

Now they can see it too well," my mother said. "No Freddie, it's not cow. Don't worry about it."

"What do you think it is, Sara?" he asked. He hadn't lost all his baby fat yet, so his smile made his cheeks bulge.

"Don't worry about it," my mother said again as my father walked into their bedroom and shut the door.

"*Muerte*," I said.

"I don't know what that means," Freddie said.

"Enough dinner, Freddie. Now go to your room," my mother said. She wouldn't even look at me until she was sure Freddie was gone.

"Why do you keep praying that Dad will die?" I asked.

"What? That's not what I'm doing."

"I know what *muerte* means, Mom."

"I'm not praying he'll die. I'm just saying the Hail Mary. Praying for his heart."

"How is he even alive?"

"He is because he wants to be," she said. "His grandfather showed him how to do this as a child. He's punishing me."

"What are you talking about?"

"I told him he was an unfeeling bastard and now he is."

I went to pick up the heart-bottle and my mother stepped in front of me. I'd never seen her look that old. She didn't have any makeup on and I hadn't seen her without it in a long time. Tiny splotches she called sun spots dotted her cheeks. She told me about them every time I watched her put on her makeup. She said I was still too young for it since I didn't have any spots.

"Don't touch it. He shouldn't have made you do it. It's not natural for a man to live without a heart. He told me he'd cut it out, but he shouldn't have made you help."

"He couldn't have finished by himself," I said.

"He should've asked me. I'm his wife."

After that we washed the dishes in silence. My mother rinsed and I dried everything with a thick cotton towel. I couldn't think of a single thing to say. What woman wants to help her husband cut up his heart?

My mother handed me a tall water glass, but I didn't grab it in time. It shattered against the floor. We looked at each other and before my mother could say anything, I walked into my bedroom and slammed the door. She could pick up her own mess.

By the next week my mother was very cranky with all of us, but my father didn't seem to feel a thing. He'd gotten in trouble at the hospital where he worked in the maintenance department. He kept bleeding through his blue work shirt. He had tried to stitch up the wound, but did a poor job, so we took him to the doctor.

Everyone at the hospital called my father "Ed." My mother hated it. She said it made him sound common and boring. The doctor was only a little surprised to hear about his heart. He said he saw this kind of thing every once in a while, but most people didn't talk about it. Then he cleaned and properly sewed up the wound on my father's chest. The doctor made jokes the whole time. Apparently, my dad liked to laugh with people at work. He was never like that at home. My father didn't laugh with the doctor that time. He just stared at the wall.

My mother, still angry with me for helping my father, gave me even more chores than normal. Dishes had to be done after supper and breakfast; I had to start picking Freddie up from daycare; I had to wash all the clothes every other day instead of once a week. At night before bed, I had to iron my father's shirt and put it out for him. Ironing was the one chore I enjoyed, mostly because my entire family left me alone while I did it. I always ironed when my mother was giving Freddie a bath. I'd pour just a little water in, plug in the iron, and stand out on our apartment's little balcony while it warmed up. Sometimes there'd be a breeze. Sometimes it would be windy and leaves would hurl by in a dust storm. Usually my father would stay in the bedroom, but one night, he sat at the kitchen table smoking his Marlboro 101s while I ironed. My mother hated the smell, but I kind of liked it. It hurt my chest a little and made me want to cough, but the smell was interesting.

My dad had smoked three cigarettes in a row. I pushed the iron down and listened to it gasp. "Why'd you make me help you?" I asked. "Mom's pissed."

"I couldn't do it myself. Your hands are smaller and I was too tired to cut it up."

"Why not wait for her?"

"She would have tried to stop me," he said, blowing yet more smoke into the air. It mixed with the smell of chorizo from dinner.

"Why'd you do it?"

"You aren't old enough to understand."

I imagined pressing the hot iron into the side of his face and just watching it burn. Would he even feel it?

"Whatever, Dad," I said. I didn't want to be around him. I unplugged the iron and set his pressed shirt on the couch. I went into my room and tried to focus on my homework. I fell asleep instead, but the yelling woke me up.

"Why would you make your daughter do that?" my mother asked. "How do you think that made her feel?"

"She's fine," my father said. "She's a good girl and she did what needed to be done."

It was strange—my father wasn't yelling. On nights when they'd fought in the past I was surprised no one called the police. His screaming was so loud that even if I took Freddie for a walk, we could hear them a block away. Now, without his heart, he didn't have any fight left in him. But my mother sure did.

"I didn't want you to be the way you were," she said.

"And now?"

"Now, it's like you're nothing. You don't smile, you don't yell, you don't cry."

"You don't like that?"

"I don't know," my mother said.

My mother tried to have this fight, and several others, every night for the next week. She would rage and my father would speak quietly or say nothing at all. I could imagine him pouring a glass of Jack Daniel's and just staring at her while Freddie and I hid in our room. I imagined him trying not to give her the satisfaction of getting angry, but he couldn't have gotten angry now even if he wanted to.

Freddie would climb down from the top bunk into my bed when my mother screamed. He never cried, though. He just asked lots of questions about why he had to go to daycare and couldn't come with me to school or why our parents were the way they were. Sometimes he'd ask about the heart-bottle and I'd just pretend I didn't hear him. Then one night he asked again and I couldn't help myself.

"It's Dad's heart. That's what's in the bottle."

"Cool," Freddie said. "I mean, that's gross." He looked at me and when I didn't say anything he asked, "How did it get there?"

"Dad cut a hole in his chest and made me pull his heart out. He made me cut it up for him and then stuff it in there."

"Why?"

"I don't know."

"Sara, can Dad live without a heart?" He put his hand on mine as our mother continued her tirade in the other room.

"I think so."

"Then why is Mama so sad?"

"I'm not sure if she's sad or mad or both."

"Why'd you help him?"

"If Dad asked you to do something, you know you'd do it."

"Yeah, I guess so," he said.

Freddie slept in my bed that night. He said he didn't want to be alone.

I couldn't concentrate the next day at school. In every class I asked for a pass to go to the bathroom. I'd just sit in there for a while, on a toilet where I wouldn't have to talk to anyone or I'd wander by the lockers and duck down as I passed classrooms so the teachers wouldn't see me through the windows. During Spanish, I went by the art room. It was empty so I walked around, looking at everyone's projects. They were working with clay so lots of lopsided pots were spread out around the room. James, one of the annoying white boys who laughed when my

friends made fun of me for not speaking Spanish, came through the
door.

"What are you doing here?" he asked.

"I don't know," I said.

James walked over to me and looked into my eyes. For a second I
thought he was going to kiss me, but instead he slid his hands over
the front of my green dress. I felt embarrassed. Suddenly my boobs
seemed so small and I wished that I had waited to let someone touch
them. I looked into his face to try and see what he was thinking, but
he left without looking at me again. I'd always imagined that when
this finally happened, when a boy noticed me, he'd kiss me too. I tried
not to think about it as I went back to class because I didn't know
where else to go.

After school, I tried not to make eye contact with any of James'
friends as I walked to the daycare center a few blocks away to pick up
Freddie. It was windy again. The yellow leaves rushed along the sidewalk. Pamela, Freddie's favorite helper, pulled me aside right before I
went in. Pamela was old and her boobs were way bigger than mine.

"Have you and Freddie been watching a lot of horror movies
lately?"

"What? Why?" I asked, looking up from her chest into her face.

"Well, he was asking about zombies and said something about
your father keeping his heart on the kitchen table? He really frightened some of the smaller children," she said as she pulled her sweater
closer to her body. The sun wasn't setting yet but the air was becoming
chillier. We'd have to walk home fast.

"Oh, right. We did watch a zombie movie the other day. That's
completely my fault. I'll talk to him," I said.

As we walked home, Freddie grabbed my hand. I wanted to shake
him off, wanted to say: *You're going to have to learn how to take care of
yourself someday.* But I didn't.

"Dude, you can't tell people about Dad, okay?"

"Why not?"

"Well, it's nobody else's business and they won't understand
anyway," I said.

"Because Dad's a zombie."

"Seriously? No, Dad is not a zombie."

"Then what is he?"

"He's just Dad. He cut his heart out because he's weird and sad."

"I think he did it so he won't be mean, anymore."

"Maybe," I said. "But if he can't be mean, then he can't be nice either, Freddie. He can't really be anything."

We turned onto our street and walked toward the apartment complex. We could hear yelling. It was definitely Mom, which didn't make sense. Neither of my parents should have been home from work yet. My mom worked at the hair salon until six every night except Sundays. Did they come home just to fight or did something happen? Freddie tightened his grip on my hand.

"Sara, let's not go home."

"I can hear your stomach rumbling. We're both hungry. Maybe if we go home they'll stop fighting."

"That never works," he said.

I thought about maybe taking him to the park, but as we got closer I could hear my mom.

"I should have been the one to help you! You shouldn't have made one of our children do it."

"I needed help. I didn't want you to do it. I couldn't give you the satisfaction, Izzy. Now you'll always feel this and I won't feel anything, just like you said."

My mother's voice became high-pitched, and we could barely make out what she said even as we got closer.

"Let's not go in," Freddie said.

I opened the door and my mother turned to look at us. She had rubbed most of her makeup off, but she wasn't crying anymore. My father just sat on the couch, smoking.

"This is how it had to be, Izzy. You said you wanted a better man. Now I am one."

I dragged Freddie past my parents into our room.

"Stay in here, okay? Just color or something and I'll make you a sandwich."

"Sara, don't leave me in here."

"I'll be right back."

I didn't look at my parents as I walked into the kitchen. My mother kept yelling about everything. How was she supposed to spend the rest of her life with a man who had no feeling? Now he didn't love her. My father kept saying he was sorry, repeating it like a chant. My mother screamed that he didn't mean it.

I got a paper plate out as fast as I could. I slapped some bologna and American cheese on bread, added a squirt of mayo and mustard. I headed for our room and left the kitchen just in time to see Freddie walking to the balcony with the heart-bottle.

"I want you to still be my dad," he said.

Freddie threw the bottle off the edge of the balcony. It landed with a crash as it split open. Jagged glass and black meat were scattered everywhere, dark purple oozing and pooling in the cracks on the sidewalk. I grabbed Freddie's hand in my own as my parents came to stare off the edge of the balcony at the leftovers of my father's heart.

"Go get the pieces," my mother said.

Freddie put the pieces in a bowl and carried them back upstairs. I got on my hands and knees and scrubbed at the dark stain with bleach. It started to rain and still the stain wouldn't come up. Even though I was freezing, I must have scrubbed for at least an hour. I dreaded going back inside, but when I did, everyone had gone to their rooms.

The bologna sandwich I made sat on the living room table. I went into our bedroom and Freddie was already in bed. He rolled over and threw the blanket off as soon as I shut the door.

"Did you see that?" he asked.

"What the hell were you thinking?"

"Dad, didn't even get mad and nothing happened to him. He's like invincible."

"Damn it, Freddie! Just eat your dinner," I said. "You're going to be in so much trouble when Mom finally comes to deal with you."

"But nothing happened," he shouted.

"That's never stopped Mom from yelling at us before."

Freddie climbed down from his bunk to get his sandwich, and I got under the covers in my bed. I pulled them right up over my head. I was so angry. We were lucky Dad didn't have a heart anymore. Lucky he couldn't have felt mad or done anything to us. Who knew what Mom would do. But she never came in our room.

I woke up after midnight shivering—I'd fallen asleep still in my wet clothes. The door to our bedroom was ajar. Freddie wasn't in his bed. I flicked the bathroom light on. He wasn't in there. I ran to the kitchen and turned the light on. Not there. That's when I saw my mom sitting on the couch in the living room.

"Where's Freddie?" I asked.

My mother said nothing, but looked at the kitchen table. I followed her gaze and felt as if my whole body was tumbling through space. A second bottle—less full and containing smaller chunks—had joined the bowl of my father's shattered heart-bottle pieces on the table.

"Your father asked me to help him this time," my mother said. Her hand shook as she lifted a glass of whiskey to her lips.

"I guess you got what you wanted," I said, sitting next to her on the couch. I hated myself for saying this, but I had to. I squeezed her bloody hand. Did we do this? Was this our fault? I tried not to think about what would happen to us now that we were two women alone in a house with men who weren't really men anymore.

KATHLEEN KAYEMBE

You Will Always Have Family: A Triptych

ISOBELLE:
THE WHISPERS OF DOGS

Uncle says there's a pit bull in Mbuyi's old room, but he's lying, and his eyes are scared. Dogs aren't pets in Congo, they're for guarding—it's why Dad never got us one, and how I first knew Uncle had no pet dog. I tried to learn what he was hiding, but the more I asked questions, the worse his lies got, until I finally asked if I could just *see* the dog, and Uncle snapped. His fear and frustration exploded into an angry lecture about respecting my elders; and how I'm too much like spoiled American kids; and that I'd better be careful—no self-respecting man wants a woman who badgers him with questions, and that's true no matter what country you're from.

I bore the tirade in silence, which my American friends didn't understand. Dad and Uncle were close friends in Kinshasa; although he's not blood, he's *family*, and his lectures carry near-parental weight. His French and Sociology lectures at UMass are far more pleasing, of course, but to hear Uncle at his best, watch him gather folklore. Once he's turned in spring grades, he travels the country collecting stories of other people from Congo, living off of grants for the eventual book these stories will become, and on the hospitality of those he interviews. Uncle records oral histories, conducting interview after interview and transcribing them.

Uncle loves stories about The Way Things Were—my favorites— but he loves stories of the old religions and witchcraft more. Those are the stories my grandparents never told their children except through actions and naming, and superstitious talk in outdoor markets with other adults about rain and harvest and what evil magic can be done to you if you don't properly dispose of your hair when it is cut, and a witch gets hold of it.

Those are the stories Uncle is really seeking. They're what made him lean forward in his seat, dark eyes narrowing and hands stilling over the scuffed cherry wood of our kitchen table. He didn't look down at his list of questions the entire time Dad and Aunt Ntshila talked about their strange dreams the week before my grandmother died. He listened—really listened—when they told him their mother had asked them to gather all of her children and bring them back home. When Dad said sometimes he feels her spirit with him, Uncle even seemed to understand.

I watched Uncle as avidly as he watched them.

And then I watched him lie about the dog shut in the upstairs bedroom. I watched his fear when I stood on the stairwell to move my suitcase from his path. I watched his panicked insistence that I stay closed in the office bedroom from midnight until dawn whenever I slept over.

Something makes noise in Mbuyi's old bedroom, but I know it is not a dog.

I climbed the stairs once, to the second floor of Uncle's apartment, when he left to buy goat meat to teach me to cook. I wanted to see what was up there, but in case he asked, the downstairs bathroom—mine for the summer—was out of clean towels, and they are stored in the upstairs hall closet. I climbed the wood stairs, black twisted railing under my hand wobbling the whole way up, and stairs creaking under my feet. I stood at the closet door with closed bedroom doors on either side of me. On the right was Uncle's bedroom. On the left was his son Mbuyi's room, before Mbuyi disappeared.

Now it is the dog's room, Uncle says.

But dogs don't bang on doors with the sound of a shoulder or a fist. Dogs don't rasp obscenities in jagged French with a voice as sweet as sugar cane. Dogs don't make fear rise up in your bones from somewhere so deep you didn't know it was there. They don't make you afraid to turn away from whatever space they could inhabit, or to sit with your back to the door they are behind, or to close your eyes—even to blink—for fear they will be in front of you when your eyes open again. They don't fill your chest to bursting with a haze of adrenaline and sluggishness. The whispers of dogs are not meant to haunt our dreams.

I never did open that door.

That night, like every night, Uncle said, "This is an old superstition," and he blessed me with wrinkled fingers pressed to my forehead, hung a necklace of beads on the lintel, said goodnight, and gently closed the door. That night, the summer of my freshman year at UMass, Uncle's odd superstition suddenly held new meaning—and wasn't enough. I locked my door. I spent that night huddled on the futon in the downstairs office, for once all too happy not to open my door until dawn, even if I had to go to the bathroom. I wait to lock it now until I hear him moving upstairs; I don't want to seem rude. I also don't want to sleep with the door unlocked while something lives up in Mbuyi's old bedroom.

I often played in Mbuyi's room when I was little. While Uncle sat with my parents downstairs, he let Mbuyi and me play mancala with his nice board, the one of polished wood with hand-carved faces of men and of women with corn-rowed hair, their nimble fingers wrapped around flowering vines. Mbuyi's scarred right hand could always hold all the beads, and he chose which hollow to scoop from faster than I did. Still, though I was younger, we were almost evenly matched. I took a long time to move each turn, but strategizing for the game came naturally to me. He was more reckless, but didn't mind losing to a girl who was younger as long as we both had fun.

Mbuyi was my favorite cousin, and although given the name for an older twin, he remained Uncle's only child. When I asked Mbuyi—once—why he had no younger twin, no Kanku, he rubbed his long scar. Then he left and stayed gone long past dark. When he returned, and Uncle yelled at him, Mbuyi asked something in Tshiluba. Uncle immediately shut himself inside his room. No one spoke of it again. Mbuyi never explained his obsession with returning to Congo, but at twenty-three he finally did. He stayed in Kinshasa with my grandfather, and boarded the plane to return to the States after seven weeks meeting family I have yet to meet, eating food I'm still not skilled enough to cook, and being exposed to a way of life my father says will "show you how some people live." That is to say, one cannot go to Congo and return as spoiled as one left.

Only Uncle knows if Mbuyi came back less spoiled; the day after his return, Mbuyi was declared missing. None of us have heard from him since. He had no car to find by the side of the road or in a ditch or the Connecticut River. His friends knew nothing about where he'd been. Uncle was distraught and cut himself off from my family almost entirely. Not until I came out to school here, where I could take a bus down from UMass to his apartment and Uncle had to let me in because I am family, did he begin to repair the rift he had created. He welcomed me with open arms and haunted eyes when I knocked on his door, and when the banging started from Mbuyi's old bedroom, Uncle told me he'd adopted a dog.

After the first afternoon I spent in Uncle's house, poring over the books in his office and avoiding the handwritten journals and the room with the dog, I visited his apartment often. Determined to drag him back into our family, I brought news, helped him clean, and begged Congolese cooking lessons from this man who knew all the best dishes because he had no wife to cook for him anymore. I stayed with Uncle for Thanksgiving because it was cheaper than going home. I did homework and helped him organize his students' papers in the afternoons, and read late into the night, then slept, in the office. And I kept the light on when I slept, because the creaks in the house sounded like footsteps, and even though Uncle's room was right above mine, I knew they couldn't be his noises, and I was afraid.

It has been more than a year since my first visit as a freshman, and I have yet to see what lives in Mbuyi's old room. It is summer now, and hotter upstairs than the heat-soaked downstairs. Every night Uncle presses his fingers to my forehead and re-hangs the beads above the lintel. Every night I hear him creak upstairs, and I lock the door and bundle up in pajamas that are too hot for sleeping with a blanket, but just right for a surprise dash into the street for safety, and wait for sleep with open eyes trained on the floor between the bookshelf and the door, where the yellow light from the desk lamp stretches to reach. I am watching for a sentient darkness. I am searching for shapes I don't want to see. I fall asleep every night on the lookout for what makes my heart beat too fast and my back prickle like an arching cat's back. I don't know what form it will take. I just know its voice, sweet like sugar cane and cruel as ice water on a slumbering child's face.

My headphones are plugged into a tape recorder the size of a hardback book. I'm typing up Uncle's interview with a man from Florida, and have been since just after washing the dinner dishes. The lethargy from the foufou and fish have worn off with the steady tapping of my fingers on the laptop keys, and now I am simply on autopilot, stopping the tape recorder every so often because my fingers don't type French as fast as they type English, and the interview switches back and forth.

Clock chimes break me from my trance. My computer says it's seven minutes to midnight. Uncle's grandfather clock always runs fast, no matter how many times you set it back. I stop the tape and close my laptop, unplugging it from the wall and taking it to my summer bedroom, Uncle's office with the futon folded out into a bed. I can't believe Uncle let me stay up so late—that either of us did. He always insists I'm in bed—in the office—well before midnight.

I have learned certain things have power. Uncle taught me this, not explicitly, but through example. Midnight has power in the West: it is the witching hour, the time of night when ghosts are most powerful. It is the time when Uncle and I are in our rooms and there are footsteps in the hall and down the stairs.

I find Uncle asleep on the living room couch. I do not want him to be around for those creaking footsteps.

I call him, shake him. His eyes open. "Time is it?" He is still groggy, his voice is slurred, but he looks at me with eyes narrowed the way they were when my father and aunt told him that on the final night, when all the children were back home, they dreamed their mother had died clutching her heart.

"About five to midnight," I say.

Uncle struggles to sit up and I try to help, but he waves my hands away. "Go to your room," he says. "Time for bed."

"I know." I want to roll my eyes, but feel this isn't the time for such casual familiarity. His back straightens slowly, he squares his shoulders, and then he takes me by the back of the neck, the way my father does when he is upset but being gentle, and herds me to my summer bedroom. He rushes me into the room, but does not rush as he places his fingertips on my forehead, and re-hangs the beads above the lintel.

He stops as he is closing the door and casts a tired smile in my direction. I am standing still, heart hammering and mind eerily quiet. He opens his mouth to say something, and then he pauses. Finally, he clasps my shoulder. "Isobelle. Don't be afraid."

He closes the door, and I am alone in the dark.

I stand there and hear the creak of his footsteps approaching the stairs. I see lights go out under the door, and realize I have not turned on the desk lamp, and now it will be harder to find.

I have not yet heard Uncle creak up the steps. A faint light still shines underneath the door. He has not finished turning off the lights. But something creaks above me, and I wonder how Uncle got upstairs without my noticing. Then the sound leaves the space above me, and the stairs start their swaying creak. It is slow, deliberate. It is not Uncle's pull-trudge-trudge-pull, railing to foot, to foot to railing, step. It is a lighter sound. It presses heavy on my chest. I feel the fear of a shapeless, shifting dark expanding in the air around me with each step, until it is hard to breathe. I have had dreams like this, where the fear in me is so great, the danger I face so terrible, that I cannot make a sound louder than a whisper. I stare at the door, invisible in the darkness but for the faint bar of light spilling onto the floor beyond reach of my toes, and I am paralyzed with fear.

I want to open the door, but I have always been told not to. I am afraid to open it, to warn Uncle away from what he must know, even better than me, is coming slowly and inexorably closer. I wish now that I knew the old stories of witchcraft that Uncle transcribes himself. I wish I had not thought I would never need such information, or even, when I first heard the stories, that they were the rickety beliefs of the old, the foolish, and the ignorant. I want the protection of something, and I want my uncle to be safe.

The footsteps stop at the bottom of the stairs, and I hear a heavy thud, and then nothing but the sound of my pulse, the AC turning down, and crickets chirping dangerously loud outside.

"Uncle?" I force the word from my constricting throat. It comes out a croak. I swallow. "Uncle?"

There are no more sounds.

I tell myself Uncle is fine, and then I tell myself I am a bad liar, that the silence is too heavy to be natural, and that the next unnatural silence will come from me. The footsteps have stopped completely, but still I wait. I count to thirty, to fifty, to seventy-five, before knowing Uncle could really be hurt overpowers my cowardice. I open the door fully conscious of the hairs rising on the back of my neck and the goosebumps prickling my arms. The sound of the beads *scritching* over the wooden door does nothing to soothe my nerves. Outside my room it is dark, but the light over the stairwell is on. I poke my head over the threshold and feel the beads from the lintel sliding cool on the back of my neck.

"Uncle?" I call softly, then again, louder: "Uncle? Are you all right?"

There is still no sound.

I grip the door frame and step one foot outside. I cannot see around the stairs. I cannot see Uncle. I feel my way slowly outside and, seeing nothing—though perhaps what had happened *couldn't* be seen?—dart into the light of the stairwell.

I nearly trip over Uncle. He is slumped at the bottom of the stairs, as if he'd started to go up, become light-headed, and sat down just before passing out. There is no blood, and no wound that I can see. Perhaps he had been walking strangely because he felt sick?

Still I am wary when I crouch over him, clutching his thin shoulder and staring down at his chest to make sure it still rises and falls. He is alive, at least, but his breathing comes shallow and fast, and a strange smell of rot covers him that is both odd and familiar—the scent of the house when I wake up in the mornings, that fades until I go to bed. The smell grows stronger, and I look from Uncle to the dark room around me. The shadows move as they always move, and yet the stench creeps closer. Rot, death, decay. That is what's coming.

The clock chimes quarter past and I think I might leap out of my skin.

I want to leave Uncle and go to my room—the room with a door I can close and beads that are supposed to protect me. But before I can decide whether bolting will remain on my conscience forever, a shadow peels away from the darkness: a dragging corpse with a face I almost recognize.

The creature before me might have been human once, but the body it wears is in tatters. Dark skin in a wash of brown and green shades hangs off of torn muscles and ligaments and bones, just as the fibrous rags of a blue pinstriped dress shirt and stained off-white briefs hang from it. Maggots wriggle in the creature's empty eye sockets and drip from the thing like blood. Its lips are gone, leaving black gums and a ghastly wide smile that never wavers. It reaches out to me with fingertips that are almost entirely bone, and a familiar scarred hand.

The corpse's mouth opens. "Cousin," it says in French, "give me your body, so I can avenge my death."

It makes the creature real when that honey-sweet, broken-glass voice pummels its way out of my missing cousin's mouth. I start to scream, but the taste of its stench makes me choke. Someone—Uncle—clutches the back of my knee, and I scream and scuttle away before realizing I have left us both alone to face the creature, the stranger who's wearing my cousin's skin. I grope toward the kitchen light, but before I can turn it on, the smell of rot is overwhelming and the creature is in front of me.

I freeze as abruptly as I moved before, and my breath stops with my body. The corpse's hands touch my face with hard fingers, pressing my forehead where Uncle touched me just before he closed my door. Darkness seeps into my vision, and a new presence crawls in from the edges.

Something pushes me hard in the chest, but it is not a hand or a body, it is that presence—who is Kanku?—in my chest and my head, stretching through my legs and my arms and my pelvis, trying to push me *out*.

With a snap like a rubber band or a sparked synapse, I am outside myself. I feel nothing. I think I must go somewhere, but I do not know or care where that place is. I only know my body is walking away from me, out of the kitchen and into the living room, and I feel nothing about this but mild curiosity: why am I not inside my body? A knife hangs casually from the hand that was mine. I wonder what it is for.

KANKU:
"MY FATHER HE KILLED ME"

SOON MY TWIN'S BODY WILL BE TOO WEAK TO LEAVE this room, and Baba will have killed me—again. Day after day, I stand at this bedroom door in Mbuyi's decomposing flesh—though it has lasted years, like it knew this shape would have been mine too if I had lived. I wait for the midnight chimes as the air grows ripe around me. My hour, once again, is closing in.

I have spent much of my life waiting. Much of my life thinking. There is little living to do without a body to do it with. There have been three long waits in my life, before and after my death. I dwell on my memories, review them, pick at them like wounds made to fester and seethe. I replay my life and my rage, and the memories give me strength to finish the task I have set for myself: I will kill my Baba.

It all began with Mama.

"Kanku, come here!"

In our bedroom, I stop playing cowboys with Mbuyi and run to the kitchen. "Yes, Mama?"

Mama is stirring a pot on the stove. "Kanku, find me my peeling knife. It's not in the drawer where it belongs."

I think it is on the television, and when I run to the other room it is waiting for me there, just like I thought. I bring it to Mama. She smiles and takes it from me, kisses my cheek. "Such a clever boy," she says. She frowns at the blade then, spits an annoyed sound through her teeth. "Wash this."

I take it to the sink.

Baba says, "Where was it?"

I tell him, "You left it on the TV."

Mama's face glows with pride as she nods, but Baba is quiet. Then he says, "You were asleep when I got it out." He does not sound proud, or even happy.

"Our son is gifted," Mama says. I dry the cleaned knife and give it back. She sets it down, keeps stirring the pot on the stove.

As I leave the kitchen, Baba says, quiet, "A gift is only as good as the person who has it."

Something crashes—Mama's spoon against the pot, I think, or the stove. "Our sons are good boys," she growls, low, like I am not supposed to hear.

"So you say," Baba bites back, just as quiet.

Inside our bedroom, Mbuyi looks up from a new wire man he is making. Expression waiting to be delighted, he asks, "What did she want you to find this time?"

I shove Baba's suspicion away from my face and my thoughts. I won't tell Mbuyi. It would hurt him to know.

Mama was proud when I knew things grown-ups didn't want me to know. She ruffled my hair and pulled me close when Baba's friends looked wide-eyed at my words. She said I had a gift, that the ancestors had blessed me. I think maybe Mama was the blessing.

Remembering the kitchen knife—among other things she had me find—I've thought about how I could have known where it was without knowing why I knew. Perhaps I followed a trail of observations: Baba sometimes used the knives in the kitchen as screwdrivers; Baba always fixed the broken things in the house; the TV wasn't working, and he'd tested the antenna while I played in the family room, but the picture was still skipping, and he was annoyed he'd have to unscrew the back to look inside; the next afternoon the TV was working, but I never saw him fix it and I was home all day. Perhaps I even saw the knife crossing through the room from the kitchen or my bedroom, and left it because Baba might still be using it. I am still not sure how I found things for her, if I even had a gift, but Mama impressed upon me that being a good man, using my gift wisely, would bring good fortune to us all. Mama told me, *You are a good boy. I know you will be a good man.*

Mama said when we die, we join our ancestors in the spirit world stretched out over this one like a mirror, like a twin. There, joyfully reunited with our loved ones, we watch over our living family members. They give us honor and we bring them comfort. They give us prayers and we protect them from witches. They beg our advice and we nudge them in the right direction. Because of this, Mama said, no one is ever truly alone. Living or dead, we will always have family.

"Mbuyi, you cannot catch me! I am faster than you!" When my twin sees me again, I stop to wave the wire man he made, laughing. When he chases me, I run to the kitchen.

"Give that back! I said give it back!"

Mama shakes her head at us, but I see her smile as I run past her troop of steaming pots, and I am happy.

Baba is in the living room. "Mbuyi! Kanku! Stop running around this house while your mother is cooking!"

We stop. "We're sorry, Baba," we say with one voice.

I hide the wire man behind my back. Mbuyi wrinkles his nose at me.

"Kanku—come here." Baba holds out his hand to my twin.

"I'm Kanku!" I almost smile. Baba still confuses us. Mama never has.

"Then you come here! Give that back to your brother."

If I give it back, the game is over. "But Baba—"

"Don't look at me that way," Baba snarls, "it isn't natural." Baba's face is hard, cold. It scares me. I look at Mbuyi, confused and afraid, and his face is a mirror of my own.

"Like what, Baba?" I am grateful to Mbuyi; I know he asks for me.

Baba only says, "Give that to me," then, "Mbuyi, come here. Here. Now go, both of you. And don't run in the house—you are not dogs, do not act like them!" He returns to his newspaper. Mbuyi grabs my hand as we go hide in our bedroom, squeezing it to comfort me. His unease is a mirror of my own.

Too soon, Mama had stomach pains, or child pains, or some pungent infection Baba would not explain. When Baba was at work, Mbuyi and I would play in Mama's room even though it smelled so bad I couldn't keep my face from curling when I opened the door. Mbuyi wanted to play outside with the other kids, and sometimes he would, but often he would keep me company in Mama's room and make wire cars and men for us to play with from the rug next to the bed. From Mama's bed, where I curled against her as she slept, I would reach down and make the men dance and sing for us, make Mbuyi's eyes light up as he held in laughter. We used the figures to tell Mama's familiar stories. Sometimes, when she woke up, she pulled me and Mbuyi close and said, *Did I ever tell you the story about*—and we would say no and beg her to tell it even if we knew it already, and she would smile through strained eyes and stroke our arms and murmur tales about the wider world.

My first long wait was for my mother to recover her health. That wait was the shortest. It lasted a year. Her death brought my own.

Mbuyi is at the neighbor's house, where I am supposed to be, but I snuck home before Baba. I hear him from my bed.

"You think he is a witch?" Baba's friend says.

"He refused to leave her, and now she is dead. He must be a witch." Baba's voice is cold. He is always cold now, when he speaks of me. When he speaks to me. I do not know how to make his voice change back.

"He is only a child—and a twin! He is good fortune! How can he be a witch?"

I am not a witch. Mama knew. Mama loved me. It hurts, always, now she is gone.

"You have seen the way he looks at people. How he moves his hands when he thinks no one sees. And now he speaks to no one!"

"It is suspicious . . . "

I talk to Mbuyi. I talk to Mama. Mama knew I have restless hands.
She used to hand me things to toy with—spoons, sticks, dolls. She knew
it calmed me. Now I have only my fingers. I move them and remember
her. It calms me.

"I will not take him with us. I will have enough trouble with just
Mbuyi anyway. What kind of father keeps a murderer with his son?"
My heart freezes in my chest. No. He would not leave me behind.
"No one will take in a witch."
"And no one should. He killed my wife—let him lie in the bed he
has made."
No. I would never hurt Mama. I love Mama.
I want Mbuyi. I want my Mama.
No.

After Mama cut our hair, she burned it in the fire. After we cut
our nails, she burned those in the fire. Mama said, Be careful whose
gifts you accept, and be careful who you give gifts to. You never know
when a witch will use a gift to curse you, sacrificing your life to gain
more power. A twin's death is powerful magic for a witch. So Mbuyi,
watch out for your brother. And Kanku, take care of your brother.
People come and go, Mama said, but you can always rely on your
family.

"Do not cry, I said!"
"Baba, don't leave me, please!"
"Oh, so now you talk?"
"We are all going to the new house in America, you said—"
"Don't you cry to me, Kanku! You killed your mother—I would not
take you to a dog's house."
"I did not! I promise, I tell you the truth!"
Baba's big hand cracks, and I fall.
"You are a liar and a witch. Stay here."
". . . but Baba—"
"Let go of me!"
"Baba, please, Baba—"
"Do not try to follow us. You are not my son—you are no one's son."

Glass breaks. Mbuyi cries out. The car horn shrieks and shrieks.

No one took me in, not even a witch to make a sacrifice. I was seven years old when I realized Mama was wrong, that Mama lied.

It is important to know where you come from. It is important to remember your roots. As I wait for dark power to swallow the air, as I wait while Baba and that girl fritter away downstairs, as I stand in Mbuyi's room picking maggots out of my cheeks and hips and squishing their wriggling bodies, I remember with religious fervor the distance that I have come, and fuel my rage.

The second long wait spanned the end of my life and lasted most of my death. For almost two decades, I waited for my family to come home.

The sun is not pretty anymore. It burns like their eyes, always watching. Warning me away. Throwing stones at the witch. Only the dogs are not afraid. They smell death. They are starved as me, their ribs showing and spines poking and dry tongues dragging from their mouths. I talk to them, but they are not friends. Their fur is spiked with ticks. They are waiting.

I stole food. I sheltered with and ran from other "witch" children cast out on the street. I grew boney with hunger, and bitter, and mean. I knew I was going to die. And where were my ancestors, who I prayed to? Where was Mama's comforting warmth to my spirit? How much of what she said was wrong when she told me of death and the afterlife?

As death knelt close, I knew I was truly alone in the only world that mattered.

I made a choice.

And Mama was right: the death of a twin is powerful magic.

They are no longer waiting.

They gorge their feral stomachs.
The people turn their eyes away.

As I hovered over my body, I waited:
. . . Mama? . . . Ancestors? . . . Anyone?
. . . No.

They ate me. Tore into my body like jackals. They ate me . . .
But . . . they are only dogs. This is not their fault.
Mama left me.
Baba killed me.
Mbuyi let him kill me.
I'll show them a witch. They will come back home.
I am waiting.

The first body I took was a witch boy I ran from once. He was twelve, an adult to my seven-year-old eyes.

When I was alive, he found me eating chicken and foufou I stole from a table when a missionary stood to hug his friend. I ran with heart in my throat through the streets until the shouting died. Then I huddled with my stolen food, my first meal in days, under an awning on a quiet street of shops. I ate like the street dogs, quick and brutal and wary. The witch boy still surprised me. He pulled me up by my wrist, stole the chicken from my slick fingers, and shoved me hard onto the ground. *These are my streets*, he said as I skittered away. He sucked the rest of the meat into his mouth as I seethed with wretched hatred. He noticed my fist, cradled to my chest. But before he said, *Give me that*, I was running.

While I lived, alone on the streets, I ran and I hid. As a dead boy, I explored my hometown fearlessly, in the open, though I could travel only a few kilometers from where I died. Whenever I got too far, my consciousness narrowed and fluttered like a fish gasping for breath. I found the witch boy again as I explored. I wondered if I could hurt him now. I meant to burrow into his chest, try to squeeze his heart. Instead I felt his spirit quail against me. I thrashed it with glee and shoved it out.

The sudden wall of sensation knocked me flat, and then his memories assailed me. I lay in the street like a drunk. It took most of the night for me to master his body. The next day I stole and I ate. I had longer legs. My new body was weak, but stronger than mine had been when I died. I survived for two glorious days in his body. Then it began to rot.

I stole more bodies while I waited for my family. People who wronged me in life. People who should have stood up for me, taken me in. People with hands in my death. Always they began to rot after a few days. I discarded them quickly so no one suspected a witch. I learned one other thing during these experiments: while cloaked in a body, my tether was gone.

More than a decade passed before Mbuyi came home to visit our old house. I watched him walk through town, ask after me, come away angry. I wanted his body, but I hesitated. In all of my memories, Mbuyi loved me, took care of me. I watched him plant his feet in the ghosts of Baba's footprints and look down the road. He did not feel my presence as he apologized to a dead boy.

If he is really sorry, I thought, he will not fight me too much.

The last wait I spent trapped in my Baba's house, in a bedroom that should've been mine: I waited for the day I could finally kill him for killing me.

I sifted through Mbuyi's memories enough to get to the airport, get to Baba's car, get to Baba's apartment without him suspecting. It was the second day, the last day I had before Mbuyi's corpse started rotting like all the others. Baba asked me about my trip and I struggled to find Mbuyi's memories in time to answer. Twice the cold look returned to Baba's eyes as we spoke, and he showed me a necklace that made me recoil. I wanted to kill him then, but he wore it and I couldn't get close, not even with a knife. He cut my hair for me, as he did when I was a child, and tottered off to his office. I was woozy from the necklace brushing against my neck as he cut. I fell asleep in the chair. When I woke, he helped me walk up the stairs, my consciousness reeling with every step. I felt like power had gone out from me, like I was trapped in a cage, someplace dark and small. Somehow, while I slept, he had taken my power. I was a child in a corpse-shell, and Baba my master.

I could not shove him away, down the spindly staircase. I could not reach for his neck to choke the life from it. I could not curse his name with a witch's power. He dropped me in Mbuyi's room and he told me, face ugly with rage, "I always knew you were a witch." He slammed the door shut.

Mbuyi's corpse didn't rot after two days, or after seven, or after two years. In that time I learned Baba's house, walking it in the night when the dark power crests with the chime of the clock. I couldn't go far into Baba's office. The necklace was somewhere inside the desk, and it sickened me to get close. He hides my power in there, I am sure. While he slept I paced like an anxious dog. I was tired of waiting. In the third year, Mbuyi's body began to rot, and the girl started visiting Baba. In the fourth year, the body grew weak, its stink thick, and the girl settled in to spend the summer with Baba. She slept in the office, Baba's necklace hanging from the door, warding me away.

But tonight the air is thick with promise. The girl closes her door. Baba starts climbing the stairs—and the clock strikes twelve. I twist the door in my scarred right hand and step into the dark.

I am done waiting.

My spirit surges with the memory of adrenaline as I reach the top of the stairs. Baba puts the necklace at the office door—his only protection besides his locked bedroom door, which can't help him now. I grin at him stuttering up the stairs, and take a step down.

Baba looks up, eyes wide. His body shakes. I step closer, closer, and his face contorts. He grips his chest. He stumbles down to the landing and sits on the stairs facing the wall.

He cannot face me. He cannot face what he has done. He cannot face the death that is coming. I step beside him and run a loving hand over his shorn hair, the balding crown spattered with gray and white. Baba is old now. He has lived longer than I ever will. His time has come. I step down again and slide my hand, just strong enough, around his throat. I step down onto the landing and bring my face close. I want to watch him die, let him feel the peace it brings me. Baba is panting already, his dark face pale and pained, beginning to sweat. He slaps at my hands, but even against this body he is weak. My thumb presses into his windpipe.

My thumb presses in.

My thumb . . .

Baba huffs and twists his head just enough. He is laughing at me. I cannot press in. I cannot kill him. He still has my power, somehow. I cannot kill him—still! Cannot even shove him into the steps where he slumps. My half-rotted face twists in so violent a snarl a maggot drops from my cheek onto Baba's heaving lap. I turn in disgust and disappear in the shadows. I need a new plan, but what can I do that I haven't tried already, many times?

"Uncle?" the girl's voice quivers through my rage. She opens the door, calls again. "Uncle? Are you all right?"

Is this the answer?

I tear through Mbuyi's memory, call her to mind. The strongest memory is half-rotted, the details corroded. They are in Mbuyi's room, my prison, but the blinds are open and sunlight gleams on a mancala board. She is much younger than him, but his memory of her is fond, like his memories of me.

> *Hurry up and go already!*
> *Shut it, Mbuyi, I'm thinking.*
> *You're gonna think until bedtime. You just don't want to lose.*
> *I refuse to lose this game.*
> *I know. That's why you're my favorite cousin.*
> *Why? Because I always beat you?*
> *You only wish that were true.*
> *So why am I your favorite cousin then?*
> *Because you don't give up.*

Perhaps her mind will think of something I cannot? It is worth a try.

She finds Baba, a brave little mouse until I approach and she screams and she runs. I leave Baba to catch her.

In the dark kitchen I burn through the weak little blessing of Baba's, buzzing like a busybody on her forehead to keep me out. My power is mostly gone, stolen by Baba, but I have enough left to break this. The blessing's light crunches and winks out. I push myself from Mbuyi's corpse into my cousin. Rage and hope propel me. Her spirit leaves like a moan. The corpse smells stronger in my cousin's body, but I pay little mind, even trailing its juices in my bare feet. My strongest hour is wasting, but this body has been in Baba's office, has touched the necklace without fear. When I break it with my woman's bare, weak hand, my new body shivers with triumph.

I tear through the desk, quick and vicious, touching everything in sight. Paperweights, folders, things I have never seen except in Mbuyi's memory—stapler, computer, tape recorder, cordless phone—I shove my way in and out of Baba's treasured things, touching and rejecting it all. These things are not *mine*, not my power that he stole, and so I treat them like trash, I break them on the floor, just as Baba has treated me all of my life. I can feel my energy in the desk, but could never get close before.

When it is not in the drawers, I claw at the walls, the inside of the desk. I may have to break it apart. But on an inner drawer wall I find a hidden compartment. My back hunches and stills: this is mine.

Slowly, reverently, I peel open the compartment. Slide my fingers inside, caress and find and pull out: a homemade, brown rag doll. It has a twist of black, curly hair sewn to the top of its head. A black-thread smile and black-thread eyes cut across its rough face. A scrap from Mbuyi's blue pinstriped dress shirt is sown onto its torso and back.

Baba has trapped my power in a doll of me, an ugly doll tied to Mbuyi's body and my spirit. For four years I have waited to kill my Baba, thwarted by his chains lashed to me by this doll.

I doubt Baba will handle chains nearly so well.

I take the doll and the knife and some rubber bands into the living room. Baba looks up. "Kanku," he rasps.

"Witch," I correct him, bending over him with the knife. Baba strains for me with the hand not clutched to his side, but his arm barely moves. I yank through Baba's beard, ripping out skin as much as I cut through hair. I slice a patch of Baba's shirt at the sweat-damp collar.

"Don't," he whispers, pleads. His face is a rictus of pain.

"Because of you, I died like a dog," I snarl.

I'll make fire on the stove in the kitchen, I decide, and leave him to wait.

"Kanku—don't . . . "

The clock strikes half past. I turn on the kitchen light, turn the knob of the front burner. The fire lights with a pop. Carefully, I pull Mbuyi's hair from the doll's head and burn each piece in the fire—just like Mama.

Something in the living room crackles. The house abruptly smells like rot and cooked meat. Baba gurgles like an infant. I ignore him and burn the shirt too.

The rubber bands are not needle and thread, but Baba's hair and shirt stick to the doll just as well. In the living room, Mbuyi's body is gone. Only the smells are left. Baba looks pained. I am glad.

Baba's eyes go wide when he sees I have trapped him. He tries to speak, but only breath sounds come out. His eyes roll to face me, and he grimaces. I savor the moment. I reach for his throat, and my thumb presses in. "Look at me," I tell him.

For a moment, Baba does. Then he looks over my shoulder, and his grimace turns up in the corners. It is almost a smile. I push at his windpipe, a warning. He mouths something that I can't catch. His mouth closes, and he slumps. His eyes lose focus. Baba's whole body goes still.

I have barely started. I had barely started. I check him for breath, but there is none. This cannot be. Baba is toying with me. He is alive, he will remain alive until I kill him at last.

I shake him and shake him, slam his back into the stairs, but Baba flops like a rag doll until I fling him with a shout.

What right has he to look so peaceful?

I laugh. I laugh like a crazed, bitter thing.

A thing robbed of its prize the moment it was within reach.

My Baba abandoned me in his life. Why should he change in the moments of his death? I waited for him. I hoped, and I waited, and I thought maybe, maybe . . .

But no. I was wrong.

And all I can think of is: I killed my brother for this.

MBUYI:

WHITHER THOU GOEST

QUESTIONS IZZY ASKED ME—ONLY ONCE—FOR which I had no answer:

> *"Why do you have a twin's name?"*
> *"Why don't you celebrate your birthday?"*
> *"How did you get that scar on your hand?"*
> *"Why did your parents only have one kid?"*
> *"Did you ever wish you had a brother? A sister?"*
> *"Did you have a best friend in Congo? Who did you play with every day?"*

When I was a child in Kinshasa, I had a brother, a twin. He was my best friend. He told the best stories, after Mama, and after she died, he spoke only to me. He thought she'd get better. I hoped she would too, but I saw Baba's face every day, and my aunt's face as she cared for Mama, and somehow I knew Kanku waited for a day no one else believed would come.

I didn't tell him what I was afraid of—Mama told me to watch out for him, take care of him, protect him. I thought, Maybe I'm wrong. I thought, If I say it, it might come true. And I didn't say it, but I wasn't wrong, and Kanku felt betrayed by everyone who had known, and he got quiet and angry and sad, and I couldn't protect him from Baba.

We were adjusting. A family of three without a woman, without a mother, without Mama. We were adjusting well, I thought.

Then Kanku told me: *Baba thinks I'm a witch and that I killed Mama.*

> *Are you a witch, Kanku?*
> *Do you really think I am, brother?*
> *I'll believe you, whatever you say.*
> *No, I am not a witch! And I did not kill Mama!*
> *I know. You would never hurt Mama.*
> *Baba does not believe me.*
> *He will if you talk to him. If you only talk to me, people will think you're a witch.*
> *I do not like talking to Baba. He gives me mean looks. They all do.*
> *Baba will change. It hasn't been long since . . . He won't always be mad.*
> *But you believe me, right, Mbuyi?*
> *Of course I do. You've never lied to me.*

I thought as a child thinks: Baba loves us both, and Mama says when people are mad they say things they don't mean. Baba was angry. He cannot really believe you are a witch.

Then Kanku told me: *Baba says he is not taking me with you to America.* I thought, Kanku is scared, but Baba would never leave either of us behind.

If I had believed him about Baba, maybe I could've changed things. I would've prodded him to talk to Baba at dinner, or to play with the kids of the family who visited, or to seek hugs from the women who watched us after school so they'd see his pain.

But I didn't, and I didn't, and by the time I believed him, it was done.

I stopped being a child the moment Baba struck my brother—my best friend, my identical twin—in the face, in the street. Kanku fell down. He held Baba's knees, screaming and whining like a dog, crawling like a wet-faced beggar in the dirt. In the car I looked the same way, held down by Baba's friend's flexing arms as I thrashed for the door. I drove my fist through the window trying to get out, to go protect him, to wrap my arms around Kanku and not let go, so Baba would have to take us both. Baba would not abandon me, I knew.

We left Kanku crying in the street.

Baba used one of Kanku's shirts to bandage my hand while his friend drove. He gave the rest of my brother's belongings to the friend who was driving, to give to his children. All the belongings I had helped Kanku fold and pack for America. He seemed sure he wasn't going, but I tried to make him excited for the trip, to ride an airplane, to see yellow hair and learn to talk like cowboys. I couldn't stop crying, even when Baba threatened to give me a reason to cry and held up the hand that struck Kanku in his face that looked like my face, that felt like my face in those moments. I didn't want Baba to touch me. He had betrayed me, betrayed us both, betrayed Mama's love for us both. I wouldn't speak to him for weeks, even when he hit me or starved me for my silence. In America I had to speak to him—he was the only part of home I had left. But still. I hated Baba for years. I prayed to Mama to take care of Kanku the way I should have. I promised them both I would come back as soon as I could and bring him home.

They arrive, Tonton Badia and Tantine Janet, and her face is like a frail peach, and his is like a sturdy wooden desk, and when they hold hands their skin clashes but their fingers lock perfectly. Tantine Janet is round, and Tonton Badia holds me in his lap while I touch and the baby kicks my hand and I jump back and we laugh.

I watched Izzy grow up in the summers. Sometimes she visited alone while her parents traveled or had busy weeks full of meetings; or I visited her family alone while Baba traveled, collecting histories of other Congolese immigrants. I didn't like going with him, but Baba took me anyway—until I asked a man in an interview whether he'd cast out his son as a witch.

Baba never took me again.

Izzy was a quiet girl, thoughtful but bright like a dandelion. She smiled much more than she laughed, but seemed to take joy in the world like a child, like Kanku, even when worries weighed her down. I was a big brother to her for years. She wasn't Kanku, though I feared in loving her I was being unfaithful somehow, replacing Kanku with a cousin. I think she looked up to me. I think she liked my company as much as I liked hers. She was my favorite cousin—I think I even told her once—but as she grew up she grew small, like a mouse; tried to entertain me, keep me happy, as if afraid I'd lose interest in her company, her existence. On a walk with Baba and Tonton Badia, I confessed this with worry—but they approved: It's good for girls to learn to keep men happy.

Neither Izzy nor Tantine Janet were there when they said that. I thought of Izzy, who laughed at my silly faces for years, who made sassy jokes when adults weren't around, who complained the boys in her class could do more pull-ups than her, who started wearing skirts even though she hated sitting with feet on the floor.

I didn't confide in Tonton and Baba about much after that.

At home, I dug up an old pair of draw-string sweatpants. They were a little too big, but Izzy wore them when we played in my room that summer, sprawled out on the floor.

Topics Izzy never brought up again—not even to me:

   —*Why I have a twin's name*
   —*My birthday*
   —*The scar on my right hand*
   —*Why I have no other siblings*
   —*Siblings I'd wish for*
   —*My best friend in Congo; who I played with every day.*

Baba looks at me with pity when I tell him I want to visit the old house. He doesn't say, *He won't be there.* He doesn't say, *I'm sorry.* He doesn't say, *I was wrong, and I regret what I did to him, and all of us.* He says, *Go visit family first. Save sightseeing for the last day. Everyone is excited you are coming.*

Baba buys my ticket, arranges for me to stay with relatives, speaks at midnight and three a.m. to bridge the time zones with family so I can cross to meet them. I seethe inside, but think, Kanku will be there. I will find him and bring him home.

The day before I leave Congo, the host of family I've only just met finally lets me go to see my childhood home. Walking through streets I played in as a boy, I have flashes of recognition: The bus took this street into town from the house. This wall surrounded our house, and the crushed glass cemented on top kept out thieves and soldiers. The house I grew up in is through this new gate.

Baba cast Kanku from our family here, on this torn up, pock-marked road.

In a car on that corner, I cut my hand trying to escape Baba's friend so I could protect Kanku—the way Mama couldn't, the way I promised her I would.

This is the last place I saw Kanku before the car turned and he couldn't catch up.

That is the house of a woman who helped raise us, who told me—without shame—my twin died in the street not long after.

I can almost feel him here, on this heat-rippled road full of patterned stalls that weren't here years ago. I tell him *I'm sorry* and whisper a prayer that he's safe and happy, is somewhere with Mama.

My skin feels suddenly cold, but the lump in my throat and chest dissolves into a warmth I haven't felt in fifteen years. I think, Kanku hears me. Somehow, he is here.

I smile. I cry silently in the street, ignoring bystanders and the market's kaleidoscopic closing bustle.

Then my vision shudders. The *Kanku* feeling punches in.

I think, Something is wrong.

I think, Somehow, Kanku is alive. He wants my body. Is he a witch?

I think, It should've been me.

I think, I promised him we would go to America.

I think, Maybe this way I can finally bring him home.

I don't fight as he pushes into my skin and my spirit leaks out beside the body I sacrificed. I tell my twin, in bruised Tshiluba, *You're safe now. Let me take care of you.*

But Kanku doesn't answer, or even seem to notice I am there.

I stay with my body as Kanku takes his first trip in an airplane, watching his eyes light up in the body he never grew to inhabit because of Baba. I felt his pain, his rage, when I left my skin to him, but that anger is gone as he looks at the world from above the clouds. When a flight attendant speaks to him in English, I share his delight when he understands.

I pass my spirit across my skin, just enough to check on my body and check on Kanku. I catch a memory as I slide through—my trip to the airport—and when I see Kanku's familiar thinking expression— same as mine—I wonder if he saw my memory too. I don't know how it works to give over one's body. I worry about something I read last year: that our cells send out a death signal, a call taken up by all our cells to shut down. It's how our bodies know to die, how we die, and all it takes is one. Our bodies are smart. I'm afraid mine will realize Kanku, though identical, is not me, and this transplant will fail, and my body will die on Kanku before he finally gets the life I promised.

I slide around the edges of my body, checking for a death signal, pushing just far enough inside that it notices my presence.

Kanku never does.

I talk to him, try to calm him with my energy as Baba picks him up and I feel his anger build again.

And then Baba pulls out a necklace an interviewee gave him years ago.

And then Baba cuts Kanku's hair and his shirt and skewers them to a doll; and leaves Kanku slumped in a kitchen chair like some back alley anesthesia victim, like he's trash.

And Baba half-carries Kanku up to my bedroom and I think, Maybe things will be okay.

And he drops Kanku on the floor and snarls at him like a rabid, angry dog.

And as he slams the door, I see Baba's face as Kanku sees

it—finally—full of pain and rage and righteousness, and I realize what this means.

Baba will not suffer Kanku to live. He will not murder my brother—murder me—but he'll cage him until he dies all over again.

For years I keep our body alive. No one knows I'm there—not Kanku, not Baba, and they are the only people who come inside the house.

I go into Baba's room, go into his office, read over his shoulder, hover through his shoes—but mostly I stay with Kanku. I try to show him I'm there, to give him comfort. I tell him stories just inside our fingernails, jostle my brain to show him my first trip to the zoo, the magic of my first automatic door, my sorrow when Izzy asked questions that reminded me of him. I don't know if they work, if he hears me or feels me, but I see his eyes when the memories curl through him. It eases my heart that in this way I can still make him smile, give him life.

Two years in, I miss a death signal. After that I struggle to keep up, to limit the spread, to chase down the signals passing with synaptic speed without dislodging Kanku's spirit. I don't have to sleep, but the body is composed of billions of cells, and I am only one man, an impotent spirit who's going to lose his brother again.

This time, it's entirely my fault.

Enter Izzy. She's all grown up. Shed some of her quiet compliance. Still curious as ever, but wary of my bedroom now. She argues with Baba. She drags family back into his life with phone calls and showing up outside. She likes his interviews, helps him one summer, has come back for this one. I tell Kanku to stay away from her, but she sleeps in the office and he crowds her door at night. I worry for her in a way I don't for Baba, but he leaves the necklace with her and it calms me that she's protected, though I don't dwell on from whom.

It's her second summer with Baba since Kanku came home. His

body is falling apart. Flies land and hatch maggots in his skin, and I hope enough of his nerves are dead so he doesn't feel crawling inside his cheeks, at his hips, in the meat of his thighs, in the fat of his buttocks. It is hard to see him like this, but it's all my fault, so I watch, I stay with him.

He doesn't know, but I know. I pretend knowing is enough.

This night feels different. Kanku waits at the door that locks only from the inside, trapped by Baba somehow, by magic, though I never believed in it until I found Kanku again. At midnight, wrath propels him out once again. One o'clock is my hour when energy's high, so when it all goes wrong I see Baba collapsed on the stairs, a heart attack maybe, and he needs a hospital, but Kanku seems bent on destruction, and I am not strong enough to intervene.

I won't help him kill Baba, but I think: If Baba dies, Kanku will be at peace, and we can all move on from this.

But then Izzy comes out of her room to find Baba, and if I had a body my heart would have dropped to my stomach and punched out my breath with one beat.

And Kanku does the unthinkable.

I watch him shove inside poor Izzy's body, leave ours in a heap on the landing. Izzy, kind Izzy, who kicked my hand when I was new to this country and she new to this world, not even born. Izzy, my favorite cousin, my adopted sister in spirit, is a spirit now, watching her body walk off.

I can't let it end like this.

Izzy.

She hears me.

Mbuyi?

And she barrels through me like a hurricane. Our memories collide in a disembodied hug fraught with emotions and eddied by pressures of thoughts pushing from one mind to the next: *Thought you were dead* and *You need to get back in your body* and *What happened* and *Kanku didn't mean what he did* and *What's wrong with Uncle* and *Kanku wouldn't really hurt anyone* and *What is he looking for* and the half thought, *Maybe he would*, and from her, *You* do *have a twin!*

The clock strikes quarter to one as I push the death signal thoughts into her consciousness. She needs to get back in her body. I need to make Kanku come out here with me. I push my idea between us. I tell myself I'm doing what's right, that I'm not choosing sides. I tell myself I'm not robbing Kanku of his life, that I'm not like Baba.

To Izzy I say, *It's time for us to push.*

Izzy's body reels against us when we thrust under her skin. Kanku flinches her into the wall. His hands slap at us across the dim stairwell. Baba sits silent on the stairs. I know he's dead.

I feel an echo of warmth, a reminder of home as it used to be. I want to fade towards it, go to it, but I won't fail Izzy and I won't leave Kanku, never again.

We push inside Izzy's body. Our memories cloud together, knowledge crowding out thought in torrential bursts as our three lives flash-flood my mind.

Kanku curls Izzy's lip when he feels us. "I killed you!" he shrieks.

I ignore how my heart breaks in three.

I press under Izzy's skin, into her brain. *Kanku, give her body back. Come with me.* He shoves me back out. When I rush back in I feel Izzy's fierce rage bashing his, her will to take what is hers like a gale. *You killed Uncle and you killed Mbuyi,* she shoves at him, *but you can't have me. Did you kill your mother too, witch?*

Kanku's stolen face twists with fury. He flings me—I barely hold on. "I did not kill Mama!" he bellows, Izzy's voice in shreds. "Baba just wanted to blame a witch!"

Izzy's voice snaps right back: *So you're a witch then, Kanku?*

I bolster her, willing my brother to see what he's done. *Are you a witch, brother?*

The rage on Izzy's face freezes. She suddenly looks very young. Fragile and solemn, her mouth speaks: "Do you really think I am, brother?"

You've never lied to me, Kanku. I'll believe you—

And I'll believe you, Izzy tells me.

—and we'll still be brothers, no matter what. Okay?

Izzy's face stills. Her eyes blink, slowly at first, then more quickly. Her expression folds into itself like a house of cards. "I am a witch, brother," her voice says in Tshiluba. "But not then. I tell you the truth: I never killed Mama." A tear slides down one cheek. "You know that, right, Mbuyi?"

I know. You wouldn't lie to me, Kanku. You never have.

Izzy's body sags. Kanku curls into himself—and out of her body—like a sea anemone retreating within its tubes. Relief tears through me as I watch him let her go.

Izzy pushes past me then, deep into her body. As she slides to refill her spaces, she sends me gratitude, love, and sadness I return with fearsome pride in who she's become. I check her for the death signal—she's safe.

Reassured, I sink like a wave after my brother.

Kanku's hovering over Baba. I float to him as Izzy thumbs her phone. I join our spirits at the edges, but my twin pulls away.

He offers up his thoughts taking my body in Kinshasa. He passes me his determination, his refusal to feel pity, to feel shame.

I give him back my memory of that moment—why did he never look?—and then I let him feel my anguish watching over him, a shadow, since that day.

Kanku reaches for me then, and sudden as a crashing wave we are one person, whole, together as the day we were conceived. The feel of *home* and aftertaste of family dinners sitting around the foufou bowl and pondue bowl and plate of fish wisps slowly through my mind. And when we realize it, we startle, shocked as one: the feeling doesn't come from us—it comes from somewhere else.

Mama.

The pull is there, sudden, deep: Mama's waiting, family's waiting there for us, *elsewhere*—the afterlife she spoke of?—and this elsewhere place is good.

Izzy passes through us, phone in hand. She's checking Baba's pulse, face wet. She doesn't feel us, and my presence in this place begins to fade as I reach toward this elsewhere. But when I let myself drift up toward Mama, I'm alone.

I stop.

Kanku, aren't you coming?

His hesitance is back, the bitter cast of fear upon him. I see memories of other bodies taken, used with glee. I don't condone his actions, and I let him feel my disappointment, but I've loved him all my life and death, and he is family, he is mine.

I'm not going without you, not again.

Kanku says, *It's okay. You go on, Mbuyi. I'll follow soon.*

But he's lying. I feel it deep: this first, heartbreaking lie, his hope I'll believe one last time, forget him, let him waste away in penance here. I turn from Mama, curl around him like a suit of armor. *I'll wait,* I say. *We'll go together.* I bare my resolve.

You would wait for me? And once again he's seven, trying to grasp why I'm not outside playing football like I want to be; why I've stayed in with him.

I've waited for you since I left Kinshasa—both times. You will always be my brother, and my best friend. I won't lose you again.

Mama's warmth is up there, in a place that's bright, familiar, feels like home, like her love as she wrapped us in her arms and told us stories. I know she waits for us and loves us both. And for the rest of our dead family, I'll hold tight to Kanku. They won't leave me; they'll have to take us both.

DANIEL
CARPENTER

Flotsam

THE ARRIVAL

N o one could recall the storm though it is true to say that a storm had passed. The evidence was there, carried in a calm wind and the smudged grey sky like a poorly erased mistake in pencil. A curious amount of detritus had blown through the town also: a single bloodied shoe, a small doll with too many limbs to be human, a rusted bayonet (perhaps not rust, but rather ancient blood instead). Amongst the artefacts was discovered an iron helmet cleaved in two, its jagged edges cauterized and blackened.

The creature had arrived during the storm. It had erupted from the depths of the ocean, fatally wounded and had hauled itself on to the pebbled beach where it had gasped a final, inhuman breath and died, leaving behind a trail of its blood, thicker than oil, which traced its path from the ocean and spooled around in a whirlpool from where it had originated.

WHAT THE CREATURE LOOKED LIKE

There was never a consensus in the town on precisely what the creature looked like. The things that most agreed on—thick black tentacles, no eyes, a ridge of spine-like hair across its back—were refuted by others who saw bright colours, scales and too many eyes. The children in the village were not scared of it, not like some of us adults. They would freely walk close by and play around it. Sometimes building it a home out of sand, or redirecting the route of the tide to create a protective moat around the thing. What did they see when they looked at it? Something friendly, or perhaps something so monstrous it could not be processed by childlike minds.

For some of us, just looking at the creature brought upon terrible headaches almost instantly. So painful that they caused bright colours to dance across your eyes. At night, those who had seen the creature dreamt dreadful things, waking up in a cold sweat, practically feverish. It would pass quickly, and after that you learned to look away.

There were a select few though, whom the creature did not appear to affect. Mrs Bradley was the most prominent, though she was always like that at any event in the village. Mrs Bradley made the best cakes for the school fundraiser, she won village garden of the year, and she grew the biggest cauliflowers around. Everyone knew Mrs Bradley, or rather, everyone had to know Mrs Bradley, and it was as though that piece of village lore had passed on subconsciously to the creature itself. When she approached it on that first day, whilst the rest of us staggered back from the pain in our heads, she was unaffected. She touched it. Stroked it. I saw an oily black residue coat her hand, dripping onto the pebbles below.

She said, "It has been brought here for a reason, and we must devour it." The way she muttered it to herself, like an affirmation.

MRS BRADLEY ARGUES HER CASE

There was some debate at first. Most of the village gathered in the Scout hut by the creek, squashed in to the space. It felt clandestine. As though we were hiding from this dead thing on the beach. The local councillor, Mr. Peabody, was angry that this meeting even had to be called in the first place. Why should we, on Mrs. Bradley's say-so, eat the creature that had washed up from some unknown place? There were stories, Brian Hargreaves, the butcher said, about fish who were caught, cooked and eaten, who contained within them immense poisons. Did Mrs Bradley wish to kill us all?

The thing should rot, claimed several people. It should be left there to rot and die. Maybe then the headaches and dreams would end. It should be forgotten about. We should not speak of it again. Cast it into history. But Mrs. Bradley was adamant. "It has come here for a reason. You all fear it and look how it treats you. I don't fear it. I admire it."

Then, someone suggested, if Mrs Bradley is so keen to eat the creature, would she be willing to be the first to consume it?

She would do it gladly. She would be so proud to be the first.

WHAT DID PEOPLE DREAM
WHEN THEY SAW THE CREATURE?

The cosmos, spiralling out and out and out, ad infinitum. Sparks of life exploding in interstellar clusters. A feeling of dread, of sinking into nothing. Facts and knowledge that you cannot understand and so they sit at the edge of your mind, on the tip of your tongue, waiting just out of reach for you. And then, the inhuman screams of something vast, echoing across the universe, touching signals from asteroids and moons like radar. It is a scream without emotion, but it instils a kind of fear within you which you have never felt before in your life. Louder than anything you have ever heard. How small you feel. How insignificant. How utterly pointless.

HOW MANY COULD TOUCH THE CREATURE?

At first just three: Mrs. Bradley, Ms. Hobson the baker, and Mr Stoakley the farmer. Just three to begin with, although over time, there were more.

MRS. BRADLEY EATS THE FIRST PIECE

She didn't cook it. She ate the thing raw.

After it was agreed that she would be the first to eat the creature, she retrieved a carving knife from her kitchen and made her way to the beach. Some of the villagers followed her, despite the onslaught of pain from the creature. They watched as she took the knife to the creature, slicing a small piece of one tentacle. It came away gently, slipping from the rest of the body and splattering into the bucket Mrs Bradley had prepared for it. A little oily black blood dribbled from the wound.

Do any of the people who were present recall the creature shifting and twitching when she cut into it? No.

Mrs. Bradley took the bucket and sat on the edge of the seafront, looking out across the horizon. The trail of blood still floated on top of the water like a scar. She plunged her hand into the bucket and took out the piece of the creature. Almost immediately she tore into it with her teeth, ripping its flesh apart. The oily black substance staining her mouth and chin, dripping down onto her clothes. She smiled when she ate it. She smiled like she had never smiled before.

WHEN DID MRS. BRADLEY DIE?

At 142. She lived the longest.

ANOTHER MEETING CALLED

No ill effects were observed of Mrs Bradley, who continued her day to day life in the usual manner. Her vegetables grew large and impressive and she tended to her garden obsessively. However, there did appear to be a marked change in how she moved, how she carried herself. It was as if she floated, or knew some piece of impossible information. Everyone saw that change in her. Everyone wanted a part of it. It was the creature that did it. Eating a piece of it had given her a kind of revelation and why should the rest of the village not be privy to the same thing?

Mr. Peabody brought the meeting to order, but almost immediately Mr Stoakley interrupted him. Mrs Bradley had been permitted to eat the creature. Mrs Bradley had seen something. Why shouldn't the rest of us get the chance?

Not all of us felt the pull of the creature. Not at this time. But after

Mrs Bradley ate the tentacle there were more who could look upon it without experiencing terrible pain. Fewer dreamers, screaming in the night.

It was decided that each man and woman would make their own choice. If they wished to eat the creature then they may do so, providing they took only a slice. If they wished to leave it be, then so be it.

THE QUESTIONS NOBODY ASKED

Where did the creature come from?

What kind of storm leaves a trace, but cannot be recalled?

What kind of creature wants to be consumed?

A QUEUE FORMS

They brought their knives from home, scythes from the wheat fields, Stanley knives shining red in the sun from the pockets of their Scout leader uniforms. They didn't surround the creature and tear it apart. No, they formed a queue, winding its way up the beach, straggling the wall at the back, and flowing up the steps to the promenade. It snaked past the fish and chip shop on the corner, passing the B&B and up towards the high street. Mrs Bradley paraded up and down, shaking everyone's hands. She didn't say anything, didn't have to. It was all in her eyes. Welcome, her eyes said. The first day of the mass consumption of the creature was a glorious day.

THE HOLDOUTS NOTICE A CHANGE

It was not immediately apparent. Life continued as normal. There were a few hundred or so who chose to abstain from eating the creature. Walking down the promenade, their heads throbbed and they couldn't help but turn to look at the corpse lying on the beach, slices of flesh missing, so that it resembled something even more alien that it had previously. It was not just in its fractured body that they saw a difference. There was an emptiness to the town.

In their nightmares they saw the villagers who took part in the eating. The oily blood from the creature cascading from their mouths. Not just that thick black, viscous liquid but the pieces of the creature itself, slipping from their mouths, regurgitating itself. The pieces came together in the middle of a supernova of light.

When spoken to, the villagers who ate the creature were cordial. They took part in small talk and asked questions about family members: How is Uncle John? Did little Sally get her silver in swimming? Is the kitchen going to be finished by Easter? But to the holdouts there was something missing. It felt like a performance.

It drove them away, one by one.

WHAT OF THE DETRITUS?

After the storm, the bayonet, shoe, doll and helmet were all taken to the library immediately to be photographed and retained for historical record. They remained there during the consumption. No photographs were ever taken and as with all things, no record was made. Instead, they were locked away. The relationship between these objects was never discussed or considered, and the whereabouts of the other shoe in the pair (a right) was not pondered.

THEY TOUCH THE CREATURE

They stood around it one morning, all of those who had eaten a part of the creature. The remaining villagers who hadn't tasted the innards of the thing on the beach caught sight of it on their way to work, or on the school run. Hundreds of them surrounding the corpse, hand in hand. Mrs Bradley right there and though the circle did not have a start or end point it seemed as though she was at the head of it. The day was quiet, no cars rumbling along the high street, no clinking of empty milk bottles being picked up. All that could be heard was the calm slosh of the tide, and the odd hollowness of pebbles shifting beneath feet.

Somewhere in the distance, across the horizon and far from the eyes of the villagers, a ship's horn rumbled in the air. Those watching the group encircling the creature turned to look for the source of the sound. Those with their hands clasped did not move.

It was as though they moved closer towards the creature, closing in on it. But they did not move so that couldn't be true. It was just as likely to suggest that the creature, dead as it was, expanded to fit the space created by the circle of hands. That it fattened itself. What remained of its skin rippled around it, following the ring of consumers. The people surrounding it shuddered momentarily as though being caught off guard whilst standing on a moving train, then righted themselves and offered no further movement. All save Mrs Bradley. Her face, an assiduous look of concentration, but for the glimmer of a smile, for just a moment.

The creature expanded to touch each of the people, pushing itself against them, bulging out through the gaps between their hands, the spaces below and above their arms. One lone tentacle escaped between someone's legs, then whipped itself back into the fray just as quickly.

Those who had not consumed a part of the creature fought the vicious headaches they experienced, some practically blinded by the pain. They fought so they can watch. They felt a need to witness this that had nothing to do with its strangeness. This appeared strange to no one. No, this felt wholly expected.

WHAT DID MRS. BRADLEY DIE OF?

Unknown causes. She was cold to the touch, and stiff as a bone. No blood was discovered either outside her body nor within it. Though a tiny patch of oil close to her body was noted in the coroner's report.

———

INSIDE THE CIRCLE

It breathed its first in an age, taking in one or two primitive minds and expelling the scraps back out into their bodies. There they were: pieces of it, inside them all. Digested and absorbed into skin and fat and blood. There was a piece of it careening around, hidden in some minuscule vein. Another breath. The sweet taste of a soul. Memories flooded through it. Unknowable things. A party by a river, the wind picking up a tablecloth. A sudden rush indoors at the first sparks of rain. It searched within for something more filling. There: a horrible thought, an anxious woman pacing in the corridor of a hospital. The news will be bad. She knows it will. That would do. It released what it hadn't devoured, broken and piecemeal though it was. All the while it grew, found strength that it forgot it had.

THE LIBRARY IS OPENED

Mr. Peabody ran from the events on the beach. He knew each and every one of the people in that circle and he watched briefly as they shuddered and lost themselves to the creature. There were shards of glass in his head, scratching at his mind. A pain like no other he had ever felt in his life. Turning tail he abandoned them to the thing that had washed up. What had happened to his town? He thought back to the day after the storm that he could not recall, when the creature appeared. His head splintered as though a bullet had pierced it. A pain that stopped him dead in his tracks.

But he recalled the detritus that washed up in the town the same night. Recalled where it was being stored.

Mr. Peabody ran.

The streets were empty. Everyone was at the beach. Those who didn't eat, watching, those who ate participating. Mr Peabody raced down the high street, passing open stores with no workers, dogs tied to lampposts, barking for owners who are far from them. From inside The Railway Arms he caught the sound of a football game being watched by no one, and heard the trickling of a tap still running. But he did not stop. He felt a burning racing across his chest, tightening his veins. Like whatever kept him running was seeping from him, being devoured piece by piece. The library could not be far.

Glass scattered on the floor when he broke the window. He found himself surprised by it. Not the act of destruction so much as the evidence left behind. Did I do that? he found himself asking as he clambered through the gap into the library.

THE CROWD ATTEMPTS TO WATCH

The pebbles all around the circle shifted, as though being trodden on. Pain cascaded through all of the non-eaters though they could not look away. The thing that had washed up on their shores roared in their minds. All of them. A terrible indecipherable speech that tore through them. Some were knocked to the floor, others staggered back. One or two stood their ground. No one dared get close to the events taking place at the shoreline. Those who formed the circle clutched each other's hands, but their bodies appeared limp. All except for Mrs Bradley. Mrs. Bradley's smile was as terrible as the creature itself. She stared right at the creature. Smiling. What was the creature saying to them? What was it saying to her? Whatever it was, to those watching, it felt like the end of all things.

A BAYONET, A DOLL, A HELMET, AND A SHOE

They were hers once. Torn from her as she dragged the thing into the rift. The doll she had been given by her mother, so many years ago. So long that she couldn't even recall it not being in her life. It was apt then that in that moment she would lose it.

ON THE BEACH

Mr. Peabody sprinted towards the circle. The closer he got to the creature the more the pain in his head intensified. Pain unlike anything he had ever experienced. As though his brain was pouring out through his ears. But it wouldn't stop him. Brandishing the bayonet, he ran forward towards the eaters. The creature, a writhing mass, was a negative space in front of him, an absence of light. It had nearly engulfed all of the circle now, close to breaking free. Where a part of it had been eaten, it was regrown, the wounds zipped together and closed. Tentacles sneaked around the area, combing the beach, lifting pebbles. A screaming sounded in his ears and Mr Peabody understood what it was. The creature was laughing. Laughing at his attempts to do what he was trying to do. No matter. He reached the edge of the circle and, raising the bayonet above his head, he leapt forward, toward the screaming thing.

MR. PEABODY FALLS

The bayonet stuck in the creature and Mr Peabody fell. He clutched the doll in his hand, but his hand was weak and he could not hold on to it much longer. The creature screamed again and he thought, "It's in my head, and how much more of this can I take?" But it was not in his head this time. A great shockwave passed through the circle, breaking clasped hands, showering the promenade with pebbles, and washing the tide out. Mr Peabody felt a wetness against his cheek and he touched it, bringing back a handful of blood. The doll is a curious thing, he thought. So many arms.

So many arms.

MRS. BRADLEY WISHES FOR DEATH

At 142, don't we all? She felt a change after the creature left. A rushing of something inside of her. None of the other eaters experienced it. She understood in that moment that it was because she was the first. She was trusted and she had been gifted something. The others, they became husks. Something had been taken from all of them. Mr

Stoakley went back to running his farm, but he could never keep an animal alive for more than a couple of months. He could be seen sometimes, standing on the beach, weeping. Others who had been in that circle could be seen there sometimes too. Mr Hobson often went there and walked across the shore, picking up pebbles and checking under them. Mrs Bradley felt none of this, except that deep within her there was a terrible longing. She didn't go back to the beach, not for any of the many decades she remained in the village. The children who saw her named her Grandma Ankou and crossed the road to avoid her, lest she drag them to hell with her at night. It was curious as to how the stories they told about her took something from her each time she heard them. As though the children were carving little pieces of her, and eating them raw.

MICHAEL MIROLLA

The

Possession

As always, Amil pops out of the trunk first, rotating his head in a 360 degree circle to examine his surroundings: an empty nondescript room whose lack of windows gives the impression of a disguised bunker.

All clear, he says, looking back into the trunk.

Wolf emerges, blinking, eyes rimmed red.

I hope you're right this time, he says, dabbing at his eyes with a handkerchief. No more surprises.

The two men—somewhat past, as the saying goes, their prime—have always shared the same room. Not the same room in the sense of one room but rather a series of identical rooms accumulated over a period of many years. But it might as well have been one room for all it matters: bedroom-living room-bathroom-kitchen nook all crammed in one space. And, while they are free to leave the room and wander about, they always return before nightfall, as if tethered by some type of umbilical cord.

Contrary to malicious gossip, however, it isn't because of some mutual attraction, a lust for one another that makes everything else—even the possibility of disease and excruciating death—irrelevant. Nor are they related—at least not by blood. No, the truth, as is usually the case, seems of the much more mundane variety. You see, they own something in common which neither is willing to relinquish completely to the other. This . . . shall we say . . . possession had been acquired just prior to the sharing of that first, primal room, now so indistinguishable from the rest. And both have a vague memory of having come from different elsewheres, of journeys of some kind, a memory that seems to manifest itself in languages neither of them understand—at least not on a conscious level. What they do know is that, unless they are really forced to, they do not want to experience such vagueness or journeys ever again.

After all those decades together, filled with the cares and necessities of daily life, the unstudied routines of existence, neither any longer can actually come out and say what this possession might be—or why it is so important. Is it perhaps the antique, stretched-to-the-limit almost transparent table-lamp cover that popped up just after the last great war, after the annihilation of so much historic property? Amil says no. Wolf says yes. Or is it the massive black trunk—Prop. of A.H. & B.M. written on its side—they use when shifting from identical room to identical room? Wolf says no. Amil says yes. How about the cloudy-glassed bottles with labels that read: "Olio di ricino—Manganello"? Both shrug. The solution is obvious—to hold on to all their possessions jointly until the unique object is re-discovered. This presupposes, however, that they also have to hold on to each other, and never be out of one another's sight—at least while in the room. It is, as one might guess, this aspect of the arrangement that caused—and continues to cause—problems.

Wolf, a self-described "painter, architect, author, sensitive soul full of romantic aspirations that had been dashed before fruition," at first found this intolerable. He had fretted about his lack of privacy and his inability to act out his dreams with someone else in the room. In fact, he'd packed up to leave several times in those crazy early days when the relationship had yet to stabilize. Gradually, he has given up any thoughts of leaving. A voracious reader, spending much of his free time in the closest library he can find, Wolf claims to know about such things as symbols and metaphors and semiotics and thus inevitably develops a theory concerning the possession.

It is non-existent, I tell you, he says, pacing as he imagined Socrates might have done. Simply a ruse invented by you to keep us together, to keep our détente going. After all, what would you do without me? You would have nothing to clean up, nothing to worry your little brain about. There's no doubt who the leader is around here. And you have intentions on my body. Oh, I know. You've held them in check till now but they'll surface one of these days. They'll burst forth. You mark my words. That bulge in your pants says more about you than all your excuses and wimpy apologies put together. That bulge defines you. That and your hairy chest. Like all your kind, you allow the physical to dictate how you conduct yourself. I, on the other hand, allow culture to dictate mine.

He also knows some of the theories behind sado-masochistic relationships (having read *The Legacy of Cain, The 120 Days of Sodom, Kannibale von Rotenburg, The Serpent in Paradise, Justine ou les Malheurs de la vertu, Histoire de Juliette, ou les Prospérités du vice*). Except that in this particular case he can't decide which is which or who is who. Let alone what is what.

Every Monday, whether the urge is there or not, they strip down and fight. Evenly matched physically (Wolf short and wiry; Amil short and stocky), these bouts are usually decided by an opponent's slip, a new feint, an inventive grapple. As well, they are able to wrestle without causing too much damage to each other (except the one time when, in the heat of the moment, Amil had bitten Wolf on the buttock—and to prevent a re-occurrence Amil is now obliged to remove his teeth before combat). During these wrestling matches, the two engage in a ritual litany of insults. But, although the tone seems to mark them as insults, neither really understands the specifics or how they relate to them. An example:

Wolf: May you hang upside down until your testicles fall off.

Amil: May you spend your last days in a burning hut.

In keeping with the idea that only the joint possession holds them together, they won't acknowledge each other if they happen to meet on the street. Not even a nod or second look. They are strangers till they return to the room where, each night according to a pre-arranged schedule, first one and then the other examines and catalogues every article they own. It is probably true that most of these articles hadn't been found or bought together; nevertheless, they are now possessed jointly. Both allow this to happen—as long as the objects remain. A pair of reading spectacles ("Ruhnke Opticians") will one day be uncovered by Amil, on the next used by Wolf; pants and coats ("Lattimer Collection") are shared; a black fez with eagle decoration is worn by each on alternate days.

Amil rejects Wolf's theory. In fact, rejects all theories. Despite vague recollections of having been a teacher, or perhaps some type of civic leader or union organizer, he prides himself in being a practical man, a man of the world. He insists the possession is real—and somewhere to be found. The problem is that they haven't searched well enough. And he feels it is quite possible it will turn up at any moment, fresh and unharmed by the passage of all these years. This is possible even if nothing has appeared in the previous search. Amil's views are bolstered by the fact new things do materialize each time they examine their possessions, thus necessitating an updated catalogue daily. Not that *the* possession has turned up as yet, but it is only a matter of time before it does appear—or re-appear, to be more precise. Precision is Amil's outstanding attribute. When asked, he tells the time precisely, down to the second; measurements are precise; thoughts are precise; the world is a precise place with one word for every object or action— and should be run like a train schedule. It was his idea, for example, to examine their room nightly. Wolf hadn't been in favour at first, saying he knew its contents by heart. But he quickly changed his mind when he saw that Amil was going ahead without him and finding things never before seen.

The balance in the room—between living space, kitchen nook and the accumulation of material goods—is kept by the judicious disappearance of articles at crucial moments when the piles of clothes, furniture, baubles and antiques threatens to inundate them. There are no set rules for these disappearances, neither priority nor value of goods. Newly-found as well as ancient articles vanish; important and trivial alike. Like all men who consider themselves important, Amil and Wolf have developed a very laissez faire attitude towards these articles and they are quickly forgotten in their all-consuming search for *the* possession. This possession is conceived in terms of everlastingness or indestructibility. It has simply been misplaced for the moment and both look forward with great anticipation to the day it will make itself found.

To date, their discoveries appear to have been of a random nature, without any discernible pattern that they can make out. But, of late, the objects they turn up are becoming increasingly nefarious. In rapid succession, a shotgun (with "A.H." beneath the trigger guard), a gold-plated pistol, a silver knife and a cudgel (inscribed with "Dux") are unearthed. Wolf attributes this to Amil's evil thoughts. He's decided long before that the articles appear and disappear through the action of their minds, a fused telekinesis, a link also buried in the past. That he's never been able to consciously think up an article doesn't deter him from formulating what he calls his "thought-article-thought" theory.

Amil doesn't help. He greets the theory with laughter and denies all connection between the articles and his thoughts even when pinned to the ground by Wolf one Monday and forced to say "thought-article-thought" several times in succession. These moments of sweaty intimacy can normally be put to good use by Wolf when he comes out on top. For one thing, he is able to extract confessions which otherwise wouldn't be forth-coming. Amil enjoys confessing—that he fantasizes winning an argument on genetic purity with Pope Pius XII; that he once voted for a socialist party; that he masturbates while imagining a steam engine chugging along and pulling into a station. But, of the strange and potentially hazardous articles of late, he admits to knowing nothing, even when Wolf comes dangerously close to snapping his fore-arm. Accompanying the appearance of these weapons is the vanishing of useful and time-worn articles such as their beds, shoes and underwear, things which have never disappeared before.

Amil laughs it all away. Sticking the gun, knife and cudgel in his pants and shouldering the shotgun, he goes off singing songs in languages that he doesn't even recognize: "Salve o popolo d'eroi / Salve o patria immortale / Sono rinati I figli tuoi." He doesn't mind not having shoes and underwear. After all, revolutionaries/highway robbers/pirates seldom wore them. Beds can also be dispensed with if one is willing to curl up in a corner and cover oneself with straw.

Wolf, on the other hand, collapses into a state of intense moroseness and paranoia (something always near the surface in his case). The weapons worry and frighten him. He envisions all sorts of accidents, blood everywhere, the last room filling up with more and more possessions (without them, with no one to put a halt to them—or worse, with someone else enjoying them). Or slowly being covered with dust, an archaeological display for the benefit of future inhabitants. Perhaps suicide would be the best: a single bullet ripping through both of them. Only, who would pull the trigger? He would, of course.

He is the only one who can be trusted. Amil would move out of the way at the last moment. They'd have to fight over the honour of pulling the trigger. A combat in the heroic style. Wolf in loincloth, the knife gripped tightly between his teeth; Amil in military uniform, slapping the cudgel against his open palm. No matter how romantic such thoughts appear in the abstract, they always turn ugly—and dangerous—when the details are worked out.

These are the conditions at the time a singular event takes place to throw everything off kilter, to begin an entropic cascade. Wolf, in the hope of at last coming up with a definitive explanation for the appearance and disappearance of the articles and out of fear that Amil might become violent, invites a librarian friend to come up to the room and participate in one of the searches. When Amil takes Wolf aside and demands an explanation for this strange female's presence, Wolf informs him that, aside from Basha's book cataloguing, she dabbles in astrology and telepathy and the study of signs. But this is unheard of, Amil whispers, casting a dubious glance at the imposing woman who stands with hands on hips, nose haughtily in the air. You can't bring someone else in here, he hisses. It's supposed to be just the two of us. Too late, Wolf says with an oily smile. I already have. And, unlike you, this is one person who can carry on a decent conversation. Wolf turns his back and walks away towards the librarian-astrologer. Amil looks at him for a moment, fists clenching, then slinks off to sit in his private corner.

Wolf, busy being garrulous with his new-found friend, ignores him. After a brief conversation about her name, which she says means "Daughter of God," the two sit down and began their search in earnest, marking down what they find on the list and checking it against the previous night. Until that is, Basha comes across the tightly-stretched, translucent table-lamp covering. Her reaction, a jumping back as if the covering were about to wrap itself around her, has Wolf scratching his head. *What is that?* she asks, having trouble catching her breath and with one hand across her throat. *How dare you . . .* She takes another deep breath. *You lured me in here to show me . . . that.* No, no, no, Wolf says. I just wanted to show you how things appear and disappear. *You're sick*, she says. *You're both sick in the head. Sick*

fucks. I'm going to call the police. You can't have things like that . . . But,
but, but, Wolf says, picking up the lamp and holding it out towards
her. It's just a table lamp. Tomorrow, it'll be gone. *You hear that, God.*
She looks up to the ceiling. *Just a table lamp, he says. The police, I tell
you. They'll know what to do with you.*
   Basha takes a step towards the door. Wolf reaches for her coat sleeve
while blubbering that it is all a misunderstanding. That it is all Amil's
fault. That if she doesn't like table lamps she just has to wait and it'll
vanish. No problem. Silly old lamp. Basha pushes him away, sending
him across the room. Wolf stumbles to the floor. *You'll be sorry. There
are laws against this.* She turns and reaches for the door handle. As
she does so, Amil springs up, shouts: "Long live the squadristi!" and
hits her across the back of the head with the cudgel. With exactly the
amount of force needed to stun but not kill her.
   Amil drops the cudgel. Turning, he follows Wolf who is circling
the edge of the room. Wolf stops and looks back at him. But neither sees the other. Instead, Wolf sees a pile of human bones that
keeps growing, that keeps swallowing the space around it; Amil sees a
series of identical men, naked, skeleton-thin, squatting painfully over
chamber pots, the diarrhea pouring out of them like fetid, stagnant
water. Killer! Wolf and Amil scream at the same time before lunging
at each other.
   Assassino! Amil shouts.
   Attentäter! Wolf retorts.
   A noise from near the entrance makes them hold up. Still somewhat stunned, Basha is trying to crawl away, reaching up for the
door handle with one hand and clutching a purse with the other. She
is muttering: *Please God, not again. Don't let it happen again. Help
me* . . .
   I'm sorry, Wolf says, smiling and offering her his hand. My friend
has emotional control problems. Prone to outbursts. Neglected childhood and all that.
   I'm prone to outbursts, Amil says. That's a good one. What happened the last time?
   Please . . .
   Oh come on, Wolf says with a dismissive wave. That doesn't count.

You heard what he called himself. A Marxist-Leninist of all things. You know how those guys make my blood boil.

Please . . .

Yeah, well, Amil says. You didn't have to shove his head in the oven.

Please . . . I . . .

What's she saying? Wolf asks, leaning down. What are you whispering?

As he places his ear near Basha's mouth, she pulls out a can from her purse and sprays him in the face. He screams and falls to the ground, fists rubbing against his eyes.

Amil tries to approach but she holds out the can menacingly.

Come closer, you bastard. You sick fuck. Come on. I dare you. There's plenty more where that came from. After I'm through with you, the cops will just have the mopping up. Unlike my ancestors, I'm not going like a lamb to slaughter.

Amil looks around, spots the gun where he's left it in his private corner. But before he can reach it, she backs out of the door and slams it shut behind her, all the while shouting: *Not again. Never again.*

Wolf continues to writhe. Amil locks the door and then squats beside him.

My eyes, Wolf says moaning. I can't see.

There is hammering on the door, followed by shouts to open it or have it broken down.

We have to leave, Amil says.

He leads Wolf towards the trunk, opens the lid and helps him to get in.

You should have killed her when you had the chance, Wolf says.

Yes, Amil says, lowering himself into the trunk and pulling shut the lid just as the front door smashes open. Maybe next time, I will.

IAN
MUNESHWAR

Skins Smooth
as Plantain,
Hearts Soft
as Mango

THE BEAST IN THE FOLDS OF HARRY'S GUT HAD NO heart and it did not need one for his was strong enough to keep them both alive. It had neither heart nor mind nor eyes to see; it was only lips and teeth and fingers like needles that slipped inside his tongue and his bowels and even those places he did not know he had. Those unfilled hollows made its gums throb with an emptiness that might have been desire.

That night a man came to the house whose face Harry remembered from the dimness of a childhood memory. His thinning hair was combed forward over the shining dome of his skull, and the line of a moustache traced the contours of his upper lip. He sweated with an unnatural persistence from the pock-like pores on his cheeks.

"You remember your Uncle Amir," Father said, a statement.

Harry's eyes flickered over to Mother, who stood just behind Father, her arms crossed over her stomach. The way she sucked her tongue over her front teeth told Harry all he needed to know: this man was no brother of hers.

Uncle Amir smiled. His teeth were too large for his mouth; when the smile faded, his lips still didn't cover the thick, yellowed ends.

"It's good to see you again, Harry. It's been a while."

His English was excellent, almost unmarked. He reached a hand out, and Harry took it.

"Dinner must nearly be ready," Mother said, pulling away. "Come, Amir. Majid's been cooking all afternoon."

The dining room was at the end of the hallway, behind a heavy hardwood door. The table was set for four. White candles stood in pewter holders; Mother's best plates—white and blue chinoiserie shipped all the way from London—sat perfectly centered before

each empty chair. The tablecloth had begun to yellow—because of
the humidity of Guyana's summers, Father would always say, jovially
cursing the tropics.

Father sat at the head of the table, striking up a conversation
with Uncle Amir, and Amir immediately took the chair to his right.
Harry cursed inwardly; this meant he would need to sit next to
Mother.

Father took the white linen from under the fork and knife, shook
it open, and placed it neatly on his lap. Everyone else did the same.

The cook, Majid, burst in from the kitchen, shouldering the door
open, dinner balanced on the trays in his upturned palms. Harry
had been listening to Father talk about work—a tedious monologue
about the rising price of equipment for the mill, which had Uncle
Amir nodding in vigorous assent at the end of every sentence—but
his attention drained away as soon as Majid laid the plates on the
jaundiced tablecloth.

It was a richer meal than what they had most weekdays: two large
tilapia, one leaned against the other, their meaty sides slit open and
stuffed with lemon wedges and sorrel; plantain baked until its edges
had crisped, caramel-brown; a steaming bowl of channa spiced with
cumin and ginger and topped with rings of sautéed onion—

—and back he came with still more plates: a pie of beef and goat
(Majid's poor facsimile of Father's favorite: steak and kidney pie); okra
roughly chopped and fried in ghee—oh, he could smell the fat!; and
mango, sliced thin, spread like an orchid in bloom.

Harry reached a fork out to the tilapia, and Mother swatted his
hand away.

"We have to say grace," she scolded. Then, raising her eyes to Uncle
Amir: "Would you mind?"

Uncle Amir recited a short, elegant grace, thanking Father for
giving him and the others at the mill such fulfilling work. Father
nodded thoughtfully, and the meal began.

Harry went at once for the fish, taking a whole tilapia for himself.
He cut it open just down the middle, pulling away that sweet, flaky
meat with his fork before lifting out the spine and troublesome ribs—
he'd come back for those later. He scarfed down the fish skin and

all, gratefully swallowing and immediately returning for more. The beast rumbled pleasantly in his stomach, its jaws receiving the food Harry chewed for it, its snakelike throat slicked by Harry's saliva. He returned to the tilapia's charred head and used the point of his knife to carve out its fleshy cheeks. He especially loved the salt, the sweetness, and the softness of the cheeks—next, the eyes.

He only slowed when he noticed, after a few more throatfuls of fish, that Mother was pinching him under the table. She had dug her fingers into the skin just below where his shorts cut off, twisting the fat on his thigh.

"Harold," she hissed, mouth drawn. "You're eating like an animal again."

Harry put his fork down, pulled his leg away, and wiped his mouth with the napkin. He ignored the heat of her stare, the nettle of her prying, meddling eyes, and focused on his plate.

"That's settled then!" Father broke away from a conversation with Uncle Amir that Harry hadn't been listening to. "Harry, my boy, you're coming to see the mill tomorrow. How about that?"

Harry lifted a slice of the pie off of the serving dish.

"Sure."

He ate a heaping forkful. It was wonderful: the goat was soft, savory, fatty; the salt and animal juices and hot water crust all came together on his tongue. The beast pushed up, stretching open the base of his esophagus, unfurling its own eager tongue.

Mother put her fork down as she watched, then pushed her full plate away.

"You'll be lucky to have your Father's job one day," Uncle Amir said, wiping his moustache with the crisp edge of his napkin. "You have a few years yet, but it's never too early to get started at the family business." He gave an ostentatious wink.

Mother excused herself, saying she was beginning to feel nauseous, and Majid came to clear the plates. As he did, heaping dirty silverware on top of plates balanced expertly up his arms, Uncle Amir came and sat next to Harry.

"I have something for you," he said. "Something you might like too, Reginald."

Father leaned in, his curiosity piqued. Harry swallowed a mouthful of plantain.

Uncle Amir removed a thin magazine from his briefcase and placed it on the table in front of Harry. It was an old copy of *The Cricketer*. A player posed heroically on the cover, his bat pitched at a perfect angle, his eyes on an unseen ball spinning into the distance. Beneath the picture it said: FRANK DE CAIRES DOES IT AGAIN!

"Good lord." Father reached for the magazine. "This was your mother's, Harry. She had a dozen of these, back when we were together. She loved this man. Worshipped him. What was his name?"—he spoke it slowly, savoring the syllables—"I never thought I'd see this again. Do you know, Amir, did Bibi ever get to see him play?"

"Oh, sure! Mommy them went to Bourda whenever they could." For the first time since he'd come, Amir's accent slipped through. He corrected himself: "I remember it fondly."

Father passed the magazine back, and Harry took it gently. He didn't care much for cricket—sacrilege, if you were to ask the other boys at school—but he knew his mother had, and that was enough.

"Thank you," he said, glancing up to Uncle Amir.

"My pleasure."

"Well," Father said, pushing himself up from the table and giving a mighty stretch, "your Uncle and I have some things to talk through. You should get to bed, my boy. We'll have a long day tomorrow."

Harry was in no way looking forward to a long day at the sugar mill, but he gave Father a quick smile, thanked Uncle Amir again, and closed the dining room door behind himself.

The beast flexed its long fingers, pushing a little deeper into the warmth of Harry's groin, and settled its tongue against the lining of his stomach. There were whole hours when Harry would forget the beast was there at all, hours when he could let his mind wonder at a life that was not consumed by its needs. But it would pop another vein, gorge itself on his blood, his bile, his mucus—and then heal his broken body. He suffered it all without so much as a bruise.

Instead of getting to bed, he eased open the kitchen's side door. Majid was still there. He had his apron on while he washed grease out of dishes, his face buried in a cloud of steam rising from the sink.

"Oh!" He started when he heard the door close behind Harry. The dishes clattered back into the sink. "You scare me, boy!"

"I'm sorry, Majid. I'm just looking for a little food, if you have any left," Harry said, playing at coyness as best he could. "Sometimes I'll just get a little peckish at night."

"You not eat?" the cook replied testily, cracking open the icebox. "Look how skinny you are, boy."

"I ate. I'm just still hungry."

Majid wrapped yesterday's roti and a hunk of leftover tilapia in paper towels, then put it all on a small plate. Harry took the plate, and the cook returned to the dishes in the sink.

Food in hand, he headed upstairs. Father and Uncle Amir had retreated to the drawing room. He watched for a moment as their shadows moved behind the door's frosted glass inlay; their voices were pleasant, muffled baritones.

He padded along the hallway at the top of the stairs as softly as he could. The door to Mother and Father's room was just ajar and the lights were off. The hallway grew darker the further he went along, until he came to his room at the very end. He pulled the door just shut behind himself, slow, then switched the lamp on.

The room had been his for the twelve years he'd lived in this house, but it had been Mother's collecting room before then. She had a fascination with the tropic wildlife, a real naturalist's eye, as Father said. She trapped insects—damselflies, dragonflies, orange-spotted butterflies, blister beetles, darkling beetles, velvet ants, boring weevils—and pinned them to huge sheets of Styrofoam leaned against the walls. She'd refused to relocate the collection when Harry moved in, so he'd grown up with them here. Year after year, the bugs' hollow carcasses would be eaten away by mites, but there was an infinite number of insects in the jungle and Mother never tired of finding more.

Harry was allowed the two bottom drawers of the dresser in his room; all the others were filled with longhorn beetles and boxes of pins. In the very bottom drawer, tucked in a corner behind his always freshly-starched school uniforms, he kept the few things he had that reminded him of his birthmother: a fishing hook, a photo of her in front of her old house, and now, *The Cricketer*. On his knees, he took out the photo. She wasn't especially beautiful. Her skin was dark—at least, because of Father, Harry was light enough to pass as British—and, like Uncle Amir's, her front teeth stuck out when she smiled. But his only memories of life with her were golden, sweet things—memories that didn't include the beast.

"This is disgusting, you know."

Mother stood in the doorway. Harry shoved the picture back into the drawer, slid it shut. She stepped into the room, blocking the lamplight, and reached a finger down to the plate of food. She flicked the corners of the paper towel apart, revealing the heaping roti and half-eaten fish.

"What're you going to *do* with all this?" She adjusted the bow at the neck of her powder blue nightgown, pulling it breathlessly tight.

"I get hungry at night."

"You should be eating downstairs. With a fork and knife. At a table." She crinkled her nose at the lukewarm tilapia, covered it again. "I'll tell Majid not to let you upstairs with food anymore."

She left, and Harry closed the door tightly this time. Even cold, the roti smelled of garlic and mustard oil—he had to stop himself from reaching out. He was hungry now, but the beast would be much hungrier before the night was over.

He turned the light out and lay on top of his sheets. He listened until Majid finished in the kitchen, Uncle Amir said goodbye, and Father had come upstairs and eased the bedroom door shut behind himself and the house was entirely silent, entirely still.

Harry packed the food into his schoolbag, slung it over his shoulder, and made his way downstairs. He knew just which floorboards would groan under his weight, just which stairs would squeal in the early morning's dusty quiet. He never left through the front door—the clunk of the deadbolt as it slid open would wake Mother from her shallow sleep—so he padded down the hall, to the kitchen. Majid was long gone by now, back in his home with wife at the far end of town. The kitchen had a door that opened onto the backyard so Majid could take garbage out unseen by Harry's parents. Harry gently opened this door, left it unlocked, and slipped into the warm night.

The waxing moon split the world into pale greys and slanting darkness. No light came from the queer, square houses of the compound, but even in the dark Harry knew his way across the lawns and to the break in the wooden fence that separated British families from the town itself.

The beast lurched as soon as he stepped onto the street and the fence hid the compound from view. Harry expected this, though. He feared, sometimes, that the beast knew his mind as well as his body; he stayed up some nights imaging that if it pressed its long tongue to curve of his brain it could taste his intentions in the sparking of his synapses.

The beast settled, pressing its weight into his bowels, and Harry walked on.

Provenance was a long city, a strand of streets and homes clinging to the hem of the Demerara's silty waters. He walked to the river's edge, turning off of the paved roads and onto smaller, muddy paths, and continued west. The city changed the further out he went. The British Officers' groomed, orderly houses gave way to smaller homes: squat, wooden constructions, balanced on stilts, that overlooked the swollen river and the jungle beyond.

He finally had to stop just before he reached the docks. He could stand a little pain from the beast: a clip of its teeth, a prick of its fingers. But it grew more incensed the further out he went, sinking its fingertips into the knobs of his spine and drawing its teeth over the tendons holding his kneecaps to their muscles. He fell heavily onto his hands and knees, his breathing labored.

He slid the backpack off and took out the tilapia and roti. He ripped off a chunk of the roti and crammed it into his mouth, barely chewing before choking it down and readying another fistful. He felt the beast heave upward out of his stomach and reach its greedy jaws to the base of his esophagus. It downed the food heartily, thoughtlessly. Harry ate and ate until there was only a thin layer of roti remaining and the beast had settled back into his intestines, gorged for a time.

He came to a narrow pier at the end of the street. It rocked gently with the current, the water sloshing beneath. A girl, Alice, stood at the far end. She raised a hand to wave; Harry smiled and waved back.

"Wasn't sure you'd make it," she said when he got to the pier's end. She sat back down, dangling her bare feet over the edge.

"Every Friday." He took a seat beside her and scrounged a lighter out of his backpack. "Wouldn't miss it."

Alice slipped two loose cigarettes out of her jeans pocket. She was an Arawak, one of the people who lived in the jungles before the blacks and coolies were brought by the British, and before the British, too. She lived on the other side of the river with her brothers, who fished the Demerara by night.

She put a cigarette between her lips, and Harry fumbled with his lighter, rubbing his thumb raw against the wheel.

He didn't care much for girls at school—another failing in the eyes of his cricket-obsessed classmates—but Alice was different. He wasn't sure that what he felt for her was sexual: she was older than him, and boyish, too, with her close-cropped hair, square face, and jeans. She smoked with a practiced, world-weary ease, and when he first told her that he'd never even lit a cigarette before she did not laugh or condescend; she simply showed him how.

Harry finally got a steady flame from the lighter and he lit the cig, breathing in deeply. He let the smoke settle in his chest for as long he could stand. The beast was quiet while the tobacco lingered in his throat and pricked his gums; for the time it took for the cigarette to burn itself low, Harry could try to forget that his body was not his own.

"My father's taking me to the mill tomorrow," Harry said after a while. "He wants me to be ready to work with him when I'm done school."

"Is that what you want to do?" she asked.

"I haven't really thought about it."

Swarms of gnats hung low over the river, rising and falling as if touched by the breath of an unseen giant. A fish broke from the water, leaping high in a flash of silver, its sinuous body curved with the effort of flight. When it fell it hit the river with a crack like a gunshot.

"It's not such a raw deal," Alice said, tilting her head to look at him.

"You'll have all the money you'd need, and a job lined up. Better than fishing this river for money. Better than cutting cane."

"You know," Harry said, regretting he'd brought up the mill at all, "I've never been on the other side of the river. At least not since my mother died. It's so long ago, I don't remember."

Alice laughed her dry laugh. A cloud covered the moon, and for a moment the only light came from the reddened ends of their cigarettes.

"I'm not sure you'd like it. It's not like Provenance. No shops, no bakeries, no buses to take you to school."

She pulled her feet out of the water and positioned herself closer to Harry, her elbow on the pier and the back of her head cupped in her hand. She looked up at him, and smoke drifted lazily from between her lips. Her eyes flickered upward, made contact with his. The urge to lean down and touch her—to just kiss her—overtook him suddenly, and he slid his hand along the pier's pulpy wood, closer to hers.

The thought must have occurred to the beast, too, for it rumbled awake out of its nicotine-coated sleep. Its fingers pried clumsily at the bottom of his esophagus; its tongue slithered up, soft and wet.

Harry let it rise in his throat. He felt a warmth spread through his chest, a confidence he'd never before possessed; he felt he could lean down now and kiss her on the lips and it wouldn't change their friendship, wouldn't change that at all, it would only—

A motor rumbled downriver. Alice sat up, pulling herself away, and the dream collapsed. The beast slithered back, dragging any confidence Harry might have felt down with it. Alice took a last, long pull, then stubbed out the cigarette on the pier.

"Sounds like my brothers are almost back. You'd better get going."

"Yeah," Harry said, giving a small, false smile. He felt the heat of his face going red; he couldn't let her see the shame that filled hollow where the beast had been. "Time to get home, anyway. Thanks for the smoke."

He put his lighter back in the bag, waved goodbye, and started back down the pier.

———

The beast had been with him from the time before he was. It found its skin off the stone-cradled coast of Baleswar and took teeth from the mouths of sightless catfish slicked in the muds of the Hooghly; it found fingers in the splintered iron wreck of a sunken steamer—those half-eaten Company men suspended in the deep watched, unseeing—and then pushed onward, upstream, to break the surface off Kolkata's restless, sweat-streaked banks. Its lips—what practiced, deceitful lips—it pinched from a gora in a white cotton shirt and crisp straw boater, bent at the waist over the rail of a ferryboat, his clean-shaven face so close they all but kissed as it rose to meet him.

On the banks it found a Bengali farmer, a devout Muslim and a newlywed, too, and it buried itself deep inside him. It stayed with him for a year, in guileless sleep, until the man and his wife sailed that unbordered ocean to a place they knew nothing of, a world they could hardly imagine but was richly described by their sahibs and Her Majesty's Officers.

One night when the ocean churned and the ship's passengers cowered in darkness, all lanterns gone out, the merchant lay with his wife. The beast slicked itself inside the man's heavy cock and spread itself inside his wife and when, at last, they emerged from the belly of that ship and stepped onto Georgetown's streets, the beast lived inside yet another: a child who would be born to this unknown country, this ancient jungle.

Father had a motorcycle that had been brought by ship from London; a sleek, chrome-buffed Norton Manx painted a royal oxblood and fitted with all the most fashionable accoutrements. Though the sugar mill was only just over a mile from the house, Father still drove the bike there and back every day.

"She's got enough space for the both of us," he assured Harry as they readied themselves the following morning. "Just be certain to hold onto me good and tight—they need to have another go at paving this road."

They puttered down the main road slowly, Father steering around rain-filled potholes but still managing to hit bumps and stones that jarred them both. The other Officers' homes spun by, just beyond the wooden fence, and when they had passed the compound he took a turn that put them on a dirt road that traced the edge of the river. Indian and Arawak fishermen worked the banks, hauling crab pots out of the water, throwing nets, dragging buckets out of their mud-streaked boats that writhed with the morning's catches: eel, chiclid, bushymouth catfish, snook, croakers, and lungfish as long as Harry's arm.

This flew by them, too, and soon they were past all the houses, past the docks. Harry knew they were close when they came to the prison: a building as uncannily tall as it was narrow, set back from the road, with rows and rows of blacked-out windows. A hundred years past, maybe more, it had been one of the colony's first sugar refineries; its thick walls and iron-barred doors made it a prime candidate when the British decided the city needed holding cells.

Father's mill was just back from the prison, over the railroad tracks. It was, from what Harry could see beyond the stepped fence running the perimeter, like a small city itself. Several small, shack-like build-ings encircled a three-story, whitewashed structure with a slanted roof. They crossed the fence, and Father slowed the motorcycle.

The mill was already busy. Sweating men—Indian and black alike—heaved six- and eight-foot bundles of sugarcane out of the backs of trucks parked in the lot. They pressed the cane along what looked like a low gate that was banded together by a long iron bar along its top. The bottom of the gate swung inward, and the loose cane fell onto a conveyor that rolled it into the mill. Men stood on the other side of the low gate, huge bamboo rakes in hand, pulling the cane down onto the conveyor belt.

"Come," Father said after he'd parked in front of the mill. The motorbike's polished, red chassis seemed alien amidst the white-and-brown tedium of the cane workers. "Let's find Uncle Amir."

The interior of the mill was darker and noisier than Harry had expected. The conveyor belt carried the sugarcane into a central chamber filled with machines whose purposes he could hardly guess at: steel-sided shredders with rows of spinning teeth, thick pipes that ran the walls and hissed with steam, and vats filled with dark, boiling liquids. Men with heavy gloves moved like ants in an underground colony: each knowing exactly where he was going, but none saying a word to the others.

"He should be up here," Father said, shouldering open a door labeled *Management Only*. They climbed a steep flight of stairs that doubled back on itself and opened into a small room with a glass wall. The whole mill was visible beyond the glass, much as fish could be watched in a child's aquarium.

"Harry! So glad you came today." Uncle Amir stood from behind a small oak desk, came over to shake his hands. "I haven't seen you in so long, and now we get to see each other twice in one week! What grand luck. Would you like milk tea?"

Harry shook his head, but Father insisted on tea for the three of them.

While Amir boiled water, Father enumerated the job's various daily tasks—invoices, vendor inquiries, customer relations, and management. "It's tough keeping the coolies on track and making sure production is where the bosses need it to be. So much slips through the cracks. Right?" he asked, looking to Uncle Amir.

"Right," he said with a nod as he poured tea from a steaming pot.

Father sat Harry down at a chair with a stack of invoices—"clerical work keeps the mind organized, son"—and retreated to his own desk to answer the ringing rotary phone.

Harry's concentration left him after alphabetizing the first six. He sat beside the only window in the room that looked outside. The view was bleak—mostly men hauling cane from the trucks, staggering with the weight—but the window had a small, wooden ledge and on the ledge was a dead caterpillar. It was an enormous, bloated creature that had only recently died. He peered closer: he recognized the markings. Mother had several moths in her collection with the same rows of dots on the wings, the same shallow—

—Harry blinked. The caterpillar was dead, clearly dead, yet could have sworn he'd seen its skin ripple. Just a slight protuberance, as if some small heart, deep inside, beat once.

His stomach turned at the thought, though the beast inside him didn't move. In fact, despite being so far from the compound, the beast had hardly protested at all. It purred complacently—content-edly, even—from the thin lining of his intestines; he could barely tell it was there.

Somewhere inside the mill, men started yelling. This was followed by the sound of metal shrieking against metal and a long hiss of steam.

"Amir?" Father said.

Uncle Amir looked up from his paperwork, keeping his gaze away from the window onto the workers.

"Amir," Father repeated, hanging up the phone. "Would you go look into that?"

Uncle Amir feigned surprise. "Oh yes! Yes, of course. I'll—I'll just be back." He nearly tripped over himself getting down the stairs.

Father gave a pained sigh and, when Harry didn't inquire as to the reason for the sigh, he elaborated: "He's been having trouble with the men. He's usually so good with them, but this blasted People's Progressive Party is driving them apart. Amir's a reasonable man—he understands the benefits of us being here, running things. All coolies are not as reasonable as your Uncle, Harry. That's a good first lesson."

The caterpillar's skin had started moving again. First, one pulse—a single, small heartbeat—but then it came again, more strongly, pushing up against the necrotic flesh, distending it. The caterpillar's skin tore with the pressure, and a small mouth emerged from inside: two black mandibles, sharp as sickles. A pin-waisted wasp pulled itself free, its wings slicked with the caterpillar's viscera.

Another wasp crawled up through the hole, and the caterpillar's body began to boil: ten more heads pushed up into the dead skin, biting hole after hole until the caterpillar was nothing more than a heap of dislocated parts, a first meal for a host of sickly-orange wasps with legs sharp as needles.

"Reginald!" Uncle Amir called from the bottom of the stairwell. "Might you—might you come down, please?"

"What's the trouble?" Father asked from his desk. The shouting from the men downstairs grew louder as Uncle Amir kept the door propped open.

"You should bring the boy with you!" Amir yelled, and then they heard the door slam shut.

Harry pulled himself away from the caterpillar—there were just two wasps left, now; the others had taken off into the midday heat—and he followed Father downstairs.

The mill's workfloor was chaotic: workers ran back and forth, some with pails of water from spigots outside, others with burlap tarps. The far end of the chamber was starting to fill with black smoke, and the room reeked of burning timber. One of the workers, a tall, broad black man, was yelling at Uncle Amir. His accent was too heavy for Harry to understand much of what he was saying.

Father stood paralyzed at Harry's side. He gripped the back of Harry's neck in his hand, squeezing just too tight.

"Should you see what's wrong?" Harry asked.

"I—I think we should just—"

Uncle Amir jogged over. "It's one of the processors, Reginald," he said, his voice hoarse with inhaled smoke. "It's lit the cane chips somehow. You should get him out of here."

"Are you sure? I could stay if there's anything—"

"It's under control," Amir retorted. He turned to go back to his men.

Father took Harry by the hand and they started out of the facility. Harry turned just before they got out, though, to see the workfloor one last time. His gaze slid from the billowing smoke to the black worker, who was standing there, watching them go. His face dripped with sweat and was streaked darkly with ash and his eyes went wide and wild with such fear, such rage, that Harry had to turn his face away.

The fires were put out, and the mill and all the cane workers survived. The mill would need some time for repairs, Father explained, but it would be back in no time at all. The fire started due to faulty machinery. All of the processors were years too old, but that wasn't *his* fault, he was careful to say, that was something Amir should have told him about long before it had gotten *this* far.

He spoke with the bluff of bravery, but he was clearly shaken by the incident. He kept to the drawing room, fingertips stained from the endless chain of cigarettes passing through them. He came out for short, silent meals with Harry and Mother, then excused himself.

The image of the mill worker had stayed with Harry, too: he had never seen such terror carved into one man's face. Father's immediate retreat from the mill filled him with embarrassment, but he couldn't bring himself to talk to Father about it, or to be there when Mother found out what had happened.

So he stayed away from the compound. Later in the week, after a day spent in too-hot classrooms thinking about his mother and her love of Frank de Caires, he found himself wandering back toward the Demerara, picking his way along a road he'd walked many times when he was a child. His mother's house had been down this way, he thought. He had few memories of the place—he'd been so young when Father took him away to live at the compound—but there were still feelings that stayed: the croaking calls of toucans with beaks the color of ripened papaya; the static joy of hearing cricket games in countries across an ocean, broadcast over transistor radio; his mother coming home from work, her apron curry-stained, her smile wider than the river.

As it always did, the beast grew restless. It smelled the river's sucking mud and the jackfruit trees in bloom; it tasted the brick-red dirt he kicked up from the road and the winds that brought clouds from the west blue with rain. But Harry had pilfered the kitchen before he left for school, taking what little Majid had left after breakfast: a pine tart and a tennis roll. He took a starchy bite out of a tart, and the beast quieted itself.

He came upon a house he thought he remembered. It was a split-level with wide, screenless windows, a green-tiled roof, and small yard full of mango trees. Two boys, one his age and one much younger, played with a ball and cricket bat in the front yard. Harry thought he recognized the older boy. He watched them play for a while, and, when the younger boy went to fetch the ball after a particularly enthusiastic hit, the older boy came over.

"I remember you," he said, to Harry's surprise. "You're Harold, right?"

"Yeah. I'm sorry, I don't remember . . . "

"We grew up down the street. You're Auntie Bibi's kid, yeah?"

"That's right," Harry said. He flushed with the embarrassment of not remembering anything about this boy.

"Yeah, I remember. You always looked white. You know, like your father."

Harry, opened his mouth, unsure of what to say.

"Well, I'm Bobby," the boy continued, rapid fire. "Want a turn with the bat?"

He offered it over. Harry paused, startled. He wasn't any good at cricket, and he had very little food left for the beast. It had started its rumblings again; slipping itself around the pit of his stomach, prodding those tender walls with its tongue.

"It's gonna rain soon," Bobby said, gesturing with his full eyebrows to the changing sky. "Might as well get a few hits in while you can."

Harry took the bat, and walked to meet Bobby's little brother.

He played for fifteen awkward minutes, missing more throws than he should have and failing to catch any of the balls that came his way. The other boys were good sports, though, and Harry found himself laughing more than he had in a long while.

Then, while he stood between the mango trees, watching the younger brother, Abed, pitch to his brother, Harry saw a man coming down the road. He came from the direction of the prison and the mill, dressed in a fine suit and a starched shirt. He walked haltingly, swinging long arms and drunkenly swaying.

The boys stopped their game; the ball went rolling through the grass, into the thickets beyond.

"Do you know who it is?" Harry asked.

"No, I can't quite—"

The man staggered closer, and Harry saw that there was something wrong with his face. Half was swollen, his left eye nearly shut, and his lips were distended and purpled. Blood had run down his forehead and dried over his eyebrows, caking them.

He came near enough that all three boys could make out the rest of his face: his thin moustache, his teeth so thick his lips could hardly cover them.

They all went running.

"Uncle Amir!" Bobby called as they neared.

He looked at them but there was no recognition in his eyes, no light behind them at all. He half-fell into Bobby's arms, and the boy couldn't hold his weight so they collapsed together into the dirt.

"Run and get Bhauji," Bobby said to his brother. "Run!"

The boy took bolted for the houses far down the road.

"And you, go and get the ferryman's wife. She's a nurse," Bobby said.

Harry balked; his heart stuttered in his throat.

"I don't know who that is."

Bobby looked up. He had taken the corner of his shirt, wet it with his tongue, and was wiping blood off of Uncle Amir's face. Uncle Amir's one open eye closed.

"Down this road. Left at the fish market, left at the baker—"

Harry was nodding but he was hardly listening. The beast had grown hungrier still; it pulled at the inside of his guts with its practiced fingers; it licked at the base of his throat so he had to swallow, and swallow, and swallow—

"Shit, man," Bobby said. "I'll go. You stay here with him!"

Bobby ran in the opposite direction, puffs of dust rising behind him.

Harry got to his knees beside Uncle Amir. He had never felt a hunger like this before; it opened his mouth for him, wet his tongue. A long line of spit trailed from the corner of Uncle Amir's mouth; as it moved down his cheek it crossed a line of dry blood. The beast hummed inside Harry, it pressed lips to the back of his frantic mind.

Harry leaned down. His nose brushed Uncle Amir's cheek and his lips touched the line of spit and the flaking blood. Oh, what sweetness, what sugar! His tongue lapped out of his mouth and he soaked in the rest of Uncle Amir's spittle and blood. He licked the face clean of dirt and sweat and the beast rejoiced with the flavors: the salt, the tang, the sticky sweet!

Harry pulled back. He was filled with the desire to take a bite— Amir's cheek was so full, so fatty. The beast asked, then begged. Then it didn't beg, it demanded. Pain ripped through his bowels like the sting of spider-killing wasp boring through his intestines. He leaned forward at once, opening his mouth—

—and pulled back. He couldn't feed the beast, if this was what it needed. He couldn't, and yet no tennis roll had ever look as soft and as perfectly firm as Amir's licked-clean cheek. It was plump as a quail's breast, and it smelled like ghee. He leaned in once more and fitted his teeth into the thin, soft flesh just above Amir's jaw. He pressed in, his crushed nose breathing in the savory warmth of his Uncle's skin: the scent of freshly fried pholourie. Amir's blood seeped into his mouth, washed in along his gums.

"Amir!"

Harry pulled away from his Uncle's face and wiped the blood off his lips. Abed came hurtling back down the road with Bhauji. She was a small woman who wore a purple-flowered headscarf that flapped at the nape of her neck as she hurried to keep pace. She was out of breath from running, and her words came through in spit-racked sobs:

"He done vex those mill men now!"

She dropped to the ground. Amir seemed to be coming to himself again; his right eye blinked open when he heard her say his name.

"Come here, boy," Bhauji said to Harry.

"Come on!" Abed implored. He pulled at his Uncle's hand, trying to get him to sit up. "Help us get him up!"

But Harry could go no nearer. It was not the pain that stopped him, not the beast's razor-toothed insistence that he return to the man's broken body. It was the shame. It was the taste of Amir's sweat and blood and spit still lingering in his mouth and the pleasure that came of tasting it. He couldn't tell if it was the beast's pleasure or his own.

"I'm sorry," Harry said, backing away. "I'm so sorry."

He started running in the direction Bobby had gone to look for the nurse. The storm was all above them now; the rain started with slow but heavy drops that cratered the dirt road. It started coming faster, harder, and he turned and was running along the river, back to the piers. He didn't think about where he was going; the beast kept him from that. It had started growing inside him, swelling his small stomach, pushing into the surrounding blood vessels and yellow fat. It crowded his lungs and his breaths brought less and less relief with each step but he still kept running until he came to a pier where some fishermen were untying their boat, readying to set off.

"Hey!" Harry called, but his voice was lost as the rain crescendoed. He knew one of those fishermen—they were Arawak, and one was Alice's eldest brother. He ran to the end of the pier. "Hey!"

But the men were already pushing off, their boat's small motor kicking into life.

Harry looked back. Provenance was behind him: the nurse and the ferryman he didn't know; Abed and Bobby and Bhauji, who he hardly even recognized; Amir, broken, bleeding. Beyond them was the compound, where Father and Mother were probably starting to worry, if they'd even noticed he was gone.

Harry heeled his shoes off, took off his pants, and jumped into the Demerara.

The beast howled. It ripped at soft, pink tissue; it sunk its teeth into flexing muscle; it wrapped its long tongue around his spongy lungs and squeezed. It did not stop to heal him.

Harry swam with the current. He tasted the blood that was coming up from his throat, but he could not see it as it mixed with the murk-brown water that filled his mouth. He couldn't see where he was going for all the rain—it was driving now, cutting—but he knew the Arawak were somewhere downriver.

He swam until he couldn't anymore, until the pain shuttered his vision blue and black. His muscles burned and his knotted stomach cramped and distended in ways he had never felt before. The water was starting to come over his head now; the silt stung his eyes and he felt himself begin to go under. So he turned onto his back and simply floated. The rain filled his mouth, and washed his dark blood out toward the sea.

A light broke the beat of the rain. The curved bottom of a boat came into view, and an Arawak man bent over the edge and reached a hand down. Harry took it; the boat tipped and righted as he scrambled on board and the hands of six and eight men pulled at his sodden clothes, his chilled skin.

The men spoke amongst themselves in their native tongue, and then—

"Where you from, boy? Where is your home?"

Here, in the middle of the river, Harry approached a place beyond pain. He wiped the blood and snot off his lips, and swallowed his senseless, ocean-deep craving.

"Please," he said, "please let me come with you." Then, louder, so the rain would not silence him: "I don't have a home."

The rainy season will come to an end, as it must: the rivers recede, the land dries, and the lungfish bury themselves. They open their gasping mouths and tunnel into the cool mud where the sun will not touch their earthbrown skin. They sleep these long months curled tight, swaddled in a film of their own dried mucus, their bodies slowly decaying as their muscles and fat are consumed to nourish what little is left to nourish.

Some will die like this.

But the rains will come again—with a brutal crack like the sky cleft open—and the land returns to itself: the rivers swell, the swamps fill, and the dirt is gorged, sated. The lungfish wake as their cauls dissolve, and they thrash themselves free of the clay. As they writhe their slick bodies across the storm-soaked land they are so consumed by hunger, by the nerve-deep need to return to the water, they will not remember that they had ever lived before.

CLAIRE
DEAN

The

Unwish

ONE STEP INSIDE AND AMY KNEW THERE WAS something she'd forgotten. She heaved her rucksack over the threshold and counted the carrier bags she'd lugged up from the Co-op in the town. Four, which was right. There might not be enough wine, though. With the front door key between her teeth—metallic tang on her tongue—she dragged the bags inside and stopped. The room hadn't changed at all. She'd been eleven when they last stayed here.

She'd never been back. How could it have changed so little in twenty years? She placed the key on the table and heaped the bags beneath it. Her boots were caked with mud. She tiptoed towards the kettle rather than battle with the filthy laces to get them off.

She cradled her tea on the bench by the front door. The river was insistent in her ears, though it was hidden by the trees. The opposite valley-side shifted with the wind, the trees forming an agitated creature that could not rest. The wood of the bench had warmed in the spring sunshine, but clouds were collecting now. A narrow path beside the cottage climbed to the road. She watched for the arrival of her sister and parents. They'd have to leave their cars further up the hill and carry everything down. A goldfinch perched on the gate for just a breath before lifting off again. She'd reached for her phone to take a picture, but the moment had gone. She couldn't get a signal to send it to him anyway. And he'd be here before too long. They could sit on the bench together. The goldfinch might return.

Her cup was empty but still warm. She let it rest against her collarbone. She picked up her phone again and read through their last messages: "Can't wait to see you tomorrow x," she'd sent from the village. "See you soon," he'd replied. No kiss. She tackled her laces and dirt powdered the flagstones. There was a hole in her left sock. It was a good job she'd worn that pair today. She left her boots beneath the bench and headed inside to unpack.

Her parents would take the main bedroom in the front. Should she claim the other decent-sized one? Sara had it when they'd stayed here as kids. They'd fought over it but Sara won, as always. Amy had ended up in the tiny room off the kitchen downstairs. Dad said it was like having her own den. But there was another room upstairs, she realised now. She pushed open the door at the end of the hall.

How had she forgotten it? It was single-sized, but a double bed and narrow set of drawers had been squeezed in. Blue blankets on the bed lapped against the window wall. Beech leaves pressed against the glass and green light filled the room. She climbed up onto the bed and unlatched the window, letting the sounds of leaves and the river into the room. Sara could keep the big room. It would be cosy in here when he arrived. She emptied all her clothes out of her rucksack onto the bed. Ordinarily, she'd leave them balled inside her bag and extract them as she needed them, but she didn't want him to see she was messy. She folded her creased T-shirts and the two lace nighties she'd brought. Maybe she should have brought pyjamas as well.

She'd be cold that night in bed alone. She kept her stuff to one side in the drawers, leaving space for him. She put her washbag on top and then hid it back in her rucksack. He didn't need to see all that crap. Lying on the bed she tried to imagine him into the room. His arms around her. She read his last text over and over. Why had there been no kiss?

"Bolognese, really?" Sara set her grey leather weekend bag down on the table.

"Nice to see you too," Amy said.

"Is that mince organic at least? You know, turkey mince is so much better for you." Sara leaned over the pan and sniffed. "I'll cook tomorrow night. Are Mum and Dad here yet? Mum, Dad, hellooo!"

Amy stabbed the mince with the spatula, trying to separate the claggy brown clumps. "They're not here yet," she said.

"And when's what's-he-called-again arriving?"

"Aidan will be here tomorrow night. He couldn't get time off today."

Sara raised her eyebrows and lifted her bag off the table. "I really don't know why we had to come back here."

"Dad wanted to come. Mum said he was insistent about it." Amy turned back to the mince as her sister pounded up the stairs. She tipped a tin of tomatoes into the pan and attempted to liquidise them with a potato masher. She sloshed a little red wine into the pan and more into her glass.

When her parents finally burst through the door in a flurry of bags and arms and kisses, the bottle was empty.

Sara picked it up. "Do we have recycling here?" she said. "Sorry we're late," Mum said. "Your Dad got us lost."

"I didn't get us lost. They've changed the road layout up in the village."

"You got us lost." Mum upended her handbag on the table and retrieved her tablets from a mound of tissues.

"Let us get the bags for you," said Sara. "Let's go and get comfy and light a fire. Do you remember how Amy used to hide the wood so we couldn't burn it? She said it screamed. Amy, can you take all the bags upstairs?"

Amy hadn't bought dessert. She never had dessert at home.

Didn't wine count as dessert? Apparently not. They were already dangerously close to the end of the second bottle and Sara had barely touched her glass.

Mum started to clear the plates. "It doesn't matter. I couldn't eat another thing anyway."

"Pasta can sit so heavily, can't it, Mum?" Sara said. "I'll go out in the car and find the nearest Waitrose tomorrow. Get us properly stocked up."

"Shall we play a game?" Dad headed off into the snug as Mum began to clear the plates.

The Scrabble set still had old score sheets inside. People had made a palimpsest of them over the years. Sara pored over them. "See I won," she said finally. "I always got the triple word scores."

"You were older than me," Amy said, looking over her shoulder at the sheet.

"I'm still older than you. It's not an excuse for losing." "Actually, who's K? It looks like they won," Amy said. "That's someone else's game."

Amy lifted a battered Trivial Pursuit box down from the shelf. "There were pieces of pie missing when we last played this."

"You replaced them with beech nuts you'd all collected," Dad said.

Now there were just the empty pies. Amy put the lid back on the box.

"So you'll have to face me at Scrabble," Sara said, dishing out the tiles on the coffee table.

Dad pushed his back. "Actually, just you two play. I'm happier watching."

Mum came through from the kitchen, glass in hand, and pulled a Danielle Steel novel from the shelf. She crumpled into the armchair and took another of her tablets with the last of the wine. "I probably read this last time," she said. "Good job I never remember how things end."

There were other books on the shelf: a Ruth Rendell, some hard-backed Dickens, a couple of Catherine Cooksons. "Do you remember that book that was here, full of weird fairy tales?" Amy said. "It was small, had a brown cover. There was that horrible story about the cat mother in it and—"

"No," Sara said as she placed five tiles on the board. "T.R.I.C.K., with the K on a double letter score. That makes 16."

Amy placed an O beneath the C. If only she had a W. She added a D instead. "C.O.D. That's 6," she said.

Dad stood up. "I've left the map in the car."

"Well you don't need it now," Mum said without looking up from her book. "We're here."

"I'd like to have a look at it. See what's going on with those roads in the village."

"Get it in the morning."

"It'll only take a minute." He was already getting his boots on. "D.E.U.X." Sara placed each tile with emphasis.

"You can't have that," Amy said.

"Of course I can. And the X is on a triple letter score, so that's 28 for me."

Amy shuffled her tiles about as though it would make a difference to how useless she was at seeing words in the random letters. The fire guttered as cold air flooded the room. Dad mustn't have shut the door properly. Amy shuffled her tiles again. What was she going to do with two Fs? "I'll go with Dad," she said.

"Thanks, sweetheart," Mum said. "Well, I'll come too then," Sara said.

"Good girls." Mum sipped her wine and went back to her book.

Bluebells held on to the twilight. Tree branches reached up into the falling dark. Amy walked quickly, until the air was sharp in her chest, but there was no sign of Dad.

"So are you sure it's going to work out with this one?" Sara said from behind her.

Amy focused on trying to follow the lighter stones that made the path.

"Because you're not getting any younger. And after Gareth . . . " Sara let the memories out in a studied exhalation. The same way she used to blow smoke rings when they were teenagers and leave them to hang in the air.

"Mum said he's married," she said.

"He's been separated for a long time. They're getting a divorce." "But he's still married?"

The stones were all mud-slick now. Amy stopped looking for the path and just kept heading upwards. They had to reach the road at some point. And Dad. How could he have got ahead so fast?

"So what is it he's doing that couldn't be put off?"

"He had to work. I already told you that. Where's Richard anyway?"

"Closing a deal. The partners needed him there. Anyway, he's arranged a special meal for Mum and Dad at The Cottingdale when they come to stay with us at the end of the month. We'll have a lot to celebrate."

"Great," Amy said. There was a scuttering overhead as birds swapped places on the branches. She stopped.

"It's only the birds, Amy. God you're still scared of everything."

"In that fairy tale book there was a story where all the leaves were really birds and they flew down all at once and trapped the children. And they had to live for years in a house of wings. Do you remember?"

Sara overtook her. "Come on, we're never going to catch up with Dad."

"And there was that story about the sisters. They were trying to collect wishes from . . . was it from a tree? Do you remember?"

"No. I don't."

"But that one was your favourite. You made us act it out. There was a hollow tree down by the river . . . I'd completely forgotten about it until now, but there was a tree down there that we used to hide things in."

"I don't remember."

"There were three sisters and the eldest—" "You're making things up again," Sara said.

A shuffling and cracking ahead announced their father. In the last light he could have been a badger, stooped in his worn grey coat.

"I left a . . . I left something in the car. Went up to get it," he said.

He didn't have anything in his hands.

The morning was cold against her shoulder. Amy huddled under the blankets and watched shadow leaves flitter on the wall. Tomorrow she'd get to wake up beside him. It was worth having to put up with a few days of Sara for that. She hadn't actually spent a whole night with him yet. He said it was too difficult to get to work from her house. When he rolled out of her bed before midnight to retrieve his clothes the extra space was crushing. The smell of him never lasted long enough on her pillows.

She couldn't hear anyone else up. She dressed and crept downstairs. The front door was wide open. Dad's boots were gone. She headed out down the hill. The bluebells were still the colour of twilight. The river sounded heavy and urgent in the trees, drowning out any birdsong.

Dad was on the small stone bridge, curled over its side, staring down into the water. She watched as he turned, then crouched to the ground, crossed to the other side of the bridge and rushed back to his starting position like a creaky old automaton.

"Morning, Dad," she said. The dank mouth of the bridge held ferns and boulders and old bricks tumbled until their corners were gone. The water that frothed through it all looked more like bitter. She pressed her fingers into the moss growing on the stone, expecting it to be cool and damp, but it was warm and dry.

Dad scrabbled for more leaves. One, two, three, he let them go. "You always enjoyed playing this with your sisters," he said.

Sister, she corrected in her head, but she let it go. He seemed fragile. Something wasn't right.

Two oak leaves raced through. The third must have got caught. "Are you coming back to the cottage, Dad? I can make you some breakfast."

"I'm waiting," he said, "for the other one." "It's got stuck, Dad, come on."

Sara had already laid the table for breakfast and arranged several pans on the hob, but she'd disappeared upstairs to the bathroom. Amy took over and had served a full fry-up to Mum and Dad before Sara came down.

"Would you like some?" Amy asked.

"No, thanks." Sara sat at the far end of the table. Amy filled her own plate and sat right next to her.

"What's the plan today then?" Sara got up and leaned against the sink.

"I don't want to go out there," Mum said. "I mean, I would like to stay here and finish that book by the fire."

"I need to go food shopping, of course," Sara said. "What time's your new boyfriend arriving, Amy?"

"Sixish. Although he said it could get to seven." "I'll do a late dinner then, if he can't be sure." "I'm going to go for a walk today," Amy said. "You've just been for a walk," Sara said.

"A longer one. Maybe cross the river and climb the hill on the other side."

"There's a good view from the top," Dad said. "You all loved it up there when you were younger."

Each barely-there filament of the feather added to its delicate Rorschach pattern. Amy twirled it between finger and thumb as she set off down the hill. She might give it to him when he arrived. What would he do with it, though? Would he keep it because she'd given it to him? What if he just discarded it? She wanted to tell him she loved him when they went to bed that night. The words had been in her mouth so many times, but she'd been too nervous to let them out. What if he didn't say it back? He'd said he needed to take things slowly after his marriage. Did the fact he'd already been married mean he wouldn't want to do all that again? She'd never fantasised about a big fancy wedding like Sara's, but still. She let the feather fall back to the ground.

He didn't like to hold her hand. He'd never said that, but she could feel it when she let hers touch his as they walked. He never took it. It was a small thing really. But did it mean he didn't like her enough, or that he was still in love with his ex? Maybe he would never want to hold her hand. Would that matter? As she stumbled down the slope she couldn't pull apart the rush of wind in the leaves from the sound of the water. For a moment she felt as though she was walking beneath the water, and its surface was up above the branches. She might drown in the trees. She had to stop. She leaned against a tree and then sank to the ground between its roots. He thought it was fine for them to not see each other all week. She felt a longing for him that scared her. She checked her phone for him constantly. Every message from friends and every marketing email she'd never signed up for hurt, because she believed for a split second it was going to be from him.

Damp was seeping through her jeans, but the leaves around her felt
dry beneath her hands. She stood up and looked at where she'd been
sitting. There was a deep crevice, not much more than a hand's width,
in the trunk. It was the hollow tree. She slipped her hand inside and
pulled out mounds of desiccated leaves. With her face against the bark
she reached in further. There was a smell of wet soil and something
sickly. She dislodged an object deep inside the tree. Twisting her wrist,
she managed to pull out an old ice cream tub. The label on the lid had
disintegrated but there were initials scratched into its sky-blue plastic
sides, SP, AP, KP. Inside there were seven ring pulls tied to a length of
string, a rusty needle and the book. The fairy tale book they'd taken
from the cottage. The text block came away from its sodden cover in
her hands. The page edges were mildewed and it was difficult to prise
them apart with her nails, but when she did, the printed words were
remarkably intact. "The Cat Mother", "The Bird House", "Devil's
Bridge", "Three Green Baskets", "The Fox and the Leaf". There were
pages missing where the final story should have been; only its last page
remained:

*The last wish, the un—, had to be hidden from the world. The good sister
folded it up and asked me to put it into this story. And a fine story it makes
too, but, dear child, take heed; it must never be taken from here.*

Amy shoved the book back into the tree. She stuffed the tub and lid
after it, scraping her arm on unseen ridges. She remembered finding
a tiny bone in the tree and pretending it was a key from one of the
stories. Was that before, or after? They'd been playing in the woods.
She remembered being piggy in the middle. She was always piggy in
the middle. She remembered following a tangle of red thread through
the trees. That was after. They found a little cairn of white pick-up
sticks by the river. Sara threw stones at it. There were other parts, not
attached to their names, that lay swollen and shining like jewels in the
mud. There had been three of them. But by the time Dad had called
them back for lunch they were two. There had been nothing left of

her little sister: no bones, no eyes, no heart. The woods were empty of her. Before she was gone it was like her body had tried to hold on to the world, to make itself so viciously present they could never forget it. Forget her. But they had forgotten. What was her name?

Sara was making the dessert, stirring a thick chocolatey mess in a bowl. Mum and Dad were sitting at the table drinking tea in silence. They all looked so normal.

"Your boots are filthy," Sara said.

It was you, Amy thought. It was you, it was you, it was you. You unwished her.

"Cup of tea, love?" "No, thanks, Mum."

She sat and fought with her mud-thick laces. We had a sister. We had a sister. We had a sister. Maybe if she kept saying it to herself she could stop it falling out of her mind again. She tried to picture her, but couldn't see her for the river water and leaves.

"Look at the state of me!" Sara laughed and wiggled her chocolatey fingers.

Amy watched Sara wash her hands and pat them dry on a towel before letting them rest lightly on her belly. A baby, Amy thought. Sara's going to have a baby. Of course she was. She always had to be the centre of attention.

"Are you okay, love?" Mum asked. "I'm going to have a bath," Amy said.

"Yes, best to make yourself presentable for your new boyfriend." Sara's hand remained on her belly.

The water ran in a scorching stream. She tried to imagine her little sister into being, but every time her thoughts got close to the edge of her, her mind pulled away. She wiped the steamed-up mirror with her sleeve. Her face was streaked with tears, eyelids thickening. She'd look a mess when he arrived. She needed him to arrive. To hold her. Things would feel okay in his arms.

She folded her clothes neatly in a pile on the floor. How would she explain all this to him? Would he think she was mad? Would he let her cry? Gareth had always hated it when she cried, said she should go on tablets like her mum. Sara was having a baby. A baby. She shouldn't think about the baby. She couldn't breathe. Her skin was burning. She added more cold. What would he think of her, a beetroot with puffy eyes? He'd never seen her like this, or first thing in the morning, or kissed her morning mouth. Would she be what he wanted? Maybe he'd leave her too. She remembered the pages of the book washing under the bridge. Was that before, or after? She tried to imagine he was with her. Why wouldn't he hold her hand? Did he still love his wife? It was all her fault. How could she think he'd love her?

There were candles and napkins on the table. "We waited," Sara said. "Sorry."

It was raining outside. They ate their lamb steaks in silence. Sara made no pretence with the wine and poured herself a glass of orange juice instead. After dinner, Amy washed up. In Scrabble she got F.O.U.N.D. on a triple word score and wondered why it made her want to cry.

Green light leaked into the room. Amy shivered and hugged the blankets around herself. At least she was going home today. Stuffing her clothes back into her rucksack she wondered why she'd bothered unpacking in the first place. She had so little stuff with her that it only took up half the space in each drawer.

KRISTI
DEMEESTER

Worship
Only
What She
Bleeds

THE HOUSE BLEEDS AT NIGHT. I KNOW NOT BECAUSE I have seen it but because I can *hear* it. The blood moving through the walls, a singular drumming heartbeat that presses against me, fills me up to the point where I think I might scream. But I don't. It wouldn't matter. The blood comes no matter what I do.

Momma tells me that there's no such thing as bleeding houses and that she ought to whip me for sneaking and watching *The Amityville Horror* even after she told me not to, but her ears are old, and she can't hear it. Not the way that I can. Every night the house pours itself back into the dirt. The blood finding its way home.

Even more than the sound there's the smell. A hot, metal smell. Like in the back of your throat in winter when you've been running and can feel all the raw parts of you exposed and open. It makes me sick. Plenty of mornings I wake up dizzy, my stomach heaving and rolling. Momma gets me on the bus anyway. Even the morning I threw up because the smell had found its way inside my throat.

"Stop being so dramatic, Mary," she said, and tucked me into my green raincoat.

"A daddy would fix it. They fix things," I told her last night.

"You don't have a daddy anymore." She wouldn't look at me after that, picked at her bowl of lettuce and cucumber for an hour before tossing it in the garbage. Later, when I should have been asleep, I watched her pluck out her eyelashes one by one, transparent half-moons drifting toward the ground as she watched the mirror, her eyes unfocused, distracted. The blood roared through the house, and the stink rose, but she still didn't notice. I fell asleep watching her hands rise and fall against her face, the violence she committed there a small, quiet thing. In the morning, I don't ask her about it, and she doesn't mention that she found me out of bed, and we eat our toast in careful bites.

"I think," she begins but stops. She wipes at her lips with the back of her hand. A smear of red jam lingers in the corner, and she brings the same hand to my forehead, huffs as she sits back down, her swollen belly bumping the table. I think of the baby there, floating in the quiet dark. I wish I could trade places with him.

"You're warm," she says. She doesn't look at me, and her eyes are strange without their lashes, too big and wet, like massive pools of murky water threatening to spill over the shore line. A red scab has formed over her right eyebrow, and she scratches it, her fingers scrubbing against flaking skin.

"I don't feel warm," I say, but she shakes her head, her mouth turning down at the corners.

"You're sick. Very sick. A very sick little girl," she mumbles and scratches again at the scab. It looks bigger now, the size and color of a strawberry.

I reach across the table and pull her hand away. "You're sick, too. You could stay home, too. With me."

"It's just a rash. I'll put some ointment on it. I'll be fine." She pulls her lips back and grins. Teeth like an animal. Like Princess when we took her to the vet because she had to go to heaven. Like even though she was a dog, she knew something was wrong.

"Don't you want to stay home?" she says, and I nod my head. Outside, the morning light is covered in dark, and fog creeps against the windows like little fingers tapping. *Let me in, let me in.*

When she leaves, I hold my breath. Quiet. Quiet. Wait for the house to do something, for it to show that it knows that she is gone, that I am alone. But there is only the sound of my heart whooshing the blood to my head and a dull pain building in my lungs.

Maybe the house sleeps during the day. I try to sleep, too, but the fog rolls against the windows, and I can't settle down. It's too quiet and too loud at the same time. Instead, I turn on the television, but the fog has knocked out the antenna, and white and black ants crawl all over everything. I shut it off, and write my name in the dust covering the screen.

For a long time, I stand at the window and watch the fog. Wave after wave of white smoke crushing against the house. I press my face to the glass and cup my hands around my eyes to block out the light, but I can't see anything. It's like the house is floating away, the fog lifting and carrying us somewhere not solid.

"Where are we going?" I whisper, but there is nothing there to answer me. I want to go out into the fog, to float in it the same way that the house does. To be cocooned and protected inside of its breath. To sleep. Maybe I would forget the look on Momma's face when the police came to tell her about Daddy. Forget the worm crawling through the dirt I threw into the hole we put him in. Forget that he had been going to get ice cream for me. For my birthday. Forget that it was my fault.

Momma left the door unlocked when she left. I can't think of a time when she has done that before. She's always telling me stories about people who go around testing doors to see who's stupid enough to roll out the welcome mat for intruders.

"There's men out there just looking for juicy little girl bits like you, Mary. Looking for places to sneak in and find them and hurt them real bad," she would say but now the door is unlocked, and I want to float, so I open it and go out onto the porch. The fog licks against my feet, and I take off my shoes, curl my toes against the wooden slats.

Behind me, the door closes. It won't, I think, ever open again.

The smell lives in the fog now. Stronger than ever, and I gasp against it, pull my shirt over my nose so that I won't retch. It worms against my skin, tries to open me up, little razors seeking something soft. It hurts, and I back against the house, try to get away. But the door is closed, and I can't go back.

The fog reaches grey fingers down my throat, twists inside of me until I gag, and I claw at the wood beneath my hands. *Let me in. Please let me in.*

The wood gives way, splinters into nothingness as I press harder, a hollow space yawning wide and warm. It's nothing at all to make it bigger, the wood breaks easily under my fists, and there is a hole large enough to crawl into, a place to hide from the sharp teeth of the fog. From somewhere deep in the house, the heartbeat starts up.

I creep into the space, careful not to catch myself on the jagged edges of the hole. The air here is softer, the smell not as strong, but dull, the reminder of a smell instead of the smell all by itself.

I should be afraid. Should leave here. Find a way to open the door. Go back to sleep and hope that I wake up when Momma gets back home, listen to the sharp sounds of her cutting vegetables, pulling meat from bone. But it's so nice here. So warm, and the heartbeat is like a lullaby.

Just like a little mouse, I think and giggle. Inside and outside at the same time. In the guts of the walls, under the floor. The hole tunnels forward, getting smaller as it goes on. I have to hunch my shoulders and duck my head, but the tunnel is just big enough for me to fit. I push myself forward.

My fingers brush against the edges of the tunnel, burrow into piles of something soft. It feels like fur, like petting Princess, only it's longer and stringier. Like my hair when I haven't washed it in a few days and Momma practically pushes me into the shower.

It's wonderful to be inside the house, to squirm along just behind the walls, snug and safe where no one can see me. I have to hurry. Momma will be home, and she won't want me here. Will say it's strange to be inside the walls, and I don't want her to know that I found this place. She'll roll her eyes again; tell me that I'm imagining things. Like she did when I told her about the blood, about the smell. Like she always does.

She never *believes* me.

My hands are wet and sticky, but I don't know how they got that way, and when I push a clump of hair out of my eyes, something gets all gummed up in the strands. It's too dark to see what it is.

There's light coming from up ahead. Probably an opening into the house. Behind me, the tunnel is all closed up, and the fur stuff pulses and moves. I don't like it. I don't like that it's wet and looks like it's reaching out for me. I don't want it to touch me, to smear its damp fingers across my arms, my legs.

A round pinprick of light shines into the tunnel, and I stop my burrowing, stand before it, look out and out and out. I blink, shake the stars from my eyes, wet my lips with my tongue.

Momma's home. I can't see her from my spot inside the wall, but I can hear her humming. I don't know the song, and the notes don't sound right together. They're all jumbled up and screechy, and her voice slides over them like oil.

I'm inside the wall of her bedroom and can see her bed, the corners tucked tight and pillows propped just so. The dress she put on this morning is draped across the mattress, the shoulders placed across her pillow, as if she laid down and the bed swallowed her skin and bones and left the dress behind.

"Mary," I think I hear her say, but the words slip into something else, something that sounds like another language. The warm air in the tunnel has turned cold, and I shiver. The humming stops. Starts again. But it is different this time. Ghosts of words dance in the air, and I strain against the house to hear them. Underneath everything, the beating grows louder, and the fur stuff twitches.

When Momma steps into view, I scream. She is naked. Her legs bend impossibly, the joints crooking the opposite way, and she walks with slow, jerking steps. The scab on her forehead covers her face now. She's scratched at it, torn open the flesh, and blood drips across her neck and chest. Her mouth is open, a wide O, the tongue a fat, wet piece of meat, and her teeth are pointed and sharp.

She turns slowly, stares at the wall. Surely, she can see me hiding here, just behind the plaster. A small, quaking animal waiting to be gobbled up. She cocks her head and watches the wall, eyes flickering back and forth, nostrils flaring.

"Little pig," she says and grunts, reaches her hand toward my hiding place in the wall. I push away from the hole, but the tunnel has closed up even more, and the fur stuff snatches at me. Cold fear clenches my stomach, a grasping, hungry thing.

"Can you hear it, Mary? You were able to hear it before. Can you hear it now?" she says. From the other side of the wall comes the sound of her raking her fingernails across the plaster.

"The blood, Mary. I've always heard it. Come and see.

Come and see," she says.

"Please, Momma. You're scaring me."

"Nothing's wrong, love. Come and see what I've brought you."

My face is wet when I press my eye to the hole again. Momma stands before me cradling a squirming bundle. She resumes her humming, and a tiny reddened hand reaches out, the fingers flexing.

"See what it's given back to me? To us? After all this time, Mary. A daddy. Just like you wanted. A daddy to fix things and to make everything better," she coos. A gurgling rises from the blankets she clutches to her chest. The sound of drowning. The sound of blood leaking from a cut throat.

"It's not a daddy. It's not. It's wrong," I say, and she bares her teeth.

"What do you know about it, girl? What do you know about the places daddies go? How they rut against you, their stinking meat between your legs? They all come in and go out the same way. Pushed out with the shit and the blood into the dirt, and they always *leave*. One way or the other. But not this time. It heard me. Heard *us*. Heard what we wanted, what we needed. And the blood gave back. Everything I've poured into this world, it finally gave back. Aren't you happy?"

The fur stuff has wrapped itself around my arms, my legs, and it pushes upward, envelopes me like a second skin. I don't mind any more. It's like velvet, soft and smooth, and I run my hand over the flesh sprouted new.

Inside the house, the new daddy cries, and Momma shushes him, brings him to her breast.

"Hush now. It'll all be all right. Everything will be all right," she says. I want to scream at her, to tell her to throw it away, to burn it, to cut it open and pour the blood back into the earth. But the house is in my throat now, the fur pushing further and further down, and I'm so tired.

Beneath me, the world opens its teeth, stretches its mouth wide as my body splits open, empties itself into the dirt.

The new daddy sings to me. His voice merging with the heartbeat of the house. The light fades. Blinks out. And I sleep.

DAVID
PEAK

House of
Abjection

W HEN THE FATHER PARKED HIS LONG, BLACK SEDAN at the bottom of the hill, he saw reflected in the rearview mirror the rambling, vine-choked mansion, its hideous and chipped paint bleakly visible beneath the street's lone light. He put his hand on the mother's knee and she immediately stopped her fidgeting beneath the commanding weight of his silver-ringed fingers.

"If you stay in the car, you're going to get cold," the father said to his wife. "We might be in there for half an hour, maybe even an hour, and they're saying that the night is supposed to get quite cold."

The mother sat quiet and still, only slightly turning her head to the side window. Outside, in the early evening dark, the blue and low-hanging leaves of the massive white oak trees shuffled soundlessly. She barely breathed out something like a whispered *no*.

"You can't just sit out here alone and get cold," the daughter said from the back seat. She turned to her husband, the son-in-law, and did something with her face that made him quickly sit forward and say, "She's right, mother. If you sit out here alone in the car you're likely to catch cold."

"I won't run the heat for you," the father said. He turned the keys and the car's engine went dumb. "I refuse to leave the keys here in the car. It's not safe for a woman on this side of town—in this neighborhood. This is not a good neighborhood. It's unclean, improper."

The mother breathed a final, limpid protest and removed her husband's hand from her knee. "Okay," she said to no one in particular, "I'll go inside, but I resent being made to feel scared."

It's important to note here that the daughter had been the one to initially suggest a nighttime drive to the mansion.

The four of them had spent the afternoon at the county fair, where the seemingly endless tractor pull had brought down stubborn clouds of all-encompassing blue smoke, swallowing whole the

mud-streaked grandstand and dulling the streaked red lights of the
carnival rides. The smell of the smoke was sweet and it was everywhere. The old woman calling the bingo numbers in the pavilion at
the end of the fairground hacked her way through the penultimate
game of blackout. Unsupervised children stalked one another in
thuggish groups, playing "Jack the Ripper." Although the father's
patience with his son-in-law had grown strained toward the end of
the day, they'd all gotten along rather well, which wasn't necessarily
abnormal.

Originally constructed in the late 1800s, the mansion had first
functioned as an inn, serving the laborers of the area's once-booming
coal industry. Running a brothel, however, had proved significantly
more lucrative, and so the owners, French immigrants, a husband
and wife with the surname of Kristeva, had ingratiated themselves
with the local peace keepers, offering steep discounts in exchange for
their turning a blind eye. By the turn of the century, the mansion was
well-known as a place of ill-repute. It's said that several unspeakable
atrocities were committed within its walls.

No one knows how or why, but eventually the house went vacant;
it stayed that way for decades.

Only recently, there was talk that the mansion had reopened its
doors, this time as a spooky haunted house—a tourist attraction
designed for the purpose of entertainment. And so this is how the
daughter had come up with her idea. She resented being made to
feel like she was missing out on something others were talking excitedly about. "Spooky tours are given throughout the night," she said.
"Everyone is talking excitedly about it." The father, who almost always
deferred to the wishes of his daughter, said it sounded like fun. The
daughter's husband agreed.

Only the mother declined and yet she'd had no real choice in the
matter. "Maybe I'll just wait in the car," she'd said, to which, for the
time being, no one had said anything further.

When they arrived at the front door of the mansion, a handwritten
sign above the buzzer read, "Press me and wait." The father did as
instructed and a shrill bell could be heard from within the house. "I
guess we just wait here then," he said. "That's what the sign says to

do." The daughter made a face that clearly conveyed impatience and the father shrugged sheepishly in response.

Within a few moments, a metal slot in the center of the door slid open, showing two slightly squinted eyes. "How many in your group?" a woman's voice said, her accent French, thick.

"There're four of us," the daughter's husband said, barely finishing his sentence before the slot slid shut. The door opened and swung wide, revealing a drab, wood-paneled hallway, its lights dimmed and the runner an awful, faded red.

The father motioned for his wife, his daughter and her husband, to enter before him. When they were all inside, cramped together, the door closed, and there stood the woman who'd spoken to them. She was dressed in black, and though she was obviously quite young her face was heavy with make-up.

Something about the color of the rug reminded the daughter of her menses—more importantly that she was a few days late. She felt a cramp in her gut; instantly a white-hot line of sweat stippled her upper lip. Although she desperately wished to not be pregnant, she was unable to articulate this to herself. The thought that her cramps were actually an impending bowel movement brought on by the rich foods she'd consumed at the county fair—the elephant ears and pulled pork, fudge sundaes and lemon crushes—slightly calmed her sudden panic. Her skin would react poorly to the sugar, the grease, and this too caused her great concern. She'd have to find a restroom during the tour, she decided.

"Please," said the woman with the French accent, "find your way into the drawing room and have a seat. Your host will be with you shortly. He's finishing up a tour of the house with another group at the moment." Then, almost as if it were an afterthought, she said, "My name is Julia." With that she disappeared into the shadows down the hall, the floor-boards squeaking softly beneath her steps.

In the drawing room, the father sat alone on a loveseat opposite a television set of some vintage. The daughter and her husband sat together arm in arm on an adjacent—and also quite old—fainting couch. The mother chose to stand in the far corner, her clutch held tightly in both hands.

"How funny," the daughter's husband said, inspecting the fainting couch. "There's a small plaque here that says this very couch belonged to Freud. I'll be." He turned to his wife's father. "You think that could be true, Father?"

"How should I know?" the father said curtly, feigning an intense interest in his wrist watch. He had very little patience for his daughter's husband—the man who'd ripped his little girl from his life—and did his best not to speak to him beyond brief exchanges of necessary information.

The walls of the drawing room were cluttered with bric-a-brac. There were dozens of spooky masks, battered instruments with broken necks, wild and tangled strings, timeworn posters for silent horror films. A nylon rope hung from a light fixture in the center of the ceiling, tied in a noose.

"Lovely," the daughter said, staring at the rope. And then the room suddenly went dark.

The tube television flicked on, flooding the room with silver light. The thick glass screen looped an over-scanned black-and-white image of the drawing room, the father sitting on the loveseat, his daughter and her husband on the fainting couch, and the mother, his wife, standing in the corner. The image of the drawing room was suddenly wiped clean of its inhabitants, the grain of the film altered, as the room was devoured by decay. It came on as heavy layers of drifting dust, settling into the crevices of the furniture, forming sloping piles where the walls met the floor.

Abruptly, the screen's harsh light pulled into itself, a small gray dot, and then the room fell into total darkness. It had to have been some clever optical effect, the son-in-law thought, a filter placed over security footage, overexposed images acid-burnt and half-eaten by ravenous dust.

And then the television was on again, shedding rapid-fire images one after another: an obese man on the toilet, his genitals hidden by the lip of the bowl; a cat vomiting; gulls pulling flailing and panicked crabs from oceanic whitecaps; an erect and stubby cock, its urethra glistening a compact pearl of pre-seminal fluid; a stallion mounting a mare; the corpse of a rabbit succumbing to decay, swarmed by insects and picked clean, its crumpled and greasy bones piled loose in the long blades of grass.

In the corner of the room, near the mother, a lamp buzzed metallic like an alarm clock in a cartoon. The loveseat the father sat on pneumatically lurched forward before hissing back to the floor. All the lights turned on and then off, buzzing. A junked cuckoo clock mounted on the wall hatched a baby-beaked bird, its wired wings flapping.

To everyone's immense relief, the room went dark—and silent—once more. The mother was overcome with the unmistakable feeling that someone had just brushed past her. "Someone just brushed past me," she said, surprised by the eerie calmness of her voice. "There's someone else in the room with us."

A flashlight clicked on in the center of the room, its yellow beam illuminating a face from below, its features freakish and contorted and orangish pink. Although it was somewhat difficult to discern details, the face—seemingly floating there in mid-air—appeared to belong to an elderly man with wild hair. His mouth hung open; his eyes were shut. The room went silent with the collective vacuum of held breath.

The lights turned on—the ghoulish face of the old man filling out and suddenly growing a somewhat hunched, disheveled body, arms and legs and all—and the daughter, once again, clapped her hands. "Amazing," she said. "Where must he have come from?"

"Thank you for choosing to spend your evening with us," the man in the center of the room said, clicking off the flashlight and lowering it, his thick French accent rendering his words near unintelligible. "My name is Louis-Ferdinand." At this, Louis-Ferdinand did something of a bow, sweeping his hand to his side. "I will be your host for the next hour, personally leading you through our awful home." He giggled before he continued.

"They say," Louis-Ferdinand said, scanning the room, leering, "that a man's home is his castle, no? Well, I happen to believe that my home is not only a castle, but a fortified castle. What do I mean by that, you ask? Aren't all castles, by definition, fortified? By that, of course, I mean that the walls of this castle cannot crumble. I exert total control over my domain and everything within it. How is this different from a prison, you ask? And the answer, unfortunately, is that for you tonight this house will be no different from a prison."

Louis-Ferdinand then proceeded to deliver an oral history of the mansion, occasionally pausing for dramatic effect after a particularly horrific anecdote. During this telling, the room would occasionally plunge into darkness. It was a cheap trick, perhaps, but upon being repeated three or four times, its effects became profoundly disturbing to the son-in-law, who grew increasingly conscious of the sound and speed of his breathing, the uncomfortable heat of the blood coursing through his hands, the horrifying idea that anything could be lurking about in that darkness, in all that nothingness. He desperately wished to get on with the tour—and out of this stuffy, cramped room. A wave of nausea brought the acidic sting of bile into his throat when he caught himself thinking that, perhaps, there was nothing beyond the walls of the drawing room—endless and infinite nothingness.

Just as the son-in-law's discomfort was becoming unbearable, the lights came on, seemingly taking Louis-Ferdinand off-guard. "*Quoi?*" A small, hidden door opened in the wall behind the mother, and Julia, ducking low through the archway, came quickly into the room, her heavily shadowed eyes wide with fear.

She barked something harsh in French, something that went against the naturally fluid contours of the language, which quickly shushed Louis-Ferdinand. Then, turning to the group, she said, "I am so sorry to interrupt, but I feel the need to let you all know that there is some news in the area. There has been some atrocities. People are dead—perhaps many. It is horrific. These crimes, they occur one town over and I have just heard that the person who committed these crimes—a well-dressed gentleman, according to preliminary reports—has been witnessed as stalking around the shadows near this very house."

The father turned to his daughter and said, "Darling, isn't this just fiendishly clever?"

To this, the daughter clapped her hands. "Oh yes," she said. "Brilliant." In an exaggerated voice she said, "Perhaps this maniacal fellow is lost somewhere in this spooky old mansion, just waiting to jump out of the dark and scare us."

Louis-Ferdinand set his flashlight on the mantle behind him. "*S'il*

vous plait, mes amis," he said, turning back to face everyone, "this is
not part of the tour. *Ce n'est pas* a joke"

"Well of course he's going to say that," the son-in-law said, laughing.
"It's all in the name of verisimilitude, isn't that right?" He winked at
Louis-Ferdinand.

The Frenchman was visibly repulsed by the son-in-law's attempt at
non-verbal communication. He turned and took a few quick strides
across the room, standing near the door that led into the hallway.
"The chateau is quite old and has many windows," he said, addressing
the entire room. "I must ensure that they are all locked, that the castle
remains fortified. This place is larger than you could imagine and
filled with many *astuces*—unnamable things." With that, he left the
room and disappeared into the bowels of the mansion.

Julia lit a cigarette and leaned against the wall. She took a long
drag—performing a highly practiced French inhale—and crossed her
arms. If she was concerned, her face did not betray it. She seemed to
be staring at a memory, through the very walls of the house, staring at
something miles away.

Time passed, it's impossible to say exactly how much. The guests,
understandably, grew quite restless.

"Listen, Julie—" the father said.

"*Julia,*" Julia said, her voice stern. "My name is Julia." She stood
up straight, dropped what was left of her cigarette to the floor and
crushed it with the heel of her black leather boot.

"Listen, Julia," the father said, seemingly unembarrassed by his
faux pas or perhaps oblivious of Julia's scorn, "do you have any idea
when your father might be coming back? We've already been waiting
for . . . " He looked down, with great interest, at his wrist watch.
"Well, we've been waiting for quite a long time."

Julia laughed. "My father?" she said. "Louis-Ferdinand? No, *vous
vous trompez.* Louis-Ferdinand is my lover." She covered her mouth
with her curled fingers, a behavior she hadn't entertained since she'd
been a young girl in school, hiding her gossipy giggles from her
teachers. She pointed a long finger at the father's daughter and her
eyes went wide, surprised to be singled out in such a crude manner.
"Just like she is your lover, correct?"

The daughter gasped. Her husband noted his wife's reaction out of the corner of his eye, though he kept his face angled toward Julia and did his best not to convey anything other than the kind of boredom that stems from familiarity. The father's face turned blood red, or so thought his daughter, who was once more reminded of her unpunctual menses. When the father spoke, he spoke slowly. "That is my daughter," he said. "And that," he continued, motioning toward his wife, who remained standing near the wall, holding her clutch, also with a carefully studied look of familiar boredom on her face, "is my love—" here he stopped himself short, "that is my wife."

Julia continued to giggle through her fingers. "Ah, of course. How silly of me to get it perversed."

The father, the mother, their daughter and her husband, the son-in-law, watched horrified as Julia attempted, multiple times, to stifle her laughter only to rupture into further fits of something approaching hysteria. "I meant to say *reversed*," she said between gulps for air. "My language is . . . not so good sometimes." Tears formed in the corners of her eyes. She waved her hands in front of her face, blurted out a quick "*Excusez-moi*" and fled through the door and down the dark hallway, in the general direction of her lover Louis-Ferdinand.

"What an awful woman," the son-in-law said.

"Quite rude," the daughter said.

The occasional sound of an old window slamming shut echoed through the long and empty hallways. These echoes drifted apart in time, the distant softness of their sounds correlating directly with their growing infrequency, before stopping altogether. The house buzzed with the raw tension of silence.

The father abruptly took to his feet. "Come on," he announced, apparently addressing the entire room. "This must be some sort of trick—a test of courage or something. It's part of the tour. If we don't get on with it, we're likely to sit here all night."

"We really should find a restroom," the daughter said.

"Are you not feeling well, my dear?" the mother asked, her voice icy. In response, her daughter merely pouted. She knew better than to solicit sympathy from her mother.

"I think we passed a restroom when we entered the house," the son-in-law said, making his way to the door leading into the hallway. He turned the knob and found that it was locked. "It's locked," he said. He turned to the others. "They've locked us in. Doesn't that violate the fire code?"

The mother pushed in the hidden door Louis-Ferdinand had used to sneak into the room. The door's hinges creaked as the door slowly swung inward, revealing a dark passageway, their horrible noise attracting the reticent stares of her husband, her daughter and the son-in-law.

"We'll have to go through here," she said, taking time to relish the apparent discomfort of her family.

The father went first, ducking his head to fit through the archway—his wife, her daughter and the son-in-law followed—and as a group, they moved slowly, one step at a time, the father feeling ahead into the darkness with his hands. Soon enough, a dull light glowed in the distance, evidently showing where the passageway spilled into a larger, concrete room. Hissing and dripping pipes lined the walls, occasionally letting off great charges of steam, their serpentine circuits ornamented with grease-slicked valve-wheels and infinitely complex meters.

"They sure did do a good job preserving all this old plumbing," the son-in-law said.

"Keep up the pace," the father said. Although he was loath to admit it, he was feeling claustrophobic. His eyes played tricks on him: more than once he thought he saw a glowing red exit sign, only to watch its letters morph into incomprehensible shapes before disappearing altogether. Still, he pushed on, leading the way. His instincts paid off, as they often had throughout the course of his life, because the concrete and exposed plumbing eventually gave way to drywall and plywood flooring, the darkness replaced by strings of mining lights hung near the ceiling. The air suddenly became less stuffy. "It's this way," the father said. "I can smell fresh air."

A small ramp led up to a flimsy cellar door, the distinctly blue tint of moonlight seeping through the break of its shutters. The father pushed through, half expecting the door to be padlocked from the outside, only to find that the shutters flipped over effortlessly.

They appeared to be in the courtyard at the center of the mansion. The moon—for it was quite full—illuminated a terribly overgrown and pungently rotting garden, a black gazebo choked with ivy and filled with broken down and rusted machinery. Three floors of windows enclosed the vegetation, much of which appeared Jurassic, overtaking the haphazard stone steps of the walkway, its paths forming something of a circle around a white stone fountain, its large bowl bone-dry, the headless statue of a nude woman rising from its center toward the sky, one of her breasts broken away.

Upon setting foot in the courtyard, the four guests split up, each exploring different corners of the garden. The father angled the glass of his wristwatch in the moonlight in order to make out the hours while the mother watched him judgingly from afar. The daughter inspected the statuary of the fountain while her husband, the son-in-law, was drawn to what appeared to be a long metal cylinder emerging from a wild tangle of broad-leaved plants. Indeed, upon pulling away great amounts of foliage, the son-in-law discovered, to his utmost surprise, that he'd uncovered an almost perfectly preserved battle tank, a Panzer III.

"I'll be," he said. "I guess this is what the Frenchman meant when he was talking about fortification, wouldn't you say, Father?"

The father grunted in response, but he hadn't actually heard his son-in-law's question—in fact, he had mistakenly thought his son-in-law had asked him about *fornication*, which greatly annoyed him, reminding him of that insipid French girl's giggles—for his attentions were fully engaged by the unbelievably strange behaviors of his wristwatch, whose second hand appeared to be spinning backward at a rate he couldn't quite figure out, as if it were irregularly set against the standard, sixty-second minute. For that matter, the minute hand had disappeared altogether, having been replaced with what looked like an earwig pinned in the center of the watch face. The hour hand had turned upward, pointing him accusingly in the face.

Annoyed that his father had once again shirked his attempts at conversation, the son-in-law climbed on top of the tank and opened the hatch. He was tired of being ignored by his wife's father, having spent year after year seeking his affections, made to feel invisible at family functions, like he was nothing. Where he had hoped there would be deep wells of feeling, there was nothing. The word sent a shudder through his body, *nothing*. He wanted to hide. He wanted to be unseen, and so the son-in-law climbed inside the tank and shut the hatch behind him.

Inside the tank, there was only darkness. The son-in-law reached above his head to try to find the hatch but there was only air above him. He reached out to his sides but felt nothing. For a brief moment, the son-in-law felt as if he were in free-fall, his guts queasy with weightlessness—but that couldn't be possible. It wasn't possible. In the blackness, the son-in-law thought he could make out the shape of a door. He made his way to it. It was an ordinary door. He opened it. Through the door there was another door, in the blackness, this one perhaps twice as far away as the first had been. The son-in-law stepped through the door and it disappeared behind him. Or at least he thought he had, but that couldn't be possible. He had no choice but to continue forward. He made his way to the second door and opened it. In the distance he could just barely make out a third door, this one farther than the distance of the first two doors combined. He almost got lost trying to make his way to it, nearly giving into the temptation to turn around, to try and retrace his steps. Or had he turned around? He couldn't remember. He couldn't see the door in the distance. There was nothing behind him. He didn't know which way *behind* or *in front* was. He was lost in an infinite blackness. He tried to scream but his voice was too small to fill the impossible void which now engulfed him.

"Did you hear that?" the daughter said. "It sounded like a toilet flushing, I think." There was no response. She looked around the courtyard and could see neither her father nor her mother, nor could she see any sign of a restroom. It occurred to her that maybe the sound she'd heard was some sort of a gurgle, perhaps water bubbling up from within the bowl of the fountain, or, and she was unwilling to think about this in any sort of detail, perhaps it was the unmentionable doings of her own digestive system.

In an effort to distract herself from her own bodily functions, the daughter once more focused her attentions on the fountain's statue, thinking how uncanny the resemblance was to her own physique. Of course, the daughter wasn't missing one of her breasts, but that was beside the point. The proportions were almost identical. Double-checking to make sure her mother or father weren't watching her, the daughter quickly undid one of the buttons on her blouse and cupped each of her breasts in her hand, first one and then the other. It did feel as if one was smaller than the other, but that was normal. She repeated the same action, first cupping her right breast and then her left. This time, however, one breast felt significantly smaller than the other.

The daughter stepped into the bowl of the fountain in an effort to more closely inspect the statue. The white stone was badly worn by the weather, discolored in some places, chipped and flaking in others. She thought of her own skin and the stress she'd put it through today—the unhealthy foods, the smoke from the tractor pull—and became intensely fearful that her best days were now behind her. She wished that she could freeze herself in time forever, preserving her beauty for others to admire, and, while contemplating this, unknow-ingly climbed up onto the stone pedestal with the statue, wrapped her arms around it, and joined it, leaving her unreliable and mortal flesh behind.

At that very moment, it suddenly became clear to the daughter's father that he wasn't looking at his wristwatch at all; in fact he was looking at a compass, which would go a long way toward explaining the insect-shaped needle straining toward the other side of the court-yard. "We have to go this way," he said, calling to his wife. "The signs are all pointing northward, or southward, whatever."

The wife's husband stumbled his way through the knee-deep veg-etation without bothering to check whether or not his wife followed. He found a door, opened it, ran down a long hallway, nearly tumbled down a steep flight of stone stairs. The insect on his compass was buzzing wildly, its thorax glowing green, its spiracles flexing, telling him he was very nearly there. He made his way down the steps, care-fully, one at a time, his hand on the iron railing, the endpoint of his descent lost in a swirling pool of inky shadows.

Now alone in the garden, the woman looked up into the sky and saw a rather sinister thunderhead rolling over the face of the moon.

The night-time air suddenly grew quite cold and she began to shiver. Across the courtyard, she noticed that one of the first-floor windows had been left ajar—Louis-Ferdinand must have missed that one—and so she made her way to it, carefully climbing over its sill, shutting it quietly behind her before locking it in place.

She made her way down a hallway and up a flight of creaking stairs, occasional pulses of blue lightning beaming in through the windows, showing her the way, and then another flight of stairs, yet another, this one spiraling upward into what had to be some sort of steeple. In the room's center, a chair set before a small screen.

She sat down. The screen was split into four smaller screens, each intermittently flipping between various nooks and crannies of the mansion—security footage.

Eventually, the small screen in the upper right hand corner showed what appeared to be a man resembling her husband. She instinctively reached forward and pressed the image with a single finger, enlarging it to fill the screen. Indeed it did appear to be a man who resembled her husband, in what appeared to be a wine cellar, a massive, floor-to-ceiling rack filled with bottles of indeterminate age, the cobble-stone ceiling over his head arched, a few massive wooden barrels on the other side of the room.

The man who resembled her husband seemed to drop something, getting down on his hands and knees and staring at something on the floor. He tracked nearly across the room for a while before standing, his back to the camera. Stepping out of the shadows just below the camera's view, creeping up to the man who resembled her husband's turned back, was a tall man wearing an elegant suit and top hat. The woman was unable to see clearly, but he appeared to be holding something before him with both hands. And then, in a flash, the man in the top hat lunged forward, throwing his arms up into the air, a tight string wrapped around each gloved hand. He wrapped the string around the man who resembled her husband's neck and cinched it tight—just as the security footage cut out, the screen blank, showing only the woman's own reflection, surprised, reflected in the light of a particularly intense bout of lighting.

She resented having to think of a grown man being weak, unable to care for himself. She turned to the window at her side, the sprawling view of the town below showing endless rows of other homes, their windows filled with husbands and wives, daughters and husbands, everyone lost and searching for something they would never find.

This was the woman's greatest fear—the wondering. Were they all in it? Was it all an attempt to make her feel scared? It wouldn't be the first time they'd excluded her from their fun. In fact, her daughter had a lifetime of stealing her husband's attentions, perverting them into her own.

The coldness of the night seeped in through the old window, profoundly discomfiting. The woman looked down into street far below and saw a long, black car parked beneath the wind-swept leaves of a massive white oak tree. She waited, her heart aching with dread, hoping beyond her wildest dreams that she shouldn't have to see her family get into that car and drive away, leaving her alone and cold and forgotten in this dark tower.

HELEN MARSHALL

The Way She is With Strangers

I⟧ WAS ONLY AFTER THE PAPERS WERE SIGNED, THE dissolution of the marriage arranged and witnessed, that Mercy Dwyer finally moved to the city. She had never lived in a city before. She had known only the sleepy village of Hindmoor Green in which she'd been raised, a place where no street needed a name because there were few enough that they could be recognised, like children: everyone knew what they were, everyone knew where they went, no question as to their identity had ever been raised and for all she expected from now until Judgement Day none ever would be. Hindmoor Green had been comprised of a small circle of buildings clustered around a post office, a one-pump petrol station, and the local pub. Beyond the village boundaries was the hazy sameness of rolling hills and ancient woodland. There were fields too, and pastures; but all of it was so similar that if you looked in one direction, you saw exactly the same view as if you had looked in the other entirely.

There was a legend, she had heard, that the universe had been created and destroyed three times: each time it had been built smaller than the last. Mercy believed it. Hindmoor Green was the smallest version of the universe she could imagine. It was complete. She knew its borders, and she respected them. But the city was, to her surprise, much, much smaller. To herself she called it New Manchester or sometimes New New Manchester. It was claustrophobic, folded up like a paper bird, wing touching breastbone touching foot touching beak. Once she dropped a penny from a bridge. She watched it flutter through the sky, turning end over end, winking. It crashed through her skylight, three miles to the north. She found it on the kitchen table like a gift, nestled amongst ribbons of scattered glass. She knew it by the date, by the tiny indent in the Queen's chin her thumb had scratched. She didn't wonder at this. She wondered only about the inevitable suicides. Every city had them. Bridges were portals not just

to the next city over but to the next world. But what happened to the
bodies? Were there families who woke to startled guests at the breakfast table? Mercy liked to imagine these unexpected meetings, how the
children in their school clothes would welcome the visitor with joy
or exasperation, cream or sugar with the coffee, eggs on toast. How
much could be healed with such simple accommodations?

It was a kind thought, and Mercy thought it because she was a
kind person. She had a kind face. In her childhood she had smiled
often, and there were lines because of it now. Not deep lines, more like
shallow cuts or old scar tissue. But it made people trust her immediately. The first time someone stopped her in the street she was a bit
frightened. It was only that day she had moved into the townhouse
terrace, and she was still learning her way. But it was a woman and
her child, foreigners clearly, just as she was. The woman had sad eyes,
sensible shoes, and a smell like wood smoke. She wanted to know how
to reach a particular street. "I'm sorry," Mercy told her, "really, I don't
know. I've only just arrived myself." The silence after this seemed to
last an eternity. Mercy felt her heart breaking. She wanted to help.
The boy was soft-looking, his flesh hadn't sharpened into adulthood
yet. He turned away from Mercy and stared down the street. It was
getting dark, but the lamps hadn't come on yet. The darkness pressed
the cobblestones flat. She shivered. The boy was shivering too though
he hadn't noticed yet. "That way," said Mercy, guessing desperately.
The mother gave her a look—grateful but anxious. "Thank you," she
whispered. Then she tugged at the boy's hand. They set off into the
gloom.

Mercy had a daughter named Comfort who came to stay with her on
weekends. Comfort was a sweet girl, eight years old, but almost nearly
very grown up. She took the train from Hindmoor Green to the city
by herself with no one but the conductor to watch out for her. Mercy
had feared for her daughter the first time she made this trip alone, but
lo and behold, when the train had pulled into the station, there was
Comfort exactly where she should be. She was always full of questions after the trip. Mercy didn't know many of the answers. Mostly

she made things up. "How many stars are there in the sky?" Comfort would ask her. "Only twelve," she would say, "but the sky is a mirror maze so it seems like there are many more."

Mercy had loved her husband, but they had married very early. She had been seventeen, he had been twenty. She didn't remember what the rush was. It hadn't been Comfort. Comfort came later. When Mercy looked back on the early months of her engagement to Noah, she remembered the warm glow she had felt in the pit of her stomach, a furnace fueling the engine of her days. In Hindmoor Green he had seemed larger than life: always laughing, big hands, square palms. But they hadn't really known each other. Had they moved too quickly? Her parents said so. "Build the foundation," they said, "test it, make it perfect. Don't put all your weight onto something that may not hold." But she had never lived like that. She knew all things had a crack at the heart of them. They would fall apart eventually. This had never scared her, not even as a child, when someone—a teacher—had first explained what death was. She had known death was inside her already, she hadn't needed someone to tell her. The only houses she feared were the ones that were built to stand forever. Those she did not trust. She loved the houses of snails and sea creatures. They grew or were discarded. She loved her life by the same principles. When things with Noah fell apart, she knew how to pull herself from the wreckage. How to start over. She built her life up again, but smaller this time, less expansive, less willing to admit visitors.

"Is this my bedroom?" Comfort asked the first time she saw the townhouse terrace. "Is this where I shall play?" Mercy allowed that it was. Later there were other questions: "How far is it from your room to mine? Why do the stairs make that sound when I stomp on them? What shall we keep in the cellar?" In a fit of exasperation, Mercy said: "Bodies," and she blinked twice afterward in surprise. It was an accident really, she hadn't meant to say that. But one of the city's builders had told her a story in the pub, and it stuck with her. "This building? What it is, right, is a boneyard, this and every other," he said, spitting on the ground. His eyes were glazed with alcohol. His breath shone. He sniffed his palm, scowled, then whispered into her ear: "The foreman's dead corrupt. He takes the money for it, gets a heavy bag, about so big, wrapped like so. Bodies. They put them in the foundation. For luck, maybe. Or to seal up the cracks. Me? I dig the hole." Mercy hadn't been able to sleep after she heard that. When she walked to the shop where she worked, she couldn't look at builders. She couldn't look at the buildings. She was afraid that Comfort wouldn't be able to sleep either. But Comfort slept through the night like a darling. She didn't stir once. In the morning she wanted to make mudcastles in the back garden. She filled her orange plastic bucket with dirt, and upended it gleefully. "Can I bury you, Mummy?" she asked. "Not today, pet. Maybe tomorrow."

Mercy glimpsed the woman and her boy sometimes. They stared at her from the reflections in glass panels of certain buildings. When she saw them, she would turn quickly, whether away or towards she didn't know. She resolved to do better in the future. So she bought maps of the city. Just a few at first, then more and more until her house was filled with them. Comfort draped them from strings. She built enormous mansions from them. Mercy would find herself crawling through tunnels bridged by paper folds. The hallway lights glowed behind onionskin levees. Streets swirled around her like fingerprints, the snaking lines of the canals. She touched them, and whispered their names. She didn't know why someone would want to go to one place more than another. They seemed equally strange to her, equally inhospitable. But she had promised herself she wouldn't lead anyone astray, not if she could help it.

In autumn, the night rain crawled like a stream of black ants down the window. When winter came, an unexpected snowfall made the faucets drip. Water snaked over the counter and seeped into the warren that Comfort had constructed, left the sodden paper hanging like old towels. Now it felt as if Mercy was crawling through seaweed. The tunnels could have been on the bottom of the ocean. The builder told her, afterwards, that it hadn't been the snows. Something had crawled into the pipes and died there. It had created a blockage. Still, the ink ran. It painted her fingers, her cheeks. It was as if the city was sealing itself onto her. But she didn't mind. She was learning.

There were foreigners everywhere, and they all came to her: shy, distraught, eager, afraid. Mercy learned their gestures. "How far now . . . ? Which is the way . . . ?" She came to measure distance in five languages, and then six, and then she learned that she didn't need words at all for what she wanted to tell them. The ones who asked her knew the way already. The city was printed on them as well, only they couldn't see it. Not yet. But she could. She felt the tracery lines glowing beneath their skin like thin, blue veins. She only needed to help them remember. And that, she learned, required very little: a kind smile, shy look, her hand touching theirs.

"Are you happy then?" the builder asked her. It was Wednesday. They were sitting at the pub, him leaning against the bar with a pint of bitter and her balanced on a stool, not talking to him, not listening to him. He was a big man, his body seemed to be stacked from successive layers. He reminded her of the mudcastles that Comfort built, only in reverse. "You look happy," he said, spreading his fingers. "You look dead happy." The question caught Mercy like a hammer blow between the dull eyes of a bull. She thought about the range of possible answers: "I make do" and "No more than anyone else" and was afraid to admit the truth: she *was* happy. It was easier with things as they were, with her tiny world, with her daughter present but not permanent, her husband regretful but never angry.

"If you're willing," Noah would say to her as he slipped into their narrow bed together, him already pressed against her. Afterwards, his mouth would tickle her ear: "How I love you," he would tell her, "my bright star, my darling." She could not imagine that all he ever wanted was her: slim-wasted, flat-chested, almost boyish in the coarseness of her hair. But Noah loved her. She saw it in the way he longed to sink himself into her so deeply that direction would reverse itself, like a tidal flow, and he would come back to himself: but complete this time. She could not tell him that she felt incomplete. She was not capable of holding that much love, of returning it unspoilt. It slipped out of her like water through a drain. Now there was a quiet space in the middle of the day when nothing was required of her. It was during these hours she took to the streets, looking for the strangers. Hoping they would stop her. "You could take me home," Mercy said to the thick-handed man beside her. She wanted to imagine him crawling through the tunnels that Comfort had made, on his hands and knees, surrounded by the smell of creeping damp. "Nah," he said. "A happy woman is no woman for me."

When Mercy left the bar it was on tottering feet. She felt unwell. She couldn't see the stars. The city blotted them out. There were towers where there used to be stars, and clouds, and a dull glow of silver from the streetlights, atoms of light bouncing between cloud and sodden sidewalk. But the stars. She had owned a telescope when she was younger. She loved the fierce red of Mars, gleaming like desert rock or a newly minted penny. She had read recently about the moon of Mars, Phobos: named for fear, daughter of Venus and Mars. She had read that tidal forces were ripping the moon apart. Its lifespan was now predicted to be 30 million years, a long time, no doubt, but finite. It was not forever. Above Mercy, the moon was shredding itself, its centre a pile of rubble, shallow stress grooves lined its skin. She would be long dead by the time it fell apart, but it made her sad anyway, and strangely frightened, to think about what was happening. It was all invisible anyway, out beyond the lambent atmosphere, but it was happening and it was terrible. Like a premonition. "You should have come home with me," she whispered into the darkness. "See, I'm sad and I'm tired and I'm frightened. Just like you are."

In the distance she heard the sound of glass bursting. The terrible fraying of metal. She did not stop. She did not turn around. Three days later she learned the builder had been struck down in the street. It was an accident. She did not go to the funeral. The papers did not mention where he was buried.

Two weeks later, Mercy saw the builder. He was standing at an intersection of Potato Wharf and Liverpool Road with a dazed expression on his face. His jaw hung slightly slack, as if death had loosed the muscles that had formerly hinged it together. Normally Comfort was anxious, almost shy, when they walked the streets together. The city, she had been told, was different than Hindmoor Green, more dangerous. She would dog Mercy's footsteps, fitting comfortably into the space her shadow carved in the sunlight. But today she was eager. She had skipped on ahead, never once glancing back to be sure Mercy was following.

When Mercy saw that awful figure slouched against the terracotta facing of an old canal warehouse, she reached for her daughter. But Comfort had already passed beyond the range of potential interception. "Are you drunk?" she exclaimed, a mixture of delight and skepticism. Indeed, he smelled of something faintly boozy, dark and yeasty-sweet . But the builder did not speak to her daughter. His eyes raked upwards, met Mercy's, and a sharp spark of light leaped up into the pupils. "Please," he said desperately, "I don't know the way." Mercy's tongue was thick, it plugged the cave of her mouth like a rockslide. "Come with me now," she said. "Let me show you." His hand was clammy but unexpectedly warm. She squeezed it gently.

In Hindmoor Green, they burned the bodies of the dead. The ashes rose in a feathered bloom from the chimney of the crematorium and resettled upon the fields with the softness of snow. The dead became dust: comfortable, comforting, a velvet veil over sacred things, objects too precious for daily handling. The dead inhabited lungs, they etched themselves under fingernails. The dead were lifted gently from the inner canthus of the eye by tongue or tears. They did not come back. It was different in the city, Mercy realized. Perhaps it was that the buildings were settled too deeply, perhaps their towers soared too high. The city was small, yes, but it was expanding, colonising those parts of heaven and earth that had since been left vacant. When Mercy took the hand of a stranger, she was never certain of where they had come from and where truly they were going.

Her own first train journey from Hindmoor Green had been a revelation. She had never imagined the size of the country she lived in, the glow of white chalk in the hillsides, the copper and tan waters of the ship canal snaking inland from the sea. There was terror too, yes, the sense of hurtling into the unknown like a silver arrow, but mostly it was the joy that Mercy remembered afterward. How her eyes devoured the sight of the men disembarking onto the platform in their crisp suits, briefcases in hand, slouched children, dainty women in sensible shoes, used to the journey. She did not know what the city would look like, and the tallness of the buildings was a shock. How could such things exist? Distantly she had always imagined the sky as a thin blue film but these things revealed that as a lie: they gave it depth, they were a measure stick for its enormity. She had not known what she would do when she arrived, only that she was empty, and the city would imprint some kind of shape upon her. She wondered if it was the same for the dead man. He had been a builder after all. He had known the city better, more intimately, than she ever would.

But it was the memory of the dead mother and her child that hurt Mercy the most. She had not known what to tell them, had not properly understood their questions. She had pointed blindly, and they had followed her directions. But where had she sent them? Once she had believed that one place was as good as another, but she was learning differently now. When she looked at the strangers she could tell: some of them were going to good places. There was a brightness in their eyes, a calmness, a sense that things would be easier when they got wherever they were going. But for others there was only exhaustion, an aching look that spoke of the miles behind and the miles ahead. When she woke from dreams of those two, she would go to her daughter's bedroom and crawl into the narrow bed. Mercy had always thought her daughter was exactly as she was named: a comfort, somehow extraneous to Mercy's existence, a delight, to be sure, but unnecessary, nothing to seal the gaps. But when she breathed in the smell of the sheets, which she refused to launder until the day before Comfort arrived, she knew this was not the case at all. Comfort had become her centre, the smallest, purest part of her. The foundation stone of her entire life.

Now it was Friday morning. Mercy had walked to the train station to meet her daughter. Her eyes skimmed the eyes of those she passed, careful not to linger too long. Today was not a day she would give over to the strangers. Today would belong to Comfort. It was her birthday. In the kitchen sat a little sunken cake clothed in nets of sugar and glazed orange slices. Mercy had eaten the ones that hadn't set properly so that only the best remained.

The train arrived. The doors flung out a stream of people, men clutching briefcases, women clutching the hands of their children, children clutching at whatever caught their eye as they passed: sunshine on the rails, pigeons, flutters of paper. Mercy waited. She had become more at ease with the crowds. She knew they would part, and there would be Comfort looking sleepy and sensible and not at all uncertain of where she was. But as the platform cleared, Comfort did not emerge. A worm of panic crawled into Mercy's heart. This had never happened before. She went to the platform attendant. He spoke in a slow drawl, "Perhaps she's on the next train, mum."

Comfort wasn't on the next train. Nor the one after that. Nor the one after that. Mercy's hands were shaking now. Noah had left at her at the station in Hindmoor Green. He had kissed her on the cheek. He had watched her climb the stairs. Mercy spoke to the station master, a close-shaven man with weepy, blue eyes. He was apologetic. He was baffled. He would do everything in his power to find out what had happened. Then there were the police, sure it had been a misunderstanding, a mistake. "Did you have problems with your daughter?" they asked. "Was she unhappy?" Mercy let them talk. At home, she remembered, was a labyrinth of old paper and a cake with perfect slivers of orange. They would dissolve on her tongue like snowflakes if she let them.

There was a comradery among the dead, Comfort discovered. She awakened in their city, a city of twisted glass lit by a warm, flaxen glow whose source she couldn't see. The dead crowded around her. She knew they were dead immediately because they had no smell. When she kissed their cheeks, they had no taste. The dead insisted on touching her, on hugging her close to their chests. It reminded her of past birthday parties when her father's family, a large and noisy crew, would descend upon her home to pinch her cheeks and exclaim over her height. It was not an unpleasant feeling. Comfort asked them questions, and they answered immediately. There was a joyfulness to their speech, even if it was strange to her. They remembered what it was like when they first arrived. They were frightened too. "I'm not frightened," she told them, and she realized this was true. She was happy. She felt as if she had stumbled upon some marvelous secret, and, in many ways, she had.

Time lost its urgency. She was unhooked from its rhythms. She watched it flow past her the way one might sit on the banks of a river, watching the passage of boats. She grew older. She fell in love. She married. She had a daughter of her own. She named her Solace, for her mother. Solace Dwyer. Time passed. Comfort believed once that time would have no meaning after death, but this turned out not to be the case at all. To exist, she learned, was to be in time. But time was not the problem in the city of the dead. Space was the problem. The city was shrinking, moment by moment. Comfort could see the horizon approaching with the height and mass of a standing wave. Soon it would topple and pin her in place. She knew this. The dead stood together. They had lost their joyfulness. They smelled of nothing, they tasted of nothing, but even so, it was very bad. Perhaps it was the fear. The dead had learned to fear what was coming. She clutched her daughter's hand.

There was a story Comfort's father told her about a man named Jacob. She did not miss her father. She did not, if she was honest, remember her father. But she remembered the story. Jacob was favored by God. He was the father of many children. One night God sent him a dream. He dreamed of angels going up and down the sky on a vast ladder. Comfort imagined this would be how she would leave the city of the dead. But the way out of the city of the dead, Comfort discovered, was nothing like that at all. You couldn't leave by regular methods. The city had no borders, or rather, its borders were turned in upon themselves. Walk as far as you could in one direction and at some point you would find yourself retracing your footsteps. There was only one way to leave. The city had a crack at the centre of it. The road through the crack was very long, so long it seemed impossible. Comfort tugged at her daughter. They would begin at once.

They walked. Their shadows fell behind, always. Sometimes Comfort imagined dragging them like a weight. There were others walking too, but conversation was difficult to keep up. Although the dead couldn't feel pain, they could still feel despair: the slow enclosing of hope. This did not break Comfort. For her despair was only a sort of pressurisation. Her hope, made smaller, had become harder, sharper. Eventually she found herself in another city. It too was made of spires of glass, but these were frightening rather than familiar. "Where are we, Mum?" her daughter asked. But the glass confused her senses. It reminded her of how birds must feel when they see lights in the windows of tall towers and think they are the stars.

There was no news for Mercy in the days that followed. The loss of Comfort was a crack that ran down the centre of her life. She felt as if it had cleaved time in two, before and after. Noah came to stay with her. The first night he slept in Comfort's room, which made Mercy inexpressibly angry. She did not want him to have that. He was covering over one of the only things that remained of her daughter with his own male smell. At breakfast, she hurled a teacup at the wall. It broke into three pieces. Noah swept these up without comment. He cradled her in his arms. She fought him bitterly, but his arms were exactly as she had remembered them, strong, those hard square palms like shovels patting down the earth. He kissed her, and she let him do it. The second night he slept in her bed. He did not touch her, but she could feel him lying alongside her, taking up space that used to belong to her. He snored gently. She turned her back to him, but the heat of his limbs snaked over her anyway.

For a time Mercy became a shut-in. She was afraid to leave the house. She kept imagining the look on Comfort's face if she returned to find her mother missing. Noah folded up the maps. Her living room became a living room again, ordinary, thick with dust in the corners where she had not bothered to look. In Hindmoor Green, she might have discovered a piece of Comfort tucked away there, but in the city she knew the dust was simply dust. Comfort had been buried elsewhere, in a basement, perhaps, or the foundations of the new bank: her tiny bones curdling in cement. Comfort did not like the dust. She was appalled by the open space of her living room. She had become so used to following the paths that Comfort made: here, along the sofa, two feet, three feet, then over the chair, then a rest, perhaps, under the old oak table whose tablecloth formed a perfect shelter. But Noah set it right. The chairs were placed neatly where they ought to be so the two of them could sit together over a breakfast of eggs on toast, coffee with sugar or cream. Simple kindnesses to help her cope.

And just like that Mercy realized it was not that she didn't love Noah. She did. She loved his kindness, the hot snort of his breath as he slept, the sound of his footsteps on the stairs. It was just that she had traveled so far in one direction that she hated the feeling of having returned home, just like that, just that easily. So one morning, while he was sleeping, she levered herself from beneath him, put on her winter coat, and left. She did not know where she was going. Mercy took to the streets, circling the waterfront piazzas, and following, apparently at will, the paths that lined the canals. There was a smell in the air, something heavy and brooding. She knew the streets by name though many she had never visited before: Market Street, Bridge Street, Oldham Road, Stockport Road, New Street. They were what they were. They said what they were, where they were going. Nothing else in her life had ever been so straightforward.

She did not know what she expected to see until all at once, she did know, because there was Comfort. She looked older than Mercy remembered, taller. She had cut her hair at some point, and now it hung short and feathery beneath her ears. There were lines on her face. She clutched the hand of a tiny girl, three years old. "Comfort," she cried, "please!" But the look her daughter gave her was uncertain, confused, exhausted. There was no recognition. "Sorry," she muttered. Her voice was deeper now too, robbed of its sing-song quality. "I seem to have lost the way. How many streets are there in the city?" she asked. "Only twelve," Mercy said, "but the glass is like a mirror here so it seems like there are many more." They stared at each other like strangers. But then the girl smiled. Her lips were soft and delicate, she had her grandfather's chin, her grandfather's blunt nose. "Where do they lead?" the girl asked. Mercy touched the girl's hand. It was cold and clammy, but Mercy could feel the pulse of something—new life—beneath her skin. It stretched the fabric of her, but she did not crack. She felt her heart expanding, she felt herself growing larger. She had anchored herself so firmly in heartache, and now the heartache was dissolving like sugar on the tongue. The touch was all she needed. Calmness washed over her. "I don't know," Mercy said, "I've never known, not for certain. But come with me, both of you. Let me take you home."

JOSHUA KING

The

Anteater

It'd been two weeks since the anteater had moved in next door and already things were starting to change. At first it was hardly noticeable, like the bush on the shared patch of grass at the end of their driveways had grown all out of control. The previous neighbours had trimmed it, but evidently the anteater didn't think it was his to take care of.

If that had been it, Peter wouldn't have been bothered, but that was just the beginning.

The village Peter lived in was quiet and everyone knew each other, whether they wanted to or not. At one end of the street was the park with its swings, a football pitch and surrounding houses for local farmers. At the other end was the church, houses for the schoolchildren and their families and the vicar. Bridging the two ends were the rest. This is where Peter and his wife lived, with the anteater next-door.

The previous owners of the anteater's new house had only recently moved out. Their daughter had turned eleven and wanted to go to a secondary school in the city, which had a strict catchment area entry policy. So they left the rural life behind to seek better things. One day they were there and the next the anteater had replaced them.

When the anteater was moving his few pieces of furniture in from the van, Peter couldn't help watching through the curtains. Twice the new villager caught his eye, but Peter would be damned if some anteater was going to just turn up and pretend like he was the one who should be self-conscious. He'd lived here his entire life.

It takes everyone a while to get used to somewhere new. Peter knew it took him close to five years to admit to himself that this little village was his home, having moved almost seven miles from the village where he was born.

Waking up to the sound of different farm birds and heavier-duty lawnmowers and inconvenient distances to the post-office was hard to get used to. He could admit that. This new chap though, well, he looked as though as he'd fit in here like a hoof in sandals. There was just something about him, Peter supposed it was a look he had, or the way he carried himself. It made him mysterious. Not knowing who he lived next door to was a sort of mental torture, and it was made all the more acute by the fact that the anteater never seemed to leave. Never went anywhere. Maybe he left at the times Peter wasn't watching, then came back during those moments too, but that would take some coincidences.

Come away, his wife, Maggie, would say, pulling Peter back by the shoulders and turning the volume up so loud on the television that he got distracted and eventually fell asleep in his chair.

Every week at the church Peter and the five other husbands in the village would meet and talk about politics. They'd been doing it for years. There wasn't anything else they had in common, and they didn't even have politics in common come to think of it, but everyone can talk about politics and they had to stay sane somehow. When you're detached from the rest of the country by miles and miles of field and motorway, entertainment can come from the simplest things.

This tradition started after a village party someone decided to throw for the vicar's birthday, with music and wine in the church hall. The husbands stayed on drinking and talking. It wasn't planned, only a natural result of the high-spirited evening. It was such a success—they got so unashamedly drunk without being told they had to stop—that they decided it should become a regular thing, and so from then on they all brought a bottle, took a seat and every Sunday night put the world to rights. That is, as long as the vicar remembered to leave them a key when he didn't join in himself.

It was more a slip of the tongue—Peter often drank before going out in order to ease himself into socialising—than rudeness, but when the anteater sheepishly walked in and drew up a chair to their circle, Peter asked who had invited him. He didn't mean it to come out the way it did, which was abrupt and suspicious, though of course his motivation was cruel, and rightly so. Who did this newcomer think he was?

A friend, a farmer, piped up and said it was him who had given the invitation. It'd been two weeks, he said, it was about time the anteater got to know the benefits of this sleepy little village. The farmer then waggled a bottle of whisky and poured himself a large glass. Of course, Peter laughed, saying he would have done the same if he'd bumped into their new friend here. This is, after all, the real beating heart of the place, the back room of the church.

Popping open the bottle of wine and offering a glass to the anteater, Peter wasn't surprised to find the guest raising his claw to say *no thank you*. Here we go, he thought, but smiled at him and topped up his own glass.

It was an awkward evening, touching on news stories with less zest than usual and considerably less alcohol. It was only half past ten when Peter made it home, and having dropped behind the anteater on the walk back, he fumbled with his keys while listening to his neighbour lock his own door from the inside.

There were as many wives in the village as there were husbands, but more women overall. Maggie and Peter had theories as to why this was. He thought that a man was less likely to end up in a place like this, because if he was single he would likely have made more money than a woman in the same situation and anyway, men would be more likely to live in the city, wouldn't they? There were a couple of reasons why, so Peter said, because firstly, a man had to show off a little more, to get women and all that, so they wanted to live where there were people to see all the showing off, otherwise what would be the point. And secondly, a woman didn't need all the things a man needed for excitement. She was happy with a little house in the middle of nowhere. Women were humble and practical.

Maggie thought that it was because men died earlier, as a rule, and it was always likely that a place full of old couples would eventually become a place dominated by old women.

Besides, wouldn't somewhere full of lonely woman just attract the men Peter was talking about?

"What's the neighbour like then?" Maggie asked, as Peter stumbled through the door.

"Bit quiet."

"Oh really? You think so?"

"Yes. In my opinion. Why? Someone else say different?" "I just didn't get that impression."

The next day stones were being disturbed on the neighbour's driveway and the noise distracted Peter too much to read the newspaper. It wasn't a car or anyone's footsteps. It was loud enough to sound like some sort of small industrial machine. There was a crunch as the surface gravel was broken, then a scoop, then a scatter of the stones being tossed somewhere before the scooping returned.

The window offered no clues. Even the view out of the bedroom upstairs was conveniently obscured by a walnut tree. Slinking back downstairs to rest in his armchair, Peter almost entertained the thought of going outside to investigate when he heard Maggie, taking a break from her watering, call a *hello* over the garden wall. The churning of gravel stopped. Kneeling again on the sofa and looking out, Peter saw the humped, monolithic figure of his next-door neighbour rise above the dividing wall, his feather-duster tail shaking in the breeze, his machete claws dropping clumps of dirt and weeds.

Maggie's voice was no more than distant scatting and rather than strain himself to hear how long they chatted for, or what they chatted about, Peter instead fell asleep and woke to the smell of a roast dinner, which they ate in front of the evening soaps as the sun set.

"You know," Maggie said, "it wouldn't kill you to do some weeding once in a while."

The big news story of that week was about a group of six men that had gang-raped the son of the boss of one of Britain's top banks. It wouldn't have been such big news amongst the group of drunken husbands if it hadn't happened in the city, only thirty miles away, where the boss' son owned flats, which of course stirred the farmers and had stirred their wives into thinking the village would soon be plagued with similar problems.

It was an outrage, that couldn't be denied. In the backstreets of their own county on a Wednesday night. A Wednesday. *How on earth does a thing like that happen on a Wednesday?* one of the husbands said, to the acquiescent grumble of the rest of them. *A Saturday night, fine. But a Wednesday?*

Only one of the perpetrators had been caught so far, because he'd twisted his ankle during penetration. The lesson, Peter said, was to never rape on a cobbled pavement, at which a few husbands laughed while others took uncomfortable sips of their drink. The anteater hadn't said a word, continuing his tradition from the week before, and he'd neither accepted nor brought any drink. Peter wasn't sure what was going through his neighbour's head, but no one else seemed to mind his silence. The arrested rapist had told the police that in some parts of the world, a harmless gang-rape was equivalent to going to the movies. Everyone needs a way to wind down after a long day.

"Some people will just never see the world like we see it," a farmer said. "The *right* and *proper* way."

Peter could barely see as it was. He was pissed, and so was everyone else. Apart from the anteater, that is.

On the days that he didn't get drunk with the other hobbyless men, Peter took the mile or so walk to the pub in the next village. Drinking there was ideal, because most people he knew were either too lazy or simply incapable of walking a mile, so he could guarantee some peace and quiet. The fresh air was always good for sobering up, too.

Sitting near the open fireplace, Peter warmed his feet as he sipped his ale. The pub prided itself on its original ales. This one was called *Woodlouse* and the image on the pump was just a pair of antennae, under shining orb eyes, poking out from under a rotting log. It tasted like smoked meat. Four pints of whatever was on offer was usually enough to kill a couple of hours and allow Peter to deliberate on life's bigger questions. *Are the council going to build a wind turbine in the village? If Valerie stops selling eggs, where will they get them from? Will that anteater ever cut the bush between their two driveways?*

As the third Woodlouse started to hit and turn his thoughts into looser, cloudier versions of themselves, Peter gave up his own musing and turned instead to the comfortable silence of the room. Though most of the patrons were men just as averse to socialising as he was, the landlord kept it from being entirely dead by talking to whoever was closest.

"I read earlier," he said, looking around the bar for the bundle of newspapers, "that two soldiers were killed in that hellhole. My nephew's over there, too. Could have been him. I tell you, the world's out of control. Never been any fucking thing like this, has there? And they're on their way here. They're already here."

He sipped his own beer and went on.

"You know what they do—my nephew said he'd *seen* this—they strap 'em to train tracks, loose bits of railway, not attached to the ground or in use or anything, and then lift these bits up with helicopters—bloody helicopters—and then drop them in this pit they make. By the time they've done a few, these poor sods are being dropped into pits of multiple railway pieces with others strapped onto 'em. They're alive, mind. Well, not by the time it's over."

"Terrible," said the man at the bar.

"Another one was that they take the bones of whoever they killed last, then use the arm bones, you know, or whatever, the long ones, and push one into the guy's mouth and another up their *wherever* until they meet in the middle. While the others watch. Imagine having that happen to you down an alleyway up the city. 'Cause that's what's gonna happen."

The man at the bar went to take a sip, grimaced, and then completed the action.

"He said as well that they have this zoo, where they keep weird stuff like . . . snakes and scorpions and things like that, and this thing that—no joke—he said burrows into people's eyes, and–"

Peter couldn't listen to it anymore. It wasn't that he was squeamish, just that he wasn't much in the mood for these kinds of thoughts before bed. Pouring the final quarter of ale down his throat, he lifted himself up and his eye caught a silver thread that connected the sleeve of his jumper to the armchair. Spider web, he thought. This place needed a dust. Catching it between his thumb and forefinger, however, it felt too thick and brittle to be a strand of web. He rubbed it between his fingers and held it up to his eye in the light. A hair. Dark grey and tough like a fishbone.

Flicking it onto the floor, he gestured a good bye hand at the landlord, who broke from his litany of torture tactics to grunt a good bye back.

A month went by and the weather soon became too cold to do any gardening. Maggie complained about being cooped up all day and never going on holidays or even going to the city anymore. She said Peter was becoming a boring old fart.

No one, not even the hardened country people in their wax jackets and thigh-length wellington boots went out in this type of cold. Not unless they had animals to feed, which they did quickly and then got the hell back inside.

"I don't want to go far," Maggie said. "Just anywhere. Anything. How about a film?"

After twenty minutes of arguing—they hadn't been to the pictures in twenty years and Peter didn't want to start again now—he agreed to drive her there and see what was on. On the way out, despite the cold wind and icy feel outside, they saw the anteater digging in the garden, his large, dry tail bent over himself, acting as a makeshift windbreaker or blanket. Peering out from underneath it, his long tongue unravelled and tasted the air. He was pulling a small tree from the ground and filling the hole back up with rocks and earth. Maggie waved, but Peter kept his eyes fixed on the road ahead and sped off.

There had been no doubt in Peter's mind that there'd be nothing he wanted to see at the cinema, and even Maggie had to admit that the selection didn't justify having come. Insisting that they make the best of it, however, she chose a film and watched while Peter slept.

On coming home, both were more agitated than when they had left, but rather than argue in the car or niggle at each other, the two of them just sat in silence, listening to the windscreen wipers scrape away the rain. Pulling into the driveway, Peter saw that their neighbour had gone inside but had left something on their front doorstep. It must have been him, because Maggie held her chest in delight and said that only the other day they'd been talking about his garden, which he'd taken pains to fill with plants from his home country. He'd left one as a present. How sweet of him.

Peter watched Maggie heave it inside and release it from its plastic bag, spilling dirt all over the carpet. Moving some photographs and an antique clock that had been his grandfather's, Peter placed the shrub on a cabinet in the hallway, and Maggie went to write a thank you note for him to go and slide under the anteater's door.

Sunday came quick because the week had been uneventful. There had not been much news in the papers, and nothing so terrible as to spend a whole evening tutting about. The husbands still got drunk though and railed again at the news that never died away. The state of the world, the peril their way of life was in, how they wished they could go back to the fifties when life was good: taxes, migration and bad television.

The anteater hadn't shown up, for some reason or other, and Peter felt more relaxed. Every so often someone asked where he had got to, but no one knew and after getting well and truly sozzled no one cared. At half past midnight they all went home, propping each other up until they reached their respective houses.

When Peter walked into his front room, Maggie was still up, reading a book on the sofa.

"Not in bed?"

"What do you think?"

"Had a good evening?"

"You stink of wine. You smell like a brewery."

"That would be beer then. Not wine."

She turned a page and didn't reply.

"Has the kettle boiled recently?" he said for something to say, and she shook her head. Peter went into the kitchen and while he waited for the kettle to boil he tried to shift some of the drunken fuzz in his head by opening his eyes wide and blinking hard. When he got back to the front room, Maggie had gone and before long he heard her brushing her teeth in the upstairs bathroom.

Settling into his chair, Peter forced the tea down his throat, swishing it around in his cheeks. It didn't mix well with the wine that coated the inside of his mouth, but it did go some way towards clearing his head. The next thing he knew it was morning. Sunlight was shining through the French windows. Birds trilling sliced through his unconsciousness like a drill sergeant's insults. He felt sweaty and his mouth was dry and sticky.

Before anything else, he wanted to wash himself and so staggered upstairs. Hanging his clothes over the edge of the bath, he went to turn the shower on, thinking a blast of hot water would wake him up, when he noticed a crack in the bottom of the bathtub. That hadn't been there before. He ran his fingers over it, testing to see how deep it was, and jumped when the crack moved and stuck to his hand. It wasn't a crack at all, he noticed, but a brittle spike of some sort. Like a fishbone. The fog cleared and his eyes narrowed as he realised what it was, and what the same thing had been in the pub that night. It was a tail hair from the anteater next door. Checking the seat of his trousers, he found more, of varying length and thickness. The anteater had been sat in his chair downstairs and left a wig's worth behind of himself.

Before taking time to wonder about the connotations, or to put his clothes back on, he walked to his bedroom, brandishing the hair like a detective holding a fake suicide note up to the true murderer. Peter drew in a breath, ready to shout, but saw that not only was his wife not there, but that the bed had been made, the curtains opened. The bedside clock said eleven-thirty. The day had already started.

Maggie couldn't be outside gardening in this weather, nor was she at

the neighbour's. The view from the bathroom window showed that
the car was gone. What day was it? Monday. Did she have anything
she usually did on Mondays? No, but then again, she liked to do
the big shop on a Monday, so perhaps she had simply gone out to
the supermarket. Peter placed the hair carefully on the sink edge and
showered, picking it back up once he was done and taking it downstairs with him.

Even as he walked out of the front door, he wasn't quite sure what
he was going to do. The air was cold still and recent flurries of snow
had left the ground slippery. It was a wonder he'd made it home at all
the night before without falling on the icy tarmac or catching a cold.
The route to the anteater's was all gravel, though, so he stepped with
confidence until he reached his neighbour's door and knocked on it,
still holding the needle of hair between his fingers.

A dark figure appeared behind the frosted glass of the doorway and
the anteater's claws fumbled with the key until Peter heard a click and
the door opened as far as the chain would allow. A foot above Peter's
eye line, the anteater's own eye, black and shiny like a marble, looked
down at him. The tongue snuck out a couple of inches and crept
around the doorframe. The door shut, and Peter was about to knock
again when he heard the chain slide back and the door opened fully.
The anteater gestured to the front room. Following him in there, Peter
found a long sofa and an armchair, and took a seat on the former,
assuming the anteater, like himself, preferred the comfort of his own
chair. Before he had had time to think through his reason for being
there, he was sitting, admiring the décor and watching the blackbirds
in the anteater's garden.

The anteater sat in his chair, which was on the other side of the
room to the sofa, giving away nothing with his teddy bear eyes and
not making a sound. Peter thought he should perhaps explain himself,
and so held up the hair.

"Look here," he said. "I have good reason to suspect you've been
meeting privately with my wife, and I wanted to know what your
designs on her are."

Only the tongue of his host moved. Peter hadn't been offered a
drink or even greeted with a *how do you do?* which was rude. The

silence, however, was unsettling. As the anteater's tongue reached closer to the ground, Peter held in his amazement at how long it was, and felt his own tongue growing drier. Perhaps out of thirst, or perhaps due to the dehydrating amount of alcohol he had consumed the night before and the poor night's sleep he'd had.

"Well? What do you have to say for yourself?"

The fur on the anteater's back bristled and rattled like dry grass in the wind.

"There's no use in denying it," Peter said, leaning forward as far as he could. "I found this—and a good deal more—on my chair this morning. Not to mention the fact that she's been all out of sorts."

Like a retreating tortoise head, his neighbour's tongue withdrew and as Peter was about to stand and take the fishbone hair over to him, the anteater lifted itself up and dropped forwards on all fours. He seemed bigger. Not only longer, but wider and more muscular in this position. Stretched out like this, Peter suspected the anteater was three, maybe four times heavier than himself. The animal's front claws were bent over so that it was resting on its knuckles. Its tail fanned out, and was almost as long as the anteater's body, reaching back to the armchair and hiding a great portion of it. Peter had to stop himself climbing onto the sofa as if he'd seen a mouse as the anteater lumbered across the room toward him.

"Now then, calm down. What are you doing?"

Still the anteater lurched forward, his thin, heavy head lolling from side to side and his tongue sliding in and out of his mouth.

"I'm warning you."

The gap between them became no more than a metre, and feeling his heart thump in his chest and panic spread through his aching body, Peter grabbed a lamp from the table next to him and brought it down on the anteater's forehead. His neighbour fell on his chin, his legs having given out underneath him, but still he continued to crawl forwards. With adrenaline still coursing through his body, Peter brought the lamp down another time, hitting the anteater between the eyes. He had pulled his feet up on the sofa now and was leaning over, lamp in hand, looking down at his neighbour, inspecting the fresh wound he had made. The fur around it turned purple and red.

There were a few seconds in which the only thing Peter could hear was the blood pumping in his ears. The anteater gurgled for a few seconds and Peter lifted his weapon, ready to strike again. Reaching his front leg forward and stabbing his claw into the carpet, the anteater managed to pull himself forwards an inch, but it was obvious, with the direction he had dragged his head and the way he was trying to throw his leg, that he was not trying to reach Peter, but trying to get around the side of the sofa. He pulled himself another half-metre or so before he had to stop. The rise and fall of his body slowed. His tongue poked out and didn't wind back in.

Noise filled the room all of a sudden. The ticking clock seemed to be firing off gun salutes, the blackbirds screeched for the help of the emergency services, the wind beat at the door, calling for anyone inside to open up or it'd batter it down. A fringe of white noise started to creep into Peter's vision. He needed water. He went to the kitchen, filled a glass and downed it in one go. Back in the front room he found the body unmoved. His mouth was still dry so he refilled his glass. Before he entered the front room again, something made him stop on the threshold.

Covering the anteater's snout in a neat line were hundreds of tiny insects, all following one another, beginning at the skirting board around the side of the sofa and ending at the smatter of blood between the anteater's eyes. Ants. They were organised things, Peter noted, waiting their turn, following the leader, turning back once they'd got their fill and marching back towards their nest around the side of the sofa. It was not a steadily moving line, however, because by the time the crowd on the anteater's forehead had busied themselves doing whatever it was they were doing at that drying patch of open skin, tens, hundreds more perhaps, had joined in at the end of the queue. Soon there were multiple queues, then no less than a plague. Within five minutes Peter's neighbour's head was unrecognisable as anything but a pulsing, baseball-bat shape of tiny bodies, all as black as their meal's eyes, which they had by now taken apart and shared amongst themselves.

Going back to the kitchen Peter opened the dishwasher. Finding it full, he left his glass on the countertop. But that seemed rude, so he rinsed it, dried it and put it back in the cupboard.

Over the garden wall, he saw that Maggie was not back yet. She often took a long time shopping, so it was no real surprise, and besides, he could do with a bit of peace and quiet for an hour or so. Sinking back into his chair, Peter realised that he was still holding the strand of hair and heaved himself back up, opened the window, and put it outside. It drifted away, disappearing in the hedgerow. Peter knew there were still a lot on the chair and his trousers, but those could be ignored for now. He'd deal with them after his nap.

Did something move? Scanning the carpet, he couldn't see anything, so thought it must just be his hangover playing its dirty tricks.

Sleepiness came and went, and more than once he jerked his head up, having nodded off in an uncomfortable position. After a heavy ten minutes of sleeping, Peter jumped up with such energy that it brought consciousness fully back to him, and after coming to his senses he became aware of an itch on his leg. Pinching a tuft of his trousers, he scratched through the material until he was satisfied. A moment later the itch was back, so he scratched it again. Soon the itch had not only grown in intensity, but was running all the way down his leg, and scratching with both hands did nothing.

Peter realised that it was not just itchy, but painful.

Lifting his trouser leg, he saw what looked like an open wound or raspberry jam. He was covered in some kind of red paste. Bending towards it, he felt his stomach lurch. A line of ants were making their way from the rim of his sock up towards his knee. The red was not a wound, or jam, but the blood of hundreds of squashed ants. The inside of his trousers were covered too.

Jumping up from his chair, Peter brushed the insects from his leg and stepped away from the army that had gathered around his feet. There was no distinct beginning or end to them, like there had been next-door. Just thousands, in groups all around the room, darting every which way. Peter took off his shoes and socks and threw them at a couple of the vague patches of ants, closed the door and retreated to the front garden. There he stood, trying to figure out where they could have come from. Out here there was no sign of the swarm within. But he could hear them, climbing over his furniture and in his shoes.

A shout came from across the road.

"You too?"

"All over!" their neighbour replied.

Choruses of horror were springing up all down the road. Everyone was rushing out into their gardens to check if their neighbours were similarly overrun with the plague of ants. Peter's feet were freezing on the cold grass. He just wanted to be back inside in his chair, reading the paper, sipping his tea, watching the clouds pass over his little village.

JENNI
FAGAN

When Words Change
the Molecular
Composition of Water

As she watches her life back, the thing that strikes her most is the number of times she's been saved. She is on her belly. Watching. One screen. She is in a long, slim pod and it reminds her of the capsule hotel she once slept in in Japan, for a whole week; it was $30 per night and felt like a well-lit coffin. This pod doesn't feel quite the same. The screen takes up the entire end wall and she has to be careful to focus on exactly what she's seeing or fast forward or replay or return is activated and it all becomes too confusing. What she is aiming for is chronological order.

She is trying not to get upset anymore. It does not help one bit that this is not how she expected it to be. There was no white light. No familiar faces greeted her, just a small dog walking ahead, leading the way, nodding her toward the pod and her climbing in and the door mercifully staying open and that is how it begins.

She is naked. More comfortable naked now than she ever was, although she is still lumpy and bumpy and the L-smile scar across her tummy is still there, where they took the baby. She hasn't watched that bit yet. Not yet. Not that bit.

What is striking her again and again as she watches herself is how many times she only just avoids death, or being raped, or walking in front of a car, or choking on Spam (it was a trip to South Korea) or the time she has a pencil jabbed just to the side of her ear and it misses her brain by millimetres. Her younger cousin, the culprit, is in the footage now, crying and crying, and her bleeding, and later she is walking through a meadow. Later still, through a park with trees, it is 5.37am and cherry blossom falls and she is still moderately high after a party, a first date, and two streets away there are four men who do not turn down the alley where she would have bumped into them. She is wearing a loose, full-length skirt and she looks happy and free.

Outside the pod, light does not appear to change; she does not know if she has been here for a day, a year, or something in between. She has no hunger. She cannot blink. It's not that she cannot remember how to blink, it is just the case that blinking doesn't happen here. She senses this naked body is just a way for her to feel more comfortable until she can accept something that is too big for her mind, or heart, or soul.

Her pod is in a row of pods and when she steps out and looks along them, it is not possible to see where they end—they trail off into an apparent infinity. There are skies. There are grassy hills on either side. Feet hang out of the ends of some of the pods, and in the one next to her, on the right, a pair of legs, black, with pins in the knees. When the legs step out, they turn white at the thigh and the lower area appears as a bruise, as if the legs themselves died but only up to the thigh. The man looks at her.

On the screen she is waving to herself. A silly thing to do, but once she'd had the idea, every so often on a street corner or in bed or walking along the beach, she would wave. To a stranger she would appear to be waving at nothing, but what she was waving at was her future self, who would one day sit down and watch her entire life back—she thought that might be an arduous process, so a wave might help. At this exact moment she is stood at the top of a castle in Bodrum; she is waving from the parapet. She waves and her hair blows in her eyes and behind her there is a large stone penis. It is pretending not to be a penis, but nobody is convinced.

She begins to file how long she spent in life doing each activity. 789 hours spent watching home-improvement shows.

1836 hours watching reality programmes about people much wealthier or better looking than she ever would be.

9 years waiting for things, for letters, wages, people, love, stuff, health, hope—waiting to become something she could tolerate living with.

That didn't happen.

She climbs out of her pod and looks along the row. Tonight the sky is pink and there is a moon slim as a fingernail. It is nice to sit outside and take in the breeze. The man in the pod on the right is twitching his feet. Sound out here in the open air is muted; she hears nothing. The volume has been turned off, as if by parents who know their children will only sleep, or concentrate, when all extrasensory stimulation is removed.

She is in the aisle of B&Q looking at the expensive paint and wondering which colour to pick. Once she has chosen, she will find a member of staff and give them the expensive shade—so they can mix up the exact same colour in the cheaper house brand. A toddler in a trolley gums a mobile phone; his mother picks up some colour samples then turns out of the aisle. She is on her own again and eventually she decides on bowler-hat grey, then a chapel green for her bathroom. This footage calms her. Sensible hours spent changing the colour and tone of her world. She picks up some solar lights. They soak up the sun, and even though the sun only arrives occasionally in winter, she buys them. They are dragonflies and during the daytime clear glass will soak up sunlight and at night they will glow red, green and blue—a little loud, but she needs something cheerful when she looks into the back garden at night and all she can see is black.

She has her hand on a door. The door to university, to a classroom, to a life she is not sure she can engage in, and she is hesitating, sweating. She knows her heart rate is climbing and what she is really scared of is having a panic attack in front of someone else, of hyperventilating on the floor while an unbearable fear pummels her consciousness, and she has always been terrified of this, she realises, as she plays back to her first day at school, and every lunchtime, every break time it is not always so painful and she does not even understand it in life—all she knows is: she feels uncomfortable around people.

She is in the university classroom in the back row and she has some diazepam in her bag and she keeps her head down and takes careful, precise notes.

Age seven, she is stood in front of a drawer with a monkey on it and being told that is her drawer and that is her name and that she must put her new jotters in there and a rubber and at break time they will gather in front of a crate of small bottles of milk and they will be given this to drink and a square of cheese, and it is meant to be a treat but when she gets there, she will find the milk is warm and the cheese is sweating, and she will eat it anyway because that is what they all must do.

The man to the right often sits looking down the hill behind the pods. There does not appear to be anything at the bottom of the hill and she wonders if they are only playing a night and day sky to appease them. Last evening the sky was impressive; she saw several satellites and forgot her discomfort at being unable to blink. She wants to ask him how long he has been here. Nobody asks anyone anything; they do not speak. There are thousands of them—one old lady seven pods along does Tai Chi every morning. The silence is astounding. It might be because of the lack of vocal cords, or the inability to work them, although occasionally they hear singing and look in the direction of this sound with utter awe and somehow it makes the whole place feel peaceful.

She cannot get used to how rare it is to hear anything here. In your pod, of course, you can hear every sob and fart and grunt and orgasm; and every sneeze and every laugh, and every sigh and every snore, and every plea to another for love—enough to heal the hurt—the past—the things within themselves they had all evidently found too difficult to bear.

That is what she struggles with as she looks at the others along the line and realises if this were a class, they would all be getting Fs and maybe that is why they are here. She cannot take the footage again and decides to walk to the bottom of that hill and see what happens; it is absolutely unclear who or what is in charge here. She had been looking forward to seeing so many people but it turns out—just as in life—right now, she is alone. Making a decision. To walk to the bottom of a hill. It feels like the hardest thing she's ever done—all that space—so exposed, she goes forward feeling exposed away from the pods; she will do it so she will be more comfortable later, and maybe even rest (they don't sleep here) with ease.

She is watching the hours she has cried—it is depressing even now and she realises each area of her life can be watched chronologically or under headers such as crying, orgasms, telly, painting nails, on the telephone, travelling, ordering takeaway, walking, appreciating, seeing friends, getting dumped—dancing, cycling; she did a fair bit of that.

She spent 19 days of her life ordering takeaway food. She has spent 17 months crying. This is the most extraordinary thing and although maths was her weakest subject, she still knows that is quite-a-fucking-lot.

No waves today. She needs another one of those. Everything here feels more unreal than it did down there, but more than that, the guilt is utterly unbearable. The man three pods along left yesterday. He walked down the hill and has not come back. She will go down the hill tomorrow; she only made it about 30 feet yesterday before she had to return.

She is laying in a hospital parting her legs as a woman inserts four fingers, and the little sticky tabs on her tummy are blue and the screen is beginning to beep and people are running into the room and she is asking if the baby is okay.

The man with black legs looks in her pod at her. She looks back. He smiles. She gets out of the pod and the two of them just stand there for about an hour, looking at each other. The sky turns orange. He writes something in the sand.

Are you okay?

She writes back with her toe—I don't know. How did you get here? I don't want to talk about it.

You got here the same way I did, he says.

She is so shocked that she climbs back into her pod.

Every so often, she glances back without turning her head and she can tell he is still there. To soften her deep unease, she replays a field of lavender and as she walks through it she lets the long grass skim her hands. There is a plough two fields away from her and it is throwing up earth and yellow spikes of hay; a young farmer turns it around. She takes her shirt off to sunbathe unseen while mice burrow and make nests. Above her was a sky. Azure. Hopeful. She fell asleep like that and a tick settled on her arm, opened its arachnid mouth, and bit down.

She goes back to that moment, zooms in on the thing, millions of years of evolution creating black legs, an exoskeleton and the ability to infect. In the field she dreams on, happily unaware. It is quite beautiful. Her face is not as saggy as she thought it was. She does things in her sleep that she has never seen before. Words muttered under her breath. Scratching. A twitch on her right eye and turning often, this way, then that. As if sleep is an uncomfortable place but she cannot remember that, not that day, sleeping in the sunshine, the sound of the wind and the smell of honeysuckle and long grasses swishing gently as a broom on a wooden floor.

Later, she walks home with burnt shoulders, at peace.

It is the day her brain broke. She is walking across a green and a tractor appears to be circling around her; she is getting angry, she is muttering—what's-your-fucking-problem! The tractor is cutting grass and spraying it out and the noise is so loud she is holding her ears.

Grey sky, no bench, vast expanse, walking to the bridge, baby is with Grandma, the doctors have tried, one tablet, another, none of them work, they make her feel as if she is on LSD. It is winning, the exhaustion, years of it. Her face registers nothing. She cannot watch what comes next. She cannot watch. She slips out of the pod and wishes she could close her eyes.

A vast expanse of grass and feeling her head actually break and if she panics (she was panicking) there will be nothing to grab for support, her legs may give way, she has to slow down, but the panic attack gains speed as she reaches an outdoor ladies' toilet and realises that instead of being able to just run in and hide from the street (hyperventilate in peace, as she has learned to do, to cure the agoraphobia—evidently not a foolproof cure), what she is realising as she begins to hyperventilate outside the ugly, small building is that you need 30p, in change; then you have to pay the woman (whose back of head is curly haired and tabard is on, blue, checked, over a jumper, as it is cold), so instead she walks across the road and goes into a store where the lights glare and she realises that whatever has happened to her is not going to go away.

A million years of fight-or-flight giving her enough adrenaline to outrun a dinosaur and at the counter in the supermarket, it is only the girl who always has eyeliner on and braces on her teeth, the one she saw (and was surprised to see) in a sports car with a man. She is serving her and she is not a dinosaur, but her body does not understand the difference anymore.

While paying, she grips onto the credit card slot, types in 9765, puts her groceries into the bag, all the while wanting to run, screaming, from the store. When she walks out of there (still upright, nobody else any the wiser), she is convinced she is a national hero. A superhero. The overcomer (or accepter) of fear.

It is barely the beginning.

When the man with the black legs holds his hand out to her she notices there is a flower tucked behind his ear. She holds his hand. It feels warm. She wants to know where her grandma is. It's the only thing she really looked forward to in coming here. The man is writing a word in the sand. Love. The word he writes out is 'love'. The effort tires him out, quite evidently and she feels ashamed that she wants him to explain this place to her, explain everything to her, but she doesn't know who else to ask. He hobbles back on his swollen legs with their metal pins and she notices that his toes are mashed and short. She will not push him for answers even although he is the only one who will communicate with her; she must wait until he is stronger.

It's a moon. It's far away. Further away than our moon. Perhaps it is Venus's or just some other moon (equally pretty). She is glad it is here and she is walking down the hill again and nobody seems to notice. The grass is cool under her bare feet, it is soothing to her and she needs this walk, this space; the part of her life she watched today is a part she'd forgotten and had not wanted to watch again and she will not think of it now, not even to herself; she will repeat the word 'love'. Love. Love.

Love. Love. Love. Love. Love. Love. Love. Love. The thing about words is they can alter the molecular compositions of things; this is most noticeable in water—a Japanese scientist said different words to a glass of water and depending on which words he said, the molecular components changed accordingly. 'Love' is the word she must say. It is not the first time she has had to retrain her brain—the areas of her brain dimmed in a scan, showing damage, unable to continue, needing respite, the lights going out from the inside.

Inside, out.

What she does when she wants to commit suicide: is dance. She picks a CD. It takes a while. She closes the curtains (light is not her friend), she hooks up her vintage amp and the two Marshall speakers that make up her stereo and she presses 'play'. Everything in her is utterly unable to bear this pain, but she has no choice. There is no deadline. There is no out-date. There is no guarantee she will ever feel better and in fact she might only feel worse and to this—fact—she chooses to dance.

Her cats on the back of the tiny sofa, nose to nose, watch her as she stretches her arms up and shakes her hips and she might be crying, but she can still move!

She is leaning against her pod and so is the man with the black legs who, it turns out, is called Jim. He wrote it with his short toe. She wrote hers. They are sitting against their pods and it is starry and the breeze is cool, although she has never been cold here, not yet. They are watching two women a few pods along who are dancing with each other, a waltz; one lets her head fall back and the other expertly supports her waist and her body flips back up and they turn like that, the sand underneath their feet patterned with swirls, indents where heels have slammed into the ground, trails where feet have skimmed the sand that they all walk on. Later on, she sits on top of her pod and Jim sits on top of his and they are happy. Even later still, they go to get back in their pods but at the last minute she looks at Jim (who has been holding her hand for the last hour) and—they swap.

They swap pods.

She didn't know they could do that.

It's time to make a Christmas cake with her grandma. It will take three months. The first part is the most important part. She goes to the store with Grandma. They buy a bottle of gin, a bottle of some cherry stuff, some brandy. Fruit. Dried. Four bags. Home up the hill, past the stone square in the middle of the council estate that was built to be used as a paddling pool for the kids in the summer

—as a focal point, as a place where families might meet and picnic, but the water founts broke and it laid empty all her lifetime. She would jump in and out of it to play there, though. Take skipping ropes in and jump for hours. At Grandma's, on the side path she once found a war-time coin and it was worth money and she got slapped for suggesting she could keep it (not by Grandma) and in the footage they are unpacking bags in her long, thin kitchen and there is a cupboard at the end that Grandma made into a larder. A radio plays and there is a table with a Formica top where they are laying out the fruit and alcohol and the glass bowl with curved edges at the top in the shapes of fruit and the glass ladles and Grandma is telling her about when she was in the Wrens in the war and they used to stand on that table (her girlfriends) and they would use teabags to stain their legs brown when they could not afford stockings, and then go out dancing. She always said that the wartime years were the best years of her life.

She wishes she were back next door in her pod watching that instead of Jim, who is walking through the city. He has stepped out of an office, he is upset, he has an engagement ring in his pocket and he is wearing a mack and when he gets to the bridge she wants to shout out and the cars just whizz by and it is windy and he walks along and there are boats. Further out there are platforms, small rigs, there is a tall ship in the distance with four white sails and his face, as he climbs over; she is crying now and she has her hand up against the screen, her fingers splayed out as he jumps and his coat billows like a balloon—it slows his fall by only a fraction of a fraction, but it is enough.

Impact.

Under water.

Pressure above like the earth itself is on top of her head, like she is Atlas, unable to bear the weight, like nothing she could possibly imagine and only the deepest, instant, most complete regret.

She cannot watch her funeral. She cannot see the faces of those she loves, she cannot see her child without experiencing a pain more unbearable than any she knew in life, Jim is outside her pod holding her foot and in the sand he has written the word—'forgive'.

Jim doesn't die; as he hits the water his leg bones break in 103 places, the coastguard boat drives by at that minute, fishes him out, a helicopter is called in, the noise of the whirrs as it lands, he is taken to a hospital and his lower body placed in a cast for three years.

How could he do it again?

Jim goes back to work. He has black legs. Nobody knows. He sits on buses. He goes to the swimming pool and makes himself stand at the edge holding onto the metal ladder until he stills and then he swims.

He swims free of the edge.

She cries as she watches it. They have swapped pods but she must go back to hers and she will, in a minute, but for now she watches his head dip under the water, his face rising up, his goggles, steamy around the edges, the echo of the pool, the glimpse of a beach outside the window. He looks happy.

They sit on top of the pods, holding hands. She knows he has watched the bits she can't watch yet and he knows she has watched the unseen bits of his life and neither of them can walk down the hill yet. But in her head, every day, she is practising words that might positively alter the molecular composition of water.

ALISON LITTLEWOOD

The Entertainment Arrives

THE PROFESSOR DROVE SLOWLY DOWN THE RAIN-lashed promenade, passing sign after dispirited sign that marked the boarding houses still clinging to whatever sorry living this place could afford. Westingsea in early May, and the angry sky flung handfuls of rain at its houses and pavements and the battered old black Wolseley he drove, drowning out any other sound. He could see the sea, black and heaving to his right, shifting in as surly a fashion as it always did, but only the rain was listening to any murmur it made. He knew without looking that the belligerent clouds, fierce as he'd ever seen them, were indifferent to whatever lay beneath. Of humanity there was no sign, unless it was the mean slivers of light trying to escape the windows of the blank-faced, three storey properties along the front.

None of it mattered to the Professor. In fact, it was probably better this way; there was no one to see him arrive and no one to see him leave. He required no witnesses, no applause; there would be enough of that later. He knew where he was going and he knew what he would find when he got there, since it was always the same. The jaded, the worn out and the mad: that was who he had come for. Momentarily, he closed his eyes. *After the strife,* he thought, *after the rain, the entertainment.* He could almost smell their clothes, redolent of over-boiled potatoes and their own unloved skin. He could almost feel the texture of it on his hands, and his fingers, resting on the steering wheel, twitched—though sometimes it seemed to him that the car responded to his thoughts, or someone else's, rather than his touch. He suddenly wanted to look over his shoulder at the things on the old and clawed back seat, but he didn't need to look. He could feel them, as if their eyes were fixed on his shoulder blades, boring into him. Punch had woken, then. He must be nearly there; he saw the spark of irritation from a neon sign to his left, HO EL, it said, the T too spent to play its part any longer, and he spun the wheel, or it spun under his hands; he wasn't sure which. The even movement of wheels on road gave way to the jolt and judder of potholes and the car drew to a halt facing a crumbling brick wall, drenched and rain-darkened. He stared at it. He still didn't want to turn around, though he never eluded what he did; it was his—what? Duty? That seemed too mild a word, for duty could be shirked. It's who he was. He was the entertainment, and he was here to entertain, and entertain he would. *After the rain . . .*

But for now the rain showed no sign of ceasing. It hammered on the roof and spat at the windows, and he switched off the engine and thus the wipers, and the deluge blurred the world entirely. He realised he hadn't even looked for the name of the hotel, but he had no need to do so; it had called him here and he had answered, just as he always did, even when the day wasn't special, as this one was.

He pushed open the car door, his right sleeve soaked through at once, but that didn't give him pause. Rain seemed to follow him even in the height of summer, and at least this smelled right: of ozone and tarmac and, peculiarly, of dust. He stepped out, retrieving the heavy duffel bag from the back seat before heading for the hotel entrance. He heard the cackle of the neon sign and turned to see that the 'O' had also given up the ghost. A matching spurt of electricity ran down his spine, and he savoured it; he hadn't felt anything like it for a long time. It was a special night indeed. The shadow of an echo of a smile tried and failed to touch his lips, and he reflected that such a thing hadn't happened for a long time either.

The glass doors slid aside at his approach—unusual for the establishments he frequented—and the rain was suddenly cut off and other sounds, human sounds, returned. From an opening to one side came the clink of glasses. Somewhere someone was vacuuming, which made him frown, and he stared down at the dust-free carpet. His shoes were as wet as if he'd emerged from the sea and he shifted them, watching the moisture darken the floor with something like satisfaction. Then a voice, a cheery voice, said: "Can I help you, sir?" A young woman with sleek hair pulled back against her head was seated behind a reception desk, smiling at him with reddened lips. The desk was grey, as was her uniform, and the wall behind her, and indeed that too-clean carpet. It looked anonymous; the hotels he frequented were often shabby and dirty, but they were never anonymous. The Professor frowned in answer, but he felt a sudden jolt of—what? Hunger? Eagerness?—from within his bag, and the contents shifted as if they were settling, or perhaps its opposite. He walked towards the girl and simply said, "Snell?"

His voice was dry and cracked. In truth he was unused to using it; his real voice, anyway. Sometimes he used his clown voice, or his jolly comedian voice, but not today. Generally, until it was time, he didn't need to; he certainly didn't like to.

"Welcome, Mr Snell. One night, is it?" She wrinkled her nose as if she could smell something unpleasant, then covered her expression by parting those red-painted lips once more. It wasn't quite a smile. "No." He leaned in closer until he could sense her wanting to recoil, needing to recoil, and he stared at her and he did not blink.

"The manager. Snell. Booked the entertainment. Snell."

Her forehead folded into wrinkles. "Our manager—Miss Smith—she's not on tonight, I'm afraid sir, but I don't—"

"Snell."

His voice was implacable, and she knew it was implacable, he could see it in the way her eyes struggled to focus when she raised them to meet his. "Of course. I'll get someone for you, sir. I'll only be a moment."

She was as good as her word, trotting into the room from whence he'd heard the sound of glasses and returning a few seconds later with a gangling lad in dark, ill-fitting trousers and a waistcoat with grey panels down the front. He looked puzzled, was muttering something to her, but he fell silent when he stood in front of the Professor, who stared at the pock-marks in his skin until he was forced to look away. "I'm sorry," the lad began, but suddenly another voice rang out behind him, so bright and full of excitement and somehow pure that they all turned to look.

"Punch!" the voice cried. It belonged to a small boy of maybe six or seven, his hair curling and golden, and he grinned and pointed at the Professor's bag.

The Professor looked, though as soon as he saw the shadow of a hand reaching across the carpet towards the child he knew what he would see. The crimson sugarloaf hat with its jolly green tassel had escaped the fastening and was poking from the top of the bag, along with the beaked nose, the hooked chin, the single avaricious eye, staring and endlessly blue.

"Mr Punch!" the boy said again, his voice disturbing the very air, which seemed to reconfigure itself around them. "Is there a show? Is Judy in there? Can we go, Mummy, can we?"

The child looked up at the slender woman with the fond gaze who was holding his hand, and she smiled back at him. "We'll see."

"We will," the Professor said, but it was like being in the car, that odd feeling that he wasn't always the one steering, the one forming his lips into words. It was better when he had the swazzle in his mouth. Everything he said felt right then, even though the sound emerged as a series of shrieks and rasps and vibrations, words that no one else could understand. He realised he didn't know if Judy was in the bag, as the boy had asked. Sometimes it was the earlier one, the older one: Joan. Sometimes it was the newer one, the one he never quite knew where she came from: Old Ruthless.

The waistcoated lad who'd only managed to say *I'm sorry* drew a sigh. "I suppose we could—in a corner of the bar, if it's just a booth."

The Professor answered him with a look.

"Just the one show, is it? Just one? Because we're kind of busy."

"And dinner."

The boy looked puzzled. "I'm afraid service just finished. Chef might be able to plate something up for you, before he goes."

The Professor scowled. "I'll be fed."

He nodded in relief. "Our manager—she left no information about paying you—"

"I'll be paid." The Professor started to walk across that grey, too smooth carpet, leaving the youth to follow in his wake. A special night, and nothing was ready: he did not suppose his theatre would be set up waiting for him, as it usually was, nor his watery soup turning tepid upon the table. It was lucky he always carried his booth; and his puppets—his special puppets—were always at hand, as they should be, or he wouldn't deserve the name Professor, or Punchman, or, as some were wont to call the entertainment, Beach Uncle. And without such a name, what would he be? He supposed, once, he had borne some other moniker, but if he had, he could no longer remember it. The space opened around him, larger than he had expected; perhaps the night was special after all. The walls were painted a slightly paler grey, too bright, but it was flaking in the corners and the edges of the sofas were scuffed. The bar was grey too, and the high ceiling, lost to the dim lighting, was a deeper shade. He saw at once where he would set up his booth. There was a little nook off to one side, too small to be of use for anything else, where he knew the floors would not have been swept and the dim corners would have been abandoned to the spiders or whatever else cared to take up residence there. Yes: that was the way to do it.

He did not look at the faces of the occupants of the room, not yet. It wasn't time. But his gaze went towards the wall of windows, which were dark, reflecting the interior of the bar and the deeper shadow where he stood. He nodded with satisfaction. The rain, finally, had stopped.

In the long pause, in the silence and the darkness, the Professor waited. He was on his knees, his back bent; the bag was at his feet with Mr Punch still supine, half in and half out of the opening. Above the Professor's head was the little waiting stage and beyond that was the bar, entirely stilled, its patrons gathered in to a row of chairs hastily brought forward by the lad who'd said I'm sorry.

Outside the booth nobody spoke, but he could picture their faces, all turned expectantly to the little rectangular opening draped in fabric that had once been brightly striped in red and white. Without looking, the Professor slipped the swazzle from his pocket and into his mouth, tasting the old, cold bone, and he held it in position with his tongue. He could still sense the excitement creeping from the bag and towards his hands. It was *the* night. Early in May on the seafront, and not just any day in May: it was the 9th, the evening that was recognised throughout the land as Mr Punch's birthday.

In answer to that thought a faint wheezing, a little like a laugh, emerged into the quiet. He was not sure if it came from his own breath passing through the swazzle or the bag on the floor or from the air around him. It didn't matter. Soon they would begin and everything else would end. It was almost time. He reached down, his fingers seeking out Mr Punch's hat, passing over the soft nap of its fabric and finding the opening into which he would slip his fingers.

He couldn't see it but he pictured the soft brown substance; its touch felt like skin against his hand as he pulled it home.

He closed his eyes. *That's the way to do it.*

He pictured the little boy's face. Is Judy in there? He knew, despite his excitement, the child would not be watching. He was too new, too fresh for any of this. The show wasn't meant for the likes of him. He knew who would make up his little audience: ladies in voluminous chintzy skirts, their face powder clogging the wrinkles beneath; old men, tired from years of stale marriages and disappointing jobs, disillusioned and spent; the worn out, the mad and the lost. That's who would be waiting for him, who was always waiting for him.

In the next moment, he had poked Mr Punch's head up over the stage and an odd sort of sigh rose from the audience. With his other hand he stretched down and rummaged in the bag, finding another soft, leathery opening. As Mr Punch began to shout for his wife, he slipped it on. It wasn't Judy, he felt that at once. It was the original: it was Joan, though he knew the people watching wouldn't know the difference. Sure enough he heard a call of "Judy, Judy!" as he used her little hands to grab her baby from within the bag's innards and sent her up to join her irascible husband.

He spoke through the swazzle, every word and gesture coming as if from somewhere miles distant, the show drifting over him as if he wasn't the one in control at all, and yet it was the same as always; a sense of being in the very right place at the very right moment, though he felt discomfited at that, and an image of that hotel sign rose before him, flashing its maimed sign as a woman's voice said: *Mr Snell. Mr Snell . . .*

As he thought of it, Mr Punch dropped the baby, Joan screamed, and the couple set to, her beating him with her hands, he fighting back with his stick until the sound the swazzle made rose to a scream. Joan fell, though within reach, as she always did; he pulled her into the dark with the tip of his shoe. He knew that she was waiting; she was only ever waiting. And then he realised that no one had yet laughed.

He listened, hearing only silence on the other side of the booth, and felt the stillness creeping from that side of the grimy fabric and into the dark, and the little twist of discomfiture inside him grew a little. But of course all was still; nothing was happening, and he grasped in the bag for the policeman and sent him up to make his arrest until Mr Punch beat him too and flung him into the void.

At last there came a titter, too high and too clear, but there was no time to think of it. The words were forming, the next puppet fitting itself slick and snug onto his hand.

"It's dinnertime." The words were clear, even swazzle-distorted as they were, but as he said them the Professor *thought No, it's not, I haven't had my dinner*, and he knew something was wrong even as Joey the Clown entered stage right and waved his string of sausages at the onlookers. Punch descended once more into the dark and nestled in close. He didn't speak in words, not exactly, but the Professor heard him anyway: *Hungry.*

I know. I know you are.

It's my birthday. I want cake.

The Professor swallowed, carefully, around his swazzle. Punchmen had been known to die that way, choking on the thing that made them what they were: when their time was up. He felt suddenly very tired. His time would never be up, he knew that. The characters were all there, in his bag, waiting: Scaramouche and the skeleton; the hangman; the ghost; the lawyer; Jim Crow; the blind man. The crocodile, who would soon go up and wrestle the clown for his sausages. All had made their appearance in his show so many times, appearing in the very right place at the very right time. Old words ran through his mind:

> *With the girls he's a rogue and a rover He lives, while he can, upon clover*
> *When he dies—only then it's all over And there Punch's comedy ends.*

As if in answer, laughter finally came from the other side of the curtain, as the sausages and then the clown went to join Mr Punch's wife in the nothingness beyond the booth. It wasn't the right kind of laughter though, he knew that, felt that, and he found himself wondering if tonight was the night and an odd kind of hope rose within him. Tonight, the devil might come, the one character from the show who never did; the devil might come and take them all.

That's the way to do it, he thought but didn't say, because it wasn't yet time: he always knew when it was time. First Punch went back to dispose of the crocodile and then the doctor tried to treat him only for Punch to beat him with his slapstick—"Take that!" said the swazzle— and he too was thrown into space, emptied and wrinkled without the enlivening force of the Professor's hand, nothing but an empty skin.

Another delve into the bag and a jolt of that same electricity he'd felt earlier crackled through him. Jack Ketch, the Hangman, was soft yet cold against his hand. Suddenly, he knew he had to look. He didn't know why but he felt almost sick with the need to do so, and he used Ketch's arm to draw the awning back, just a slit.

The breath seized in his throat. The golden haired boy he'd seen earlier was there after all, sitting in the front row, his smiling mother on one side and a man who must be his father on the other, all of them smiling, not used up, not worn out, not ready. It wasn't right. None of it was right, and he realised he'd known it when the steering wheel had turned in his hands and he'd felt the greed rising from the back seat where Mr Punch lay, watching with his blank blue eyes and hungering, always hungering, but especially today.

I want cake.

The Professor closed his eyes. He knew suddenly it was not the right time; it wasn't the right time and it wasn't the right place. It never had been. Snell was waiting, he knew that too. Mr Snell had called him and booked him, the entertainment to follow the strife, to follow the rain, but Mr Snell wasn't here.

The Professor opened his eyes and saw Punch's blue orbs staring back. "I don't know how to do it," he said, except it came out in a series of wheezing growls, the words lost, because this was what he did: a duty that could not be shirked. Mr Punch whipped his head back up onto the stage and Jack Ketch chased him with his noose, Punch pointing at it, condemned but not ready to go quietly, not yet. "I don't know how to do it." The words, this time, were clear.

Here, the Professor knew, was where the hangman would put his own head in the noose to show Punch how to do it, only to be kicked off the stage and hung himself. That's what was supposed to happen. It wasn't what happened in his show, however, because Joan was back, taking Ketch's place, holding the noose herself and looking about, shading her painted eyes with one hand.

"I need a volunteer," she said, every word crystal-sharp despite the swazzle, the old bone that was cold in the Professor's mouth. He recalled that it was sometimes called a strega. The word meant 'witch'. He had never known why, not properly, and yet somehow he had always understood and had felt strangely proud of the fact, because it showed that he belonged: he was the Professor, the Punchman, the Beach Uncle.

He realised the boy was staring directly at the slit in the curtain, looking straight at him. He nudged it back into place even as the child pushed himself to his feet.

"A volunteer!" Joan shrieked, waving her little hands in excitement, jangling the noose, beckoning him on, and the Professor heard footsteps approaching, too soft and light.

For a moment there was silence. Then Joan made prompting noises, little wheezy nudging sounds, and she waved the noose, and he heard:

"I don't like it," spoken softly and with a little breathy laugh at the end, and the same footsteps retreated, and Joan shrieked more loudly than she had ever shrieked, so loudly that it hurt the Professor's ears. Then came another voice, a louder, smoother voice, which said "Don't worry, it's fine, I'll show you," and louder, more tappy footsteps approached, and the Professor knew without looking that the child's mother was coming forwards; that she was going to show him the way to do it.

Joan showed her the noose. She slipped it over the woman's head. And then there was a pause because Mr Punch wanted a souvenir; he always wanted a souvenir. He bobbed down and reached his camera from the bag—an old, heavy, Polaroid camera—and he bobbed up and had her pose, trying this angle and that before there was a loud bang and a flash drowned the world in light, just for an instant, and the woman's son caught his breath.

The camera whirred and spat its picture onto the floor. The Professor could just see it, below the old tangled fringe that ran around the bottom of the booth. Faintly, like a ghost, the woman's grin was appearing in the photograph: only that, her lips parted in the strained semblance of a smile, revealing teeth a little less white than the paper. Then Mr Punch stepped forward and hit her with his slapstick.

There was another bang, this time so loud that everyone would be forced to close their eyes, just for a moment, just as long as it took, and the woman was hung, her body limp and falling, emptied of enlivening force; nothing but an empty skin.

"I don't know how to do it," said Mr Punch. "I need a volunteer," said Joan.

A rough shout came from the other side of the booth, of mingled surprise and awe, followed by loud clapping, albeit from a single pair of hands. The Professor peeked out to see the woman's husband looking impressed, grinning and clapping. They always grinned and clapped. And he realised that the child and his father were the only ones watching the show. There were no worn-out old ladies, no tired and ancient men. The boy wasn't grinning and clapping, however. He was peering to left and right of the booth at the blank grey walls and the grey floor, no doubt wondering when his mother was going to appear again, laughing at his surprise and perhaps, too, his fright. But his mother didn't appear. Instead his father was coming forward, his smooth-soled shoes making hardly any sound on the carpet. Joan placed the noose over his head. There came a bang—flash—whirr, and a photograph drifted to the floor, the ghost of another fixed smile already beginning to form.

"Dad," the boy said from his place in the front row. "I don't like it."

"Come on, son!" his dad replied, his voice full of humour. "It's all jolly good fun!"

The words didn't sound right, even to the Professor who didn't know the man, who should never even have seen him, and yet Joan tightened the noose about his neck and held him steady for Mr

Punch, who grasped his slapstick in both little hands and spun, and the man slid to the floor, as empty and used up as his wife.

This time there was no laughter; there was no applause. There was only a pensive little boy looking up at the stage, waiting for his mum and dad to come back.

"I need a volunteer!" said Joan.

The boy shook his head. The Professor peeked once more through the curtain and thought he saw, in the dim light, the glisten of a tear on his cheek. Don't, he thought, don't you do it, that's not the way, and something in the child sagged and he pushed himself to his feet, as weary as any old lady in chintzy skirts, as any man waiting to use up his retirement, and he stepped forward.

The Professor felt his hands carry out the motions as Joan slipped the noose over the boy's golden head. He felt it as she tightened the rope. He heard the bang and the whirr but he didn't see the flash because his eyes were already pressed tightly closed. He realised he hadn't felt much at all in a very long time. He wasn't certain he ever wished to again. There was only the darkness behind his eyes and then Mr Punch said, "That's the way to do it!" and it was so full of excitement, so full of triumph, and the Professor opened his eyes to see another little square of white, a photograph of a child's clean smile. He knew the boy hadn't been smiling, that he would never smile again, but Mr Punch's camera had caught it anyway, just as it always did.

He lowered his hands, feeling the strain in his elbows and shoulders, feeling suddenly very old. He caught only disjointed words as he started to thrust puppets, without looking at them, back into their bag. Soon he would be on the road again. He would be driving somewhere else, anywhere, and he knew that it would be raining, and that the rain would smell inexplicably of dust.

Dinnertime, said Joey the Clown.

Birthday, said Joan.

Cake, said Mr Punch, and his voice was the most contented of all: Cake.

The Professor slipped his hands under the booth's fringe and felt for the puppets that had fallen. He grabbed Joey and the crocodile and the doctor, feeling the old, cold skin, and then he grabbed the new ones: those who had fallen. He paused when he felt their touch on his hands.

The skin was still warm, and it was supple, and smooth, and soft. He drew them towards him and picked them up, holding them to his chest, then stroking them against his cheek. He felt them and their warmth went into him. It awakened parts of him he had rather hadn't awoken because it was wonderful, conditioned by their love, seasoned by their life. They weren't used up and they weren't jaded. They weren't mad or spent or lost. They were fresh and new and something inside him stirred in response.

Cake, Punch murmured again, and the hard unyielding surface of his face pressed up close to the Professor's. Cake.

The Professor pressed his eyes closed, though he could see everything anyway. There were beaches outside, not just rain-tossed promenades. There were hotels limned in sunlight. There were roads he had not yet taken. All he had to do was see where the Wolseley wished to go, and grip the wheel, and force it to go somewhere else. The entertainment would arrive, and he did not suppose they would welcome him in. He had a sudden image of Mr Snell, thin and bent and grey, twitching the dingy curtains of a faded boarding house and waiting, fruitlessly waiting. The Professor decided he did not care. He had tasted cake, the only kind he wanted; he had not had his dinner; and he found he was very, very hungry indeed.

One day, he supposed the devil might come and take them all. Until then, he would find them: the golden little boys and girls who did not laugh and did not clap. He would find every one of them. He whispered under his breath as he emerged from the booth into the empty and quiet bar. He began to dismantle the stage, his whisper sounding different as he slipped the swazzle into his pocket, speaking in his own voice at last the words that were always waiting there for him: That's the way to do it.

CHAVISA WOODS

Take the Way Home that Leads Back to Sullivan Street

"ZYPREXAOLANZAPINEZYDISWITHFLUOXETINESYM-byaxothan." She pronounced this word with familiar ease. "This drug was recalled from the pharmaceutical market, but I still have a renewable prescription. The doctor said it works best for me, regardless of the side effects."

Why are smart people always so fucking crazy? Or maybe it's not that smart people are crazy, it's just that crazy people present themselves as being super-duper smart. She did. She clung to the notion of her genius like her life depended on it. But you know, if I pull it apart, nothing she ever said was really that smart.

"Geniuses are always considered a little crazy by their generation," she told me. She told me she had a photographic memory, then she recited the names of the presidents in alphabetical order, then in the order of their presidencies. Then she did the same with the names of philosophers from Aristotle to Žižek.

But that's not really genius, is it? That's just memorizing needless shit, which I now know she probably does to keep herself from picking her toenails down till they bleed or shaving all the hair off her entire body for the third time in one day. She told me she can feel it growing.

Kali also told me she has two alternate personalities: a man whose name she doesn't know, and he is very shy, and a woman named Rose, who is a very horrible person, who slugged her first boyfriend in the face once. But she never remembers anything Rose does.

She said when she becomes these other, more horrible people, it's like a door closes in front of her and she can sometimes peek though the keyhole and see the blurred images of Rose doing things to people she knows, and she hears the muffled noises from outside, but she can't quite make out anything clearly, and she certainly can't control anything they (she) do(es).

She told me she was terrified of worms, and that at night she had dreams that copper worms were eating their way through her skin. That's why, Kali said, she could never make it through *Dune*—because of the worms. I said that probably wasn't the only reason.

Kali told me she could talk to turtles and smell architecture. She tried to make me register Libertarian. She told me she had a *feeling* about me. The first time we made love, she told me that a blinking red light named Alganon had been visiting her in the night. Alganon blinked to her from the upper corners of the bedroom as a means of communication. Alganon said that I should move in with her.

It's not like no one told me to stay away from her. Everyone who knew her, and come to think of it, even my friends upon first meeting her, told me I should run as fast as I could in the opposite direction. But Kali knew this would happen. She'd warned me.

"People don't like me," she told me. "People think I'm crazy."

"Are you?"

I guess her eyes were always a little dilated and her mouth was always smiling, especially when she was upset. She was thinner than a skeleton and cold. I don't know what that feeling was that I had for her. Was it love? Was I just mesmerized? Maybe I wanted to save her from something. Or maybe, most likely, I, like everyone else who let themselves get close to her, believed her insanity *was* some kind of genius. Her family sure did. They all thought of themselves as geniuses. I guess that's a big part of why it was so important to her. I guess that's why her whole identity depended on it.

Jesus. Now I'm picking *my* nails. My bags are all packed in the backseat. She didn't hear me leave, I don't think. It's three in the morning. I'm just driving around East St. Louis, aimlessly. There's a line of whores waving at me from the side of the road. They all have really impressive jewelry that glints in my headlights as I pass. I'm just sort of circling this strip. It's disgusting. There's like a little mini-mall of peep shows and porn stores and strip clubs I keep passing, right before or after I get to the whores, depending on my direction. The peep-show mini-mall wouldn't be so bad, if it weren't placed directly beside what is obviously a grade school, which shares a playground with the parking lot of the sex strip mall.

I guess I could go live in my dorm. I can't go there tonight, though. It's late and my roommate is scared enough of me as it is, even though she's only met me four times.

I have a dorm at a university in Southern Illinois. It's part of my package. I haven't even spent one night in it. I got this college package before I met Kali, when my family was still going to help me pay. They already knew I was a dyke. But when I put a face on it, *her* face anyway, they stopped helping me pay for anything. Not that they had it to give at all, anyhow. So now I have this stupid dorm I never used that I probably won't ever be able to pay for, or that I'll be paying for forever. God. Just crossing the river from St. Louis to Illinois: East St. Louis, what a shithole. And she's still there, freaking out in our fancy apartment in the West End, the one I lived in but never paid for.

Funny, I'm paying for the crappy dorm I never lived in and not paying for the fancy place I've actually been living in for the past year. I should have known, when she asked me to move in with her and I told her I couldn't afford it because of college and the dorm and all, and she said, "Don't worry about the rent," I should have known she needed me too much. Why else would a rich, straight girl overlook the three major facts that (a) I'm a dyke, (b) I'm poor as hell, and (c) I have a small drug problem?

Her parents have lots of money and a fancy house in the city, and she has a fancy apartment in a neighborhood too hip for her. Her mother is a failed actress with stock in Walmart and a permanent glass of red wine attached to her right hand. She's the spitting image of Shirley MacLaine.

When her mother met me, she asked me if anyone had ever told me that I was also the spitting image of Shirley MacLaine; a young Shirley MacLaine. I said yes, that I had heard that a lot.

She said, "Oh yes, well, women always seek out women like their mothers. Isn't that what they say? Or is it something *else* they say?" She asked me this with a resentful grin blooming on her face and a sarcastic lilt in her voice. She's a little passive-aggressive about her daughter's newfound lesbianism.

The first time I met her parents, they were hosting a Mensa party in their home. Mensa is a club for people with high IQs. They take a test, pay a due, and then hang around upper-middle-class dinner parties with a bunch of academic liberals who have no social skills. It's great.

Her mother and father are both members of Mensa. The first time I came to one of their dinner parties, I found fifteen middle-aged frumpies sitting in a circle passing around a helium balloon and reciting dirty limericks in high-pitched voices. *Ahh-ha!* I thought, *This is why she's terrified of worms and drinks soap.*

When we moved in together, she told me two things. One: she told me there was a headless woman in our kitchen who paced back and forth swinging her own head by its hair (which she always sees in kitchens, but only ever in kitchens), and Two: she told me she didn't want to take her medication anymore because she didn't need it. "I probably just needed to come out as a lesbian," she told me. "Denying that big of a part of yourself can cause serious problems," she told me.

For a while, I thought maybe she was right. When she stopped taking her medication, at first she seemed better. She didn't mention the headless woman again. She didn't vomit in the mornings. She stopped shaving every day. She even started talking to people her own age, making some friends at her college and hanging out in the radio station after classes. For a while there, yeah, when we went out, I enjoyed having fairly normal conversations that didn't involve detailed global statistics, the sniffing of old buildings, or cryptic discussions of the possible repercussions of her having been named after an ancient god.

Maybe, I thought, the medication *was* the problem after all. But something did bother me about the fact of her diagnosis. I hadn't really ever heard anyone complaining that schizophrenia was an over-diagnosed disorder. And there were still moments, even during those peaceful times, I noticed her staring intently at nothing, moving her lips softly, or squeezing her wrist till it bruised. Once, I asked her if she was really feeling more mentally stable, or if she was still seeing and hearing things, but trying to hide it. She snapped out of it, held my hand too hard and explained to me that this (I) was her first real relationship, and she wasn't going to fuck it up. She wasn't going to let me get away by being crazy. She didn't want me to get away at all. She never wanted me to go anywhere actually, and if I did, not without her.

My sort of unyielding urge for danger was probably what attracted me to her in the first place. Our codependent, peaceful life wasn't enough excitement for me. After five months of living with her in close-quarter domesticity, I started going out with my friends again. I think it was spurred by the big Y2K party. Everyone was sure it was going to be the end of the world. So we all totally obliterated ourselves. It felt like the end of the world that night. But other than everybody getting obliterated, nothing happened.

I took massive amounts of hallucinogens, stayed out partying until the sun came up and returned home smelling like Vicks VapoRub. She hated it. She wanted me with her all the time. She said she didn't understand why I wanted to go to parties with my dumb friends, who, incidentally, think she's too dorky for words. And she thinks they are not intelligent enough to have the privilege of my presence.

That's the other thing she started doing when she stopped taking her medication, obsessing over calculable intelligence levels, namely, her

IQ. She'd been dragging me to at least one Mensa dinner a week, most of which are held at her parents' house. She started threatening to take the Mensa entrance test a few weeks ago. But then, she ruminated that she didn't need to take the test because she's already an unofficial member. The truth is, she was terrified to take the test . . . terrified she might fail. Everyone just assumes she is an out-of-the-ballpark genius. Her parents excuse her schizophrenic tendencies, which mostly show up as small moments of quirky darkness or anxiety in their presence, as side effects of her genius. If she took the test and failed, her insanity would no longer be viewed as the residue of a great mind at work, but just what it was—crazy for the sake of crazy. And I knew being exposed in this way would totally unhinge her.

I never encouraged her one way or another. She could take the stupid test or not. I openly found the whole idea completely dull.

Yesterday morning, Kali asked me to go to a Mensa party with her, but I had other plans.

"Please," she begged. "It'll be different this time. It's gonna be wild."

"It's never been *wild*, honey, come on. The wildest it's ever gotten was when they decided to play strip Trivial Pursuit, and that was really just kind of uncomfortable."

"No," she said, "I promise, it's gonna be wild. The guy at the radio station gave me something. I've been saving it for tonight."

"What did he give you?"

"It's a surprise. I've been saving it for tonight. Please. Just this once? I promise you, this *thing* he gave me will make the conversations much more interesting."

I guess she thought she needed to make her life more interesting to me in order to keep me in it. I was sure she had some coke or maybe pot or something, trying to lure me away from my drugged-up friends by becoming my drugged-up girlfriend. But hey, it worked. I thought it might be kinda funny to interact with the Mensans high. So I went with her.

I grabbed a hitter and a mirror just in case Kali didn't have the foresight, and we drove to her parents' house.

The party was already under way when we pulled up. A few of the Mensans were still filing into the small, near-mansion, colonial-style house, which she said smelled like grapes (colonial architecture, that is). The lights were all lit up and I could hear the sound of drinking songs coming from the living room. They were singing, "A ghost that's meshugenah makes Mendelssohn go drown."

She turned to me and held out her tiny, closed fist. "You ready?"

"I brought a mirror, and a hitter," I told her. "Which is it?"

She opened her hand. Sitting in her palm was a small, folded piece of tin foil.

"Oh my God, you're not serious."

She opened the tinfoil. Inside were two little stamps bearing images of the pink elephants from *Dumbo*, which smiled up at me.

"Acid? You want to do acid at your parents' dinner party?"

She smiled excitedly at me. "Yeah. What? You've done it before, haven't you?"

"Yeah, I've done it a lot. Enough to know you shouldn't do it at your parents' dinner party."

"Oh, but cocaine would have been all right?"

"Yeah, somehow, it *would*. I mean, it's very different. Have you ever even done acid?"

"Yeah, I did it once. It wasn't intense. It didn't really even have any effect on me. Everyone else was tripping but, I don't know, I have a high alcohol tolerance. Maybe I just have a high tolerance in general."

"For acid? An acid tolerance?"

"Yeah. It had virtually no effect on me. Everything was just black-and-white for five hours. But other than that, I felt totally normal."

"Mmmm-hhhhmmm."

"Listen, we don't have to stay the whole time. If it gets too weird, we can go for a walk or just go upstairs and hang alone."

We put the little papers on our tongues and let them dissolve. I wanted to stay outside for a while, smoke a couple cigarettes and prepare myself. But in the time it took to "prepare myself," the acid started kicking in. And I realized, as I always do the first ten minutes of a trip, that there is no way to prepare one's self for tripping. You can tell yourself all sorts of dumb shit like, *Just keep quiet and no one will know.* Or, *use the drug, don't let it use you* . . . la-di-da. But acid always surprises you. It always comes up with something you had no way to prepare yourself for. My friend Rob swore acid never got the better of him, swore to all sorts of meditation techniques that helped him get the most out of his trips, "to control it," he said. Why, then, did his mother find him barreling naked through a cornfield on all fours, the words jesus christ why? written backwards on his forehead in red lipstick?

Because there is no way to foresee that these sorts of things might happen. And if there is, how can the before-acid-you tell the post-acid-you not to do these things, no matter how much you want to? How can you foresee that you might *want* to strip naked and etch the words jesus christ why? backwards on your forehead in red lipstick? How can you control that kind of insane wanting? There's no way to explain this, really. Let's just say, there is no way you can prepare not to react to self-inflicted schizophrenia.

Self-inflicted schizophrenia. That's what tripping is. I never saw it so clearly before that night. But seeing it as such brought up in me a big question, which I probably don't really want to know the answer to: What is insanity?

When we walked into her parents' house, everything was normal. And that's what I kept telling myself, *This is normal, and this feels normal. I'm still acting normal.*

Jan, her mom, came up, handed me a glass of wine, and kissed me on both cheeks. "That's normal."

"What's normal?"

Fuck did I say that out loud?

"It's normal . . . in Europe, to double-kiss like that," I told her.

"Mmm. You're so worldly, aren't you?" She never missed a chance to make me feel dumb. "Come in here then. There's something I want to show you. I think you're really going to be intrigued by this. You just can't believe it."

The way she said it, I thought she might be leading me into a secret laboratory, and perhaps we would find Dr. Strangelove sitting there with the red button. Whatever it was, it seemed very important the way she kept turning to me and nodding, saying, "Yes, yes it's coming any minute now," and smiling with pride and anticipation. "I've got this really terrific *thing*, you just *have* to see it. And tell me what you think. Don't be afraid to give me your real opinion," she said, an eerie, almost ravenous smile spreading across her face.

All this anticipation culminated in her taking me into the den and showing me an antique lampshade.

She talked for literally ten minutes about the history of the lampshade, the design, where she bought it, who owned it before her, and why it was a relevant historical piece. Rich people are hard enough to deal with not on acid. The things that excite them are confusing and hilarious enough without a psychedelic lens magnifying everything. As she went on about the lampshade, I was biting the inside of my cheek very hard to keep from laughing, and I suddenly realized I'd bitten it too hard and I could taste blood in my mouth. My eyes opened up very wide and I said "Oh!" She thought I was pleased, so she moved on to the cabinet the lamp was sitting on. At this point I became worried that my feet might be melting.

"This, on the other hand, is not actually an antique," she said of the cabinet.

I made some sort of very surprised expression, because I had just relearned how to cross my toes.

"I know," she said. "It's amazing! Jerry made this. He just finished it yesterday. I didn't know my husband was such a wonder with wood. He stained it this way and la-di-da, and the cut is intended to represent designs from the something-something era." (I wasn't totally listening.) "And do you know what we're going to do?" I stared at the cabinet blankly. "We're throwing a birthday party for the cabinet." She laughed gleefully at herself. "We're having a birthday party for it next week!" she repeated.

"I'm sorry."

She took this as if it were a question: a request for an explanation. But it was very simply an expression of the deep and pressing sorrow I felt for her at that moment.

"A cabinet birthday party!" Liz boomed, suddenly beside me. Liz

was a soft-spoken poetic type who always had to wear something purple. Even if it was "just a dash," she never, and I mean never, left the
house without at least a bit of purple. She was a rich, pseudo-hippie,
Buddhist, Jewish journalist. She possessed all of the categories that, at
least one of which, most people at the party fit into. "A cabinet party
for the cabinet!" she squealed, excitedly, clapping her hands. "I'm wearing my new purple dress." She was so excited, her oversized tits were
shaking beneath her purple sweatshirt. I stared too long at them.

"Are you coming?"

"No!" I said, too forcefully.

"Why not? Do you have other plans?"

"I don't know what my plans are," I said, anger showing in my
voice. "But I'm not coming."

I usually had an all right time at the parties, but I never felt a connection with these people like my girlfriend did. Mostly I just drank
wine and made sarcastic comments when they hurled their trivia
disguised as conversation at me. They seemed to like me, though.
They were always sort of awed by the fact that I have no interest in
appearing super smart, and I can't quote statistics, but I can quote
Skunk Anansie, Warhol, Bill Hicks, and Jello Biafra. My clothes
always fit me, and I do my hair before I leave the house. I am the cool
kid come down amongst them.

It always gets tired for the cool kid, though. Tonight, I worried my
sarcastic comments might soon become too close to just being out-
and-out malicious. This sudden burst of irrational anger startled Jan
and Liz, probably even more than the time I freaked out on Walter,
the linguist pedophile who showered his undying affection on me
until I turned nineteen.

He'd given me a piece of manganese with the word "Manganese"
inscribed on it from his actual elemental table. That's right, he kept
a real elemental table in his house. It took up an entire room, the
table laid out as a vinyl print on the floor and actual samples of all of
the elements in the appropriate place, with the exception, of course,
of a few radioactive ones. It was rumored, though, that he had two
of the minorly radioactive elements locked in a safe by the dresser.
He'd cornered me at every party for three months (during the time I

was only just eighteen), attempting to deconstruct the origin of my strange name. He'd begun invoking some sexually explicit phrases from Africa, and I finally told him, in so many words, to go fuck himself, loudly. Speak of the devil.

There was a tap on my shoulder. It was Walter; the sixty-two-year-old self-admitted pedophile with a PhD in linguistics. It's not like he's constantly proclaiming his pedophilia. He just lets it slip from time to time toward the end of some of the more drunken dinner parties. He has no children of his own and has placed a swing set in his back-yard for the neighbor kids. He justifies this action by saying he never actually interacts with the neighbor children, he just watches while they swing. So no one gets hurt. It's a win-win. After he lets shit like this slip, he always finds some "clever" way to remind everyone that he has a PhD in linguistics, like it's okay to be a pedophile as long as you are very smart.

"What's that joke you told me last time?" he asked me, pinching the end of his greasy gray beard. "Ladies," he said, motioning for the two other women to pay attention, "she told me this amazing joke last time, did you hear it? It goes, *A Buddhist walks up to a hot dog vendor and says, 'Give me one with everything on it.'*"

The ladies looked very contemplatively at him and, I suppose, because he had a PhD in linguistics, they were wondering if perhaps it was just that his joke was over their heads and he was very smart, or if it was that I was very dumb and he was just being nice by retelling my ignorant joke.

He seems like a really skilled pedophile compared to his skills in linguistics. The joke was supposed to go, *A Buddhist walks up to a hot dog vendor and says, "Make me one with everything."*

I tried to correct him, but the walls were melting, as were my feet. I shook my head slowly, no. It took me several long seconds to force out the words, "Make me one with everything," slowly . . . loudly . . . meaningfully. And I am not sure anyone connected my statement with the joke Walter had just told incorrectly, or if my statement existed autonomously, in their minds, from that conversation. "Make me one with everything," a desperate plea I was suddenly lobbing at them.

Jan raised an eyebrow at me, and nodded.

There was the sound of an elephant honking from the other room. I jumped. Jan and Liz made disgusted faces. "Why do we invite him?" Liz whispered to Jan.

"He's a chapter member," Jan said in a singsong tone, throwing up the hand that was not attached to the wineglass, as if to say she had no power over the situation.

The sound of the elephant booming had come from Ed. He was an obese math wiz with Coke-bottle glasses who had recently been fired for excessive flatulence from his job in military intelligence.

"I swear to god, if he eats all of my penguin hors d'oeuvres, I'm going to kill him." He'd also once been kicked out of an all-you-can-eat buffet for pulling his chair right up to the buffet and eating directly out of the food bins.

Jan tugged on my shoulder. "Have you seen the penguin olives?" I shook my head no. She led me excitedly out of the den and into the dining room where a statue of Baucchus laughed down at the table, joyfully watching over the impressive spread of cheeses, mini-sandwiches, and fruit. Kali came up beside me and took hold of my arm. Her eyes were wide and she was smiling an oversized smile. She was also sweating. Her mom asked if she was feeling all right. She replied too happily that she was a little nauseous, but it was probably just the medication. (She hadn't told her mother she'd stopped taking her medication nearly a year ago.)

Jan ran her finger around the rim of her glass and swayed her hips proudly. "These took me hours to make, but I did it myself. Have you ever seen anything like this?" she asked, holding up an olive that had been cut to resemble a tiny penguin. "I just cut the stomach out and made it the head. It's stuck on with a toothpick, see. Then I stuffed the stomach with cream cheese. The beak is a carrot, and the little wings are easy to make, just two slits in the sides." The penguin was flapping its wings and waddling in her hand. It squawked at me. My stomach turned queasy. "Here," she said, "try it."

"I'm a vegetarian," I told her.

"Oh, it's not really a penguin! Don't be silly!" Then she grabbed the bottom of my chin and literally shoved the penguin hors d'oeuvres in my mouth. "I spent nearly three hours making these," she told me as she shoved it in. "You have to try it."

I closed my mouth and tried to chew while she watched with near reverie, but I could feel the oily flesh of the penguin struggling against my tongue. I heard the miniature penguin squealing and squawking in there. It was too much, I opened my mouth and spit it out into my hand, the black-and-white muck of it just lay there, immobile. Jan let out a long disgusted "Ewwwee," and backed slowly away from me.

My girlfriend started laughing uncontrollably as I dumped the remains of the dead penguin into the trash can. "Sorry," I told Jan. But she just shook her head at me and left the room. This wasn't going well.

My girlfriend took my arm. "It's okay. Let's go sit with them."

I protested but she pulled me in. We sat on the couch with Liz, across from Walter and Jerry, my girlfriend's father, and some others. "So, when are you going to take the test?" Liz asked, patting her on the knee.

A look of horror struck her face. She looked to me for some answer, pulled her shoulders up and down and let out a long sigh. "I've been thinking about it, and I think I'm not taking it," she said. "I probably wouldn't pass anyway, and I'm fine being an unofficial member of Mensa. You guys are my family, anyway. You're my best friends."

I scanned the room, Ed, Walter, Liz, her father, and two frumpies in the corner playing chess, only taking a swig of their gin and tonic when they lost a piece, and something in my stomach flipped.

These were her parents' best friends.

These were *her* best friends.

These were the people who saw her most and never see her at all.

These people were all at least twenty years older than her.

These were the only people she wasn't terrified of.

Except for me.

I was her lover.

I was the only peer she ever interacted with on any intimate level.

"Nonsense. You would pass! You are so obviously smart. Gee, just becoming a lesbian . . . " she motioned to me and winked. "To hell with men. That's just smart," Liz said.

"That *is* smart," one the frumpy hippie-dippies told her.

"I wish I had thought of it, don't you, Jan?" Liz asked Kali's mother, who'd come to stand in the doorway. Jan took a big gulp of wine and nodded with a passive-aggressive, not really, but really kinda homophobic, "liberal" clench-toothed smile.

"I don't feel well," Kali told them. "It's the medication. It's giving me a headache."

"Well, you do look a little clammy," her mother told her.

It had been about thirty minutes since we took the acid. We were just getting to the top of our climb. We both desperately needed to get away from them. Everything was getting too meaningful, and for me at least, it was still also melting. We excused ourselves to go upstairs.

In the guest bedroom I immediately got very caught up by a piece of rogue taxidermy mounted on the wall—a deer head with a red bulb in place of its nose. "Rudolph," they always joked, "a small-game prize from Christmas Eve, 1976." I sat on the edge of the bed, wavering and pondering the fate of dead things.

She sat next to me with her hand on my knee. I thought she was staring into my ear, but she was probably trying to get me to look her in the eye.

"Could you imagine," I asked, "if someone made a joke of your dead body like this?"

"I can't imagine, 'cause I wouldn't know. I'd be dead. Anyway, who's to say that gravestones and mausoleums aren't funny?"

I looked into her eyes. They were dilated and shining, almost completely black.

"Think about it," she said. "It's kind of hilarious."

We sat there thinking about the hilarity of gravestones and mausoleums.

"All the giant gray angels."

"The Taj Mahal."

"The Louvre."

"The Pyramids."

"The Pyramids." We took up with a laughing fit that sent us into tears and collapsed us on the bed.

"You know," she said, "I was named after an ancient god of destruction?"

I laughed harder. "Oh no, really? You've *never* mentioned it. Not once. Not every other day."

I was on my back, holding my stomach because it hurt from laughing.

Her laughing had settled. She rolled over on top of me and bit at my neck. She whispered in my ear in a voice that did not differentiate between malice and seduction. "You know, the French call orgasms 'a little death.' Why don't people build monuments to really good orgasms?"

She grabbed my nipples with her thin fingers and twisted. All of her touches felt distant and abstract. I thought she could twist my nipples off and it wouldn't matter. It would just be my body. Maybe it would even look pretty, my little pink nipple resting hard in the palm of her hand. I grabbed at her wrist and held her hand up to my face, inspecting it. Was there a nipple there in her palm? I saw it for a second, but then it disappeared. She rubbed my forehead. I was sweating.

"Are you tripping hard, baby?"

"Yeah. Aren't you?"

"I don't know." She wiped the sweat off her forehead. "Maybe I can't tell the difference. I just know I want you really badly." She sucked her fingers and pushed her hand down the front of my pants. Then she pinched my clit between her thumb and finger and tugged at it with little tugs. "You like that?" she asked.

I nodded yes. I did like it, but not in the way I usually did. I liked the thought of it—the image it put in my head—a little pink pebble between two little fleshy things. It looked like a Dalí painting. We were moving, and I was on a ship traveling to Egypt. I was a slave lying on my back at the bottom of the boat, and there was an Egyptian god in the shadows of the ceiling laughing at me.

She had gotten us both undressed somehow, and was pulling me under the covers. I felt like I was sinking below the waves. It was all happening to me. I wasn't doing it. There was wetness in my ears, her tongue, and something moving inside me to the motion of waves. I felt suddenly panicked and out of control. I looked to the shadow god on the ceiling. It spoke. *You have free will,* the Egyptian god told me. *Become . . . become.*

I grabbed her hips and flipped her on her back, placing myself on top. We stared into each other's dilated pupils. She slipped one leg between mine and the other around my hip. My clit was sliding against hers and she was moaning. I fucked her like that for a few minutes, but again, it didn't necessarily feel sexual or even physical. I just saw it. I saw our two cunts together sliding and pushing. They looked like two flowers smashed together on a rainy sidewalk. Hers was swollen. Mine was flat. It wasn't hot. It was just kind of sad and pretty.

Then I got the thought that it didn't matter what I was feeling. That this was something I had begun, and I had to finish it, like a monument. My purpose was to make her come.

I put two fingers inside and circled her walls methodically. She was shaking and tears were coming from her eyes. *Good,* I thought. *It's working.*

I sat up and she raised herself halfway to my mouth. I bowed down put my tongue against her, and moved my fingers inside of her. She got very wet till it was dripping down my wrist, which felt strange. She writhed and smashed herself against my face. This move completely overwhelmed me.

It was as if a giant pink butterfly had landed in my mouth and was beating its wings frantically against my face. But it wasn't just "as if" that were happening. I was tripping. It *was* happening. The pink butterfly's giant bug body was in my mouth. Its giant wings were beating my face. It was a terrifying ecstasy. *This must be the beginning,* I thought. *We are beginning to change, "to become."*

The thing about acid is, your perception of what you're doing and what you are actually doing are often two very different things. I thought I was kneeling in a field with my hand inside a plump yellow melon, a frantic butterfly in my mouth, and an Egyptian god watching over me.

I was actually kneeling on the floor in front of her parents' guest bed, motionless for the past minute, with my motionless fingers in my girlfriend, whose cunt was in my open, motionless mouth, and I had apparently begun humming in one loud steady "Ohmmm" tone. In short, she had kept having sex and I had begun meditating.

"What the hell are you doing?" She pulled away from me and sat up.

I opened my eyes. We were still in her parents' guest bedroom. I shook my head and let it drop into my hands. She came over and held me. "Are you okay, baby? What's going on? What are you thinking? What did you feel? You can tell me."

I tried to explain the haze. "I just thought," I told her, "that if I made you come, you would turn into something. You know, whatever you really are, what best represents you. Like a monument."

Her face grew cold, grave. "And what exactly did you think I would turn into?"

"I don't know."

"Tell me," she insisted very intently.

"I guess I thought you would sprout wings or something. You know . . . like a gargoyle, or like . . . " I searched for words, "a demon."

"A demon?" she squealed, angry and accusatory.

"That's not what I meant. No, never mind. Wrong choice."

She stood and started pacing. "So you think you know everything now, huh?"

"What are you talking about? Just calm down."

"You think you know what I really am?"

"Aw, come on. I didn't mean demon, *exactly*. I mean, I guess it kind of is—"

"What else did it tell you?" she shouted.

"What else did what tell me?"

"What else did *he* tell you?"

"Who?"

She pointed to the ceiling. "Him." Then she said some Egyptian name I don't remember and my hairs jumped off my body.

The Egyptian god on the ceiling was *my* hallucination. I hadn't shared it with her. I stared up at the Egyptian god and she stared at him too. We both saw him there, hovering above us, growling through angry brick teeth with a face that kept turning to sand and reconstructing itself. It's very off-putting to share the same hallucination with someone. It makes you wonder whether it's really a hallucination.

"This is getting too crazy," I said, collecting my clothes. I didn't dare make eye contact with her. I just headed to the bathroom and locked myself in. It probably took me twenty minutes to get dressed. I splashed some water on my face and checked to see if I looked presentable. But there was really no way to tell, the way my face kept shifting and changing color like that. How long had we been up here? An hour? It felt like about an hour.

When I came out, she was seated in a chair in the hallway. She must have been waiting for me, but she didn't turn when I came out. She just stared straight ahead at the wall, keeping her hands folded in her lap and her back upright, ridged, like she was in a trance. But she was whispering to something. I knelt beside her. "Baby, it's gonna be all right. You just need to act fairly normal for the next ten minutes. We're gonna get out of here and take a little walk. We'll come down in a couple hours. Then we can go and eat cheese sandwiches."

She stopped whispering to whatever it was and tuned her head mechanically to face me. Her eyebrows twisted into a point reminiscent of Joan Crawford as she intoned "Cheese sandwiches? Cheese sandwiches!!!" like these two words together created the most hateful and absurd of concoctions.

"All right. Here we go." I lifted her by the shoulders, keeping my grip on her as we headed down the stairs. We'd have to pass through the kitchen, the dining room, and the hall before we were out. We'd also have to say goodbye to her mother, and for her part at least, I could blame any strange behavior on the medication her mother did not know she'd stopped taking. I was getting it all planned out. It seemed doable.

We reached the bottom of the stairs. As we turned into the kitchen I felt her tiny arm begin to tremble under my grip. She set her pointed gaze at the far corner of the room like a hound spotting a rabbit.

"You see her?" she whispered.

But I tried to ignore her inquiry. "Just in one door, out the other, babe. Just say bye-bye to mom, and here we go."

She turned on me, tearing her arm loose from my clutch. "I'm not fucking tripping!" she said, sort of stage-whispering, like a whispering scream. "I have to live with this every day. Now you're in *my* world, apparently. You can see it too, so *try*. She's right there!" She pointed to the corner.

I knew who she was talking about, the headless woman she always saw in kitchens. I glanced over quickly. Maybe I could have seen her too if I'd tried, but I really, really didn't want to. I shook my head no. "No, I don't see anything."

She tapped my arm. "She's coming over here. She sees me too. Oh God. She's never looked at me before."

"How can she be looking at you if she doesn't have a head?"

"She's *carrying* her head!" she snapped, as if it were obvious.

"Honey, this is just a bad fucking trip. Calm down. Remember what I told you. Use the drug, don't let it use you."

"Don't give me that raver shit. The headless woman can see me. This is fucking serious." She grabbed her chest and gasped.

"What?"

"She's right here in front of us, next to you. She's talking."

At this point there was nothing I could do but watch her listen. I was absolutely tripping hard myself, but trying not to show it. I had my own problems, like the way the yellowish kitchen light was sliding down the walls and dripping from the cracks in the paint, and, as always, my melting feet.

I guess I must have been pretty distracted by this sort of stuff, 'cause when I started paying attention again, my girlfriend was holding a butcher knife.

There's nothing like the sight of a person on acid holding a foot-long knife that brings you that sobering feeling one so often longs for just after their peak.

I swear to god, I flew four feet to the opposite door, away from her. She was holding the knife up by her head like she was Elmer Fudd hunting rabbits.

"Honey, whatcha doing?"

She didn't look at me. "She put her head back on her neck," she told me. "She wants me to cut it off again, or wait, no, she's shaking her head no. What's that? What?"

"No, honey. Don't cut it off again. Just leave it on. That's the nice thing to do," I tried.

"No, no. She's speaking."

"What's she saying?"

She turned her black eyes to me and smiled like she was one of those women on a cooking show and she was about to show me how to bake a cake . . . made out of children. "She wants me to cut off someone else's head," she told me.

I took another step back, literally straddling the doorframe, ready to bolt. "You fucking ignore her, do you understand me?"

She tilted her head like she was trying.

"Good," I continued. "Now one of two things is going to happen: either you are going to put down the knife, or you're not going to put down the knife, but I'm gonna leave you alone here with your mom and your headless friend, and you are never, do you understand me, NEVER going to see me *ever* again." That was the best I could do.

She stood there pondering her options.

"You have three seconds to put it down or I (pause) am (pause) gone (pause) *forever!*"

She looked from me to the headless woman.

"One."

She shook her head no in the direction of the headless woman.

"Two."

She tilted her head at me again, like a puppy, and nodded.

"Two and a half."

She laid the knife on the counter.

"Walk over here, slowly. Don't look at her."

She came over slowly like she was walking a tightrope. When she was finally within my reach, I grabbed her, tugged her out of the kitchen, and hugged her hard. She buried her head in my shoulder and breathed slowly, deeply. We stood there wrapped in each other like we'd just escaped from a horror movie, our eyes shut tight from whatever might be waiting for us.

The terror wasn't in any way gone from me. I couldn't help wondering what exactly it was acid did to your brain, and wondering how she'd been able to see the same impossible thing I saw. Were these things really there? She said she could see them all the time, but acid just opened up the possibilities for normal people, like me.

While I was thinking about all this, I became aware of another presence in the room. An invasive, cold, ominous presence. I opened my eyes. Her mother was standing in front of us sipping her wine and watching us like we were a bad stage performance, as we were deeply entangled, shaking and petting each other.

"What is this, *The Children's Hour*? What's wrong with you?" She raised her right eyebrow at her daughter. "I've been looking all over for you. I thought you were upstairs."

"I've just been having a headache, Mom."

I realized that she must be used to her daughter's bouts of . . . whatever, but she treated her daughter's apparent disarray with nothing more than a little annoyance and feigned ignorance.

"Well then, have a seltzer. You're probably dehydrated. There are some bottles in the fridge."

"*I'll* get it," I said abruptly, and skipped back into the kitchen.

I heard her mother through the door. "Pull yourself together. We've been planning a surprise for you. I mean, you don't *have* to do it, even though we've been planning it all week. I mean, if you really don't feel like it, dear."

"Planning what?" I stepped back in and handed her the seltzer. She unscrewed the lid, gulped down half the bottle, then burped.

"There, that's more like it," her mother encouraged her. "Have a seat." She walked her daughter over to the dining room table and dimmed the lights. Waving her hand in the air at no one, she hollered, "All right! She's ready!"

What ensued was the strangest and dorkiest ritual I have ever been privy to, live or on video, ever. Ten Mensans marched in slowly, in single file, singing the philosophers drinking song from *Monty Python's Flying Circus* at the speed and tone of a druidic hymn. It was creepy. They then found their places standing around Kali, who was seated at the table. She was smiling her overwide smile and laughing a silent laugh that looked like little convulsions. When they had all made their way in, they stopped singing and declared happily, three times in unison, "One of us! One of us! One of us!" before placing the twenty-page IQ test on the table in front of her. This IQ test would decide if she could become an official member of Mensa or not, and I knew this was the single most important thing in the world to her: to be acknowledged as a fellow genius by her parents' friends. I just didn't think this was something she should undergo while peaking on acid.

Liz handed her a pen. Her mother nodded approvingly. "I don't think you should do this right now," I tried. "You're not feeling well." Her dilated eyes smiled up at the Mensans. Totally ignoring my comment, she tore open the paper that kept the sides of the booklet sealed, then beamed up at them, shaking with apparent joy and surprise. "Of course I'll do it," she said. "I am. I'm one of you."

I'm still circling this East St. Louis strip. I've taken to waving back at the whores. They are very polite. This is my last time around, though. I'm gonna go ahead and drive to my hometown for the night. To hell with this.

She failed the test, of course. And the rest, it's hard to explain. She just sat there quietly in the car as we drove away from the house and the scene of her worst embarrassment. When they tallied the results and announced them, her mother just quietly excused herself from the party. She started trembling, and the other guests comforted her, saying that she could try again soon, that she just wasn't feeling well.

But she bombed. Of course she did. She was tripping. I drove her home in a drug haze, finally starting to come down, and she didn't say a word until we got into the apartment, and then, well, I finally got to meet Rose, the person she becomes who does things she doesn't remember doing.

The apartment is destroyed. Most of her breakable things are broken, in pieces. There is a golf-ball-sized welt on her head (her own doing, not mine) and I have a swollen jaw, and she is sleeping now, as a result of many anti-anxiety medications I insisted she take so she would stop ramming herself headfirst into the walls and tearing her things to pieces. I am driving this disgusting strip of a road, over and over again, trying to figure where to go for the rest of the night . . . for the rest of my life.

There's that fucking song playing on the radio, the one that always made me think of her, even when I was with her. I should have noticed this as a sign before tonight— *"Where all the bodies hang on the air"*—that's not a sweet song at all. The fact that this is the song I most associate with my romantic relationship, there is definitely something very wrong with that. She's gonna miss me. She destroyed everything else. She's gonna tell me she can't go on without me. And she probably can't. Pretty soon now, though, I won't really care. I crossed the waters. I'm gonna go home through the town. I'll pass the shadows that fell down from when we met. But I'm gone from there.

CARMEN
MARIA
MACHADO

Eight
Bites

As they put me to sleep, my mouth fills with the dust of the moon. I expect to choke on the silt but instead it slides in and out, and in and out, and I am, impossibly, breathing.

I have dreamt of inhaling underneath water and this is what it feels like: panic, and then acceptance, and then elation: I am going to die, I am not dying, I am doing a thing I never thought I could do.

Back on Earth, Dr. U is inside me. Her hands are in my torso, her fingers searching for something. She is loosening flesh from its casing, slipping around where she's been welcomed, talking to a nurse about her vacation to Chile. "We were going to fly to Antarctica," she says, "but it was too expensive."

"But the penguins," the nurse says.

"Next time," Dr. U responds.

Before this, it was January, a new year. I waded through two feet of snow on a silent street, and came to a shop where wind chimes hung silently on the other side of the glass, mermaid-shaped baubles and bits of driftwood and too-shiny seashells strung through with fishing line and unruffled by any wind.

The town was deep dead, a great distance from the late-season smattering of open shops that serve the day-trippers and the money-savers. Owners had fled to Boston or New York, or if they were lucky, further south. Businesses had shuttered for the season, leaving their wares in the windows like a tease. Underneath, a second town had opened up, familiar and alien at the same time. It's the same every year. Bars and restaurants made secret hours for locals, the rock-solid Cape Codders who've lived though dozens of winters. On any given night you could look up from your plate to see a round bundle stomp through the doorway; only when they peeled their outsides away could you see who was beneath. Even the ones you knew from the summer are more or less strangers in this perfunctory daylight; everyone was alone, even when they were with each other.

On this street, though, I might as well have been on another planet. The beach bunnies and art dealers would never see the town like this, I thought, when the streets are dark and liquid chill roils through the gaps and alleys. Silences and sound bumped up against each other but never intermingled; the jolly chaos of warm summer nights was as far away as it could be. It was hard to stop moving between doorways in this weather, but if you did you could hear life pricking the stillness: a rumble of voices from a local tavern, wind livening the buildings, sometimes even a muffled animal encounter in an alley: pleasure or fear, it was all the same noise.

Foxes wove through the streets at night. There was a white one among them, sleek and fast, and she looked like the ghost of the others.

I was not the first in my family to go through with it. My three sisters had gotten the procedure over the years, though they didn't say anything before showing up for a visit. Seeing them suddenly svelte after years of watching them grow organically, as I have, was like a palm to the nose; more painful than you'd expect. My first sister, well, I thought she was dying. Being sisters, I thought we all were dying, noosed by genetics. When confronted by my anxiety—"What disease is sawing off this branch of the family tree?" I asked, my voice crab-walking up an octave—my first sister confessed: a surgery.

Then, all of them, my sisters, a chorus of believers. Surgery. A surgery. As easy as when you broke your arm as a kid and had to get the pins in—maybe even easier. A band, a sleeve, a gut re-routed. *Re-routed?* But their stories—*it melts away, it's just gone*—were spring morning warm, when the sun makes the difference between happiness and shivering in a shadow.

When we went out, they ordered large meals and then said, "I couldn't possibly." They always said this, always, that decorous insistence that they *couldn't possibly*, but for once, they actually meant it—that bashful lie had been converted into truth vis-à-vis a medical procedure. They angled their forks and cut impossibly tiny portions of food—doll-sized cubes of watermelon, a slender stalk of peashoot, a corner of a sandwich as if they needed to feed a crowd loaves-and-fishes style with that single serving of chicken salad—and swallowed them like a great decadence.

"I feel so good," they all said. Whenever I talk to them, that was what always came out of their mouths, or really, it was a mouth, a single mouth that once ate and now just says, "I feel really, really good."

Who knows where we got it from, though—the bodies that needed the surgery. It didn't come from our mother, who always looked normal, not hearty or curvy or Rubenesque or Midwestern or voluptuous, just normal. She always said eight bites are all you need, to get the sense of what you are eating. Even though she never counted out loud, I could hear the eight bites as clearly as if a game show audience was counting backwards, raucous and triumphant, and after *one* she would set her fork down, even if there was food left on her plate. She didn't mess around, my mother. No pushing food in circles or pretending. Iron will, slender waistline. Eight bites let her compliment the hostess. Eight bites lined her stomach like insulation rolled into the walls of houses. I wished she was still alive, to see the women her daughters had become.

And then, one day, not too soon after my third sister sashayed out of my house with more spring in her step than I'd ever seen, I ate eight bites and then stopped. I set the fork down next to the plate, more roughly than I intended, and took a chip of ceramic off the rim in the process. I pressed my finger into the shard and carried it to the trashcan. I turned and looked back at my plate, which had been so full before and was full still, barely a dent in the raucous mass of pasta and greens.

I sat down again, picked up my fork and had eight more bites. Not much more, still barely a dent, but now twice as much as necessary. But the salad leaves were dripping vinegar and oil and the noodles had lemon and cracked pepper and everything was just so beautiful, and I was still hungry, and so I had eight more. After, I finished what was in the pot on the stove and I was so angry I began to cry.

I don't remember getting fat. I wasn't a fat child or teenager; photos of those young selves are not embarrassing, or if they are, they're embarrassing in the right ways. Look how young I am! Look at my weird fashion! Saddle shoes—who thought of those? Stirrup pants— are you joking? Squirrel barrettes? Look at those glasses, look at that face: mugging for the camera. Look at that expression, mugging for a future self who is holding those photos, sick with nostalgia. Even when I thought I was fat I wasn't; the teenager in those photos is very beautiful, in a wistful kind of way.

But then I had a baby. Then I had Cal—difficult, sharp-eyed Cal, who has never gotten me half as much as I have never gotten her— and suddenly everything was wrecked, like she was a heavy-metal rocker trashing a hotel room before departing. My stomach was the television set through the window. She was now a grown woman and so far away from me in every sense, but the evidence still clung to my body. It would never look right again.

As I stood over the empty pot, I was tired. I was tired of the skinny-minny women from church who cooed and touched each other's arms and told me I had beautiful skin, and having to rotate my hips sideways to move through rooms like crawling over someone at the movie theater. I was tired of flat, unforgiving dressing room lights; I was tired of looking into the mirror and grabbing the things that I hated and lifting them, claw-deep, and then letting them drop and everything aching. My sisters had gone somewhere else and left me behind, and as I always have, I wanted nothing more than to follow.

I could not make eight bites work for my body and so I would make my body work for eight bites.

Dr. U did twice-a-week consultations in an office a half an hour drive south on the Cape. I took a slow, circuitous route getting there. It had been snowing on and off for days, and the sleepy snowdrifts caught on every tree trunk and fencepost like blown-away laundry. I knew the way, because I'd driven past her office before—usually after a sister's departure—and so as I drove this time I daydreamed about buying clothes in the local boutiques, spending too much for a sundress taken off a mannequin, pulling it against my body in the afternoon sun as the mannequin stood, less lucky than I.

Then I was in her office, on her neutral carpet, and a receptionist was pushing open a door. The doctor was not what I expected. I suppose I had imagined that because of the depth of her convictions, as illustrated by her choice of profession, she should have been a slender woman: either someone with excessive self-control, or a sympathetic soul whose insides have also been rearranged to suit her vision of herself. But she was sweetly plump—why had I skipped over the phase where I was round and unthreatening as a panda, but still lovely? She smiled with all her teeth. What was she doing, sending me on this journey she herself had never taken?

She gestured, and I sat.

There were two Pomeranians running around her office. When they were separated—when one was curled up at Dr. U's feet and the other was decorously taking a shit in the hallway—they appeared identical but innocuous, but when one came near the other they were spooky, their heads twitching in sync, as if they were two halves of a whole. The doctor noticed the pile outside of the door and called for the receptionist. The door closed.

"I know what you're here for," she said, before I could open my mouth. "Have you researched bariatric surgery before?"

"Yes," I said. "I want the kind you can't reverse."

"I admire a woman of conviction," she said. She began pulling binders out of a drawer. "There are some procedures you'll have to go through. Visiting a psychiatrist, seeing another doctor, support groups—administrative nonsense, taking up a lot of time. But everything is going to change for you," she promised, shaking a finger at me with an accusing, loving smile. "It will hurt. It won't be easy. But when it's over, you're going to be the happiest woman alive."

My sisters arrived a few days before the surgery. They set themselves up in the house's many empty bedrooms, making up their side tables with lotions and crossword puzzles. I could hear them upstairs and they sounded like birds, distinct and luminously choral at the same time.

I told them I was going out for a final meal.

"We'll come with you," said my first sister.

"Keep you company," said my second sister.

"Be supportive," said my third sister.

"No," I said, "I'll go alone. I need to be alone."

I walked to my favorite restaurant, Salt. It hadn't always been Salt, though, in name or spirit. It was Linda's, for a while, and then Family Diner, then The Table. The building remains the same, but it is always new and always better than before.

I thought about people on death row and their final meals, as I sat at a corner table, and for the third time that week I worried about my moral compass, or lack thereof. They aren't the same, I reminded myself as I unfolded the napkin over my lap. Those things are not comparable. Their last meal comes before death, mine comes before not just life, but a new life. You are horrible, I thought, as I lifted the menu to my face, higher than it needed to be.

I ordered a cavalcade of oysters. Most of them had been cut the way they were supposed to be, and they slipped down as easily as water, like the ocean, like nothing at all, but one fought me: anchored to its shell, a stubborn hinge of flesh. It resisted. It was resistance incarnate. Oysters are alive, I realized. They are nothing but muscle, they have no brains or insides, strictly speaking, but they are alive nonetheless. If there were any justice in the world, this oyster would grab hold of my tongue and choke me dead.

I almost gagged, but then I swallowed.

My third sister sat down across the table from me. Her dark hair reminded me of my mother's; almost too shiny and homogenous to be real, though it was. She smiled kindly at me, like she was about to give me some bad news.

"Why are you here?" I asked her.

"You look troubled," she said. She held her hands in a way that showed off her red nails, which were so lacquered they had horizontal depth, like a rose trapped in glass. She tapped them against her cheek-bones, scraping them down her face with the very lightest touch. I shuddered. Then she picked up my water and drank deeply of it, until the water had filtered through the ice and the ice was nothing more than a fragile lattice and then the whole construction slid against her face as she tipped the glass higher and she chewed the slivers that landed in her mouth.

"Don't waste that stomach space on water," she said, *crunch crunch crunching.* "Come on now. What are you eating?"

"Oysters," I said, even though she could see precarious pile of shells before me.

She nodded. "Are they good?" she asked.

"They are."

"Tell me about them."

"They are the sum of all healthy things: seawater and muscle and bone, I said. Mindless protein. They feel no pain, have no verifiable thoughts. Very few calories. An indulgence without being an indulgence. Do you want one?"

I didn't want her to be there, I wanted to tell her to leave, but her eyes were glittering like she had a fever. She ran her fingernail lovingly along an oyster shell. The whole pile shifted, doubling down on its own mass.

"No," she said. "Then, have you told Cal? About the procedure?"

I bit my lip. "No," I said. "Did you tell your daughter, before you got it?"

"I did. She was so excited for me. She sent me flowers."

"Cal will not be excited," I said. "There are many daughter duties Cal does not perform, and this will be one, too."

"Do you think she needs the surgery, too? Is that why?"

"I don't know, I said. I have never understood Cal's needs."

"Do you think it's because she will think badly of you?"

"I've also never understood her opinions," I said.

My sister nodded.

"She will not send me flowers," I concluded, even though this was probably not necessary.

I ordered a pile of hot truffle fries, which burned the roof of my

mouth. It was only after the burn that I thought about how much I'd
miss it all. I started to cry, and my sister put her hand over mine. I
was jealous of the oysters. They never had to think about themselves.

At home, I called Cal, to tell her. My jaw was so tightly clenched, it
popped when she answered the phone. On the other end I could hear
another woman's voice, stopped short by a finger to the lips unseen;
then a dog whined.

"Surgery?" she repeated.

"Yes," I said.

"Jesus Christ," she said.

"Don't swear," I told her, even though I was not a religious woman.

"What? That's not even a fucking swear," she yelled. "*That* was a
fucking swear. And this. *Jesus Christ* is not a swear. It's a proper name.
And if there's ever a time to swear, it's when your mom tells you she's
getting half of one of her most important organs cut away for no
reason—"

She was still talking, but it was growing into a yell. I shooed the
words away like bees.

"—occur to you that you're never going to be able to eat like a
normal human—"

"What is wrong with you?" I finally asked her.

"Mom, I just don't understand why you can't be happy with yourself. You've never been—"

She kept talking. I stared at the receiver. When did my child sour?
I didn't remember the process, the top-down tumble from sweetness
to curdled anger. She was furious constantly, she was all accusation.
She had taken the moral high ground from me by force, time and
time again. I had committed any number of sins: Why didn't I teach
her about feminism? Why do I persist in not understanding anything?
And *this*, this takes the cake, no, *don't* forgive the pun;, language is
infused with food like everything else, or at least like everything else
should be. She was so angry I was glad I couldn't read her mind. I
knew her thoughts would break my heart.

The line went dead. She'd hung up on me. I set the phone on the receiver and realized my sisters were watching me from the doorway, looking near tears, one sympathetic, the other smug.

I turned away. Why didn't Cal understand? Her body was imperfect but it was also fresh, pliable. She could sidestep my mistakes. She could have the release of a new start. I had no self-control, but tomorrow I would relinquish control and everything would be right again.

The phone rang. Cal, calling back? But it was my niece. She was selling knife sets so she could go back to school and become a—well, I missed that part, but she would get paid just for telling me about the knives, so I let her walk me through, step-by-step, and I bought a cheese knife with a special cut-out center—"So the cheese doesn't stick to the blade, see?" she said.

In the operating room, I was open to the world. Not that kind of open, not yet, everything was still sealed up inside, but I was naked except for a faintly patterned cloth gown that didn't quite wrap around my body.

"Wait," I said. I laid my hand upon my hip and squeezed a little. I trembled, though I didn't know why. There was an IV and the IV would relax me; soon I would be very far away.

Dr. U stared at me over her mask. Gone was the sweetness from her office; her eyes looked transformed. Icy.

"Did you ever read that picture book about Ping the duck?" I asked her.

"No," she said.

"Ping the duck was always punished for being the last duck home. He'd get whacked across the back with a switch. He hated that. So he ran away. After he ran away he met some black fishing birds with metal bands around their necks. They caught fish for their masters but could not swallow the fish whole, because of the bands. When they brought fish back, they were rewarded with tiny pieces they could swallow. They were obedient, because they had to be. Ping, with no band, was always last and now was lost. I don't remember how it ends. It seems like a book you should read."

She adjusted her mask a little. "Don't make me cut out your tongue," she said.

"I'm ready," I told her.

The mask slipped over me and I was on the moon.

Afterwards, I sleep and sleep. It's been a long time since I've been so still. I stay on the couch because stairs, stairs are impossible. In the watery light of morning, dust motes drift through the air like plankton. I have never seen the living room so early. A new world.

I drink shaking sips of clear broth, brought to me by my first sister, who, silhouetted against the window, looks like a branch stripped bare by the wind. My second sister checks in on me every so often, opening the windows a crack despite the cold—to let some air in, she says softly. She does not say the house smells stale and like death but I can see it in her eyes as she fans the door open and shut and open and shut as patiently as a mother whose child has vomited. I can see her cheekbones, high and tight as cherries, and I smile at her as best I can.

My third sister observes me at night, sitting on a chair near the sofa, where she glances at me from above her book, her brows tightening and loosening with concern. She talks to her daughter—who loves her without judgment, I am sure—in the kitchen, so soft I can barely hear her, but then forgets herself and laughs loudly at some joke shared between them. I wonder if my niece has sold any more knives.

I am transformed but not yet, exactly. The transformation has begun—this pain, this excruciating pain, it is part of the process—and will not end until—well, I suppose I don't know when. Will I ever be done, transformed in the past tense, or will I always be transforming, better and better until I die?

Cal does not call. When she does I will remind her of my favorite memory of her: when I caught her with chemical depilatory in the bathroom in the wee hours of morning, creaming her little tan arms and legs and upper lip so the hair dissolved like snow. I will tell her, when she calls.

———

The shift, at first, is imperceptible, so small as to be a trick of the imagination. But then one day I button a pair of pants and they fall to my feet. I marvel at what is beneath. A pre-Cal body. A pre-me body. It is emerging, like the lie of snow withdrawing from the truth of the landscape. My sisters finally go home. They kiss me and tell me that I look beautiful.

I am finally well enough to walk along the beach. The weather has been so cold the water is thick with ice and the waves churn creamily, like soft serve. I take a photo and send it to Cal, but I know she won't respond.

At home, I cook a very small chicken breast and cut it into white cubes. I count the bites and when I reach eight I throw the rest of the food in the garbage. I stand over the can for a long while, breathing in the salt-pepper smell of chicken mixed in with coffee grounds and something older and closer to decay. I spray window cleaner into the garbage can so the food cannot be retrieved. I feel a little light but good; righteous, even. Before I would have been growling, climbing up the walls from want. Now I feel only slightly empty, and fully content.

That night, I wake up because something is standing over me, something small, and before I slide into being awake I think it's my daughter, up from a nightmare, or perhaps it's morning and I've over-slept, except even as my hands exchange blanket-warmth for chilled air and it is so dark I remember my daughter is in her late twenties and lives in Portland with a roommate who is not really her roommate and she will not tell me and I don't know why.

But something is there, darkness blotting out darkness, a person-shaped outline. It sits on the bed, and I feel the weight, the mattress' springs creaking and pinging. Is it looking at me? Away from me? Does it look, at all?

And then there is nothing, and I sit up alone.

As I learn my new diet—my forever diet, the one that will only end when I do—something is moving in the house. At first I think it is mice, but it is larger, more autonomous. Mice in walls scurry and drop through unexpected holes, and you can hear them scrabbling in terror as they plummet behind your family portraits. But this thing occupies the hidden parts of the house with purpose, and if I drop my ear to the wallpaper it breathes audibly.

After a week of this, I try to talk to it.

"Whatever you are, I say, please come out. I want to see you."

Nothing. I am not sure whether I am feeling afraid or curious or both.

I call my sisters. "It might be my imagination," I explain, "but did you also hear something, after? In the house? A presence?"

"Yes," says my first sister. "My joy danced around my house, like a child, and I danced with her. We almost broke two vases that way!"

"Yes," says my second sister. "My inner beauty was set free and lay around in patches of sunlight like a cat, preening itself."

"Yes," says my third sister. "My former shame slunk from shadow to shadow, as it should have. It will go away, after a while. You won't even notice and then one day it'll be gone."

After I hang up with her, I try and take a grapefruit apart with my hands, but it's an impossible task. The skin clings to the fruit, and between them is an intermediary skin, thick and impossible to separate from the meat. Eventually I take a knife and lop off domes of rinds and cut the grapefruit into a cube before ripping it open with my fingers. It feels like I am dismantling a human heart. The fruit is delicious, slick. I swallow eight times, and when the ninth bite touches my lips I pull it back and squish it in my hand like I am crumpling an old receipt. I put the remaining half of the grapefruit in a Tupperware. I close the fridge. Even now I can hear it. Behind me. Above me. Too large to perceive. Too small to see.

When I was in my twenties, I lived in a place with bugs and had the same sense of knowing invisible things moved, coordinated, in the darkness. Even if I flipped on the kitchen light in the wee hours and saw nothing, I would just wait. Then my eyes would adjust and I would see it: a cockroach who, instead of scuttling two-dimensionally across the yawn of a white wall, was instead perched at the lip of a cupboard, probing the air endlessly with his antennae. He desired and feared in three dimensions. He was less vulnerable there, and yet somehow, more, I realized as I wiped his guts across the plywood.

In the same way, now, the house is filled with something else. It moves, restless. It does not say words but it breathes. I want to know it, and I don't know why.

"I've done research," Cal says. The line crackles like she is somewhere with a bad signal, so she is not calling from her house. I listen for the voice of the other woman who is always in the background, whose name I have never learned.

"Oh, you're back?" I say. I am in control, for once.

Her voice is clipped, but then softens. I can practically hear the therapist cooing to her. She is probably going through a list that she and the therapist created together. I feel a spasm of anger.

"I am worried because," she says, and then pauses.

"Because?"

"Sometimes there can be all of these complications—"

"It's done, Cal. It's been done for months. There's no point to this."

"Do you hate my body, Mom?" she says. Her voice splinters in pain, as if she is about to cry. "You hated yours, clearly, but mine looks just like yours used to, so—"

"Stop it."

"You think you're going to be happy but this is not going to make you happy," she says.

"I love you," I say.

"Do you love every part of me?"

It's my turn to hang up and then, after a moment's thought, disconnect the phone. Cal is probably calling back right now, but she won't be able to get through. I'll let her, when I'm ready.

I wake up because I can hear a sound like a vase breaking in reverse: thousands of shards of ceramic whispering along hardwood toward a reassembling form. From my bedroom, it sounds like it's coming from the hallway. From the hallway, it sounds like it's coming from the stairs. Down, down, foyer, dining room, living room, down deeper, and then I am standing at the top of the basement steps.

From below, from the dark, something shuffles. I wrap my fingers around the ball chain hanging from the naked lightbulb and I pull.

The thing is down there. At the light, it crumples to the cement floor, curls away from me.

It looks like my daughter, as a girl. That's my first thought. It's body-shaped. Pre-pubescent, boneless. It is 100 pounds, dripping wet. And it does. Drip.

I descend to the bottom and up close it smells warm, like toast. It looks like the clothes stuffed with straw on someone's porch at Halloween; the vague person-shaped lump made from pillows to aid a midnight escape plan. I am afraid to step over it. I walk around it, admiring my unfamiliar face in the reflection of the water heater even as I hear its sounds: a gasping, arrested sob.

I kneel down next to it. It is a body with nothing it needs: no stomach or bones or mouth. Just soft indents. I crouch down and stroke its shoulder, or what I think is its shoulder.

It turns and looks at me. It has no eyes but still, it looks at me. *She* looks at me. She is awful but honest. She is grotesque but she is real.

I shake my head. "I don't know why I wanted to meet you," I say. "I should have known."

She curls a little tighter. I lean down and whisper where an ear might be.

"You are unwanted," I say. A tremor ripples her mass.

I do not know I am kicking her until I am kicking her. She has nothing and I feel nothing except she seems to solidify before my foot meets her, and so every kick is more satisfying than the last. I reach for a broom and I pull a muscle swinging back and in and back and in, and the handle breaks off in her and I kneel down and pull soft handfuls of her body out of herself, and I throw them against the wall, and I do not know I am screaming until I stop, finally.

I find myself wishing she would fight back, but she doesn't. Instead, she sounds like she is being deflated. A hissing, defeated wheeze.

I stand up and walk away. I shut the basement door. I leave her there until I can't hear her anymore.

———

Spring has come, marking the end of winter's long contraction.
Everyone is waking up. The first warm day, when light cardigans
are enough, the streets begin to hum. Bodies move around. Not fast,
but still: smiles. Neighbors suddenly recognizable after a season of
watching their lumpy outlines walk past in the darkness.

"You look wonderful," says one.

"Have you lost weight?" asks another.

I smile. I get a manicure and tap my new nails along my face, to
show them off. I go to Salt, which is now called "The Peppercorn,"
and eat three oysters.

I am a new woman. A new woman becomes best friends with her
daughter. A new woman laughs with all of her teeth. A new woman
does not just slough off her old self; she tosses it aside with force.

Summer will come next. Summer will come and the waves will be
huge, the kind of waves that feel like a challenge. If you're brave, you'll
step out of the bright-hot day and into the foaming roil of the water,
moving toward where the waves break and might break you. If you're
brave, you'll turn your body over to this water that is practically an
animal, and so much larger than yourself.

Sometimes, if I sit very still, I can hear her gurgling underneath the
floorboards. She sleeps in my bed when I'm at the grocery store, and
when I come back and slam the door, loudly, there are padded footsteps above my head. I know she is around, but she never crosses my
path. She leaves offerings on the coffee table: safety pins, champagne
bottle corks, hard candies twisted in strawberry-patterned cellophane.
She shuffles through my dirty laundry and leaves a trail of socks and
bras all the way to the open window. The drawers and air are rifled
through. She turns all the soup can labels forward and wipes up the
constellations of dried coffee spatter on the kitchen tile. The perfume
of her is caught on the linens. She is around, even when she is not
around.

I will see her only one more time, after this.

I will die the day I turn seventy-nine. I will wake early because outside a neighbor is talking loudly to another neighbor about her roses, and because Cal is coming today with her daughter for our annual visit, and because I am a little hungry, and because a great pressure is on my chest. Even as it tightens and compresses I will perceive what is beyond my window: a cyclist bumping over concrete, a white fox loping through underbrush, the far roll of the ocean. I will think, *it is as my sisters prophesied.* I will think, *I miss them, still.* I will think, *here is where I learn if it's all been worth it.* The pain will be unbearable until it isn't anymore; until it loosens and I will feel better than I have in a long time.

There will be such a stillness, then, broken only by a honeybee's soft-winged stumble against the screen, and a floorboard's creak.

Arms will lift me from my bed—her arms. They will be mother-soft, like dough and moss. I will recognize the smell. I will flood with grief and shame.

I will look where her eyes would be. I will open my mouth to ask but then realize the question has answered itself: by loving me when I did not love her, by being abandoned by me, she has become immortal. She will outlive me by a hundred million years; more, even. She will outlive my daughter, and my daughter's daughter, and the earth will teem with her and her kind, their inscrutable forms and unknowable destinies.

She will touch my cheek like I once did Cal's, so long ago, and there will be no accusation in it. I will cry as she shuffles me away from myself, toward a door propped open into the salty morning. I will curl into her body, which was my body once, but I was a poor caretaker and she was removed from my charge.

"I'm sorry," I will whisper into her as she walks me toward the front door.

"I'm sorry," I will repeat. "I didn't know."

ERIC
SCHALLER

Red
Hood

THERE WAS A YOUNG GIRL WHOSE GRANDMA LOVED her fiercely, and so made for her a suit of skin. Her grandma brined the skin, scraped it free of fat and flesh, and soaked it in a brainy mash until it was soft and milky as a baby's breath. She crafted an opening in the suit with leather cords to tie the flaps. "Promise me," said the girl's grandma, while she adjusted the fit, "that you'll always wear this when you go outside."

The girl shook her arm and the skin waggled. "It's still loose."

"That way you won't outgrow it. Now promise me . . . "

"I promise," said the girl.

Her grandma then showed the girl how to smear the blood and offal of the Risen over the skin for camouflage, including onto the hairy scalp of its cowl. The girl kept to her promise. She never left home without the blood-smeared suit, and so everyone called her Red Hood.

One day her mother gave Red Hood two tins of soup and a bottle of cough syrup. "Go, my darling, and see how your grandma is doing. She is sick and could use our help." Red Hood loaded the supplies into her knapsack and put on her skin suit. Her mother applied blood from a pot they kept by their apartment door and handed her a sheathed knife, its wooden handle split and repaired with duct tape. "With luck, you won't need this."

"It's broken," Red Hood said.

"The worth of a knife is in its blade, not its handle," her mother said. She then gave Red Hood a few last words of advice. "Don't follow the road because your shadow will show in the sunlight, and don't talk to anyone until you get to your grandma's apartment."

Red Hood descended the stairs until she reached the sub-basement of their apartment building, and then followed the dusty trail of footprints her mother called the Lost Highway. The trail twisted and turned in the darkness, leading from one building to the next. Red Hood maneuvered past hulking furnaces, octopus-armed duct systems, and grimy cars abandoned in parking garages. Sometimes her flashlight picked out the decapitated bodies of the Risen. Sometimes the dust tickled her nose. She pressed a finger hard above her lip—a trick she had learned from grandma—so that she did not sneeze.

She did not encounter anyone animated until she had completed half her journey. Tinny and wan, like the mating cry of an insect, music was the first indication that she was not alone. She swung her flashlight around. A stranger leaned against a desolate sports car. He wore a squirrel-fur hat and had kindly eyes. He held a tiny machine in his hands and cranked its handle with the tips of his thumb and forefinger. "What's that?" Red Hood asked. Then remembering her mother's admonition against strangers, she added, "Who are you?"

"A friend." The music stopped and was replaced by a silence that felt like loneliness.

Red Hood looked longingly at the tiny machine.

"It's called a music box. A genie lives inside and he sings when I poke his ribs." He cranked the handle, and Red Hood heard the startled genie's tune. This time the stranger sang along with it. His voice was rough, but the words were pretty:

Away upon a rainbow way on high
There's a land that I learned of once from a butterfly
Away upon a rainbow bluebirds sing
Of warmth and food and all the love that you can dream.

Red Hood had never heard anything so wonderful. She clapped her hands. "Please play it again." She said *please* and so the kindly stranger obliged.

"Would you like my music box for your own?" the stranger asked.

"Oh yes," said Red Hood.

"I can't give it to you, but you can earn it."

"How?"

The stranger's forehead wrinkled. He stroked his naked chin. Then his eyebrows shot up. "I have it. We'll have a race to the next apartment building. First one to tag the EXIT sign wins."

Red Hood had visited her grandma many times and knew the Lost

Highway well. She knew its dangers and obstructions: the cave-ins, the flooded levels, and, most importantly, where a Risen might lurk at a dark intersection. She gained two full steps on the stranger before he even knew the race had begun, but her skin suit slapped and dragged at her ankles. She slowed and the stranger passed her like she was a rooted in the concrete. He wasn't even panting by the time she caught up with him at the EXIT sign.

"My suit tangled in my legs," Red Hood said. "Otherwise I could have beaten you."

The stranger looked so sorrowful it was surprising his eyes were dry. He placed the music box on the floor and ground it beneath his heel until it squealed. Nothing was left of it but a mess of crushed metal and plastic. "See what you made me do," he said. "That's the music box and the genie also." There was a spot of rust on the floor that might have been genie blood.

"I'm sorry," Red Hood said.

"Will you pay the forfeit?"

"Forfeit?" He had said nothing of this before.

"I'm not asking for anything of value. Just a kiss."

Red Hood had kissed family members, even a few boys. This kiss was different, hungry, and just when she thought it over, the stranger bit her lip. She gasped, tasted blood.

"Now," said the stranger. "I have something that your mother would like." He rummaged through his pack and exhumed a plastic comb, pink and with a floral design. "Will you race me for it?"

"To the next apartment building?"

"Yes."

Why dwell on the details of this race? All happened as before. Red Hood took a head start but the skin tangled in her legs and she slowed. She would have cried over her failure but for the sympathy of the stranger. "See what you made me do," he said. He cracked the comb across his knee and threw the splintered pieces away as if to hide these from their sight.

"Is there another forfeit to pay?" Red Hood asked.

He nodded.

"The same as before?"

He nodded again.

In truth, this kiss was nothing like the first. The stranger's tongue pummeled her lips and teeth and, when she relented, pursued her own tongue like a hungry salamander. He only withdrew after he had wrestled her tongue into bruised submission.

The stranger wiped spittle from his lips and smoothed his eyebrows. He removed a crystalline flask from his pack. "If you can beat me to the next building," he said, "I'll give you this medicine for your grandma." He uncorked the bottle, swirled the amber liquid inside, and let her smell its honeyed aroma.

"I can't win," Red Hood said. She fought back tears.

"Of course you can. You just have to set aside your suit. Without it, you'd be as swift as the North Wind." This was the best comparison the stranger could make, for the North Wind is the liveliest and cruelest of the four cardinal winds. "Hang your suit on this nail where it will be safe."

Red Hood stripped off her suit and hung it on the basement wall. She felt naked without it, but won the race easily. The kindly stranger had been morose in victory but accepted loss like a champion. "You do not need a suit if you are quick," he said. He rummaged once more through his pack and found a flask that looked much like the one he had shown her. "Take this to your grandma. It will assist her health."

"Thank you," Red Hood said. The medicine was murkier than she remembered. She wondered about the forfeit she had missed. Would it have been like a rat, or a salamander, or another animal altogether? She started to retrace her steps.

"Where are you going?"

"To get my suit."

"But you are almost at your grandma's."

Red Hood was tired from the races, but knew she shouldn't leave her suit behind. Luckily, the stranger was as wise as he was kind, and proposed a solution. "I'll watch over your suit and keep it safe. We mustn't keep your grandma waiting."

"But *you* might have to wait a long time."

"I won't be lonely." The stranger squeezed his pack and it rattled merrily. Perhaps it contained miracles more entertaining than anything he had yet shared.

Red Hood glanced back once after they parted, just long enough to see the kindly stranger tip his squirrel-fur hat. If she had followed him, she would have seen him give a little skip as if he had just won a lottery. If she had followed him still further, she would have seen him take her skin suit down from its nail and try it on for size. And lastly—although of course she did not, for she continued on to her grandma's apartment—-she would have seen that the suit fitted the stranger so perfectly that he, not she, might just as well be called Red Hood.

Red Hood found her grandma shivering in bed, although her apartment was roasting hot. A fire crackled in the wood stove. Red Hood sat beside her grandma and, using the hem of her undershirt, daubed at the chill sweat on her forehead. "Where is your suit?" her grandma asked.

Red Hood flushed. "There was a tear in its sleeve and I had to leave it behind."

"Couldn't your mother repair it?"

"She's doing that now." Red Hood's excuse felt too much like a lie and she evaded her grandma's eyes by fumbling inside her knapsack. "I brought you soup and cough syrup." She set these on the bedside table. "And something better." She added the crystalline flask of medicine. It sparkled with light stolen from the fire.

Grandma reached toward the flask as if it were a source of warmth. "That's beautiful. What is it?"

"Medicine." Red Hood thought back on the kindly stranger and how he had given her the flask so freely. "From a friend."

"A rare gift."

Red Hood used her knife to break the seal of sticky stuff that adhered to the cork. "Smell this," she said. "Doesn't it smell just like a summer's day?"

Grandma sniffed the opened flask and jerked away as if slapped.

"My mother used to tell me the best medicine tasted foul. But sometimes evil cannot hide its fangs. Dump that down the sink."

Red Hood did as commanded. The medicine bubbled and fumed and its stench hung in the air. Red Hood opened a can of soup and heated it on the wood stove. It was tomato soup and it smelled wonderful. Her grandma stirred the soup, inhaled its aroma, and thanked Red Hood for her kindness. But she only sipped at her spoon, and the soup cooled in its dish.

"Will you be better soon?" Red Hood asked.

"I will never be better." Grandma pulled her nightgown down to reveal a wound that was wet and red and shaped like a mouth. It pained Red Hood to look at the wound, but she did not turn aside. Her grandma reassembled her clothing and sank back into her pillows. "You brought me three gifts from home and so I will tell you a story of three's. While I am talking, you will know that I'm alive. When I stop, you will know that I am dead. When that happens, you must take your knife and stab me through the temple."

Red Hood nodded. This was one reason her mother had given her the knife. She fetched it from her knapsack and set it on the table close at hand.

"I'm cold. Please add a log to the fire."

Red Hood fed the stove even though the room was stifling.

"There was once a young woman who lived in a small town. She knew everyone in the town and everyone knew her. One day, a handsome stranger arrived. He told comical tales of outwitting the Risen, played a scuffed guitar, and sang songs to her. The best songs were those in which he compared her eyes to pools of starlight or oceans of violets. The stranger was canny enough to also charm her parents and, with their blessings, he took the young woman away to his distant home.

"They spent the cold seasons beneath a down comforter and the following summer she gave birth to a baby boy. The baby entertained her even when her man did not. Another year passed, and the young woman gave birth to a second baby more handsome than the first. She missed her family and friends, but her man discouraged her from visiting them, sometimes with words and sometimes with blows. The young woman gave birth to a third baby boy, the prettiest of them all, and, while her man was out scavenging, she escaped with her children and began the long journey back to her hometown.

"One of the Risen caught her scent, and then another, and soon it was a fearsome pack that trailed her, howling and crashing through the underbrush. She reached a river and tried to hide with her children among the rushes. The youngest began to cry and could not be quieted. The young woman knew they would soon be discovered and so she wove a basket of reeds and set her youngest in it. She kissed her baby one last time, pinched his cheek, and shoved the basket out into the current. The baby's cries attracted the Risen and the young woman escaped with her two remaining boys.

"The meal was small and the pack was many, and soon the Risen took up the chase again. This time they caught up with the young woman in the forest. The Risen gathered around the tree in which she hid and howled for the sweetness of her flesh and the richness of her blood. The young woman crawled to the end of a branch. She knit a nest of leaves and set her next youngest in it. She kissed her baby one last time, pinched his cheek . . . "

The room was hot, and the voice of her grandma dwindled until it seemed the rustle of leaves itself. Red Hood had promised to stay awake but she could not keep her promise. When she awoke, her grandma's story was long completed and the fire almost out. She fed a log into the stove and stirred the embers into flame.

Grandma's eyes sparkled.

"Oh grandma, what big eyes you have."

Grandma pulled at her blankets.

"Oh grandma, what big hands you have."

Grandma yawned.

"Oh grandma, what a horribly big mouth you have!"

Grandma stretched her stiff limbs. She was newly dead and still slow. Yet, even dead, grandma had already cast aside her blankets. She tried to speak, but the words caught in her throat, and all that emerged was a painful moan.

Red Hood stumbled backward. She spotted her knife but in her haste knocked it off the table. It skittered across the floor.

The Risen never laugh, not even at another's misfortune, and that distinguishes them from true men and women. Grandma stood and sniffed the air. Her nightgown slipped down to expose the dreadful wound in her side, and she tore at the fabric as if it had attacked her.

Red Hood's horror was like a boulder in her belly. She still loved her grandma, even though she was now on level with a beast. Who knows what would have happened if there had not been a knock at the door? This knock was followed by two more, each louder than the last. Grandma hugged the tattered nightgown against her bony chest and hunched to the door. She pressed her eye against the spy hole and howled in delight. She undid the deadbolt and opened the door.

The kindly stranger stood outside. One of his hands was extended in greeting, the other hidden behind his back. He wore Red Hood's skin suit.

"Red Hood," grandma cried. The suit fooled her. Her words sounded almost human, but were not human enough to fool the stranger. The stranger swung his arm out from behind his back. He wielded a machete. The blade flashed and grandma dropped to her knees. The blade flashed again, and grandma's head bounced across the floor. "Go to the bathroom," the stranger said to Red Hood. "You should not see what I now must do."

Red Hood heard thumpings and rattlings and dragging noises, and sometimes a joyful whistling. Finally, after thirty minutes that carried the weight of hours, she heard the stranger's footsteps approach. He knocked politely and then opened the bathroom door. He no longer wore the skin suit and once again looked as kindly and as handsome as when she had first met him on the Lost Highway. "I need your help," the stranger said.

"What must I do?" Red Hood asked. She wanted to sound brave, but her voice squeaked. The body of her grandma was nowhere to be seen.

"Help me barricade the door." The apartment door was thick, but not so thick that it could shut out the howlings of the Risen. Even more disturbing was how they scraped at the wood, as if they might peel the door apart sliver by sliver.

"Help me with this couch," the stranger said. Red Hood and the stranger wrestled the couch into position by the door. They then flipped a table upside down onto its cushions and searched the apartment for heavy objects—-pots and pans and plates from the kitchen, drawers from a bureau, rolled-up rugs, anything and everything—to add to the pile.

"That's enough." The kindly stranger wiped sweat from his eyes. "Bring me the kitchen knives."

"Why?" Red Hood's arms ached.

"This is no time for questions."

Red Hood was too tired to debate and did as commanded. The stranger dumped the knives into his pack and cinched it shut. He then smoothed the sheets of her grandma's bed, straightened the blankets, and fluffed its pillows. "We're safe now. Sit beside me and share the warmth of the fire." He patted the mattress.

Red Hood took a seat near the footboard.

"Do you still have the bottle of medicine I gave you?"

"That's finished," she said.

"No matter. I have more." The stranger pulled a crystalline bottle from his pack. Uncorked, its honeyed aroma was just as she remembered. "Drink this," the stranger said. "It will restore your strength."

Red Hood took a sip and felt fire burn across her tongue and run down her throat. She coughed. "Have another taste," the stranger said. "Each sip is easier than the last."

The stranger, as always, spoke the truth. "Do you know why I came back for you?" he asked. He had moved so close to Red Hood that she could smell the medicine on his breath and feel the heat of his body.

Red Hood took another sip from the bottle. She felt warm and a little too comfortable. "Why?" she said.

The stranger smiled. "Because you still owe me one last kiss."

Red Hood was confused. She licked her lips clean. Kisses, she had learned, were unpredictable. "Will it be like the others?"

"It will be nothing like those." If a smile can be said to smile, the stranger's smile wore itself out with trying. The stranger loosened the cord that cinched his pack shut. The leather puckered around the cord like withered lips and, once parted, the entrance gaped like a mouth.

Red Hood leaned forward. She could see nothing inside the pack. "For this kiss," the stranger said, "you must climb into my pack." The pack bulged with its hidden freight and anyway was too small to hold a person, even someone as young and small as Red Hood. Red Hood wasn't sure if the stranger was making a joke, but she laughed just the same.

The stranger dug at his teeth with a fingernail and flicked a pinkish morsel aside. The gristle hissed on the warm bricks by the stove. "Just a little kiss. You promised."

Red Hood could not have said why she thought of her grandma at that moment. Maybe it was only because memories, like ghosts, know no barriers and enter unbidden. Whatever the reason, Red Hood remembered the story her grandma had told her earlier. Red Hood had not stayed awake to hear the story's end, but she had heard its beginning and its middle and that was enough. No matter how small the pack appeared, she knew that it could swallow her and then the stranger would take her away. "If I give you this kiss, will you carry me with you to your home?"

"I live far away but, yes, I will take you with me. We will live together and you will share in all that I own." The stranger hefted his pack and it rattled merrily, suggested the wealth contained within. There was a murmuring also, like distant voices.

"What is that?"

"Those are the voices of my hometown," the stranger said. "Before I left on my travels, I stopped by the market and I listened to the laughter and chatter of the crowd and the haggling of the merchants. I gathered just a little of what I heard into my pack so I might feel less lonely on the road."

"If I give you this kiss and join you in your travels," Red Hood said, "you will never feel lonely again."

"*When* you give me this kiss."

"*If* I give you this kiss." Red Hood bounded from the bed. She grabbed the pack's strap and dragged it past the stranger's legs. She shook the pack. The first time she shook it, the voices inside came tumbling out and echoed all around her. "Run," they cried. "Run for your life." The second time she shook the pack, spoons clattered forth and scattered across the floor. Spoons, not the knives she had hoped for. "Run," they cried with their blunt metallic tongues. The third time she shook the pack, bones tumbled forth. There were leg bones, rib bones, finger bones, knucklebones, vertebrae, and broken pieces of skull. Most of the bones were white but some were pink. "Run," the jawbones cried. Red Hood now knew where her grandma's body had disappeared. She also knew why the stranger walked the earth alone but with a full pack.

The stranger laughed. He had not moved from his seat on the bed. He smiled at her indulgently, as if she were a child easily tamed.

Red Hood looked about for a means of escape. The door was barricaded, the window three levels above the street. She had lost the kitchen knives to the stranger and his pack. But there was still the knife she had brought with her from home. She had set it on the table and then knocked it to the floor when her grandma woke from the dead. Where had it gone?

The stranger caught her eye. He reached into his boot and brought out her knife. Its blade flickered in concert with the fire. "Is this what you are looking for?" He inserted the blade's point between his teeth and picked loose another sliver of flesh. He licked the flesh from the metal. He then opened the door to the stove and tossed her knife into the fire.

"You still owe me a kiss." The stranger reclaimed his pack from the floor and shook it open. The mouth of the pack gaped. Its sides caved like a stomach accustomed to richness but which has gone hungry for too long. "Now climb into my pack."

The fire crackled behind its mica window, perhaps in laughter, perhaps in simple enjoyment of the knife's wooden handle. The remains of Red Hood's knife glowed within the heart of the fire. She remembered her mother's words: *The worth of a knife is in its blade not its handle.*

She dropped to her knees before the stove and swung its door open. Sparks cascaded forth. Her knife's handle had burned to ashes, but the blade remained. She plunged her hand into the coals. The knife seared her flesh and the heel of its blade sliced into the meat of her thumb. The stink of burnt flesh filled the room. Her skin blistered but she did not drop the knife. Tears blinded her but she gripped the knife all the more tightly. She screamed and she struck.

Red Hood's first strike cut loose a hank of the stranger's hair. He laughed and caught her by the arm, spinning her around as if he were a prince and she his princess engaged in a dance. "You owe me a kiss," he whispered, his breath tickling her ear. He twisted her arm behind her back. She cried out in pain, but this was not the arm that held the knife.

Her second strike slashed the stranger across his bicep, slicing through his sleeve and drawing a trickle of blood. He cried out in surprise and released her. "You cut me," he said. He shook his head in disbelief. "All over a kiss."

Her third strike pierced the stranger through the eye. He stumbled back. The knife protruded from his eye socket, and he crumpled dead to the floor.

Afterward, Red Hood bandaged her hand and tidied the apartment. She gathered up her belongings, not forgetting her knife, the remaining can of soup, and the cough syrup, and slipped into her suit of skin. She freshened the suit with the kindly stranger's blood and then shoved his body out the window. She watched it tumble through the air and smack against the pavement, and continued to watch as the Risen shambled from the shadows and shredded his flesh. On her way home, she passed one of the Risen gnawing on a bone. The creature growled when she approached, and followed her. Red Hood had nothing to fear. She wore her suit of skin and the creature fawned about her bloody heels like a dog loyal to its master.

REBECCA KUDER

Curb

Day

Eᴀᴄʜ ʏᴇᴀʀ ɪɴ Mᴀʏ, ᴡᴇ ᴍᴜsᴛ ʜᴀᴜʟ ᴀ ɢʜᴀsᴛʟʏ number of items to the curb. It's mandatory. For years now. We don't even question it anymore.

They start collecting the third Friday at dawn. They start at a different house each year. No one knows how they choose. We have to be ready. We have to produce. They measure what we put out.

I hate the scramble. Stacks and boxes and cabinets to paddle through. I need to touch each scrap, have a conversation before discarding. I promised myself I would start early this year: the bottom of the house, because that's where time and gravity rule the world of accumulation. In the basement last Thursday, I unfurled three new bags, thinking it would be easier to add scraps as I found them. Into one bag I tossed parts of several broken coffeemakers full of mealy dust, a chipped mixing bowl, two ancient light fixtures that will never shine again, and reams of disintegrating-rubber-band-wrapped greeting cards from when I was a child and forced by Mother to write too many thank you notes (those whimsical bunnies, kittens, now greeting no one).

Despite all this gathering, I still need more.

On the basement shelves last Friday, I found a box marked *fragile*. Grandmother's handwriting. As I opened it, the box fluttered apart. Inside I found stained lace curtains used as padding. I unwrapped them and extracted the first treasure: a Depression glass refrigerator dish. Grandmother kept butter in it. For nearly thirty minutes, I held the dish. Its lid is chipped. I don't use it, clearly. Into the trash bag nest it went, with the padding. In a rush of energy, I opened another box and found several bottles of Dickinson's Witch Hazel. One still had a lick of amber in the bottom. I held this bottle even longer than the butter dish. Finally, I opened the bottle, its corroded metal lid snowing bits of rust on my lap, and inhaled. Grandmother . . . long-dead . . . setting her hair, cotton balls of witch hazel baptizing strands of silver, twirling hair and pinning the pin curl clips . . . Next, her ancient Noxzema jar, with a layer of cracked white glazing at the bottom. The things that she touched and used. The invisible backdrop to her days. The second bag would wait. I stopped to fix lunch.

The light fixture and butter dish bag waits at the foot of the basement steps. I've been tripping over it since I left it there last week. The object (trash bag) becomes an action (trip), becomes more and also less than what it actually is. The bag is no longer a bag. What it actually *is* shifts, is another way of putting it.

All this tripping over bags. You would think I'd just stop going down there, but the yearly collection won't allow me to avoid a single corner of this gaping house. So much for starting early. Before I bring *that* bag to the curb I will have to peer inside again and confirm I can jettison the contents. Must double-check. Starting early only makes more work.

I had a visit from the local government. They knocked at the door, said they want us to produce at least a third, *one whole third* more than last year. Hard to fathom how. Last year was brutal. Last year I put out three bags and still earned a caution notice. But the more we produce, so they claim, the safer we are, and the less they will bother us. The less they will come knocking at the door, faces full of cheer, plastic-framed mouths buttering us as if we are warm toast. *Oh, excuse me, but in searching our records, we find that historically, you haven't put out enough. Our records indicate that last year, you didn't seem to be in earnest. This is your complimentary warning. We assume you plan to endure?* Words spoken in that tone of buttering, nothing in writing. I have looked in several of the mirrors recently. Behold, I am not warm toast. I am human. The plastic butter-ghosts stood on my porch with their knives to spread spread spread buttered requests and warnings, as if all we live for is to lug out some ever-increasing amount. Each year there is math, and each year the only thing that accumulates is my unwanting. Now, a fourth bag?

No one objects or complains. And with what we've seen, why should we? We follow rules and drag, drag it all to the curb. But I worry there might be something in those bags that I will need again. Some wire, some lace. Can't some of it stay in my house? Deciding what to expel is excruciating. I spent yesterday hunting an appliance until I remembered I had bagged it last year; it's gone. How will it be possible to find enough?

I have been moving up and down flights of stairs all morning. Up, down. I go to the basement. Groping through the butter dish bag, something sharp bites my hand, rips the bag. The flimsy membrane of the bag won't hold it. Why do I always buy such cheap bags? Mr. Warner next door—his bags are ridiculously sturdy. No one on our street produces like Mr. Warner does. He walks from house to curb carrying two at a time, off the ground. No dragging, not for Mr. Warner. An optimist. Yesterday I heard him whistling! Something from the '50s. Those bags of his are big enough to hold a dog's carcass, a wet one. A wet dog's carcass, I tell you. I tell you I'm going to *take* one of his bags. He puts them out days ahead, no fear of anyone taking one or two; he has so many. I would hide one or two fat ones in my basement for next year. I would.

It's going to be tight this year. Yes, I admit I have trouble letting go. But even if I didn't. The noise in my house is quieter when scraps and layers remain undisturbed. With my scraps intact it's a warmer house; my walls are safer; I can exhale. Sometimes I can relax. You might not believe this but when I keep scraps, the house exhales and sometimes relaxes. Without the scraps, the wind comes through, even on a warm day. Those scraps are all that is keeping me safe.

But they said *one third more* and my hand is bleeding. Damn that sharpness, which has now squirmed to the bottom of the frail bag. And the bag is leaking. Just now I dragged it up from the basement to the parlor and was followed by a glistening trail, something a slug would leave behind. Bile, it's more like bile than the iridescence of a slug. No slug glitter. Just gut glitter. I can smell it. I bet you can, too.

Why won't they allow us to put out casings or gears? I have plenty of those. Of course I have the old windows, but they are uncharacteristically firm: they will not take old windows. No, the plastic mouth-frames say *no*, and say it so kindly, with thick, buttery shine, *no, none of that, sorry dear, we don't deal in that.* It's Curb Day, I say, so who cares? Come the third Friday it will all get eaten by the machines anyway. What's the difference? They never answer that one.

This afternoon, Mr. Warner whistled out another two bags, show tunes, and now two more bags before nightfall! He must have skipped dinner. Where does he get all his contents? That last bag, I swear, is the shape of a commode. Hulking as if it's waiting for a fight. What else can I pry from my house to lug out there?

Before it's really dark I should go ask Mr. Warner where he gets those extraordinary bags. He probably buys them in bulk. He must have a couple of empty bags for a neighbor, but he's never shown a shred of sunshine my way, so why should I expect it this week, of all times? No, it's each for themself right now. Survival. My puny pile will make his pile look better, more correct. And to ask him, I'd have to crawl across the house and turn on the water, make myself ready to present.

I used to admire him so much, though I never told him. Should have done.

Yesterday I tried to go ask, but he was out all day, likely at the bag store. He was likely thinking ahead. But *I* go at things the right way; I *examine* the scraps. Take my time. He must have found some shortcut. There's no way he could do it all, do it properly, and have so much to put out. I have a theory he's been rooting through the alley. I have a theory he has something buried back there, waiting to fill bags. I have a theory he puts his stale food in there. Food is prohibited. Everyone knows that.

I am not going to the attic unless I have to. I can't breathe in the attic. It is thick and humid like stepping into someone's mouth.

Curse this third Thursday, bright and shiny like a slap in the face. Me with only the one bag and no more scraps to sort. I need at least four. Four! It will be impossible to avoid the attic.

The attic door is sticking. Who did that, was it the humidity and the old scraps pasting themselves in the crack? At midnight, I violate whatever is holding the door shut, yank it open and go up to find the one box I've avoided all year. I look everywhere up there in that mouth. In the layers of stacks I find plenty I must keep, but cannot find that box.

I rake the entire house; I look inside the walls. With only seven hours until dawn, I lean into bed and cough out a breath, exhale. It hurts my lungs; even the air is against me. Something, a fin beneath the mattress, jabs my side. I roll over and peel back the bedding, the heavy lumps of mattress. It's the box. She's there after all.

This box holds what remains of my mother. I really cannot put her out there, not this year.

I should not say that Mr. Warner has never shown me any sunshine. He came to my door one day with a stack of things. Months ago now, but he did come. He knocked. I had been watching, so I knew it was he. (I have that window on the top floor. If he had looked up he might have seen me. There are a lot of hatboxes in that window, but I rigged a place to watch when I need to.) When I answered the door, he was so polite, so upright, as if the only thing on his conscience was whatever propelled him toward my porch.

I tried to act surprised in the way we are supposed to do. Not seeing each other, fortresses keeping to ourselves, upholding the social contract as if he could have been anyone and not my neighbor of twenty-seven years. As if he hadn't been over there combing his tidy yard when my Joe left me, as if he didn't see any of that. *Oh, yes? May I help you?* I said to Mr. Warner, as if I didn't know and hadn't studied the (perfect/ineffable/imponderable) drape of his trousers.

He looked at me and for a moment he smiled. Finally he said *sorry to bother you, but your mail was delivered to my box.* Some of my orders, a pile of things I was waiting for and had forgotten to expect, so many items coming and going, so many scraps, too many to remember.

He could have kept my orders for the collections. He didn't have to bring them to me. But he handed me the stack and left.

Mr. Warner lives alone, now. Mr. Warner and his multitude of upright bags. Like a brood! If I had that many bags, maybe I would walk around with that straight a back, such a straight back. When he came to my door months ago I felt he had broken my skin. Months ago and I still feel it. He had never been to my porch before, never breached my front walk. He had always stayed on his side of the fence with yard work, his side so tidy, but there must be frayed edges somewhere; no one is that clean. I don't like to think of him on my porch, the time he spent there standing so upright, the crooked boards beneath his feet.

When the municipality first announced the Collection Program, they held a meeting for the town. So many years ago. Strange and almost sweet to think back. The meeting was well attended: hundreds of us went to the town hall because it was back before Distraction and Apathy. Mr. Warner was there early, and so was I, and a handful of others. Joe was already gone by then. Mr. Warner has always been upright, one of those scrubbed people who look shinier than the rest of us. At the meeting, Mr. Warner asked questions about volume and purpose, about usage. The dignitary who officiated wasn't very forthcoming, so Mr. Warner had to shift how he asked questions. He became more direct. There was a look of glee on Mr. Warner's face as he asked his questions.

If I'm honest, I'd say I thought him fabulous back then. I'd even say I felt an affinity, a peculiar crush on him. His skin so shiny and clear, how his lips moved when he asked questions. When the dignitary spoke, Mr. Warner wrote more questions on index cards, scribbling as the dignitary described the Collection Program. Every mote of dust surrounding his body was dancing, itchy and ready to learn, ready to follow the instructions if only they were clear enough.

The dignitaries probably didn't care what people thought of the Program. Our town never specialized in clarity. It has always been a place of blur and innuendo, a place where you could get around just about any obstacle by thinking it through and finding ambiguity. But Mr. Warner demanded clarity. Mr. Warner needed specifics, to understand the requirements, dimensions, and scope, essentially: how many bags would keep him, or anyone, alive. His whole posture demanded to know, and when these relatively new dignitaries announced the Program, it was as if a thing awoke in Mr. Warner, a beast with a need for order. As if this meeting liberated something that had been hiding in his spine.

He also asked what would be done with the Collections. On the stage there were uncomfortable shiftings in seats when he asked about that. I myself had been wondering and hoping someone would ask. Of the hundreds gathered in a sea of awkward yellow folding chairs, Mr. Warner was the only one who wrote questions on index cards, and asked them. I was proud he was my neighbor, at the time. Now it's all mixed up and muddy: my cheap and leaking bags and his sturdy and incontrovertible bags, if that's the word I want. It's all tangled ropes.

I don't sleep much at this time of year. When I do, it's accidental, the human body crashing against the need to emerge from under water so it can keep beating its heart. Pitter pat. How things in my cheap plastic bags do, and don't. Perry won't pitter-pat anymore, hasn't for years. Poor Perry. Perry was a songbird, was a song, so long ago, Perry such a pretty bird, didn't ask to be frozen like that, poor Perry. I will go and find Perry. Not a good true just end for that winged creature, not the best epilogue, but I must find all I have and give it over, can't give my box of Mother up, not this year, and this other winged creature, the one I sometimes fancy myself to be, must live. Perry is the way. Perry will save me, will keep *me* from being stuffed into one of those bags. My own are too cheap, but Mr. Warner's heavier bags would fit me, would carry me off the ground to the curb, elbows and all, and if I don't take Perry out there, poor little popsicle, it will be me. I have time now, before dawn, time to pickaxe Perry from his protective ice layer, poor little song, poor little mite who might have been a song forever. What's wrong with a forever song? I can't leave him for whoever would find me.

They never answered Mr. Warner about what happens with the collections, what they *do* with the collections, but I don't want to find out this year, not yet, not me in the bags, not yet.

Briefly: At the meeting, Mr. Warner was not satisfied with their answers. That honeyed, naive first year, when we were all adapting. Most people put out whatever they could. Not much different from the weekly trash collection. We had no idea of the consequences, just that it was mandatory. They called it a Pilot.

Mr. Warner, who had asked so many questions, lodged a small protest that first year. He simply put out nothing.

The second year, when Mr. Warner again put out nothing, they came on the third Saturday. I watched it all.

They came from a long car. Two men got out and came to his porch and talked to Mr. Warner for a few minutes. Then another man in a green suit emerged from the long car and walked to the porch, past Mr. Warner and straight into his house. Five minutes later the green man came back out, arm in arm with Mr. Warner's wife. She was wearing a floral dress. Everyone but Mr. Warner got into the long car and it drove away. Since then, Mr. Warner brings out the bags.

When I'm asleep I have plenty I could take out. When I'm asleep, often I have an entire wing or floor of a house that I inhabit. A wing or floor I'm just discovering. Sometimes three vast floors of well-organized belongings, or furniture, or boating equipment. Things that I have no use for, nor attachment to, not even, in particular, *my* things. Maybe I should go to sleep now. If I could have one of those dreams now, it would be grand, because I could stuff into a bag and drag any number of things to the curb, and wouldn't Mr. Warner be shocked and possibly impressed, come morning? A dream of an unencountered wing, tonight, would certainly save my life.

Just now I thought I heard something clunk in the west part of the attic. It could be anything; my imagination has whole warehouses of question marks stored inside. It's full of those clunks that happen whenever you aren't looking, whenever you stop listening. Just now it sounded like ice, like being trapped somewhere cold like inside a chunk of ice and that makes me think of Perry again, poor Perry. It's been a lifetime since he sang anything. After Perry died, my father froze him. My grandmother's bird.

Father got Perry for Grandmother, to cheer her in the final months. She named the bird for that man who used to sing even and steady, nothing upsetting or foul in his songs, just beautiful, bland, scrapless notes. The bird sang in the cage by her bed in the dining room after she couldn't manage the stairs, and then sang in the cage in the hospital when she went there. I never heard him sing in the hospital. I never saw her dining room bed. I was not around until after she died. Too far away, or something. From Father I inherited Grandmother's house, full of her items, his items, scraps that keep the wind outside. From Father I inherited Mother. Everything was frozen by time, in that way we are all of us covered and surrounded by frozen things—a chair made seventy years ago, a piece of sheet music, *They go wild, simply wild, over me*, sang my aged aunt, Grandmother's younger sister, recalling the days when she was a flapper. The manic face on the man on the *wild, simply wild,* sheet music that now hangs on my wall is a bit like the face on my father. They go wild (simply wild) over me is a bit like the bird in the cage in the hospital, doing the only thing it really knows how to do. I inherited a frozen song.

Perry in a layer of ice in a plastic bag must be in the freezer, still. No cage now except death and that ice. I am going to walk down to the freezer and look. I am. It might be possible to make my quota if I can find the dead bird that should have been buried years ago. And maybe they won't notice I've included an item that breaks the rules—*no carcasses.* They are a little vague on the rules, but I've always assumed that meant nothing you've eaten the best of, leg of lamb and so on. Nothing gnawed. Frozen canary might fly, as it were, especially if I wait until the first stretch of morning and Perry stays frozen.

Light will arrive soon. I can make it, if I stay awake long enough to chip away the ice that has certainly grown around the plastic bag that holds the songbird . . . maybe it's just as well he's no longer alive and singing. Grandmother died long ago and can no longer hear the thing warble in that soothing, uncontroversial way, and maybe Perry can help *me* now.

The ice will help, more bulk.

They won't notice the debatable carcass. Perry is not really what I think of as a carcass, anyway. Such a light thing, even with the ice, a thing of so little substance. A song gone on the wind. Mr. Warner can whistle and carry to the curb all he wants. I have Perry. I know I'll find him there in the cold; I know I'll have time to chip it all away if I start now.

ADAM-TROY CASTRO

The
Narrow Escape
of Zipper-Girl

IT WAS HER ZIPPER THAT DREW ME TO HER.
She was beautiful enough, according to what most people seemed to consider beauty. She had a black buzz cut, the kind of body that gives the impression of lankiness even on someone petite, a complexion pale as milk, and an overbite that made sure that a sliver of teeth was always visible even when her bee-sting lips were mostly shut. Everything about her face seemed tentative, as if placed there by a designer who knew just how much any given feature needed before it gained enough prominence to overpower the others; hence her tiny nose, her light eyebrows and her gray eyes. When she first crossed the room, she struck me as so light on her feet that she might have been something drifting in the breeze; but it was the long line of her neck that made me look twice, the longest and most graceful neck I had ever seen on any woman, to that point.

I'm a neck man. Some guys notice breasts first. Others are first taken by long shiny legs. I notice necks. I've always noticed necks, the most beautiful and most vulnerable attribute women have.

Hers had a zipper.

I had seen any number of studs and implants and piercings on women, but had never seen a zipper.

It stretched across the curve of her throat, drawing a diagonal line from just below the base of the jaw, to the edge of her collarbone.

Later, analyzing just what made her zipper so intriguing, I decided that the angle was crucial. Worn horizontally, it would have resembled a second mouth, worn vertically, a second vagina equipped with gold metallic dentata. Slicing diagonally, like a slash, the way it was—-and here I note how impossible it is to describe it accurately without running into the traps laid by the very language——it was its own thing, denying easy analogy.

I bought her a drink, and chatted with her long enough to allow the obvious question to arrive naturally.

She had no problem demonstrating that the zipper was functional. She touched the fingers of one wispy-thin hand to the zipper's pull-tab and drew it south. The teeth duly separated by a hair, revealing another expanse of pale skin beneath them. The zipper was, in short, a false promise, implying entry to the flesh beneath the surface but in the end just an overlay, a fraud.

I liked her a little less right away.

I still asked her what had given her the idea to implant such a thing. She had some reason I forgot within minutes of her offering it——some deep appreciation of the artificial, some philosophical point about the fictions we all embrace while navigating modern life. It was background noise, just like the band's set and the fruity flavor of the house specialty drink she recommended. Her name, some exotic spelling of a commonplace name for girls, was just a label. To me, she was always a mostly unremarkable girl who had brushed greatness with the implantation of a zipper, but had retreated from it with other lame attempts at individuality. To her, I was the guy who admired the zipper but seemed to have found other points of attraction.

I didn't like her much. I never did, though we were together for over a year, and most observers would have supposed that I was wild for her. In truth, I found her tiresome and vapid, a girl who had substituted style for substance.

But I successfully hid that.

It was the zipper that drew me.

That night and over the next few weeks I discovered what little else there was to learn about her.

She lived in a third-floor walk-up with stairways so narrow that it was hard to imagine how anybody had ever been able to move furniture into any of the shoebox apartments above. The hallways were dim places with octagonal white tiles the diameter of silver dollars, separated by grout that had gone black from decades of scuffed feet. The building was narrow, too, and there were no more than two apartments per floor, one unimpeded by the stairwell and one that assumed an eccentric L-shape to accommodate it. She had one of the L-shaped ones. I liked that. It was easy to imagine her just around the bend, minding her own business, not knowing I crouched in wait on the other side.

She had artistic pretensions. She had written poetry and performed as lead singer in small bands. She had a voice that had turned to premature gravel, and she enjoyed the character it lent her. She was extraordinarily proud of the one gothic horror story she'd written that an anthology had published, but she was not driven to produce more. When I asked her if it was about zippers, she thought I was joking, and said yeah, right. Later, I read it, and it turned out to be nihilistic vampire shit, redeemed only slightly by her facility with poetic language. It was a story where nobody's throat got cut, where the point was more the weight of the alienation her blood-sucking creation felt, and I read all of it waiting for the mood and the poetry to get out of the way so the bleeding could start. But nobody died. Nobody even bled. I didn't see the point of that, but still complimented her as she seemed to expect, and at regular intervals during our time together asked her when she was going to write another story.

She was a casual smoker, but she hated what the lingering smell of tobacco did to furniture, and so she never lit up at home, limiting herself to one a day, on the street. I liked to think of the way she would have exhaled if the zipper had opened up onto her windpipe, the fumes exiting her throat without ever rising as far as her lips. I liked to imagine her head, expressionless and unconnected from the breathing process, almost dead, floating atop a bed of smoke, like a vision.

She had two tattoos, a bleeding barbed-wire band circling her right bicep and, showing more age, a tiny rose blossom at the base of her spine. I told her that if she was already bleeding on the arm she should add a long stem with bleeding thorns to the rose. She said maybe. It was not wise to return to such ideas too often; I had to pretend other interests.

She owned a one-eyed cat. It had lost half its vision before she rescued it, in what was clearly some wound inflicted by a human being. It was uncommonly friendly to most people, especially considering what it had been through, but after a few sniffs it never came near me. I shrugged and said you could never tell with animals. It never would come near me, not even after the zippered girl and I moved in together. Maybe it knew I didn't like its asymmetrical features, the way that single slit pupil regarded me with perfect comprehension. Much later on, after the zippered girl and I had lived together for a few weeks, I climbed down the fire escape one day I knew she wasn't home, broke the window with a brick, ransacked the place, and took the cat so I could make it symmetrical again.

The zippered girl had a regular job. I wondered aloud how she managed to hold one down, let alone in the dentist's office where she served as a perky young receptionist, while sporting a zipper in her neck. She told me that it was easy to camouflage. When she wanted to, she could look quite conservative, a nice conventional girl who wore minimal make-up and had a mysterious love of neck-concealing scarves and high collars. She laughed that it was her boring disguise. I laughed and said, your secret identity, before you rip off the scarf and stand revealed as . . . Zipper-Girl!

I didn't tell her that she was boring no matter how she was dressed, that nothing about her intrigued me except for the one delightful change she had made in herself. She had no way of knowing. I wasn't interested in most people, and had long since perfected the art of seeming to participate in conversations while paying minimal attention to them. I was great at it. I gave her no way of knowing that she was only the medium for the zipper. When she lit candles and we made love, I was careful to pay obeisance to all the other stations of her personal cross, bringing pleasure to her breasts and her ass and both the northern and southern set of lips, but it was the zipper that kept me interested, the thought of it being a real portal instead of a fake one, the image of the tab pulled down and everything wet in her pulsing underneath. At one point, I bought a red light bulb and she teased me for having such a corny device in my erotic arsenal. She didn't know that red light made certain things easier to imagine. Some nights we used oils, and the sheen on her skin, combined with the scarlet glow, made her breasts and arms look like they'd been lubricated by wounds. Once in a great while I unzipped her neck and licked the pale skin between the interlocking blades, making her giggle as I felt the blood pulsing underneath, and tortured myself with the thought of how it would take only one convulsive whim, now, to get at it.

The night she blurted that she loved me, I took that as a cue. She may have thought it was inappropriate shyness, at odds with our supposed closeness, but I let my eyes dip downward just before I said me too. As intended, she thought I was talking to her.

I used the name Zipper-Girl whenever I could. She liked it, and before long, in most private conversations, I hardly had to use her real name at all. Sometimes I had to remind myself what it was. I put her name on my arm. She was thrilled. But I did it because I needed a convenient reference.

I was an efficient worker. My work duties occupied only about twenty percent of the time at the job. My bosses tried to give me more, but they couldn't keep up with my ability to arrange my work day around vast tracts of free time. I refused any promotion that required additional responsibility. They honored me with an office anyway, and I spent hours in there with the door closed, using Photoshop on portraits of the girl with the zipper. I gave her more than just the one. I airbrushed out her eyes and put a pair of sealed zippers over each one. I did the same to her lips. Who needs lips? They're imperfect sealants, and instruments for fricatives. The improved portrait became a sock-puppet, even more attractive in its artificiality and in its censorship of the personality the excised features could no longer express. I imagined her sitting in a chair, not tied there, but trapped there by blindness, waiting for me to unzip her mouth so she could eat. I imagined the one in her neck being an opening to her esophagus that I could use as the entry point for nutrients that would keep her alive but that she could not taste. Zippers gave me the option of controlling her very senses. In my fantasies, she made sounds of protest until I taught her to stop.

Then I would return home to a Zipper-Girl who was to the images in that file what a paper airplane is to a fighter jet.

I had to endure doing things with her. Clubbing was all right because the music was so loud I could pretend enough local deafness to abstain from conversation. Dining required more work, but I made myself the kind of man who spent more time listening than he did speaking. Going to museums was hellish, but I developed a particular interest in the paintings where the faces were caricatures, like the aftermath of terrible accidents where the bones had healed back in inhuman shapes. I became a fan of one artist who liked to obscure the eyes behind screens of concealing shadow. I told Zipper-Girl this was a representation of just how much human beings hide from one another. This was bullshit. I just liked to imagine that along with the eyes I couldn't see there were also concealing zippers. She got serious and said, you know, you hide more than any man I've ever known. What are you thinking about, what are you feeling, when I catch you staring into space? I made a special effort to be attentive toward her, for the rest of the evening. It wouldn't do to be so mysterious and moody that she no longer wanted anything to do with me.

One day when I was out and about without her I found a young girl's hoodie abandoned at a bus stop. This was a warmer day than expected, and the owner must have taken it off to cool down, leaving it behind when the bus arrived. I wondered how long it had taken her to realize that she'd left it behind, if her parents had enough money to replace it or if when the cold weather came again she was left walking to and from school in hunched misery, hands stuck in dungaree pockets. It wouldn't have been hard to find out, because I could have asked her. A tag bearing her name and address had been sewn to the base of the hood. I brought the garment home in a bag, hid it away, and the first time Zipper-Girl was not around used a pair of shears to amputate the zipper running from hem to collar. I zipped it open and zipped it closed. There was one section near the bottom where it tended to get stuck, surrendering to motion again only after ardent struggle. I thought of the girl needing to take it on and off, growing red-faced whenever she had to fight with it, perhaps even breathing heavily, in a battle consummated only when it once again gave her what she wanted. I imagined that the zipper knew that it was conquering her, that it made her its bitch with its recalcitrance. I imagined Zipper-Girl weeping because she had pulled the false promise in her neck halfway down only to have it stuck in place, refusing to either ascend or descend, its teeth forming an asymmetrical, vertical grimace. I put the zipper from the hoodie away where I could find it again whenever I wanted. I carried it around in a jacket pocket and fingered it, imagining that the two strips bounding the metal teeth were not material from a hoodie, but skin, taken from a breathing neck.

The weather turned cold and she bought a distressed black leather jacket for herself. It had zippered pockets on the breasts, on the shoulders, and down the arms. There were pockets too small and too tight to house more than spare change. They were not meant to be open or closed, just to display their zippers. I banged her while she wore it and nothing else, paying all due attention to all the soft and unzipped parts of her anatomy. She asked me to use her name. I called her Zipper-Girl. She asked me to call her by her real name. I was able to arrange a glimpse of my own tattooed reminder, but knew that she'd noticed the hesitation.

One night, as an experiment, she brought home a bondage hood. It was a full-face mask with zippers covering the mouth and eyes, with another zipper running down the back, to the neckline. She donned it just to demonstrate that it was too large for her, regardless of all available adjustments. She asked me to wear it. I had no choice. I had to say yes just to make it possible that she would someday wear one like it. I put it on and she drew it tight, sealing the one over my mouth, then zipping it back open, then sealing it again. In darkness, unable to see her face and therefore cut off from what she was thinking or feeling, I knew only that this had gone on far longer than I had expected. After a while she loosened the hood, removed it and left the apartment with it, returning two minutes later without it. It was just enough time to have taken it to the garbage chute. She didn't talk to me again for the rest of the night.

Sex became more and more infrequent. One night when angry she told me that sometimes she looked in my eyes and saw nothing behind them but an empty space, that it was like looking through a dirty window into a gutted building. She said that when she saw something moving in there, it wasn't necessarily something she liked. I told her she was imagining things. She asked me to name five things about her, aside from the zipper, that I liked. I was only able to come up with four. I was fortunate that she had either lost count, or been so satisfied with rote poetical evocations of her smile, her sense of humor, her singing voice, and her eyes that she let the subject drop. When we did make love, I noticed her studying me during the act, measuring my own sincerity by the negative space formed around the one feature of her body that was not currently safe for me to acknowledge.

Winter faded. Spring came. The jacket got put away. She put on a white tank top and light blue jeans. I think she chose the button fly deliberately. We went for a walk in the park, and in the first moment of easy intimacy we'd had in weeks, linked hands, a gesture I privately liked because the interlocking fingers reminded me so much of the only bond I really cared about. We watched a street mime and we had ice cream from a vendor. A little boy with a toy plane asked Zipper-Girl about the thing on her neck and she said, oh, that's just a boo-boo, honey. It'll go away before long. The little boy was satisfied by this answer. He ran back to his mommy and I watched him go, feeling a wrenching pain inside me. When I turned back to Zipper-Girl her eyes were wet, and I knew that I must have flashed the wrong expression.

She said, you know what?

I said, what?

She said, I've been trying to tell myself that I was wrong about you, you were just a little focused on one thing. But everything I've been wondering about is true, isn't it? You don't care about anything but the zipper. Not even the slightest bit.

It took me a second to say, that's not true.

She said, wanna bet? How about I go to the guy who put it in tomorrow and have him take the damn thing out? It's, like, an hour's work, tops. I'll be the same person afterward that I was before. Except I won't have this piece of shit on my neck. Is there any fucking chance on Earth you'd still want to be with me if I did that? Tell me I'm wrong. Come on. Tell me I'm wrong, you son of a bitch.

I said, stop testing me.

She said, too late, I'm testing you. I've decided. It's going. What are you gonna do about it?

I took too long answering.

She said, fuck you. Just fuck you.

And she got up and walked away.

I've read in books on such things that when relationships go sour, some injured parties replay the mistakes they made in their heads, changing the dialogue in arguments, altering what was said to what should have been said, turning moments of petulance into moments of generosity, turning passages of disastrous blindness into moments of heart-affirming empathy. I have read that people rewrite the endings. I am not immune. On the stage of my imagination, she might have still had cause to tell me I was a sick piece of shit who she never wanted to see again, but I kept her from being able to make it stick. In my version, she never got watchful friends to stay with her and keep an eye on me while I gathered my few belongings and left. In my version, one male friend of hers didn't say to me, tell the truth, you son of a bitch. You're the one who took her cat, aren't you? In my version, I denied it with persuasive shock instead of remaining silent and getting a chorus of angry voices replying that they fucking knew it all along.

In my version of the story, I did not stay away for months, busying myself with other things, only to slip unseen into the back of a small concert being given by her latest band of the moment, and I did not see that while her ink had spread down both arms, the zipper was well and truly gone, not even a scar remaining. I did not see her kiss a guy in the audience, and I did not see her face light up, the way it never had at any point during the year she and her zipper had been with me.

In my rewrite, she embraced the only special part of herself and had zippers installed everywhere imagination and medical reality rendered possible; one in her forehead that could be drawn open revealing skull, two on her cheeks that could be drawn aside to reveal teeth and gums, others on her arms and on her breasts and down her back and everywhere else she had never been bold enough to have zippers before. In my rewrite, we found a hood that fit her, and whenever she was at home and not dealing with my needs it was her duty to sit with her nasty face and her annoying personality packed away, while I spent hours and days toying with the feature we'd had enlarged to stretch all the way from her jaw line to her belly button. In my rewrite, she liked it, or knew that it didn't matter whether she liked it. That, I know, would have been ideal. That would have been bliss.

I leave her alone and write it off as a learning experience.

This is the world I actually live in. It's impossible to walk down the street, now, without looking for the zippers on the bodies of others. So far I haven't seen any. It hasn't caught on as a fad. But sooner or later I'll find someone who knows that the zipper is the only important thing; or one sufficiently eager to please, or fool, into changing herself in any way I demand.

It's only a matter of time.

In the meantime, getting ready, I'm taking classes in tailoring.

K. L.
PEREIRA

Disappearer

Dᴏʀɪ ɪs ᴄᴏɴᴊᴜʀɪɴɢ ʜᴇʀ sɪsᴛᴇʀ. Hᴇʀ sᴜᴘᴘʟɪᴇs: ᴀ tape deck ready to play, a long teaspoon for stirring the instant coffee, a swatch she cut off the couch before she left home the first time, and of course the TV, which is the conduit for everything. The show, Taxi, has been off the air since 1983, though was alive in reruns through the early 90s at least. She remembers sitting on the edge of the orange and brown plaid couch while her sister, Erin, punched the numbers on the box-like remote, waiting for the theme-song to come bursting through the sides of the Zenith. In her memories, it is always late in the afternoon, after school but before any adults come home, even before her mother, who works second shift at the restaurant only sometimes, sits chain-smoking and drinking tall glass after tall glass of brandy-laced iced coffee at the kitchen counter. Of course, if Dori and Erin are watching Taxi, it was ages before they decided to go to the edge of the river.

If Dori can make Taxi come back, it will fix everything; it will maybe even fix her. That's what spells are supposed to be: a fix. A guarantee that if you have all the ingredients, everything that it once took to make something real, all the hundreds of bones and feathers in a black bird or all the nuts and bolts and grease and smoke in a car, you can make that thing the way it was: true and happening, and just the way you remember it. Of course, nothing is ever just the way you remember it being. There's always something you forgot to remember that pricks into existence at the last minute that makes it not as great as you remembered after all. But that's ok. It's ok if it's not perfect. Dori's got pieces of everything that made the past the past and she hopes that will be enough, even for it to be the way it was for a moment. A moment is all she needs.

Her life is divided (and maybe it always was), into before Erin and after. Right after Erin left (or was taken, or disappeared), Dori felt like she was the only person who remembered her. Sometimes she felt like she was on one side of a bridge and everyone else was on another. Her mother, Erin's boyfriend, the police, they all wanted her to cross over, to move on and act like Erin had never existed, to forget. But Dori couldn't. Do you forget someone just because they're dead? Or gone? Do they forget you? Dori knew that it was painful to remember, and that's maybe why her life ended up that way it did.

"We out of coffee again?" Strummer fixed her with his one brown eye, shaking the obviously empty coffee can at the floor. He was used to Dori drinking up all the caffeine in the house, stealing his speed. She usually scrawled IOUs in black eyeliner on the mirror, the stove, his headboard.

"Tony Danza marathon," Dori answered, chewed fingertip tapping the scratched laminate.

There was a creak from the bedroom, the sigh of ancient bed springs, a flump from a pile of pillows. It could have been a cat but it wasn't.

It was okay, though. Dori didn't mind other girls in the apartment.

Strummer nodded and slipped on a pair of decaying Vans, grabbed a five from the jar marked "drug money" that sat on the top of the fridge, and headed out the door. Dori knew he was only going to the store but she started imagining what it would be like if he never came back. She decided that she didn't care that much. Not really.

Here's how Dori rediscovered that she could conjure things. One night, she succeeded in calling Taxi up from vaults of the TV station basement (where all good shows went to die). She was very drunk. Not fall-down-vomit drunk, like she got when she drank wine. The kind of drunk that comes from taking one shot of tequila every half hour all day long. She could feel the equilibrium of blood to alcohol to sweat in her body. Everything was completely balanced in that everything, her heart lungs liver were saturated and equal and now she could exist in the magic place between wakefulness and dream and intoxicated and totally fucked up.

No one else was home; they were either still at the party or passed out in the street or on the subway somewhere. Lots of kids lived here in the factory, trying to be artists but really being too drunk and high most of the time to create anything. Dori was sitting on the floor beside the television, trying to remember the thing that is always in her head, the song she had been trying to remember for years. She simply started chanting "taxitaxitaxi" long and slow like the best kisses, the plosiveness of tee and ex popping on her tongue, and then through the magic of tequila and wishes the theme song came to her, she hummed it loud against the side of the TV, its electric heat pressed to her cheek. She could see herself on the couch in front of her, sitting in the exact same spot as she always had when Erin was around; the girl on the couch is already almost sixteen16, her life already on its way to wrong. She had forgotten that she was full of magic back then. That she could make things happen, appear and disappear. But soon after then, that special time when magic lit her limbic system without her even trying, her days were taken up with blotting everything out with Jim Beam and her nights were ringed with the blue smoke of Parliaments and the memory of Erin was already almost gone, fading out like a program the antenna of her mind couldn't quite grasp onto, couldn't quite pierce with its skinny aluminum body. The show only came back on that night for a minute or two before the electric flickered off because no one bothered to pay the electric bill again, but Dori knew what she'd done.

Erin had loved Taxi. She loved that it was a way station, a port from which all the characters came and went and if they wanted to they always had a car ready to take them across one of the million New York bridges and from there, anywhere. Erin was always telling Dori that everything was a bridge, even Erin was a bridge, something Dori had to cross to get to the rest of her life. The characters on Taxi reminded her of that, she said. People who were just searching and trying not to be stuck on one side or the other. Erin said:

—They're like people we could know, you know? In New York, you could find anyone.

Dori liked Taxi for the oddballs, of course, people that she thought she'd never know, like Latkae and the Reverend. But Dori also drank jar after jar of pickle juice, licked freshly mown grass (for the taste-smell), and flushed her mother's cigarettes sometimes. Dori lived weird. When she was almost grown-up a boy she was sleeping with would tell her that she was just five degrees off of everything, which threw the whole world off kilter into outer space.

Dori knew another spell that her life had proven true: if you stopped thinking about someone, anyone, from the man who begged for change at the truck stop (Jesus H. Christ, her mother would say, get a job, as she shifted her skinny freckled legs in their wooden platform sandals), to the neighbor's dog (which was fine because Dori hated dogs), to your best friend, to the man with the blank face that she wasn't supposed to talk about, they would disappear. You wouldn't notice at first—they'd get grey around the edges and then you wouldn't see them so often, though really you wouldn't think about it, because you were in the process of forgetting already, the process of erasing them; they would go away, bit by bit by bit until one day they weren't there anymore and maybe you wouldn't even notice. This happened a lot. After Dori and Erin and their mom moved across the river the first time, Dori's best neighborhood friend forgot to send postcards or call when her mom was drunk-asleep and soon even the friend's face started to disappear in Dori's dreams, a big blank question-mark of a spot, like the bottom of a worn shoe whose size has been sweated away and then after a while Dori's mother said: Who? when Dori asked if they could take a trip across the river to visit, like the friend never existed at all.

Erin was the first one to prove that this spell worked. Everyone (Erin's sweet-dumb boyfriend, who had been the meat-packer at the Grand Union until he was fired under suspicion of murder and kidnapping and lots of other things; her mother who just smoked and drank until she pickled and ashed herself when Dori was 17, and maybe even the blank-faced man) pretty much forgot Erin until one day she was just gone for good. But that's getting ahead. The spell worked loads of times before that.

One time when Dori and Erin were bored, or maybe just fed up with the adults in their lives, they tried to cast a disappearing spell. It was September summer, early Fall, maybe-Winter-would-never-come kind of weather.

—I'll bet I can disappear for the long weekend and no one would notice.

Erin pursed her lips in a rude, grunty way, like Billy Idol in all those music videos on that new music video station. MTV played music videos 24/7 and Dori and Erin watched it until their eyes felt like they would melt out of their heads.

—But where will you really be?

Dori had read a lot of books about the secrets of the great magicians and knew that nothing really disappeared, not for good. It was always hiding somewhere obvious but where the audience would never think to look.

—The den closet. I'll keep the door closed and hide behind the coats if anyone but you tries to find me.

Erin had clearly thought this through. Erin always knew all the answers to everything.

—What about going to the bathroom? And eating? I could probably only sneak you candy.

Dori was clunky-clumsy then, didn't know how to move her already-woman's hips so that they didn't bang into walls and corners and startle the people she was trying to slink away from.

—You could sneak me a four-course meal, dweeb. No one is ever going to know. And I can go in the middle of the night when no one is awake.

Their mother almost never slept at night unless she was really drunk, so this was a risky proposition, but Dori thought it might be fun to sneak things to the closet and pretend she knew nothing. Her most important job, they decided, was going to be to make sure Erin didn't run out of cassettes or batteries. Erin had won one of those new Walkman players for selling the most subscriptions to the Reader's Digest or something. Erin was good at making the things she wanted appear, just like that. Dori suspected that she was just as good at disappearing things, too. Dori was extremely jealous of this ability but always agreed to help with whatever Erin wanted to do anyway because really, she loved Erin and there was nothing else to do. They'd hadn't known about the river's edge or met the blank-faced man yet.

Dori was glad she wasn't casting the spell, only helping. She was terrified of the closet. There was a mirror on the back, and once, when Erin was angry at Dori for something, she pushed Dori inside and sat with her back against the door and wouldn't let Dori out until she chanted Bloody Mary Bloody Mary Bloody Mary in front of the mirror. Dori was extra scared because she knew that Bloody Mary came from mirrors. You only had to call her and she would come, just like that.

—Keep going! Erin said, her back heavy against the door. Don't stop until you feel her stinking breath on your neck.

Dori wanted to stop but she knew she couldn't or else Erin would never let her out. She sucked in breath after breath between hic-coughing out Bloody Mary's name until someone wrenched the door open and screamed at her:

—Who the hell are you talking to? It was their mother. She had a cigarette that was mostly ash, dangling from the filter like one of those impressions of bodies from Pompeii, the ones that looked like they would collapse if you breathed on them.

—Erin. Dori said. She locked me in and made me—

—Jesus H. Christ. Stop talking to yourself all the time. Her mother slammed the closet door but it only bounced back, Dori's reflection coming fast towards her then quickly away again, like there were two of her moving at completely different speeds.

Erin never stayed mad at Dori for long, though, and that's why Dori couldn't stay mad at her either. She would always help Erin, no matter what. Especially when she wanted to do magic—disappearing and appearing and other spells.

In the end, they almost won, almost made Erin utterly and

completely disappear. They would have totally won but it was Easter, the only only time their mother made them dress in one of their pale plaid dresses that hadn't even fit last year and go to church. When their mother couldn't find them, she stood in the kitchen with the fish-limp dress hanging by its faded tag off the hook of a metal hanger and she'd screamed until Dori felt like her ears were bleeding. It wasn't clear to Dori until much later that their mother had completely forgotten about them and had been on her way out the door until she realized she couldn't very well show up to Easter church alone. How would that look? At the time, Dori was more worried about what their mother would do to them, especially since she'd threatened no more TV ever if Dori didn't reveal her secret hiding place. Dori thought about this hard, her too-small dress cutting into her ribs (the black velvet one that her mother was always calling morbid and trying to throw away) and making it hard to breathe, until, finally, she was forced to open the closet door, the mirror catching the early light and making copies of all of them, the reflection in the cheap glass showing several mothers and Erins and Dories.

—This is where you've been? Jesus H. Christ. Take that goddamn morbid thing off and get your ass to church. Their mother shook the dress, making its mothball smell dance with dust particles in dim light of the closet.

Erin shrugged and pushed herself up off the floor. She pressed past both Dori and their mother and instead of going out the front door, climbed out the window. Dori knew Erin was going to go find her boyfriend, who was probably aching for her, positively pining after so many minutes and hours and days without her (Dori learned the words aching and pining from the romance books she stole from the library; she tried to remember them and use them in everyday conversation so she wouldn't forget).

Their mother gripped the dress in her fists. Dori followed her into the kitchen and watched as she threw it on the kitchen floor and then muttered:

—You don't appreciate anything. That's why we can't do anything nice.

Then she swirled dark rum into her coffee glass, threw it back, and slammed out to her car and then probably to the Church. The dress stayed on the floor for weeks, deflating into the linoleum until it was almost flat and Dori almost didn't have to step over it. While the dress was being disappeared by being ignored, Erin was disappeared by being forgotten like this, over and over and over. Sometimes Dori would talk to Erin and their mother would tell her to knock it off, which also didn't help Erin stick around. Their mother never really understood Erin, anyway. Never really loved her. At least, Dori didn't think so. Erin hadn't ever seemed to care about that though.

Dori was like the dress: not so much forgotten as ignored. She could read her stolen romance novels and secret magic books and comics and sit in trees and be the one that was remembered at supper time, at bedtime, whenever she did something just five degrees off of everyone else. The only time she wasn't ignored was after Erin was truly gone for good and then the police questioned her but it was too late and they didn't believe her anyway.

When Dori told Erin's boyfriend what had really happened, he asked her this: Are you crazy or something?

What could Dori say that she hadn't said already?

Dori didn't think she was crazy. She didn't even think the blank-faced man was crazy with his skiff and robe and bag of coins. She hadn't even known what was in the bag until the third or fourth or fifth time that Erin had dragged her into the weeds, their sickly green and skinny-sharp razor bodies cutting her shins as they skulked along the river's edge.

Nothing had really happened before that. Erin would stand there and just wait, while Dori got bored and started to imagine decaying fingers of people who'd been murdered or the slimy sharp mouths of crocodiles in the river. The last time they went together, she'd just about convinced herself that an enormous croc was about the jump out of the water and eat her when she felt Erin press against her.

—Be quiet. Erin had breathed, her words clammy against Dori's neck. Watch.

Dori watched and for a long time she didn't see anything. It was the middle of the morning but somehow clouds came or maybe the sun went down and suddenly it was twilight and the torn lip of a low skiff appeared out of the reeds and the water. In the skiff was a figure who Dori thought was a jedi maybe but the robes hid everything until he turned toward them and there was nothing in his face that she could see (so not a jedi, not a real one like Obi Wan Kenobi). No eyes or mouth or anything human. Nevertheless, the robed figure (who over time, minutes, hours, became a man, a man with features and hands but still had nothing in his face, a blank screen) looked at them and held out his hand and Erin leaned over the water, her body suddenly skinny and sharp like the razor weeds and would have gone to him then but Dori held her arm tight tight in her small brown fists with their sharp sharp nails.

—You're hurting me, Erin said.

Dori felt Erin's skin break away from her own and she knew she couldn't stop Erin. Not now. Maybe not ever. Erin waded through the murk until she was up to her thighs in the river. The water made it look like Erin was bleeding but that was only because her skirt was red. Now it was red and wet. The blank-faced man grasped Erin's chin very lightly, like he was holding a ripe plum and was worried he'd bruise its sensitive skin.

Dori wanted to scream but couldn't: when she saw the blank-faced man (he was so grey, his robes covered everything about him) she thought she might never breathe again.

Erin opened her mouth and held out her tongue. There was a gold coin on it, the twilight caught it like it was an early star, and suddenly her mouth was full of light. Dori wondered if Erin had swallowed the sky.

—You shall pass. The blank-faced man said, or maybe only thought. It was hard to say. His mouth wasn't moving at all, but Dori definitely heard, or maybe just knew he said it. Maybe it was a trick, like ventriloquism. The blank-faced man plucked the coin from Erin's mouth and placed it in his bag.

All the light in the world flicked off.

———

I'm going to show you a trick, Erin said.

Erin's clothes clashed brilliantly with the orange and plaid couch. She was wearing one of their mother's Stevie Nicks skirts and a sparkly scarf, all broomstick witchy. A bruja, her father would have said, if he'd still been alive. It had been such a long time since anyone had seen him; Dori just assumed he was dead at that point. She couldn't even remember what he had looked like or even what he wore. She couldn't have remembered him back, even if she had wanted to. Which she never did.

—I'm wearing an orange and plaid couch suit, Erin commanded. Even my face and neck are covered in itchy fabric.

Dori tried not to giggle, even though her stomach felt giddy. She didn't want to break the spell that Erin wanted her to believe in.

Close your eyes and count to 11, Erin whispered, making her voice fade slowly like a warm breeze snaking through the tops of trees. When you open your eyes I'll be gone. Eventually you'll forget me completely; it will be like I never existed.

Dori completely believed this was possible because she loved Erin and knew that magic worked and if you stopped seeing, whatever you didn't see would just disappear. She knew this, too, because she would lay in her bed at night and make herself stop seeing the blank-faced man, his hands, his bag of coins. She stopped seeing the flash of metal on Erin's tongue, Erin's fingers in his palm, the sparkle of money dropping into his fist.

But Dori didn't get to 11 because her mother came in screaming about how her car was missing again and if Dori knew anything about it and wasn't telling she'd beat her with her espadrille shoe. She sounded ridiculous but Dori tried not to laugh. She even kept her eyes closed so she wouldn't have to break the spell, wouldn't have to see her mother crazy angry. And when she opened her eyes, Erin was gone.

They found the car two weeks later at the edge of the river. Erin had been hiding since the morning with the couch. Dori knew she was still around because at night Erin would sit on the end of her bed and tell her stories about the places she hid and the secret things people did all day when they thought no one was watching. Dori would turn her face to the opposite wall and look out of the corner of her eye toward the window and see Erin reflected there: a wisp of blond, a sparkle, a sneer. Dori stopped being able to see Erin, though, once her boyfriend pressed his face up against the window looking for her. After that she could only hear Erin, though she had to listen very hard. After a while, Dori kept falling asleep during their visits and in the morning could not always remember what was said. Eventually, Erin stopped coming because Dori stopped remembering to look for her. At first, Dori thought that maybe Erin had found their father and would never come back. She hated Erin for that, and sometimes even tried to forget she had even existed. Their mother didn't even care that Erin was gone, though she'd stopped yelling at Dori for mumbling to herself, one of their mother's pet peeves, which was something.

—One more time. The cop said. What did the man in the boat do to you?

Dori had already told them everything.

—Not to me, she said. To my sister.

—Your sister.

The cop looked at her mother, who was frowning at the floor and massaging the bridge of her nose.

—Yes. She got all wet walking through the river to the boat. She gave the man her coin. I didn't want her to go. But he grabbed her face and then she started glowing and then . . .

—Goddamnit, her mother interrupted. What the hell happened to my car?

—Erin—Dori started to explain, how she'd made her come with her, how the car would be faster, how with it they'd be back before their mother even woke up, how they'd cross the bridge and back and go wherever they wanted and maybe even never come back, they'd be escape artists, disappearers.

Dori's mother stood up and reached over the desk, grabbed Dori's chin hard. Not like the blank-faced man had. Not like she was a ripe fruit, a sensitive plum.

—I don't want to hear that name ever again. Her mother whispered. Dori was so frightened that she agreed. She never mentioned Erin to her mother again. She tried not to even think about her.

Dori feels bad about that now. She thinks that Erin would have come back for good if only Dori had remembered to think about her more, to talk to her more, even if she couldn't quite see the wisps of her hair reflected in the window. It was just that it was hard. After the thing with Erin and the car, her mom had been down on her for being just five degrees off a lot and she wasn't even allowed to climb trees or walk to the Grand Union by herself. Not that it stopped her. Dori became a trickster after Erin left, stealing rides with strangers and drinking behind the school with older boys. She even tried to bleach her hair so it would look like Erin's, but because it was so dark naturally, it just came out orange. Eventually, she figured out how to make it perfectly white, bleached out and spiked like the punkers on TV, like the bird and fish and other animal bones down at the river's edge. She still did all the things she had always done—drank pickle juice and spent spare moments in the tops of trees reading her stolen books—but now she did all the things that Erin had done, or had always wanted to do.

Dori stopped waiting for Erin's boyfriend to show up at their bed-room window and started waiting for him at work. Erin's boyfriend's hands were like long, thin cuts of roast beef, cracked from running the slicer and light pink where his callouses split in the winter. They were warm and soft like good meat, too. Dori would press her cheek against the cool metal of the walk-in freezer at the Grand Union and when she felt the cold of the wall and the hot of his body at the same time, she imagined kisses light like the touch of a flower beneath her chin.

It took Dori a long time to remember Erin's forgetting spell (count to 11 and close your eyes) and an even longer time to remember, to know that she could conjure things, that she could make tv shows just happen from blank snowy screens and maybe other things by thinking about them, by crossing the bridges in her memory, back to where things started, where instead of being just one girl alone inside and out, there were two, : the girl she really was, and the girl, her sister, that she loved.

The second time Dori conjured Taxi, she was walking in Times Square, back when it was dirty all the time, with some guy who wasn't her boyfriend at all but was pretending to be and she was trying very hard to make him go away but she needed money so she decided to bring him back to Queens (where she'd been living with a bunch of other girls and guys who brought their dates home a lot, who all seemed to wear the same clothes and push the same grunts and gasps from their throats instead of talking). At that moment, Dori missed Erin so fiercely, so completely that the TVs that lined the shop window she was leaning on, trying to ignore her not-boyfriend, flickered on and there it was: Taxi. She stared and stared and still couldn't believe it. It stayed on for hours and Dori just stood there, watching and she even thought that maybe the girl that was standing behind her in the window, almost right where she stood with the bleach-blond hair and the sneer and crucifix dangling for fashion only was really Erin. Erin who before she had disappeared made life better, made life magic, made spells and wove stories that made all of the bad, scary things ok.

—Erin, she whispered, ErinErinErin.

But perhaps her voice was too soft, her mind too awake for conjuring. Perhaps her magic wasn't powerful enough. She'd practiced as often as she could since the night when she'd pressed her cheek to the heat of the metal television box and chanted taxitaxitaxitaxi until she almost huffed herself out. Almost every time, the show would come on and so Dori hoped that she could make Erin really be there, could remember her back. She decided that she was going to just stand here until she could actually feel Erin's skin beside her again and then she would turn around and they would go home to her apartment in Queens together.

She must have fallen asleep waiting for Erin to materialize completely because the cop and the store manager were yelling way too loud:

—Miss? Miss? You gotta move. You can't just stand here all night. I gotta a store to run.

Dori didn't want to open her eyes or turn around or leave because she knew that by falling asleep she had broken the spell.

—What channel are they on? What channel? Dori's voice sounded strange to her, blond and sneering and it didn't belong to her anymore. It was like she was someone else now. Someone she was just remembering.

—TVs been off for hours, the store manager said. Off since the Late Late Show.

His voice was full of water, of rivers, bridges; it was drowning and she couldn't grab hold.

—What channel? What channel? Dori could feel the cop and manager look at each other even though she didn't have her eyes open, not yet. She had to remember first. To really remember all of it. Everything that happened that September summer. The river, the river.

—Seven. It was channel seven.

When Dori got home, she dragged the old black and white portable into her room to try again while her roommates were sleeping but no matter what she did, channel seven was only static, black and white water pushing violently against the glass of the screen, like it hadn't been on ever, like it couldn't remember that it was a station that was supposed to play.

The TV she has now is color, which she hopes won't interfere with her spell. Since she moved in with Strummer, close to the edge of the river, she's successfully reappeared many things: the friend's cat Dori lost while she was stoned, her mother's beat-up Dodge Dart that she either left in Tucson or was stolen, and now, maybe hopefully Erin. She knows that now the smaller things are accomplished (since leaving New York for good, she has spent so much time training her mind, making small things happen), Erin will be a piece of cake.

To prepare she digs out her and Erin's old cassettes, the flashlight (which only worked that one September summer, the summer Erin disappeared), and a pile of batteries. She turns on the tape deck (it was a Walkman, yes, she knows, but she thinks inaccuracy can be forgiven here, because the sounds and pictures need space to move, roam, gel together into an Erin form in her living room). She turns on the TV (MTV isn't MTV anymore, no, no all-the-time videos or remote control game shows, but it's still the same channel, yes still the same number on the big black box). She spreads the cigarettes and brandy-iced coffee and a smooth piece of the orange and plaid couch, moldering with her in this basement by the water's edge, where nothing moved or really lived in so so long.

But she can't think about that yet. She's got to make Erin real again, and all the things that Dori has done and become can disappear, float away in the static snow of the TV screen.

CAMILLA GRUDOVA

The

Mouse

Queen

Our apartment always looked like Christmas because the shelves were laden with red and green Loeb books in Greek and Latin. Peter's uncle gave him one every year for his birthday, and we had bought more from second hand shops. Whenever we had guests over, Peter had to point out that he had covered the English translation side of the Latin books with sheets of coloured paper. He and I met in Latin class at university. I was drawn to Latin because it didn't belong to anybody, there were no native speakers to laugh at me. There were private school kids in my classes who had studied Latin before, but I quickly overtook them. Peter, who was one of them, slicked his hair back like a young Samuel Beckett and had the wet, squinting look of an otter.

He looked down on Philosophy and Classics students who planned to go into law. Under his influence, so did I. Peter wore the same type of clothes every day: heavy striped shirts from an army surplus store, sweaters that hadn't been dried properly after washing, khakis, Doc Martens and a very old-fashioned cologne whose scent vaguely resembled chutney. He had bought the cologne at a yard sale, only about a teaspoon had been used by the previous owner. It wasn't until we had dated for some time that I learned his parents were lawyers, that he had grown up with much more money than I had.

Peter and I were married in a church with a replica of Michelangelo's *Pietà*. We only invited one friend, an English major who loved Evelyn Waugh, as we thought he was the only person we knew who would understand we wanted to be married in such a manner. Of course our parents wouldn't want us to be married so young—before we had jobs—so we didn't tell them at all. We didn't move in together until our last semester of university, into an apartment above an abandoned grocery store. The landlord had stopped running it years before and left it as it was, with a faded 'Happy Canada Day' poster and popsicle advertisements on the dusty glass windows. It was cheap for a one-bedroom, because not many people wanted to live above an abandoned but unemptied grocery store—the threat of vermin seemed too much, and the landlord just couldn't bring himself to clean it and do something with the space. It seemed he thought he might open it again some time in the future, to sell the mouldy chocolate bars and hardened gum that remained there.

There was a hatch in our floor that led to a back room in the shop downstairs, and into the shop itself. Down there, Peter found some old cigarettes which seemed safe in comparison to all the old food, and newspapers that dated from when we were five years old. In our living room we had a parlour organ that had belonged to his grandfather. Peter loved the organ—it was a much, much older instrument than the piano. Organs were invented in the Hellenistic period. They were powered using water. In Ancient Rome, Nero played such an organ.

On the organ's mantel, Peter put a plaster model of a temple which fits in the palm of one's hand, a statue of Minerva bought at an Italian shop, a collection of postcards of nude athletes Peter got from the British Museum, and a large framed copy of Botticelli's portrait of St Augustine. Sometimes I was woken up in the middle of the night by the sound of Peter playing the organ, wearing nothing but his bathrobe, his hair in his face.

We turned a little chair too rickety to sit on into an altar. We made a collage of saints and Roman gods, a mixture of pictures and statues, and oddly shaped candles we had picked up here and there—beehives, trees, cones, owls, angels. Sometimes Peter left offerings, grapes, little cups full of wine and, to my dismay, raw chicken breasts and other bits of meat he bought at a butcher's. A friend told us it was dangerous to worship such a large, mixed crowd.

After graduating, we planned to live cheaply and save up to move to Rome. We both thought there was no point in applying to graduate school unless we first spent a period of time in Rome researching something original to write about.

In the meantime, I found work in a doll's house shop. We sold tiny things to put in them, from lamps to Robert Louis Stevenson books with real, microscopic words in them. Peter got a job in a graveyard, installing tombstones, digging graves, helping with Catholic burial processes, and cleaning up messes. He would find diaphragms, empty bottles of spirits, squirrel skins left over from hawks' meals, and dozens of umbrellas. He brought the umbrellas home, until our apartment started to look like a cave of sleeping bats. I had an umbrella yard sale one Saturday when he was at work:

ALL UMBRELLAS TWO DOLLARS AS IS

It was an overcast day so I did well for myself.

Peter was sombre-looking and strong so everyone thought him ideal, and his Latin came in useful. He was outdoors most of the time. He developed a permanent sniffle, and smelled like rotting flowers and cold stones. There was a mausoleum that was a perfect, but smaller replica of a Greek temple—Peter spent his lunch breaks smoking, reading, and eating sandwiches on the steps. It was built by the founder of a grand department store that sold furs, uncomfortably scratchy blankets, shoes and other things. Peter threw his cigarette butts through a gated window leading into the mausoleum, as he didn't think such a man deserved a classical temple. He was half driven mad by the cemetery—'a dreadful facsimile of Rome', he called it—but couldn't afford to leave. It paid very well because not many people were morbid and solemn enough to stand working in a cemetery. The owner said Peter was very dignified and he could see him going far in the cemetery business.

We both put up advertisements—' latin tutors available'—in bookstores and libraries, but received no replies.

Living together we became careless compared to how we normally acted with each other, and a few months after graduating I discovered I was pregnant. When I started to show, I was fired; the owner of the doll's house shop thought I would bump into all the precious little things with my new bulk and break them. I felt like a doll's house myself, with a little person inside me, and imagined swallowing tiny chairs and pans in order for it to be more comfortable.

When we learned we were having twins, Peter said the ultrasound photo looked like an ancient, damaged frieze. As I grew larger, I wore pashmina shawls around the house, tied around my body like tunics. Neither of us had twins in our families. It was the Latin that did it, Peter said, did I have any dreams of swans or bearded gods visiting me? He acted like I had betrayed him in a mythological manner. I had dreams that Trajan's column and the Pantheon grew legs and chased me which I didn't tell him about, as I thought they would upset him further.

One night Peter didn't come home from the graveyard. He arrived at dawn, covered in mud, his coat off and bundled under his arm. He opened the coat, inside was the corpse of a very small woman, a dwarf I suppose. She wore a black Welsh hat like Mother Goose, it was glued to her head. She had black buckled shoes and a black dress with white frills along the hem, wrists and neck, and yellow stockings. Her face was heavily painted, to look very sweet, but her eyelids had opened, though she was dead.

We buried a small, black coffin today, said Peter, I thought it was so terrible, the eternal pregnancy of death. If we are to have two, what difference will three make, he said, and laughed horribly, like a donkey. He had never laughed like that before. I dug the coffin up again, took her out and put the coffin back empty, he said, no one will know.

Peter stumbled off to bed, leaving me with the little corpse. Her eyeballs looked horrible. I thought I would turn to stone if I looked at them too long. I threw Peter's coat in the bathtub, wrapped her in a sheet, put her in a garbage bag. Then I picked her up. She was extraordinarily heavy. I decided I would stuff her in the organ, it was the only good hiding place but I had the horrible thought that it would become haunted with her, and the keys would play her voice.

I brought her down to the grocery store, and put her behind the counter. She was heavy. I hoped if she stayed there long enough she would shrink like an apple, and Peter could bring her back to the graveyard well hidden in a purse and rebury her like a bulb.

I kept thinking about her eyes, and later returned downstairs to put pennies over them. The pennies didn't cover the whole of them, they were very large eyes, but I didn't want to waste one- or two-dollar coins.

Peter slept for twenty hours. When he woke up, he didn't remember what he had done, so I didn't tell him. As he recovered his accusations against my pregnancy redoubled: I had consorted with ancient pagan gods. He sat in the bathtub with no water in it, reading St Augustine and burning incense. He left for Mass on Sundays without me. We had our own odd version of Catholicism where we went to a different Catholic church every Sunday, while on sporadic Sundays we went to a large park that was mostly forest and took off our clothes and drew crosses on ourselves with mud as Peter muttered incantations. I never knew which church he was going to. I stayed home and read my favourite passages from *The Metamorphoses*.

He boiled our marriage certificate in the tea kettle, saying he wouldn't work in a cemetery for the rest of his life just to feed the children of Mars and, finally, he left, while I was at the grocery store buying him lettuce and coffee.

When I came home, his bulky green leather suitcase, which reminded me of a toad, was gone, as were a selection of the Loeb books, the jar of Ovaltine, and my favourite purple wool cardigan which was too small for me to wear with my pregnant belly. He had left all his underwear, most likely out of forgetfulness, and they stared at me like the haughty, secretive heads of white Persian cats when I opened the clothes drawer.

I found his parents' address on an old report card. I had never met them. The house was in the suburbs, I had to take a train there. There weren't any sidewalks, only lawns and roads. I passed a frightening house with a sagging porch. Between the door and the window there was a rotting moose's head on a plaque. The moose winked at me. The movement caused the moose's glass eyeball to fall out and roll across the porch and onto the lawn.

It was a very large fake Tudor house, the white parts were grimy, and there was a bathtub on the lawn, used as a planter for carnations. There were two very old black Cadillacs parked in the drive, probably from the 1980s. I had grown up in an apartment with only a mother who didn't know how to drive. It was Peter's mother who answered the door, I knew it was her because she also resembled an otter, her grey hair slicked back from her face. She wore a very old-fashioned looking purple suit, and grimaced at my stomach.

I asked her if Peter was there, and she said no, he had gone to the States for law school, she was glad he was finally getting himself together.

I left, feeling sick, imagining the babies swimming in my stomach like otters, with the faces of Peter and his mother. I ran back to the train station, not caring if the motion killed the foetuses. Back downtown, I wondered what it would be like to be run over by a tram—perhaps like being pushed through a sewing machine.

I didn't have enough money to pay the rent the next month. I hoped the landlord would forget me the way he forgot his grocery store, but he came a few days before the month was up and asked for cheques for the next three months in advance as he was going to Wales to visit his cousin.

I had to leave all the furniture and the organ, we couldn't afford to rent movers. I scooped all the stuff off the organ's mantel and dumped it in my purse. My mother scolded me when I tried to pack Peter's clothes and other things. He hadn't taken his razor, his galoshes or his long maroon scarf. My mother and I took what we could box by box, on the tram, and once in a cab, my arms weighed down with plastic bags filled with Loeb books. I was glad to leave the old dead woman, whom I hadn't had a chance to check on.

My mother lived in a dark, ground-floor apartment, she had moved after I started university, to a smaller place. It only had one bedroom, so I had to stay on the couch. All the furniture was blue and green brocade, and there were trinkets I remembered from childhood: a wooden horse missing its two back legs, a paper clown in a music box which started to dance when you opened a little drawer on the bottom, a model ship covered in dust, a collection of toy donkeys I was never allowed to play with because they had belonged to my grandfather, and all sorts of things bought at yard sales, discount shops and in Chinatown—baskets, pincushions, backscratchers, plastic flowers, peacock feathers. It was a horrible thing that you could buy peacock feathers for less than a dollar.

There was no room for all my Loeb books, I had to put them underneath the couch where they became all dusty.

When I was little, my mother had given me a department store catalogue to read. It was full of toys I couldn't have, but I could cut out the pictures, she told me, she had already looked through the catalogue. I was amazed by a set of twin dolls: how did they manage to make them exactly the same? My mother laughed at me and said there were hundreds of them made in a factory, and everything else I owned had identical siblings, that's how the world was now.

I was couch-ridden for a month after having the twins. I felt like Prometheus, the babies were eagles with soft beaks, my breasts being continually emptied and filled. I didn't name them Romulus and Remus as Peter and I had planned—Peter thought we simply couldn't name them anything else—but Aeneas and Arthur.

My mother looked after the twins when I was well enough to look for work. She left them in strange places, under tables and in cupboards, but they weren't old enough to attend day care. I couldn't go back to the doll's house shop, the owner was more interested in a fake pristine, miniature domestic life—unused pots and pans, cradles without babies in them. She didn't even like to have children in her shop, her ideal customers were older men and women like herself, who wore brooches and would spend hundreds of dollars on a tiny imitation Baroque chair. I was too embarrassed to go looking around the university for work, or to put up any signs offering Latin tutoring—I felt like I had given birth to the twins from my head and my head hadn't recovered.

The air in my mother's neighbourhood was always sickly sweet because of a chocolate factory, and it was there I got a job. All the chocolates were sold in purple and gold packaging. Fruits, nuts, and other things were delivered and encased in chocolate, the opened boxes looked like displays of shells, eggs and rocks in a natural history museum. From my first day working there, I had nightmares of eating chocolates filled with bird bones, rocks, gold nuggets, Roman coins, teeth.

There was one other person with a university degree at the factory, a girl named Susan who studied English but couldn't find a job in that field and had a child. She had named her daughter Charlotte Fitzgerald after Charlotte Brontë and F. Scott Fitzgerald. She was a horrible, large child who carried a headless plastic doll everywhere with her, and spat into its body like an old man who chewed on tobacco. Her spit was always brown because Susan gave her sweets from the factory. Charlotte Fitzgerald was six, and didn't know how to read. She threw tantrums if Susan didn't give her sweets. I liked Susan but didn't want my babies to spend too much time with Charlotte in case she influenced them. I never took home any free chocolates. I knew my mother would like them, but I also knew she would give some to Aeneas and Arthur when I wasn't there, and sugar was like a nasty potion that would turn them into monsters. Susan often told me you could only have a limited influence on how your kids turned out, she felt Charlotte was already ruined and wished she hadn't been born. I tried to pick out the nicest toys at second-hand shops, I stayed away from garish plastic things, I took lots of books out of the library for them but they were too young to read them and ripped them apart. They learned all sorts of things I couldn't control at day care, words like 'gosh'. Once, as I read them *Aesop's Fables* translated into Latin, one of them yelled 'Batman' at me.

As they didn't have a father, I bought a male doll wearing a suit and bowtie with a string coming out of his back which, when pulled, emitted a laugh, but the laugh didn't take long to stop working, and his grin bothered me so I threw him out, longing for sombre and cruel Peter.

I saved up enough money to find a place of my own when the twins were almost two years old. It looked like a house from the outside, but was really just one small room with a bathroom built in an old closet, a concrete yard and a little fence that didn't reach my knees. There was no bathtub, only a shower, and I had to buy a plastic bin to wash the babies in. There was a tile depicting St Francis on the front of the house, beside the door.

I thought of Peter all the time. I took the twins for walks in the cemetery where he used to work, though the stroller was hard to push over grass. Whenever I saw cigarette butts, I imagined they were his. I collected umbrellas, and sold them from my front door on my days off. I also walked by our old apartment. The grocery store was still the same, and I imagine our rooms upstairs were too—the parlour organ, the bed now stripped of blankets, the shelves with no books on them—and of course the shrivelled old lady downstairs behind the counter.

I tried to remind myself of all the times Peter acted horribly: just after we moved in together, we decided to have a costume party. I wanted to dress up as Argus from *The Metamorphoses*. I bought a white dress and painted eyes all over it, as well as a pair of white gauze wings which I also turned into eyes. When I tried my costume on a few days before the party, Peter said I looked terrifying, and everyone would think I was maddeningly jealous and controlling of him and he wouldn't be able to enjoy himself. I threw the costume out, and decided to be a mouse from *The Nutcracker* instead of anything from Greek and Roman mythology. Peter didn't know anything about ballets or Tchaikovsky and neither did I, really. I had seen a production of *The Nutcracker* as a child and I remembered it as all blurry with a cardboard sleigh and fake snow. I bought a grey leotard, crinoline, and made a mouse tail, ears out of paper.

Peter decided to be a lamppost. It was quite awful, he painted his face yellow, with a red and blue line across the centre of his face, and made a kind of black paper lantern to wear over his head—it looked more like a bird cage. And he wore a black shirt with frills which he thought resembled the arabesques on some old European streetlights. I was baffled as to why he chose to be a lamp and was so enthusiastic about it, though I knew he thought dressing up as historical figures vulgar: he was furious when someone showed up as St Francis, wearing a dirty brown tunic with fake birds sewn onto it.

A girl dressed up as the full moon kept trying to kiss Peter. She smelled like talcum powder and unwashed stockings, which is how I imagined the moon to smell. For the party, Peter had bought tins of snails, they smelled nasty, and floated in grey water. Why did he have to waste money on them when there were snails in the shed behind our building? The Romans enjoyed snails, he said to me in an irritable

voice. He arranged them decoratively on bits of lettuce, that's all there
was to eat, besides the punch we made and some saltine crackers.

Lots of people came, and there were, I realized, many rich girls
from our university who had grown up doing ballet. I was so afraid
of them asking me where I had taken ballet, and if I could do a dem-
onstration, that I took off my mouse ears, tail and ballet shoes: I said
I was dressed up as a ball of dust. One of Peter's old friends from
the boys' private school he attended came in a brown fur coat, he
had silk pyjamas underneath, and played our organ while smoking
a cigar, getting ashes all over the keys. He had a cruel habit of telling
almost every girl he met that they looked like a male star he had
seen in a film long ago—so and so, what's his name, the funny chap
with the moustache, you're just the image, don't say are you related
to . . . ? Peter didn't say anything the time his friend compared me to
a well-known silent film actor. He always took on a feigned look of
innocence whenever anyone mentioned movies, as if he had spent his
whole life in churches and libraries, though I had once overheard him
humming *Singin' in the Rain* while in the bath.

The twins looked more and more like Peter. It made me howl and
pull my hair, though it meant they would be handsome. Peter once
told me I looked like an owl, my eyes were very round. His favourite
Roman god was Minerva.

On my way to work I had to cross over a bridge, and I often imagined hanging the twins from it on ropes, their little legs kicking,
saving them at the very last moment—I thought such an act would
make me love them more. The image disturbed me so much, I saw
it every time I passed over the bridge, so I took to running over it,
arriving at work sweaty and full of pity for my children. Peter sent
a postcard to my mother's house, she called me to say there was a
'Spanish or Italian letter' waiting for me. It was written in Latin and
he said he was faring well. It had an American stamp on it, though it
was an antique postcard of broken columns at Pompeii. He didn't ask
about the twins, with their heads that looked like shrunken, half-bald
versions of his own. Though I didn't have his address, I went to a
photo booth in a subway station with the intention of taking a family
portrait. Perhaps I would send it to American newspapers.

Inside the booth, the twins wouldn't stop screaming and struggling. They hadn't had their photos taken before.

In the photo Aeneas and Arthur weren't on my lap, as I had put them, but sitting on a black wolf whose eyes reflected the photographic flash. It had a horrible, fanged grin. I stuffed it in my pocket and pushed the stroller home, the twins were screaming, I had to belt them in.

After I got them to sleep, I took the photo out of my coat pocket and looked at it again. I didn't see why Aeneas and Arthur had cried so much. The wolf was handsome.

The longer I looked at the photograph, the larger it seemed, until I noticed the photograph was being held between two small black paws rather than hands. I was covered in fur the same colour as my hair—black. I was too frightened to look in a mirror so I filled a bowl with water, and looked at my face. I had a long black nose and my eyes were green, as they were when I was a human. I wasn't shocked, I didn't feel like I looked that different. I looked at the photograph again: yes it was me, the photo booth had somehow known before I transformed. I felt an urge to go outside and went through the backyard door. I ate some old apples in a rubbish bin, killed a rat and sniffed some puddles. I wandered from alley to alley, from quiet street to quiet street—I had never been in an alleyway at night-time before, it had the inhuman liveliness of a puppet show.

Every night the same thing happened. I would put the twins to bed, read a while then, yawning, at around 9, turn into a wolf. I would then turn back into a human sometime around 3 or 4, those hours of transformation were always blurry like my memory of *The Nutcracker*.

As a wolf, I had no fear of jumping through windows. I stole, from bookstores, grocery stores, clothing shops, even flower shops. I carried things home in my mouth—bouquets and novels and sausages.

I was back in human form by morning, though sometimes I had stray black hairs on my chin or lips, my ears were a little long or a few of my nails were still dark and thick like claws—I told people they were damaged after being smushed under a window frame. I had a lot of small cuts from breaking windows—I told everyone the twins scratched me.

A few times, the twins were awake when I returned home from hunting and stealing. When I approached them, they crouched and covered their eyes although I had stolen them all sorts of expensive, fanciful toys. I had more breasts as a wolf, but they refused to feed from me.

It ended up in the newspapers: 'Wild dog breaks into shops'. A man had seen me leave a toyshop with an expensive Julius Caesar doll in my mouth. 'It was a dark and horrid beast,' he said to the newspaper. 'I bet it was looking for a real baby to eat.' I needed a disguise for getting around while in wolf form.

On a weekend, I went to a costume shop and purchased a nice pink rubber mask of a girl's face, stretchable enough to fit over my long wolf's nose, with yellow braids attached to it, a blue and white Alice in Wonderland dress, and a dainty pair of Victorian boots perfectly sized for my back wolf paws. I felt I could trust the girl who worked behind the counter at the costume shop. She looked somewhat wolf-like herself, with a long nose. She gave me the toy pistol for free, and indistinguishable, fluffy animal ears for the twins to wear, though they cried when I tried to put them on their heads. At home, I had a Red Riding Hood cloak someone had left at our costume party. It was made out of felt and had a copper clasp.

When no one was in sight, and I found a store I wanted to steal from, I took off my costume in a hidden spot, and jumped through the windows, taking what I needed. I was much greedier as a wolf. I decided to take care of the old woman in the old home Peter and I had lived in. I broke in through the back of the shop, but when I went to eat the woman, still in a bag behind the counter, the smell of embalming chemicals was so repulsive to me that I couldn't do it. She seemed to have shrunk. I thought it would be better to leave her there than bury her in a nearby park. Instead, I chased a fat raccoon I found rooting in a compost bin, then stole a bag of pomegranates from a fruit and vegetable store.

The next morning, when I woke up, the twins were nowhere to be found. Not in the cupboards, or the bath, or the rubbish bin. I ran up and down the street and the alley, my belly and breasts flapping like the sad wings of a fowl. They were gone. I must have eaten them in the late hours of being a wolf. Usually I remembered my wolf hours clearly, but I had no memory of making a meal of my children. Yet my stomach was stretched, as if I had eaten something large. I retched, but nothing bloody or hairy came out. I drank cupfuls of coffee, trying to digest them as quickly as possible so they would be out of my body. After I went to the bathroom I looked into the bowl to see if there were any bits in my excrement. I found a tiny white bone. It could have been from a pigeon—I loved pigeons while in wolf form.

I sold all of Arthur and Aeneas's things, which didn't amount to much, around forty dollars. I bought myself some books and a plaid skirt which was too small for me.

Maybe Peter had come while I was asleep and taken them away. The idea very much relieved me. I imagined him raising them somewhere along the coast of the Black Sea, speaking to them only in Latin and making them herd sheep. I called the day care and their doctor, explaining that I was moving to Rome with the children. That night, I stole enough brie from a cheese shop to make it look like I had a fridge full of moons. I made myself a meal of brie cheese, pomegranates and raw pigeons. I started to write something I called *Memoirs of a Wolf*. I wrote in Latin first—Latin is the human language wolves know best—then translated it into English when I was in human form again the next morning.

Sometimes Susan arrived at work with a few stray brown hairs around her mouth, or a spot of blood, but I didn't say anything and neither did she, and we stopped asking each other about our children.

BRIAN
EVENSON

The
Second
Door

I.

AFTER A WHILE—WE HAD BY THEN LOST TRACK OF not only the day but of what month exactly it was—I realized that my sister had begun to speak in a language I could not understand. I cannot mark a moment when this change occurred. There must have been a period where she spoke it, or some mélange of English and this new tongue, and I, somehow, didn't notice, responding instead to her gestures or to what I thought she must be saying. But then something, some sound, a clatter of metal falling, caught my attention and I looked for the tin or the pan that had been dropped and realized the sound was proceeding from her mouth.

Was it me? I wondered at first. Some slippage in my brain, some malfunction of my hearing apparatus? I shook my head to awaken my mind, scraped the inside of each earhole out with my smallest fingers.

"Come again?" I said.

Her brow furrowed. She spoke again, that same clatter of metal, incomprehensible. It was not the sort of sound that it was possible for a human throat to make, and yet her throat was making it.

But I am getting ahead of myself. I have lived alone now for long enough to no longer have a proper sense of how to convey a story to another being. Even before I lived alone, it was just my sister and I, and our relationship was, shall we say, peculiar. Even before she lost her ability to speak in the way humans do, she was odd, and we had lived together so long as to make the need to converse with one another nearly superfluous. We did speak, occasionally, but gestured more often than moved our lips, and in general lived in that brusque and silent accord enjoyed, if enjoyed is the right word, by certain long-married couples. Or so my sister suggested to me. Besides us, I have not met any couples, long-married or otherwise, so I cannot say with certainty.

Not that we were living as if married—no, our relations were at all times innocent and chaste, as if we were merely those children's dolls that give every appearance of being human until you remove their clothing and see the smooth plane where genitalia would otherwise be. Still, we had been so long in one another's company that she knew nearly always what I was thinking and I knew the same about her. We shared that odd intimacy that comes from living partly in one's own head and partly in another's.

I loved my sister deeply, or as deeply as any sexless doll could. Perhaps I have exhausted that metaphor. I do not wish to suggest I am, or ever have been, anything other than human. I was born in the usual way, the issue of a mother and a father—so I have been told. I have no memory of my parents, but my sister always insisted that yes, we had a mother and a father. It is important to note this fact, though I cannot independently verify it. By the time my memories began, my parents were dead.

My sister would sometimes recount their death to me late at night, as she was trying to coax me to sleep, acting this out with the two posable dolls that we possessed. To comfort me, I suppose. An odd notion of comfort, indeed, but somehow hearing stories about their deaths allowed them to be alive again for me for just a moment, before they were once again consigned to death. She told the story each time in a different way so that I was never quite sure what the truth was. Indeed, I half-suspected that one evening she would not recount their deaths at all, but confess that my parents were still alive and waiting for me somewhere—in a concealed room in the house, say, or through the door set in one side of the house that we never used. But whether she intended to tell me this or not, she did not do so before her speech changed and she could tell me nothing at all.

———

In many of the versions she told of the story, my parents were set-tlers, pioneers, the first in this place, and because of a failure of some kind, left alone just the two of them. Sometimes she said we were in a remote area of a southern continent and my parents had been the only survivor of a boat that sunk. Sometimes it was a separate world entirely and they had arrived through the air or by slipping under-neath the usual order of things or by passing through a mirror.

"Separate world," I mused. "Separate from what?"

"From where they came from," my sister said.

"And where was that?" I asked.

But she just shook her head. For her, this was not part of the story.

There they were, the two dolls that represented my parents, my sister's hands making them jump up and down slightly as she moved them across my blanket. She made my father speak in a voice that was lower then hers, my mother higher. They stopped, looked around.

"Do you suppose it's safe?" asked my mother in her high voice. "Should we turn back?"

"We can't turn back," my father said. "We have no choice."

And then they were screaming, moved by sleight of hand under my blanket, vanished, simply gone.

"Again," I said. Smiling, my sister obliged.

Whatever the case, whatever had happened to my parents, it had something to do with our house, which was not, as my sister informed me, properly speaking, a house. Its windows were circular and made of thick glass and could not be opened without removing a series of screws and prying off a rubber seal and a sturdy metal ring. There were two dozen of these windows, strung down a long cylindrical central hallway that constituted the majority of our dwelling. At one end, traveling gently downslope, was a hatch that led to my room. It had the same circumference as the cylindrical hallway but a depth of no more than seven or eight feet. At the other end of the hallway, upslope, was a hatch leading to the room that had become my sister's room, a kind of tapered cone with glass walls that had been burnt a smoky and opaque black.

In the middle of the central hallway, on both sides, was a door, a window in its upper half. One looked out on what seemed to be a flat and barren plain—as did all the windows in the hallway not on a door. The other door's window opened onto deep darkness, as if onto nothing at all.

The first door, to the plain, could be used in time of need, my sister taught me. The second door, no, never. To open the second door would be to invite the end.

"What do you mean by the end?" I asked.

Again, she just shook her head.

"What's out there?" I asked, peering through the window of the second door, through the only window that looked out into darkness. "Is anything out there?"

"Don't open that door," she said firmly. "Promise me."

Despite my promise, I tried once, to open the second door. There was a procedure required for this to happen, a process inscribed on the door itself. First the door had to be primed, then a countdown would begin. Then, finally, I would have to throw a lever and the door would spring open.

I got as far as arming the door. I had not realized that this would also trigger a dimming of the lights and the peal of an alarm siren. The sound brought my sister running from her room. She immediately unprimed the door and scolded me. The whole time she was doing so, I was wondering if I had the strength of will to disable her and continue the process.

Apparently I did not.

When my sister was still alive, we kept mainly to ourselves, to our own quarters. My sister referred to them as quarters and so I did as well. We would meet for meals in her quarters, feeding off the provisions that were stored behind the panels of the central hallway.

Eventually, my sister never tired of informing me, our provisions would run out. In preparation for this, she had begun to forage outside. Sometimes she would slip through the door—the first door, not the second—and come back with something to eat. She would be gone mere minutes sometimes, other times hours. Often, when I was young especially, I would stand by the door and await her return. Sometimes I would go instead to the second door and consider pursuing the procedure to open it, but I worried that my sister, who, after all, knew my thoughts almost as well as I knew my own, was waiting for this, just outside the first door, and would stop me if I tried.

I often placed my hand on this second door. It was cold to the touch. It would have taken a mere flick of the wrist to activate the sequence, and yet I never did.

When she returned, it was dragging a carcass, of a sort of creature unlike anything she had taught me about: a tangle of legs, oozing clusters of eyes, limbs that continued to throb even in death. Or simply gobbets of flesh, still oozing fresh with blood, cut from what creature I couldn't say. Out of breath, she would drag her latest find into her room and close the hatch. When she next opened it, there would be no sign it had ever been there.

"What's out there?" the dolls who are my parents would sometimes say as they were propelled across my blanket by my sister's hand. "Why does the view out the first door's window look so different from the view out of the second? Why is there darkness out only one window?"

But they never had an answer.

"Shall we go through the first door?" one would say to the other.

"Shall we go through the second?" the other might respond.

If the dolls went out the second door, they would die immediately. If they went out the first door, they might wander for a time before eventually dying.

"Either way, they die," I pointed out.

"Yes," said my sister. "Remember that. In the end, they always die."

———

Why did the view from one window look so different from the others?

I asked my sister this, expecting her, like the dolls of our parents who she in fact spoke for, to have no answer. I was surprised when she gave the question serious consideration.

"It is as though we are in two places at once," she finally said. "One door opens onto one place, and the other onto another."

"Then," I said, steadying myself on the wall beside me. "What place does that make this?"

"No place," she said. "This is not a place at all."

But if something is not a place, what is it? Can it be said to be anything? And what can be said of those living within it?

2.

My sister had always been the one to instruct me. In the absence of my parents, she fed me, clothed me, reared me. Everything I know about what it means to be human I know from things she said to me or from images, moving or still, she showed me on the still-functioning screen in her quarters. Now that she is gone, the screen will not work for me. I wonder sometimes how much of what I think I know is embroidered falsely upon these images, is my mind working with what it was given to create another, fuller, more promising world.

"Can you understand me?" I asked her.

She nodded.

"Say yes," I said.

A distressed screech, proceeding unnaturally from her mouth, though she did not seem unsettled by it. Indeed, she seemed placid, calm.

"Do you not hear that?" I asked. "How you sound?"

A long hesitation, then she shook her head. She opened her mouth and it was suddenly as if I were inside a vehicle as it crashed, metal buckling and crumpling all around me.

I fled.

Another attempt, an hour later, perhaps two, once I had steeled myself again. There I was, knocking on her hatch until she opened it.

"Hello," I said.

When she responded, in a low whisper, it was as if a pot was being scoured by sand. I winced, and she immediately fell silent.

I extended to her a writing pad, a pen. "Perhaps this will work better," I said.

She nodded and took them with a little bow. Furiously she scribbled on the pad, filling first one page, then a second. When she finally, triumphantly, handed the pad back to me, however, it was covered only in senseless script, clotted and gnarled: gibberish.

For a time we simply avoided one another. I hoped from one day to the next that something would change, that I would simply awaken one morning and find everything to have reverted back to normal, to have us both speaking the same language again. Instead, with each day, the gap between us grew until, after a week, a few weeks, once the plain outside the first door glittered with frost, it was as though there had never been intimacy between the two of us at all. The meals we had shared before we now took separately, each in our own quarters. If I came out of my quarters to find her in the central hall, I would turn around and retreat to my own quarters, and if the situation were reversed she would do the same.

We might have gone on like this a very long time, until the day when I discovered her body lying facedown in the hall or she discovered mine. Instead, something happened.

She would still, despite everything, sometimes leave in search of food. She would go out the first door and be gone an hour, a day. She returned burdened by hunks of bluish flesh or hauling the gooey remains of a carapace.

When I heard her leave the house, as soon as I was sure I was alone, I went out into the hallway and stood by the door, the second door, and pondered opening it. I would stand with my hand on the mechanism, staring out the window into the darkness, staring at nothing, until I heard the sound of the first door opening and my sister returning. Then I would rush back to my room.

Until one day, staring into the darkness, staring at nothing, I realized that there was something out there after all.

How long I had been staring, I didn't know. Long enough to feel as if I were no longer in my body, as if I were nowhere at all. And then something, a flicker or flash of movement in the glass, caught my attention and brought me back.

It was, I thought at first, the reflection of my face, the ghost of my own image caught in the glass and cast back at me. As I moved my own face slightly, smiled, inclined my head, the ghostly image in the glass reacted just as expected. It was only when I settled again, stared out again, motionless, that I realized the flicker was still there.

I held very still. It was there, deep in the darkness beyond the glass, drawn perhaps to this face (my own) it saw through the glass. I waited. I watched and waited.

And yes, there, it was, features nearly aligned with my own reflection. There was barely anything there, and yet there was something there.

By the time my sister returned, I was back in my room, turning over what I had seen. A face, almost like my own but not quite my own, nearly submerged in the murk. I had the dolls—my sister had abandoned them in my room and had not retrieved them after her voice was transformed—and with these I played out what had happened.

The doll that had been my father I designated as me. He walked down the long, cylindrical hall, in the trough formed between my legs by the dip of the blanket. Halfway down, at the hall's knee, the doll stopped and looked out the thick circular window set in the door. Did he see anything? No, he did not. Or did he? He wasn't sure, he almost turned away, and then suddenly—

There, pushing up against the blanket from beneath, the other doll, the one who had been my mother. What was it now? The doll that was me couldn't make her features out through the blanket, not clearly, but he knew that something was there, something roughly human in form.

It was just a question of how to coax her out from the darkness.

A number of days passed before my sister went outside again. I waited impatiently, hardly leaving my room, afraid to show too much interest in the second door while my sister was still inside. But then at last, finally, she left.

I rushed immediately to the second door, peering out into the darkness. I waited. Nothing was there. And then, suddenly, though I could see little more than my own reflection, I felt something was.

"Hello?" I said. "Don't be afraid."

Nothing changed or moved, not a thing.

"Please," I said, "let me see you." But as I said it I realized that I didn't need to see to know. That something, an idea, had already begun to coalesce in my mind.

And just like that, I knew who it was.

3.

When my sister, or rather the being that had taken the place of my sister, returned to the first door, it found it locked. I had locked it from the inside. It pounded on the door, crying out in that language that was not a language. Though I could not understand a word of what it said, or even be sure that what it said was words, I knew what it wanted: to get in. It had killed my sister and taken her shape, her manners, her gestures, her whole being, but something had slipped and it could not take her speech. If I hadn't sensed my true sister, the dead one, floating in the darkness behind the glass, I would have never known.

I let the creature pound. It would not get in. Not again.

It is still there, still pounding, its face crusted with frost. I see it in those brief moments when I tear myself away from the second door. It has been there for days now. I know what it wants—its gestures are clear enough. Open the door, they say, open the door!

And yes, I have come to believe this is something I should do: open the door. Only not the door it desires me to open.

In my bed I play with the dolls. My father is no longer my father: he is me. My mother is no longer my mother: she is my sister. Not the pretender: the real one. The male doll goes down the hall and stops to stare through the dark window set in the door. He sees something. Or not sees exactly: senses. He is sure something is there. Or rather someone. Impossible, since she is dead, but somehow still there nonetheless. He waits, and watches, and then he initiates the procedure. He arms the door. The countdown begins, lights flash, an alarm sounds. And then, after a moment, he is free to throw the lever and open the door and join his real sister. There she is, billowing out of the darkness, her head torn off, coming toward him.

I record this in a language that I, at least, can understand, having as I do no other. Whether anyone else will come who can understand remains to be seen. Though not by me: I am going to step out into the dark side of our house that is not a house. I am going to rejoin my sister. The real one. The one who is dead.

I will not be coming back.

Or rather, when I do come back, as soon as I open my mouth to speak, you will know it is not me.

NADIA
BULKIN

Live
Through
This

A MONTH AFTER DANIELLE HAAS WAS BURIED, THE cemetery caretaker Mr. Wolf was found dead on the grounds with a rake in his hand and an awful look on his face like he'd just seen the Devil, or so the rumor went at school. Everybody was so convinced that he'd met the ghost of Lady Horn—the wife of the town's founder, an insane woman buried in Plot 9—that nobody noticed that Danielle's body was missing until it turned up a week later in the Roths' living room, cold and clean and stiff-as-a-board, though not light-as-a-feather. The Roths surrendered her to the morgue, which then held onto the body during a slow and meandering sheriff's investigation into possible grave tampering, and thirty days later the coroner Dr. Arnold was found dead in her office, looking just as wretched as Mr. Wolf, and Danielle was gone again.

By the time Danielle showed up on the floor of the Neumanns' lemon-fresh kitchen, people had figured out what was going on. There was a four-hour town meeting for the grown-ups in the high school auditorium, and the older kids watched the younger ones over pizza and candy, by turns scared and excited because they were finally getting a taste of true adults-only Emergency. Tegan Sauer had just read *The Giver* and was sure they were on the verge of undergoing a terrible communal transformation from which she and her brother Emory would have to rescue everyone.

"So what are we going to do?" Emory asked when their mother came home from the meeting, looking exhausted and sniffly in her oversized all-weather jacket.

"We're going to share the burden," their mother said, filling a glass of water so she could take her usual clatter of pills. "Everything's going to be fine."

"What do you mean, share the burden?"

"We're all going to chip in and take in Danielle for a month."

Upset worked its way into Emory's face. "It's not our fault that she killed herself, that was Jon Richter and Matty Böhm. Everybody knows that." Those two were always in and out of school, taking days off to talk to their lawyers, trying to settle with Danielle's family out-of-court. Their neighbor who sometimes drove their mother to work after heavy snowstorms said that the case against the two boys was so weak that they never would have been able to convict them in criminal court, and if Danielle hadn't killed herself there would have been no civil suit either. *It's really sad, but they shouldn't have to pay just because she was unbalanced,* he said. *There's a lot of pressure on young girls to be popular these days,* he added, looking at Tegan meaningfully, as if to tell her not to follow in those footsteps, to stay good and sweet.

"Because we're not that kind of town," said their mother. "Besides, this way it'll be under control, not some random . . . freak accident." She had been friends with Dr. Arnold since their father died in a random freak accident on an icy road on Valentine's Day. The two women used to go out on the back porch to drink wine, and their mother usually ended up crying.

"So we all have to live with a corpse for a month? One that can apparently *kill us?*"

"No one's going to die, I told you," their mother said, shutting off the kitchen light. In the dark she was just another pillar in a Roman temple. "That's why we're doing this, so nobody dies. Now upstairs, both of you. Chop, chop."

Tegan had that stuck in her head until dawn: the murder-corpse going *Chop chop.*

"She needs to have her revenge," said Gabby Schultz, as they watched Amy Neumann eat carrot sticks across the cafeteria. The body was staying with the Neumanns through the end of the month, and Amy Neumann had already been guaranteed a passing grade for the quarter. "You know she's doing this because her spirit is so angry."

"What do you think it's like, having her body in the house with you? Isn't she decaying?"

"Ask Amy," said Gabby, and just then Amy Neumann turned her head and stared at them with shiny blue eyes like frozen ponds. Immediately, they closed their mouths.

Everyone was holding their breath for the Neumanns to die before their 30th day with the body, but they didn't. The funeral home came to pick up the body in the only hearse in Iram's Mill and drove Danielle to her next stop: the Franke newlyweds, who lived out by the long-closed lumber factory and had so little room that they had to put her coffin in their would-be nursery. Amy Neumann started laughing again, but she also had some choice words for the boys of Iram's Mill that she shared during a Halloween sleepover.

"It wasn't just Jon and Matty," Amy whispered. "There were other boys at that party."

The other seventh-grade girls leaned in hard. "Who?" they asked, but Amy just shrugged.

"She didn't say who."

The thought of other boys terrified Tegan. She had reconciled herself with the thought of Jon and Matty, two senior football players with abrasive laughs and the tendency to sneer, raping a sixteen-year-old girl at a party. She knew Emory was scared of Jon and Matty because they were in charge of hazing the younger players and Emory once came home from one of their parties drunk and bleeding and covered in bruises. She could imagine Jon and Matty being bad. But how much *bad* could one town have? She was left scrutinizing every house on her newspaper route, wondering, *was it someone here?* What about Gabby's stepbrother? What about Emory's friends? What about Emory?

"Did you know Danielle Haas?" she asked him while they were playing Call of Duty on one of the few nights he didn't have football practice. Since Jon had gotten kicked off the team, Emory had moved up on the roster, even earned a little bit of playing time.

"Kind of," he said. "But not really. She was a year older than me."

"Were you at that party? Did you see what happened?"

Emory stared at her. "What are you saying? You think I did something to her?"

Tegan couldn't look at him. She just kept firing and reloading, firing and reloading.

"You know me, Tigger. You know I wouldn't do that. Dad would probably come back from the dead to kill me if I did." He made a little scoffing sound, and Tegan giggled despite how morbid it was. It was nice to think of it that way, like their father was just suspended in extended hibernation mode, and if he got upset enough, he would come back and fix things.

After the Frankes had their month with Danielle the funeral home took her to the widow Norma Stein, who lived alone. Gabby joked that maybe Norma liked having someone around, even if she was dead. Word had it that Norma was buying twice her normal groceries, cooking elaborate dinners for the corpse, even buying Danielle new dresses. It would have been funny if it wasn't so sad. Anyway, Gabby turned out to be right, because on Norma's 29th day with Danielle she locked the doors and boarded up the windows and wouldn't let anyone in. By the time the fire truck came and broke down the door, Norma was dead, and Danielle was gone.

"Well, Mrs. Stein was very sick," said Tegan's mother. "And very lonely." And she let out an enormous sigh, because she was also sick and lonely, and because Tegan couldn't do anything about any of these things, she just took her bike and pushed it to supersonic speeds, pushed it past Tinker Park, past the town limits, pushed it to the moon.

It was another two years before Danielle came to stay with the Sauers. After she killed Norma she was gone for three months, and the First Shepherd Church had just held a triumphant sermon likening Iram's Mill to some sinful Biblical city that had begged for forgiveness and been spared God's wrath when Danielle showed up again, this time in the mayor's bedroom. After that the churches stopped fighting it— God works in mysterious ways, and all that—and the mayor released a statement on the perils of bullying, claiming it was up to the town to make sure neither Danielle's "beautiful smile" nor her "very impor-tant" message were forgotten. He didn't mention Jon Richter or Matty Böhm or the cops or the courts; that was water under the bridge.

Danielle arrived in a coffin, but Tegan snuck a peek at her on her second night in the laundry room. Even two years after death she was perfectly preserved. With her glossy black ringlets and her milk-white skin, she looked like Snow White. She was pretty. Only her nails were out of control: long witchy talons, looking sharp enough to scrape. Staring at her filled Tegan's head with a gentle but insistent buzz, like a cloud of gnats near a summer lake. Before she knew it the sky was turning light and her mother was banging around upstairs, and Tegan had spent the entire night with Danielle. She didn't even remember how she ended up with her hand on Danielle's bony shoulder, as if trying to console a friend having a nightmare.

"That's totally creepy, Tigger," Emory said as they drove to school. He was a senior now, and thought he knew a lot about the world. "The body might have diseases on it, you know."

"Is that what you said about her, when she was still alive? That she was diseased? Because she was a slut, she was diseased?"

Emory sighed. "Jesus, Tig. I told you I didn't really know her." They stopped at a light and some of his teammates pulled up next to him, revving their Mustang's engine, teasing him for not boning Sara Klein at the party last weekend when she was *soooo* hammered and *soooo* begging for it, yelling that they wanted to race down Jefferson Street—*or are you a pussy?*

"Takes one to know one, fuckhead," Emory yelled back, and they guffawed, and it was all in good fun, because they had each other's backs and they were brothers-in-arms and Sara Klein was nothing but a piece of ass, something between a one and a ten, some kind of farm animal. Tegan wasn't born yesterday. She knew what she was becoming.

Emory saw her clenching her stomach in pain and asked if she was okay. "Those guys are losers," he added. "They're nothing. You know that."

"They're your friends," she said.

"I don't get to pick my teammates," he said, but of course that was a lie, because he could have chosen not to be their teammate, but everyone said Emory was too good, and a positive influence on the team, and talent shouldn't be wasted, and maybe he could even get a scholarship somewhere, maybe. She had been to his games; she had seen the love that the town showered on him when he completed a touchdown pass, as if he had just invented the cure for cancer. Gabby said that he was adorable, and Tegan wondered if Danielle had ever innocently sat on the bleachers with a bag of popcorn thinking Jon Richter was so adorable, Jonny the Football Hero.

That day she got into a fight with Kevin Roth because he was always kicking her chair in Computer Lab. He called her a dyke and she called him a loser, the way Emory's teammates were losers, and he kept saying *dyke dyke dyke* until she was forced to deny it just to make him stop. The incompetent teacher finally called for order, but during passing period Kevin yelled that the only way she could prove she wasn't a dyke was if she came over and sucked him off. Before Tegan could respond—that she would bite it off if she got the chance—Emory was right there, slamming Kevin into a locker, saying *if you ever talk to her like that again I'm gonna make sure you never talk again, maggot.* Only then, with his sneakers dangling a full foot off the floor, did Tegan realize how small Kevin was.

"It's awesome you have him to protect you," Gabby said jealously, and she was right.

Emory was given in-school-suspension for attacking a freshman, but he never whined, never blamed Tegan. She thanked him for standing up for her and he said glumly that he shouldn't have had to in the first place. "It's always the fucking shrimps that talk the most shit," he said. Her mother wasn't mad at Emory either. "You shouldn't be so hard on your brother," she said to Tegan. "He's one of the good ones, you know."

That night she couldn't sleep because she kept hearing someone walk around downstairs, well past the time that her mother's meds would have knocked her out, walking around and scratching the walls—then she blinked, and Danielle was standing, no, swaying in the doorway with her hideously long nails, whispering *come on Tigger I want to show you something.*

The rest of the month's days and nights and conversations blurred together like water circling a drain that was death: the guttural tunnel through which we all must travel, past stars and moons and planets, into the abyss that takes us apart. The body is nothing. Our world is nothing. But there are other things that linger. And those things grow teeth out there in the dark.

When the funeral home came to take Danielle away, Tegan actually cried a little. Watching her get loaded up like cargo was painful, and it got even worse when she heard what happened to Danielle at the next house she went to. Bill Lang turned out to be a necrophile. His wife claimed to have no idea. Tegan felt like she'd shipped Danielle off to be raped again. The Langs were barred from taking any future rotations in the communal burden—*geez I guess we should all be getting it on with her,* the boys at school chortled—but it didn't matter, because the Langs moved away.

Two more years passed and things took a bad turn for the Sauers. Emory hurt his knee on the field during his freshman year of college and lost his athletic scholarship when it failed to heal right. Their mother's fibromyalgia worsened and she had to cut her hours in half. Tegan was now the age that Danielle had been when she committed suicide, and running with a rough crowd. It seemed serendipitous that Emory had to drop out of school and move home, as if to fix things. He was looking more and more like his father. The town was happy to help out the hero who'd brought home a state championship, and in no time he had a job at the nursing home.

Tegan alone saw the overwhelming sadness in his eyes. It seemed to have gotten worse while he was away. "You don't need football," she told him, but he said that wasn't it. For the first time she could remember, he asked about Danielle.

Danielle had taken another life, but she was still hungry. Harvey Peters, a God-fearing man, strongly felt that the town should not negotiate with terrorists and that *we have all repented more than enough,* and so he tried to burn Danielle, then chop her up, and finally dissolve her in acid. Nothing worked, and Tegan figured it was no coincidence that Harvey—or rather, Harvey's plastic sports watch—was found in his own acid bath. "Karma, baby," as she told Emory.

"She's never going to stop," he said. "I guess I don't blame her. It's not like . . . "

Her head shot up. "What?"

"It's not like we ever stopped talking about it. Until she was dead."

Tegan relayed this information to her new clique as they sat in the woods on the outskirts of town, passing around a flask of Old Crow. "I knew it, man," said Amy Neumann, who was a gothabilly now. "Those fuckers took pictures. They took videos. And they passed that shit around. Probably everybody at that whole high school saw the evidence."

"It wasn't just boys," said Kit Arnold, the former coroner's kid. "Girls did it too."

"Whatever," said Amy, flicking her wrist. "My point is: what if she doesn't want us passing her around forever? What if she really is just trying to kill us all and this stupid burden-sharing, awareness-raising thing just keeps getting in her way? We should all be making like Norma Stein and treating this like the sign from God that it is. She's a missile. An atomic bomb."

"We should help her," said Zach Zimmermann, who had successfully flunked out of the military boot camp his stepfather put him in. "Help her cross that finish line."

Eventually they decided to weaponize her curse by hiding her in Tinker Park, which was where everyone hung out all summer with their pie contests and their picnics and their little league baseball. The idea of her mother and brother dying in an undeserved nuclear blast grieved Tegan, but she soon realized that her mother never made it out of the driveway let alone to Tinker Park, and that Emory was doing double shifts every day at Whispering Pines.

"Since when do you dye your hair black?" Emory said, stirring dinner. "And why are you hanging with those weirdos? What happened to Gabby Schultz?"

"Gabby's dating one of you losers now," Tegan said, with a bruised note in her voice. She resentfully pulled her hair back into a ponytail. "And I'm not some cheerleader princess."

Zach's family was up next in the rotation, so he bundled the body into his van with Kit and Amy's help and they drove it to Tinker Park in the middle of the night. Tegan had volunteered to be the getaway driver at first, but then she thought about college and chickened out. Amy called her a poser pussy and Zach said she'd better not tell, so she conceded to be the look-out perched on top of the playground fort tower. She watched for headlights and dogs and out of the corner of her eye watched as Danielle, looking like a large glow worm in her white sheet, was lowered into a poorly-dug hole. Even after the others scattered, Tegan stayed at her post, listening to owl hoots, half-expecting the dirt to start shifting and Danielle's hand to struggle out by her long nails.

"Don't you just want to stop?" she whispered, gripping the cold, oily bars. "Be at peace?"

Wind passed through trees like big water crashing, and she understood: there is no peace.

Zach's mother and stepfather freaked out when they realized Danielle was gone. She really was a weapon of mass destruction, because the cops and the firemen and the neighborhood watch searched every house, interviewed every family. *It's very important we find her,* they said, *it's possible somebody could get hurt.* Amy and Zach laughed about it at the 24/7 McDonald's, knowing everyone was still going to the now-toxic public lands of Tinker Park, crawling just a little bit closer to their end. Kit didn't laugh—he was just mad.

"My mom didn't do shit to make Danielle off herself," he said. "My mom was innocent. At least this way *some* of the people who actually bullied her will pay." He slurped his Hi-C. "I gotta say, for a guided missile, the bitch has terrible aim."

"I don't think you can aim very well once you're dead," said Tegan.

"I don't think you care," added Amy. "Shit! I feel dead right now."

But then they brought in police dogs attuned to the scent of Danielle's old hairbrush to search Tinker Park, and one of the German shepherds dug up Danielle's shallow grave before running away, whimpering the way dogs do when they come across a much larger predator—at least according to Officer Franke, who had hunted bears in Alaska. Tegan lovingly imagined Danielle as a giant bear, romping over snowy hills, chasing villagers through the tundra.

Zach took the fall for everything and was shipped off to a new military boot camp, a "wilderness experience" in the Black Hills. Supposedly he became a Satanist there. Amy blamed Tegan for how it all went down and never spoke more than five words to her again. But now all of Iram's Mill saw Danielle for the loaded gun that she was. After Jamie Walter killed Sara Klein in a drunk driving accident, Sara's father waited eight months until Jamie had to take in Danielle and then kidnapped both of them on Day 29. He turned himself in on Day 31, having watched Danielle rise like Lazarus and slowly slide toward a bound, drugged Jamie.

"Wonder how she killed him," Tegan said as she and Emory watched Mr. Klein being led away on the evening news. Mr. Klein was the only person who had ever seen Danielle's powers at work, and he looked catatonic. No, more than that. He looked *hushed,* like all the irrelevant noise that had been the building blocks of his existence had been subdued by . . . something.

"Massive retaliatory strike," Emory replied, lifting the bottle to his lips. In the back corner of the house, their restless mother coughed.

Tegan got a job as a waitress at Sparrow's Bar and Grill during her senior year of high school to pay for things like college application fees, and that was how she met Mike Bergman, who everyone called Pony. Mike was one of Emory's ex-teammates, and after he learned her last name, he claimed to recognize her from the linoleum hallways of Iram's Mill High School.

"Yeah, yeah, you were friends with Brittany Sommer right?" he said.

"Not really," she said, trying to remember if he had ever been to the house with Emory.

"Aw no? Well, that's just as well. She's a bitch anyway." She smiled a little, because Brittany Sommer was indeed the kind of boss-bitch everyone had to pretend to like. "Say, how's Mr. Goody Goody Two Shoes doing? How come he never comes out these days?"

It was odd to think of Emory as a Goody-Goody; he was sullen, impatient, drinking when he wasn't working. "My mom's real sick, can't work much anymore. Em's gotta work a lot."

"Yeah, I hear he's changing bedpans." He wrinkled his nose like a rabbit. "Must suck, I'm sorry."

He got her to give him her number, and then he showed up on St. Patrick's Day when everything was a mess of broken bottles and green food dye and kept pushing her to drink with his crew. They were chanting *Tee-gun Tee-gun Tee-gun* and she was outdrinking the older girls with their trying-too-hard eyeliner and she wanted to outdrink the guys too, she wanted to keep pace with Pony Bergman to show how fucking badass she was. Then sometime later, sometime after, they were outside and he wanted to give her a ride home and she was saying she would walk, don't touch her, she would walk, and he was getting all, *oh come on, Sauer, don't be such a fucking cock tease!* and she was throwing up in the parking lot and one of the older girls who smelled like cigarette-apples was holding her hair back while Pony was saying *fucking trailer trash* and another one of the older girls was shouting into the void, "Did somebody call Emory?"

She woke up in a polyester backseat and immediately thrashed herself upright, but it was Emory's truck, and he was driving through what was now rain. He hissed at her to lie down.

"I'm sorry, Em," she tried saying, but he was so mad he couldn't hear her. She passed out to the sound of him muttering profanities to himself like bullets, and had a bunch of dreams she wasn't sure were dreams of Danielle lying on the floor of the truck, grinning up at her with eyes like black marbles.

Tegan felt too sick to move for most of the next day, finally stumbling out of bed sometime between three and four in the afternoon. Emory was sitting on the couch staring at the television that he hadn't turned on, with a beer he hadn't opened in his hand. Tegan saw herself in the television's black mirror as she crossed behind him on her way to the sink, where she ran the water extra cold. She needed something to cauterize the shame.

"I have to talk to you," Emory said, his voice so flat and steady it didn't seem to be his.

Water cooled the taste of burning garbage in her throat, though she could barely keep it down. "I said I'm sorry. You didn't have to get me. I could have walked home."

"I have to tell you something."

And in that instant, the haze lifted and the darkness withdrew and it was as if all of God's angels and fallen angels had landed on Earth to announce with trumpets the triumphant arrival of *The Truth.* And for the first time since she first heard that a girl in high school had committed suicide thirty days after being gang-raped at a party, she realized that The Truth wasn't something she wanted to hear after all. *Chop chop*, said Danielle. *I want to show you something.*

She actually found herself saying, "wait, wait," but the distant screeching of fingernails scraping against drywall canceled out her voice.

Emory didn't turn his head. "I was there. At the party. In the room. I was taking the video." Then he sucked in a deep, ragged breath that was halfway to a sob and added, finally spinning around, "But I promise I didn't touch her!" But by then it was too late, and Tegan was already on the floor, her hands locking behind her head as if in a falling airplane.

"I was a stupid kid, I made a mistake . . . " *Brace, brace, brace! Heads down, stay down!* "Jon and Matty told me to film it and I didn't know how to say no . . . " *Brace for impact!*

"Don't touch me," she whispered as his shadow approached.

"I'm so sorry, Tigger. I fucked up." He let out a little moan and she could tell that he was in pain and that only made everything that much worse. "I didn't know how to tell you."

But the sin wasn't hers to forgive, so instead he had just ended everything.

Tegan decided to attend the most faraway college she got into. She stopped speaking to Emory—no matter how much her mother begged—and she took to cycling again, hard and fast and wicked, and leaving yellow roses on Danielle's empty grave. She told the ghost that they could switch places, if she wanted. Danielle's mother was the only other person that ever came to the gravesite, and she left things that she believed her daughter would have wanted: a blank journal and a fountain pen, her stuffed rabbit, her violin, a favorite scarf. Then she would sit for hours on a nearby stone bench in a mismatched jumble of clothes, and sometimes she would give Tegan a mint from the local Italian restaurant, of which she seemed to have an endless supply.

"Dani wouldn't wish harm on anyone," Mrs. Haas said. "That thing haunting this town . . . it isn't her. It might look like her. It might have taken her body. But Dani wouldn't do this." She meant the five deaths that had followed Danielle down the great universal drain: Mr. Wolf, Dr. Arnold, Norma Stein, Harvey Peters, Jamie Walters. But there had been other deaths too, other calamities both undocumented and incidental: divorces, miscarriages, addictions.

"What do you think it is, then?" Tegan asked.

"Their guilt," said Mrs. Haas, widening her eyes as if it was the most obvious answer in the world. She was looking over the crests of the headstones at clouds roiling like sea serpents. "When I was a little girl there was a monster in the lake near where I lived. Lake Bodéwadmi. My grandparents used to say that it wasn't conjured up from the tears of the families that had lost someone in that lake, but from the tears of the families that had never known such a loss."

Then she popped a mint in her mouth and tightened her scarf under her chin and shambled away.

If Danielle Haas really didn't want to be forgotten, she succeeded. Her message spread far and wide. Amy Neumann moved to Herrod City and showed a collection of oil paintings called *Long Live the Queen,* substituting Danielle's face into iconic images of famous queens: Elizabeth I, Antoinette, Victoria, Hatshepsut. Brittany Sommer started a community mentorship program through her sorority called Danielle's Angels and franchised it around the country. Kit Arnold wrote a well-received memoir dedicated to his mother called *The Girl in the Morgue.*

The New York Times came and did a story on Iram's Mill and the town's "unique manifestation of collective guilt," though it ended up implying that they were all insane, and when *20/20* came calling, the mayor said no. Religious groups came to investigate Danielle as an incorruptible, but her coffin would seal shut whenever they tried to see her. Eventually the town established a memorial in Tinker Park, a six-foot-tall granite statue of a young girl releasing a dove. "Dani loved this town," Mrs. Haas said at the unveiling ceremony, eyes sparkling with happy tears, but for everyone else hers was a smothering blanket, a rib-crushing embrace.

Tegan was assisting a psychological study on conformity and the "cruelty contagion"—her professor nicknamed it Asch II Milgram, but she privately called it The Danielle Project. She had not been home for four years; she had spent her breaks reading Hannah Arendt and John Rawls in silent dorms. But then funding for Asch II Milgram got pulled, and she got an email from Gabby saying that her family was up next on the Danielle rotation, and as everybody in Iram's Mill knew, families had to come together to care for Danielle. *Danielle is the force that gives us meaning,* Tegan wrote in her diary as she curled on a window seat of a Greyhound, groggy in the half-light, *Danielle is the reason for the season.*

Iram's Mill seemed to have shrunk, hardened like vines freezing into brick. She expected to see their surly old neighbor sitting in his lawn chair, yelling, *how could you leave your poor mother?*—but his house was dark, and a for-sale sign was staked into the dead grass.

"He kicked the bucket a couple months ago after a turn with Danielle. One time he came over at one a.m., saying she was trying to scratch his eyes out. There ought to be an age limit."

Emory was standing on the front step. He looked gaunt, at least for the former Johnny Football Hero, but was still wearing a faded shirt that marked him PROPERTY OF IRAM'S MILL HIGH SCHOOL ATHLETIC DEPARTMENT. She was surprised that the town hadn't taken better care of him. But he had never tried to ride his reputation, and now there were younger boys, tawny and tall, who could throw balls and win games and bring glory.

"Didn't anybody go and stay with him?" she asked.

"I did. She didn't kill him. He died after." He tilted his head. "It's good to see you."

Danielle arrived the next day, like a Christmas package from a long-lost relative. They put her in the living room and lit candles and dusted her coffin regularly. It was important to be respectful.

Tegan managed to keep a clinical distance from her family at first, but then their mother fell on a patch of ice and broke her femur, and as she slept on morphine in the backseat of Emory's truck, Emory told Tegan about a dream. "I'm trying to teach you how to drive a stick. And then we start fighting, and you get mad and jump out of the car. So I get out and I start chasing you, but you're running so damn fast I can't ever catch you. Then suddenly I look around and I realize I'm in the middle of the ocean, and I can't even see the land, and I always get this thought like, if I just dive to the bottom I'll find the road again. Of course I never do."

Tegan had had enough, by then, of conversations-not-had and questions-not-answered. "Do you ever see her?" she asked. Tegan dreamt about Danielle once a month. Usually she would just walk into a dream about something else—rescuing drowning kittens, running away from an active shooter—and just end it, the way a lightning storm might fry a television.

"She's usually waiting for me down below." He leaned back toward the headrest, drumming his fingers against the wheel. "I'm sure that's how it'll all end, sooner or later."

A sudden night chill wafted into the truck. "Whatever happened to Jon and Matty?"

But Danielle operated in a world without institutions, without human concepts of justice or even time. Of course humans still tried to exert their rules; what else but ritual could keep terror at bay? "Nothing? They moved away a long time ago. We're not exactly friends."

They passed a group of men dragging someone out of Sparrow's and into a red pick-up truck. Emory slowed down; he couldn't drive past anything anymore. Tegan caught a glimpse of the unfortunate, lingering on the bloody edge of unconsciousness. It was Kevin Roth. *Dyke dyke dyke* ping-ponged between her ears. Pony Bergman climbed in after him with a butcher's focused enthusiasm and noticed Emory's truck idling like an uncertain child in the next lane. "Hey, Sauer," Pony said. "Tegan, we thought you died."

Tegan mashed her back against the seat, trying to make herself small. Emory shouted across her body, "What are you guys doing?"

"Giving Pervy McRapist here his just desserts! Don't want another *Danielle* on the loose!" Pony looked up, grinned. "Wanna come?"

Emory rolled up the window and drove away. They called the cops, though Officer Franke didn't sound like he was paying attention, and Emory doubted anything would be done until after it was over. Kevin had roofied a girl in high school, supposedly—no one knew who, but everyone was sure something had happened. *It's Kevin Roth,* as their mother said, and that was enough. Hunters found his body in the woods a few days later, his face looking like frozen grapefruit pulp.

It was a good month, otherwise. Danielle kept her manifestations to a minimum—mostly just creaks and shadows—and they managed to get their mother out of bed and into the car to tour the town's gaudy Christmas lights and hokey glowing inflatables to the shaky soundtrack of the First Shepherd Church's Christmas Eve service. Their mother fell asleep listening to Tegan and Emory argue over gin rummy and she was smiling, the fire lighting up her face.

And then came the storm. It took the town by surprise: no one even had time to buy supplies. It was forecasted to taper off on the morning of Day 29 with Danielle but then it didn't: it got worse. They lost power and they didn't have a ham radio, just cell phones with dying batteries, and although their mother insisted that someone would be along to pick up Danielle, that there was some kind of emergency plan, no one ever did. The drifts blocked their door and made the street where Emory had indeed taught Tegan how to drive a stick shift a churning white sea. They hadn't had a storm that bad since the Valentine's Day Ice Storm that killed their father, though nobody wanted to say it; Emory was the man of the house now, and he was trembling.

"We have to get her out of here." Emory whispered. He pointed the flashlight at Danielle's coffin. "It'll be thirty days at eight." He pointed the flashlight at his watch. "It's four."

"And take her where? The Voigts are in Utah. Half the houses on this street are empty."

"The Engels down the street. But we have to start digging."

They dug. They dug with spatulas and the fireplace shovel, though snow kept falling and all the empty houses stood dark and silent as giant tombstones around them. Tegan lost track of time and then suddenly Emory was shaking her, yelling, "I'm gonna go back to get her! Keep digging!" As he staggered back to the house she realized that it had to be close to eight—he had to be scared of leaving Danielle in the house with their mother—and a surge of panic-fueled adrenaline pushed Tegan into a frenzy, screaming at her arms to swivel faster, to burn less. By the time Emory came back with Danielle wrapped in a quilt they were still two houses away, and the Engels' house was dark. Tegan screamed until she felt something in her vocal chords snap.

Emory squeezed her shoulder. "You gotta go now! Go back to the house!"

Her arms kept moving like pinwheels. "Shut up. Shut up. Just keep digging."

"Tegan!" He wrested the fireplace shovel away from her. "You need to go!"

Behind him, Danielle was a still-silent lump on the ground, her face obscured by the quilt, but her black hair was swirling free in the wind. The strands were floating, in fact, as if she was underwater instead of buried in a blizzard, as if the body itself was brimming with energy from another plane. Not for the first time, Tegan wondered where human spirits go after death.

"I can't leave you like this," she whispered, though her hands were shaking so much that she wasn't sure they'd be able to hold a shovel if she had one.

"Yes, you can," said Emory, and to her horror, when he gave her a push she slowly backed away. Perhaps she had simply lost the strength to actively resist. She nearly tripped over Danielle and then Emory reached down and picked the body up, urging her to *go, go.* Then he carefully hoisted Danielle's dead weight over his shoulder and kept digging—the snow flew like big globs of wet powdered sugar behind him but it was much too slow, much too little.

And then their mother's quilt shifted and the limp neck stiffened and the dangling head started to lift. When black eyes emerged out of an icy face and fixed upon Tegan, she let out an involuntary cry. She heard Emory yelling, "No, no, no!", saw him falling on his back as Danielle tried to clamber over him, but all she could feel was her heart slowing to big, soft wallops the longer Danielle looked at her, because Danielle was the abyss. Her mouth and eyes were holes in a weak veil that separated this vile world from the even more predatory one that comes after. She had scratched them out herself. She wanted them to see. She wanted them to know.

I want to show you something, Danielle was saying, and Tegan was beginning to see—her heart pinched as she saw her father wandering in that abyss, a blind beggar pawing at the storm—but Emory never let Danielle come any closer. "No," he said to her, over and over. "No, you look at me. Look at me! I'll carry your burden. I'm enough. I can do it. I can take it."

The abyss vanished. She saw Emory at one of his old games, running alone in the backfield with the ball in his hand, looking desperately for a receiver as the roar of the frightened crowd swelled, finally lobbing it up because time had run out, *Hail Mary, Full of Grace*—and then she opened her eyes. The crumbling snow-ditch was still dark—the Engels never did turn on their lights—but by Emory's flashlight she could see that Danielle was now prying open her brother's mouth, forcing her hand down his throat, starting with the nails and then the knuckles and then the elbow and then the shoulder, and finally folding up like a little bird so she could burrow the rest of her way in, finding the spaces inside him to fill—the bones to wrap around, the skin to slide under, the muscles to tear into and spread apart. All these things fade.

But other things last. Mostly, the memory of watching Emory weep beneath the stalactite of his own mortality, his own weakness. Her brave big brother. She had never seen him cry before.

PAUL
TREMBLAY

Something
About
Birds

THE NEW DARK REVIEW PRESENTS "SOMETHING
ABOUT WILLIAM WHEATLEY: AN INTERVIEW WITH WIL-
LIAM WHEATLEY BY BENJAMIN D. PIOTROSKWI

W ILLIAM WHEATLEY'S *THE ARTIST STARVE* IS A
collection of five loosely interconnected novelettes and novellas published in 1971 by University of Massachusetts Press (the book having
won its Juniper Prize for Fiction). In an era that certainly pre-dated
usage of YA as a marketing category, his stories were from the POV of
young adults, ranging from the fourteen-year-old Maggie Holtz who
runs away from home (taking her six-year-old brother Thomas into
the local woods) during the twelve days of the Cuban Missile Crisis, to
the last story, a near-future extrapolation of the Vietnam War having
continued into the year 1980, the draft age dropped to sixteen, and an
exhausted and radiation-sick platoon of teenagers conspires to kill the
increasingly unhinged Sergeant Thomas Holtz. *The Artist Starve* was
a prescient and visceral (if not too earnest) book embracing chaotic
social and global politics of the early 1970's. An unexpected critical
and commercial smash, particularly on college campuses, *The Artist
Starve* was one of three books forwarded to the Pulitzer Prize Board,
who ultimately decided no award for the year 1971. That *The Artist
Starve* is largely forgotten whereas the last short story he ever wrote,
"Something About Birds," oft-reprinted and first published in a DIY
zine called *Steam* in 1977 continues to stir debate and win admirers
within the horror/weird fiction community is an irony that is not lost
upon the avuncular, seventy-five year old Wheatley.

BP: Thank you for agreeing to this interview, Mr. Wheatley.

WW: The pleasure is all mine, Benjamin.

BP: Before we discuss "Something About Birds," which is my all time favorite short story, by the way—

WW: You're too kind. Thank you.

BP: I wanted to ask if *The Artist Starve* is going to be reprinted. I've heard rumors.

WW: You have? Well, that would be news to me. While I suppose it would be nice to have your work rediscovered by a new generation, I'm not holding my breath, nor am I actively seeking to get the book back in print. It already served its purpose. It was an important book when it came out, I think, but it is a book very much of its time. So much so I'm afraid it wouldn't translate very well to the now.

BP: There was a considerable gap, six-years, between *The Artist Starve* and "Something About Birds." In the interim, were you working on other writing projects or projects that didn't involve writing?

WW: When you get to my age—oh that sounds terribly cliché, doesn't it? Let me rephrase: When you get to my perspective, six years doesn't seem as considerable. Point taken, however. I'll try to be brief. I will admit to some churlish, petulant behavior, as given the overwhelming response to my first book I expected the publishing industry to then roll out the red carpet to whatever it was I might've scribbled on a napkin. And maybe that would've happened had I won the Pulitzer, yes? Instead, I took the no award designation as a terrible, final judgment on my work. Silly I know, but at the risk of sounding paranoid, the *no award* announcement all but shut down further notice for the book. I spent a year or so nursing my battered ego and speaking at colleges and universities before even considering writing another story. I then spent more than two years researching the burgeoning fuel crisis and overpopulation fears. I travelled quite a bit as well: Ecuador, Peru, Japan, India, South Africa. While travelling I started bird watching, of course. Total novice, and I remain one. Anyway, I'd planned to turn my research into a novel of some sort. That book never materialized.

I never even wrote an opening paragraph. I'm not a novelist. I never was. To make a long, not all that exciting story short, upon returning home and very much travel weary, I became interested in antiquities and bought the very same antique shop that is below us now in 1976. I wrote "Something About Birds" shortly after opening the shop, thinking it might be the first story in another cycle, all stories involving birds in some way. The story itself was unlike anything I'd ever written; oblique, yes, bizarre to many, I'm sure, but somehow, it hits closer to an ineffable truth than anything else I've written. To my great disappointment, the story was summarily rejected by all of the glossy magazines and I was ignorant of the genre fiction market so I decided to allow a friend who was in a local punk band to publish it in her zine. I remain grateful and pleased that the story has had many other lives since.

BP: Speaking for all the readers who adore "Something About Birds," let me say that we'd kill for a short story cycle built around it.

WW: Oh, I've given up on writing. "Something About Birds" is a fitting conclusion to my little writing career as that story continues to do its job, Benjamin.

Mr. Wheatley says, "That went well, didn't it?"

Wheatley is shorter than Ben but not short, broad in the chest and shoulders, a wrestler's build. His skin is pallid and his dark brown eyes focused, attentive, and determined. His hair has thinned but he still has most of it, and most of it is dark, almost black. He wears a tweed sports coat, gray wool pants, plum-colored sweater vest, white shirt, a slate bow tie that presses against his throat tightly as though it were gauze being applied to a wound. He smiled throughout the interview. He is smiling now.

"You were great, Mr. Wheatley. I cannot thank you enough for the opportunity to talk you about my favorite story."

"You are too kind." Wheatley drums his fingers on the dining room table at which they are sitting, and narrows his eyes at Ben, as though trying to bring him into better focus. "Before you leave, Benjamin, I have something for you."

Ben swirls the last of his room-temperature Earl Grey tea around the bottom of his cup and decides against finishing it. Ben stands as Wheatley stands, and he checks his pocket for his phone and his recorder. "Oh, please, Mr. Wheatley, you've been more than gracious—"

"Nonsense. You are doing me a great service with the interview. It won't be but a moment. I will not take no for an answer." Wheatley continues to talk as he disappears into one of the three other rooms with closed doors that spoke out from the wheel of the impeccable and brightly lit living/dining room. The oval dining room table is the centerpiece of the space, and is made of a darkly stained wood and has a single post as thick as a telephone pole. The wall adjacent to the kitchen houses a built-in bookcase, the shelves filled to capacity, the tops perched with vases and brass candelabras. On the far wall rectangular, monolithic windows, their blue drapes pulled wide open, vault toward the height of the cathedral ceiling, their advance halted by the crown molding. The third floor view overlooks Dunham Street, and when Ben stands in front of a window he can see the red awning of Wheatley's antique shop below. The room is beautiful, smartly decorated, surely full of antiques that Ben is unable to identify; his furniture and décor experience doesn't extend beyond IKEA and his almost pathological inability to put anything together more complex than a nightstand.

Wheatley reemerges from behind a closed door. He has an envelope in one hand, and something small and strikingly red cupped in the palm of the other.

"I hope you're willing to indulge an old man's eccentricity." He pauses and looks around the room. "I thought I brought up a stash of small white paper bags. I guess I didn't. Benjamin, forgive the Swiss-cheese memory. We can get a bag on our way out if you prefer. Anyway, I'd like you to have this. Hold out your hands, please."

"What is it?"

Wheatley gently places a bird head into Ben's hands. The head is small; the size of a half-dollar coin. Its shock of red feathers is so bright, a red he's never seen, only something living could be that vivid, and for a moment Ben is not sure if he should pat the bird head and coo soothingly or spastically flip the thing out of his hands before it nips him. The head has a prominent, brown-yellow beak, proportionally thick, and as long as the length of the head from the top to its base. The beak is outlined in shorter black feathers that curl around the eyes as well. The bird's pitch black irises float in a sea of a more subdued red.

"Thank you, Mr. Wheatley. I don't know what to say. Is it? Is it real?"

"This is a Red-Headed Barbet from northern South America. Lovely creature. Its bill is described as horn-colored. It looks like a horn, doesn't it? It feeds on fruit but it also eats insects as well. Fierce little bird, one befitting your personality, I think, Benjamin."

"Wow. Thank you. I can't accept this. This is too much—"

"Nonsense. I insist." He then gives Ben an envelope. "An invitation to an all-too infrequent social gathering I host here. There will be six of us, you and I included. It's in—oh my—three days. Short notice, I know. The date, time, and instructions are inside the envelope. You must bring the Red-Headed Barbet with you, Benjamin, it is your ticket to admittance, or you will not be allowed entrance." Wheatley chuckles softly and Ben does not know whether or not he is serious.

BP: There's so much wonderful ambiguity and potential for different meanings. Let's start in the beginning, with the strange funeral procession of "Something About Birds." An adult, Mr. H_____ is presumably the father of one of the children, who slips up and calls him "Dad".

WW: Yes, of course. "It's too hot for costumes, Dad."

BP: That line is buried in a pages long stream-of-consciousness paragraph with the children excitedly describing the beautiful day and the desiccated, insect ridden body of the dead bird. It's an effective juxtaposition and wonderfully disorienting use of omniscient POV, and I have to admit, when I first read the story, I didn't see the word "Dad" there. I was surprised to find it on the second read. Many readers report having had the same experience. Did you anticipate that happening?

WW: I like when stories drop important clues in a nonchalant or non-dramatic way. That he is the father of one, possibly more of the children, and that he is simply staging this funeral, or celebration, for a bird, a beloved family pet, and all the potential strangeness and darkness is the result of the imagination of the children is one possible read. Or maybe that is all pretend too, part of the game, and Mr. H_____ is someone else entirely. I'm sorry, I'm not going to give you definitive answers, and I will purposefully lead you astray if you let me.

BP: Duly noted. Mr. H_____ leads the children into the woods behind an old, abandoned school house—

WW: Or perhaps school is only out for the summer, Benjamin.

BP: Okay, wow. I'm going to include my 'wow' in the interview, by the way. I'd like to discuss the children's names. Or the names they are given once they reach the clearing: The Admiral, The Crow, Copper, The Surveyor, and of course, poor Kittypants.

WW: Perhaps Kittypants isn't so poor after all, is he?

There is a loud knocking on Ben's apartment door at 12:35 am.

Ben lives alone in a small, one-bedroom apartment in the basement of a rundown brownstone, in a neighborhood that was supposed to be the next *it* neighborhood. The sparsely furnished apartment meets his needs but he does wish there was more natural light. There were days, particularly in the winter, when he'd stand with his face pressed against the glass of his front window, a secret behind a set of black, wrought iron bars.

Whoever is knocking continues knocking. Ben awkwardly pulls on a pair of jeans, grabs a forearm-length metal pipe that leans against his nightstand (not that he would ever use it, not that he has been in a physical altercation since fifth grade) and stalks into the combined living area/kitchen. He's hesitant to turn on the light and debates whether he should ignore the knocking or call the police.

A voice calls out from behind the thick, wooden front door. "Benjamin Piotrowsky? Please, Mr. Piotrowsky. I know it's late but we need to talk."

Ben shuffles across the room and turns on the outside light above the entrance. He peeks out his front window. There's a woman standing on his front stoop, dressed in jeans and a black, hooded sweatshirt. He does not recognize her and he is unsure of what to do. He turns on the overhead light in the living area and shouts through the door, "Do I know you? Who are you?"

"My name is Marnie, I am a friend of Mr. Wheatley, and I'm here on his behalf. Please open the door."

Somehow her identification makes perfect sense, that she is who she says she is and yes, of course, she is here because of Mr. Wheatley, yet Ben has never been more fearful for his safety. He unlocks and opens the door against his better judgment.

Marnie walks inside, shuts the door, and says, "Don't worry, I won't be long." Her movements are easy and athletic and she rests her hands on her hips. She is taller than Ben, perhaps only an inch or two under six feet. She has dark, shoulder-length hair, and eyes that aren't quite symmetrical, with her left smaller and slightly lower than her right. Her age is indeterminate, anywhere from late twenties to early forties. As someone who is self-conscious about his own youthful, child-like appearance (ruddy complexion, inability to grow even a shadow of facial hair), Ben suspects that she's older than she looks.

Ben asks, "Would you like a glass of water, or something, uh, Marnie, right?"

"No, thank you. Doing some late night plumbing?"

"What? Oh." Ben hides the pipe behind his back. "No. It's um, my little piece of security, I guess. I, um, I thought someone might be breaking in."

"Knocking on your door equates to a break in, does it?" Marnie smiles but it's a bully's smile, a politician's smile. "I'm sorry to have woken you and I will get right to the point. Mr. Wheatley doesn't appreciate you posting a picture of your admission ticket on Facebook."

Ben blinks madly, as though he was a captured spy put under the bright lamp. "I'm sorry?"

"You posted a picture of the admission ticket at 9:46 this evening. It currently has three-hundred and ten likes, eighty-two comments, and thirteen shares."

The bird head. Between bouts of transcribing the interview and ignoring calls from the restaurant (that asshole Shea was calling to swap shifts, again), Ben fawned over the bird head. He marveled at how simultaneously light and heavy it was in his palm. He spent more than an hour staging photographs of the head, intending to use one with the publication of the interview. Ben placed the bird head in the spine of an open notebook, the notebook in which he'd written notes from the interview. The head was slightly turned so that the length of the beak could be admired. The picture was too obvious and not strange enough. The rest of his photographs were studies in incongruity; the bird head in the middle of a white plate, resting in the bowl of a large spoon, entangled in the blue laces of his Chuck Taylor's, perched on top of his refrigerator, and on the windowsill framed by the black bars. He settled with a close up of the bird head on the cracked hardwood floor so its black eye, red feathers, and the horn-colored beak filled the shot. For the viewer, the bird head's size would be difficult to determine due to the lack of foreground or scale within the photograph. That was the shot. He posted it along with the text "Coming soon to The New Dark Review: Something About William Wheatley" (which he thought was endlessly clever). Of course many of his friends (were they friends, really? did the pixilated collection of pictures, avatars, and opinions never met in person even qualify as acquaintances?) within the online horror writing and fan community enthusiastically commented upon the photo. Ben sat in front of his laptop, watching the likes, comments, and shares piling up. He engaged with each comment and post share, and couldn't help but imagine the traffic this picture would bring to his *The New Dark Review*. He was aware enough to feel silly for thinking it, but he couldn't remember feeling more successful or happy.

Ben says, "Oh, right. The picture of the bird head. Jeeze, I'm sorry. I didn't know I wasn't supposed to, I mean, I didn't realize—"

Marnie: "We understand your enthusiasm for Mr. Wheatley and his work, but you didn't honestly give a second thought to sharing publicly a picture of an admission ticket to a private gathering, one hosted by someone who clearly values his privacy?"

"No, I guess I didn't. I never mentioned anything about the party, I swear, but now I feel stupid and awful." He is telling the truth; he does feel stupid and awful, but mostly because he understands that Marnie is here to ask him to take down his most popular Facebook post. "I'm so sorry for that."

"Do you always react this way when someone shares an invitation to a private party? When they share such a personal gift?"

"No. God, no. It wasn't like that. I posted it to, you know, drum up some pre-interest, um, buzz, for the interview that I'm going to publish tomorrow. A teaser, right? That's all. I don't think Mr. Wheatley realizes how much people in the horror community love 'Something About Birds' and how much they want to know about him, and, hear from him."

"Are there going to be further problems?"

"Problems?"

"Issues."

"No. I don't think so."

"You don't think so?"

"No. No problems or issues. I promise." Ben backs away unconsciously and bumps into the small island in his kitchen. He drops the pipe and it clatters to the floor.

"You will not post any more pictures on social media nor will you include the picture or any mention of the invitation and the gathering itself when you publish the interview."

"I won't. I swear."

"We'd like you to take down the photo, please."

Everything in him screams no, and wants to argue that they don't understand how much the picture will help bring eyeballs and readers to the interview, how it will help everyone involved. Instead, Ben says, "Yes, of course."

"Now, please. Take it down, and I'd like to watch you take it down."

"Yeah, okay." He pulls his phone from out of his pocket and walks toward Marnie. She watches his finger and thumb strokes as he deletes the post.

Marnie says, "Thank you. I am sorry to have disrupted your evening, Benjamin." She walks to the front door. She pauses, turns, and says, "Are you sure about accepting the invitation, Benjamin?"

"What do you mean?"

"You can give back the admission ticket to me if you don't think you can handle the responsibility. Mr. Wheatley would understand."

The thought of giving her the bird head never once crosses his mind as a possibility. "No, that's okay. I'm keeping it. I'd like to like to keep it, please, I mean. I understand why he's upset and I won't betray his trust again. I promise."

Marnie starts to talk and much of the rest of the strangely personal conversation passes like a dream.

WW: I'm well aware of the role of birds within pagan lore and that they are linked with the concept of freedom, of the ability to transcend the mundane, to leave it behind.

BP: Sounds like an apt description of weird fiction to me, Mr. Wheatley. I want you talk a little about the odd character names of the children. Sometimes I'm of the mind that the children are filling the roles of *familiars* to Mr. H_____. They are his companions, of course, and are assisting him in some task . . . a healing, perhaps, as Mr. H_____ is described as having a painful limp in the beginning of the story, a limp that doesn't seem to be there when later he follows the children into the woods.

WW: (laughs) I do love hearing all the different theories about the story.

BP: Are you laughing because I'm way off?

WW: No, not at all. I tried to build in as many interpretations as possible, and in doing so, I've been pleased to find many more interpretations that I didn't realize were there. Or I didn't consciously realize, if that makes sense. In the spirit of fair play, I will admit, for the first time, publicly, Benjamin, from where I got the childrens' names. They are named after songs from my friend, Liz's, obscure little punk band. I hope that's not a disappointment.

BP: Not at all. I think it's amazingly cool.

WW: An inside joke, yes, but the seemingly random names have taken on meaning, too. At least they have for me.

BP: Let me hit you with one more allegorical reading: I've read a fellow critic who argues there's a classical story going on among all the weirdness. She argues The Admiral, The Crow, and Kittypants specifically are playing out a syncretic version of the Horus, Osiris, and Set myth of Egypt with Mr. H_____ representing Huitzilopochtli, the bird-headed Mexican god of war. Is she onto something?

WW: The references to those cultural myths involving gods with human bodies and bird heads were not conscious on my part. But that doesn't mean they're not there. I grew up reading those stories of ancient gods and mythologies and they are a part of me as they are a part of us all, even if we don't realize it. That's the true power of story. That it can find the secrets both the writer and reader didn't know they had within themselves.

Ben doesn't wake until after 1 pm. His dreams were replays of his protracted late-night conversation with Marnie. They stood in the living area. Neither sat or made themselves more comfortable. He remembers part of their conversation going like this:
    "When did you first read 'Something About Birds?'" "Five years

ago, I think." "When did you move to the city?" "Three years ago, I think?" "You think?" "I'm sorry, it was two years ago, last September. It seems like I've been here longer. I don't know why I was confused by that question." "As an adult, have you always lived alone?" "Yes." "How many miles away do you currently live from your mother?" "I'm not sure of the exact mileage but she's in another timezone from me." "Tell me why you hate your job at the restaurant." "It's having to fake pleasantness that makes me feel both worthless and lonely." "Have you had many lovers?" "Only two. Both relationships lasted less than two months. And it's been a while, unfortunately." "What has been a while?" "Since I've had a lover, as you put it." "Have you ever held a live bird cupped in your hands and felt its fragility or had a large one perch on your arm or shoulder and felt its barely contained strength?" "No. Neither." "Would you prefer talons or beak?" "I would prefer wings." "You can't choose wings, Benjamin. Talons or beak?" "Neither? Both?" And so on.

Ben does not go into work and he doesn't call in. His phone vibrates with the agitated where-are-yous and are-you-coming-ins. He hopes that asshole Shea is being called in to cover for him. He says at his ringing phone, "*The New Dark Review* will be my job." He decides severing his already fraying economic safety line is the motive necessary to truly make a go at the career he now wants. He says, "Sink or swim," then playfully chides himself for not having a proper bird analogy instead. Isn't there a bird species that lays eggs on cliffs in or near Ireland, and the mothers push the hatchlings out of the nest and as they tumble down the side of the craggy rock they learn to fly or perish? Ben resolves to turn his own zine devoted to essays about obscure and contemporary horror and weird fiction into a career. He's not so clueless as to believe the zine will ever be able to sustain him financially, but perhaps it could elevate his name and stature within the field and parlay that into something more. He could pitch/sell ad space to publishers and research paying ebook subscription-based models. Despite himself, he fantasizes *The New Dark Review* winning publishing industry awards. With its success he could then helm an anthology of stories dedicated to Wheatley, a cycle of stories by other famous writers centered around "Something About Birds." If only he wasn't told to take down the bird head photo from his various social media platforms. He fears a real opportunity has been lost and the messages and emails asking why he took down the photo aren't helping.

Instead of following up on his revenue generating and promotional ideas for *The New Dark Review*, Ben Googles the Irish-cliff-birds and finds the guillemot chicks. They aren't kicked out of the nest. They are encouraged by calls from their father below the cliffs. And they don't fly. The chicks plummet and bounce off the rocks and if they manage to survive, they swim out to sea with their parents.

Ben transcribes the rest of the interview and publishes it. He shares the link over various platforms but the interview does not engender the same enthusiastic response the bird head photo received. He resolves to crafting a long-term campaign to promote the interview, give it a long life, one with a tail (a publishing/marketing term, of course). He'll follow up the interview with a long-form critical essay of Wheatley's work. He reads "Something About Birds" eight more times. He tacks a poster board to a wall in the living area. He creates timelines and a psychical map of the story's setting, stages the characters and creates dossiers, uses lengths of string and thread to make connections. He tacks notecards with quotes from Wheatley. He draws bird heads too.

That night there is a repeat of the knocking on his front door. Only Ben isn't sure if the knocking is real or if he's only dreaming. The knocking is lighter this time; a tapping more than a knock. He might've welcomed another visit from Marnie earlier while he was working on his new essay, but now he pulls the bed covers over his head. The tapping stops eventually.

Later there is a great wind outside, and rain, and his apartment sings with all manner of noises not unlike the beating of hundreds of wings.

WW: Well, that's the question, isn't it? It's the question the title of the story all but asks. I've always been fascinated by birds and prior to writing the story, I'd never been able to fully articulate why. Yes the story is strange, playful, perhaps macabre, and yet it really is about my love, for lack of a better term, of birds. I'm flailing around for an answer, I'm sorry. Let me try again: Our fascination with birds is more than a some dimestore, new-age, spiritual longing, more than the worst of us believing these magnificent animals serve as an avatar for our black-hearted, near-sighted souls, if we've ever had such a thing as a soul. There's this otherness about birds, isn't there? Thank goodness for that. It's as though they're in possession of knowledge totally alien to us. I don't think I'm explaining this very well, and that's why I wrote the story. The story gets at what I'm trying to say about birds better than I can now. I've always felt, as a humble observer, that the proper emotion within a bird's presence is awe. Awe is as fearsome and terrible as it is ecstatic.

Ben wakes up to his phone vibrating with more calls from the restaurant. His bedroom is dark. As far as he can tell from his cave-like confines, it is dark outside as well. Ben fumbles to turn on his nightstand lamp and the light makes everything worse. Across from the foot of his bed is his dresser. It's his dresser from childhood and the wood is scarred with careless gouges and pocked with white, tattered remnants of what were once Pokémon stickers. On top of the dresser is a bird head, and it's as large as his own head. Bigger, actually. Its coloring is the same as the Red-Headed Barbet. The red feathers, at this size, are shockingly red, as though red never existed before this grotesquely beautiful plumage. He understands the color is communication. It's a warning. A threat. So too the brown-yellow beak, which is as thick and prominent as a rhino's horn, stabbing out menacingly into his bedroom. The bird's eyes are bigger than his fists, and the black irises are ringed in more red.

He scrambles for his length of metal pipe and squeezes it tightly in both hands, holding it like a comically stubby and ineffective baseball bat. He shouts, "Who's there?" repeatedly, as though if he shouts it enough times, there will be an unequivocal answer to the query. No answer comes. He runs into the living room shouting, "Marnie?" and opens his bathroom and closet doors and finds no one. He checks the front door. It is unlocked. Did he leave it unlocked last night? He opens it with a deep sense of regret and steps out onto his empty front stoop. Outside his apartment is a different world, one crowded with brick buildings, ceaseless traffic, cars parked end-to-end for as far as he can see, and the sidewalks as rivers of pedestrians who don't know or care who he is or what has happened. Going outside is a terrible mistake and Ben goes back into his apartment and again shouts, "Who's there?"

Ben eventually stops shouting and returns to his bedroom. He circles around to the front of the dresser so as to view the bird head straight on and not in profile. Ben takes a picture with his phone and sends a private group message (photo attached) to a selection of acquaintances within the horror/weird fiction community. He tells them this new photo is not for public consumption. Within thirty minutes he receives responses ranging from "Jealous!" to "Yeah, saw yesterday's pic, but cool" to "I liked yesterday's picture better. Can you send that to me?" Not one of them commented on the head's impossible size, which has to be clear in the photo as it takes up so much of the dresser's top. Did they assume some sort of photo trickery? Did they assume the bird head in yesterday's photo (the close of up of the head on the hardwood floor) was the same size? Did this second photo resize the head they first saw in their minds by the new context? He types in response, "The head wasn't this big yesterday," but deletes it instead of sending. Ben considers posting the head-on-the-dresser photo to his various social media platforms so that Marnie would return and admonish him again, and then he could ask why she broke into his apartment and left this monstrous bird head behind. This had to be her doing.

After a lengthy inner dialogue, Ben summons the courage to pick the head up. He's careful, initially, to not touch the beak. To touch that first would be wrong, disrespectful. Dangerous. He girds himself to lift a great weight, even bending his knees, but the head is surprisingly light. That's not to say the head feels fragile. He imagines its lightness is by design so that the great bird, despite its size, would be able to fly and strike its prey quickly. With the head in his hands, he scans the dresser's top for any sign of the small head Mr. Wheatley initially gave him. He cannot find it. He assumes Marnie swapped the smaller head for this one, but he also irrationally fears that the head simply grew to this size overnight.

The feathers have a slight oily feel to them and he is careful to not inadvertently get any stuck between his fingers as he manipulates the head and turns it over, upside down. He cannot see inside the head, although it is clearly hollow. A thick forest of red feathers obscure the neck's opening and when he attempts to pull feathers back or push them aside other feathers dutifully move in to block the view. There are tantalizing glimpses of darkness between the feathers, as though the depth contained within is boundless.

He sends his right hand inside the head expecting to feel plaster, or plastic, or wire mesh perhaps, the inner workings of an intricate mask, or maybe even, impossibly, the hard bone of skull. His fingers gently explore the hidden interior perimeter, and he feels warm, moist, pliant clay, or putty, or flesh. He pulls his hand out and rubs his fingers together, and he watches his fingers, expecting to see evidence of dampness. He's talking to himself now, asking if one can see dampness, and he wipes his hand on his shorts. He's nauseous (but pleasantly so), as he imagines his fingers were moments ago exploring the insides of a wound. More boldly, he returns his hand inside the bird head. He presses against the interior walls and those walls yield to his fingers like they're made of the weakening skin of overripe fruit and vegetables. Fingertips sink deeper into the flesh of the head, and his arm shakes and wrist aches with exertion.

There's a wet sucking sound as Ben pulls his hand out. He roughly flips the head over, momentarily forgetting about the size of the great beak and its barbed tip scratches a red furrow into his forearm. He wraps his hand around the beak near its base and his fingers are too small to enclose its circumference. He attempts to separate the two halves of beak, a half-assed lion tamer prying open fearsome jaws, but they are fixed in place, closed tightly, like gritted teeth.

Ben takes the head out into the living area and gently places it on the floor. He lies down beside it and runs his fingers through its feathers, careful to not touch the beak again. If he stares hard enough, long enough, he sees himself in miniature, curled up like a field mouse, reflected in the black pools of the bird's eyes.

BP: A quick summary of the ending. Please stop me if I say anything that's inaccurate or misleading. The children, lead by The Crow and The Admiral, reappear out of the woods that Mr. H_____ had forbidden them to go into, and you describe The Admiral's fugue wonderfully: "his new self passing over his old self, as though he were an eclipse." When asked (we don't know who the speaker is, do we?) where Kittypants is, The Crow says Kittypants is still in the woods and was waiting to be found and retrieved, he didn't fly away. Someone (again, the speaker not identified) giggles and says his wings are broken. The other children erupt into sounds, chant, and song, eager to go to Kittypants. The dead bird that they had brought with them is forgotten. I love how it isn't clear if the kids have finally donned their bird masks or if they've had them on the whole time. Or perhaps they have no masks on at all. Mr. H_____ says they may leave him only after they've finished digging a hole big enough for the little one to fit inside and not ruffle any feathers. The reader is unsure if Mr. H_____ is referring to the dead bird or, in retrospect, if it's a sinister reference to Kittypants, the smallest of their party. The kids leave right away and it's not clear if they have finished digging the hole or not. Perhaps they're just going home, the funeral or celebration over, the game over. Mr. H_____ goes into the woods after them and finds his gaggle in a clearing, the setting sun throwing everything into shadow, "a living bas relief." They are leaping high into the air, arms spread out as wide as the world, and then crashing down into what is described from a distance as a pile of leaves no bigger than a curled up, sleeping child. It's a magnificent image, Mr. Wheatley, one that simultaneously brings to mind the joyous, chaotic, physical play of children and at the same time, resembles a gathering of carrion birds picking apart a carcass in a frenzy. I have to ask, is the leaf pile just a leaf pile, or is Kittypants inside?

WW: I love that you saw the buzzard imagery in that scene, Benjamin.

But, oh, I wouldn't dream of ever answering your final question, directly. But I'll play along, a little. Let me ask you this: do you prefer that Kittypants be under the pile of leaves? If so, why?

Tucked inside the envelope he received from Mr. Wheatley is a typed set of instructions. Benjamin wears black socks, an oxford shirt, and dark pants that were once partners with a double-breasted jacket. He walks twenty-three blocks northwest. He enters the darkened antique store through a back door, and from there he navigates past narrow shelving and various furniture and taxidermy staging to the stairwell that leads to the second floor apartment. He does not call out or say anyone's name. All in accordance with the instructions.

The front door to Mr. Wheatley's apartment is closed. Ben places an ear against the door, listening for other people, for their sounds, as varied as they can be. He doesn't hear anything. He cradles the bird head in his left arm and has it pressed gently against his side, the beak supported by his ribs. The head is wrapped tightly in a white sheet. The hooked beak tip threatens to rent the cloth.

Ben opens the door, steps inside the apartment, and closes the door gently behind him, and thus ends the brief set of instructions from the envelope. Benjamin removes the white cloth and holds the bird head in front of his chest like a shield.

There is no one in the living room. The curtains are drawn and three walls sconces peppered between the windows and their single bulbs give off a weak, almost sepia light. The doors to the other rooms are all closed. He walks to the circular dining room table, the one at which he sat with Mr. Wheatley only three days ago.

Ben is unsure of what he's supposed to do next. His lips and throat are dry, and he's afraid that he'll throw up if he opens his mouth to speak. Finally, he calls out: "Hello, Mr. Wheatley? It's Ben Piotrowsky."

There's no response or even a sense of movement from elsewhere inside the apartment.

"Our interview went live online already. I'm not sure if you've seen it yet, but I hope you like it. The response has been very positive so far."

Ben shuffles into the center of the room and it suddenly occurs to him that he could document everything he's experienced (including what he will experience later this evening) and add it to the interview as a bizarre, playful afterword. It's a brilliant idea and something that would only enhance his and Mr. Wheatley's reputation within the weird fiction community. Yes, he would most certainly do this and Ben imagines the online response as being more rabid than the reaction to the picture of the bird head. There will be argument and discussion as to whether the mysterious afterword is fictional or not, and if fictional, had it been written by William Wheatley himself. The interview with afterword will be a perfect extension or companion to "Something About Birds." Perhaps Ben can even convince Mr. Wheatley to co-write the afterword with him. Or, instead, pitch this idea to Mr. Wheatley not as an afterword, but as a wrap-around story, or framing device, within the interview itself. Yes, not only could this be a new story, but the beginning of a new story cycle, and Ben will be a part of it.

Ben says, "This bird head is lovely, by the way. I mean that. I assume you made it. I'm no expert but it appears to be masterful work. I'm sure there's a fascinating story behind it that we could discuss further." In the silence that follows, Ben adds, "Perhaps your friend Marnie brought it to my apartment. We talked the other night of course."

Ben's spark of new-story-cycle inspiration and surety fades in the continued silence of the apartment. Has he arrived before everyone else or is this some sort of game where the party does not begin until he chooses a door to open, and then—then what? Is this a hazing ritual? Is he to become part of their secret little group? Ben certainly hopes for the latter. Which door of the three will he open first?

Ben asks, "Am I to put the bird head on, Mr. Wheatley? Is that it?"

The very idea of being enclosed within the darkness of the bird head, his cheeks and lips and eyelids pressing against the whatever-it-is on the inside, is a horror. Yet he also wants nothing more than to put the bird head over his own, to have that great beak spill out before his eyes, a baton with which to conduct the will of others. He won't put it on, not until he's sure that is what he's supposed to do.

"What am I supposed to do now, Mr. Wheatley?"

The door to Ben's left opens and four people—two men and two women—wearing bird masks walk out. They are naked and their bodies are hairless and shaved smooth. In the dim lighting their ages are near impossible to determine. There is a crow with feathers so black its beak appears to spring forth from nothingness, an owl with feathers the color of copper and yellow eyes large enough to swallow the room, a sleek falcon with a beak partially open in an avian grin, and the fourth bird head is a cross between a peacock and a parrot with its garish blue, yellow, and green, the feathers standing high above its eyes like ancient, forbidding towers.

They fan out and walk toward Ben without speaking and without ceremony. The soles of their bare feet gently slap on the hardwood floor. The man in the brightest colored bird mask must be Mr. Wheatley (and/or Mr. H____) as there are liver spots, wrinkles, and other evidence of age on his skin, but the muscles beneath are surprisingly taut, defined.

Mr. Wheatley takes the bird head out of Ben's hands and forces it over his head. Ben breathes rapidly, as though prepping for a dive into deep water, and the feathers flitter past his eyes, an all encompassing darkness, and a warmth in the darkness, one that both suffocates and caresses, and then he can see, although not like he could see before. While the surrounding environment of the apartment dims, viewed through an ultraviolet, film-negative spectrum, the bird feathers become spectacular firework displays of colors; secret colors that he was blind to only a moment ago, colors beyond description. That Ben might never see those colors again is a sudden and great sadness. As beautiful as the bird heads are, their owners' naked human bodies, with their jiggling and swaying body parts, are ugly, weak, flawed, ill-designed, and Ben can't help but think of how he could snatch their tender bits in the vise of his beak.

The two men and women quickly remove Ben's clothes. The Crow says, "Kittypants is waiting to be found and retrieved. He didn't fly away," and they lead him across the living room and to the door from which they'd emerged. Ben is terrified that she's talking about him. He is not sure who he is, who he is supposed to be.

Through the door is a bedroom with a king-sized mattress claiming most of the space. There is no bedframe or boxspring, only the mattress on the floor. The mattress has not been made up; there are no bedcovers. There is a pile of dried leaves in the middle. Ben watches the pile closely and he believes there is a contour of a shape, of something underneath.

Ben stands at the foot of the mattress while the others move to flank the opposite sides. The lighting is different in the bedroom. Everything is darker but somehow relayed in more detail. Their masks don't look like masks. There no clear lines of demarcation between head and body, between feather and skin. Is he in fact in the presence of gods? The feather colors have darkened as well, as though they aren't feathers at all but the skin of chameleons. Ben's relief at not being the character in the leaf pile is offset with the fear that he won't ever be able to remove his own bird head.

The others whisper, titter, and twitch, as though they sense his weakness, or lack of commitment. The Crow asks, "Would you prefer talons or beak?" Her beak is mostly black, but a rough, scratchy brown shows through at the beak edges and its tip, as though the black coloring has been worn away from usage.

Ben says, "I would still prefer wings."

Something moves on the bed. Something rustles.

The voice of Mr. Wheatley says, "You cannot choose wings."

CONTRIBUTORS' NOTES

Nadia Bulkin writes scary stories about the scary world we live in, thirteen of which appear in her debut collection, *She Said Destroy* (Word Horde, 2017). Her short stories have been included in editions of *The Year's Best Weird Fiction*, *The Best Horror of the Year*, and *The Year's Best Dark Fantasy & Horror*. She has been nominated for the Shirley Jackson Award five times, including for "Live Through This." She grew up in Jakarta, Indonesia, with her Javanese father and American mother, before relocating to Lincoln, Nebraska. She has a B.A. in Political Science, an M.A. in International Affairs, and lives in Washington, D.C.

Daniel Carpenter's short fiction has been published by *Unsung Stories*, *The Irish Literary Review*, and in *Unthology*, amongst others. He hosts The Paperchain Podcast, which was longlisted in The Saboteur Awards. He lives in London.

Adam-Troy Castro made his first non-fiction sale to *SPY* magazine in 1987. His 26 books to date include four Spider-Man novels, 3 novels about his profoundly damaged far-future murder investigator Andrea Cort, and 6 middle-grade novels about the dimension-spanning adventures of young Gustav Gloom. Adam's darker short fiction for grownups is highlighted by his most recent collection, *Her Husband's Hands And Other Stories* (Prime Books). Adam's works have won the Philip K. Dick Award and the

Seiun (Japan), and have been nominated for eight Nebulas, three Stokers, two Hugos, and, internationally, the Ignotus (Spain), the Grand Prix de l'Imaginaire (France), and the Kurd-Laßwitz Preis (Germany). He lives in Florida with his wife Judi and either three or four cats, depending on what day you're counting and whether Gilbert's escaped this week.

Claire Dean's short stories have been widely published and are included in *Best British Short Stories 2011, 2014* and *2017* (Salt). *Bremen, The Unwish, Marionettes* and *Into the Penny Arcade* are published as chapbooks by Nightjar Press. Her first collection, *The Museum of Shadows and Reflections,* was published by Unsettling Wonder in 2016. She lives in the North of England with her family.

Kristi DeMeester is the author of *Beneath,* a novel published by Word Horde Publications, and *Everything That's Underneath,* a short fiction collection from Apex Books. Her short fiction has appeared in publications such as Ellen Datlow's *The Year's Best Horror* Volume 9, Stephen Jones' *Best New Horror, Year's Best Weird Fiction* Volumes 1, and 3, in addition to publications such as *Black Static, The Dark,* and several others. In her spare time, she alternates between telling people how to pronounce her last name and how to spell her first. Find her online at www.kristidemeester.com.

Brian Evenson is the author of a dozen books of fiction, most recently the story collection *A Collapse of Horses* and the novella *The Warren.* He has been a finalist six times for the Shirley Jackson Award. His novel *Last Days* won the American Library Association's award for Best Horror Novel of 2009. His novel *The Open Curtain* (Coffee House Press) was a finalist for an Edgar Award and an International Horror Guild Award. He is the recipient of three O. Henry Prizes as well as an NEA fellowship. He lives in Los Angeles and teaches in the Critical Studies Program at CalArts.

Jenni Fagan is a poet, novelist and screenwriter. She is published in eight languages, a Granta Best of Young British Novelist (once in a decade accolade) winner of Scottish Author of the Year, and on lists including IMPAC, James Tait Black, BBC Short Story Prize, Sunday Times Short Story, Encore, Desmond Elliott among others. Currently completing two novels set in Edinburgh, theatre and film adaptations for her first novel and her new poetry collection *There's a Witch in the Word Machine,* comes out in Sep 2018.

Kurt Fawver is writer of horror, weird fiction, and literature that oozes through the cracks of genre. His short fiction has previously appeared in venues such as *The Magazine of Fantasy & Science Fiction*, *Strange Aeons*, *Weird Tales*, *Vastarien*, and *Gamut*. His work has been chosen for inclusion in *Best New Horror* and *Year's Best Weird Fiction* and has been nominated for the Shirley Jackson Award. Kurt has released two collections of short stories: *Forever, in Pieces*, and *The Dissolution of Small Worlds*, as well as one novella, *Burning Witches, Burning Angels*. He's also had non-fiction published in journals such as Thinking Horror and the Journal of the Fantastic in the Arts. He lives in the apocalypse that's known as "Florida" and dreams of days touched by snow. He wishes you delightful nightmares and magical waking hours.

Brenna Gomez was the recipient of a 2017 Hedgebrook residency. Her fiction has appeared or is forthcoming in *Prairie Schooner* and *StoryQuarterly*. She received her MFA from the University of New Mexico, where she was the Editor-in-Chief of *Blue Mesa Review* and the 2015 recipient of the Hispanic Writer Award for the UNM Summer Writers' Conference in Santa Fe. Brenna is a reader for *Electric Lit's Recommended Reading*. She currently teaches composition at UNM and hosts author events at Bookworks Albuquerque.

Camilla Grudova studied literature and art history at McGill University. Her collection of short stories, The Doll's Alphabet was released in 2017. Her stories have appeared in The White Review and Granta. She is currently working on a novel and lives in Scotland.

Kathleen Kayembe is the Octavia E. Butler Scholar from Clarion's class of 2016, with short stories in *Lightspeed*, *Nightmare*, and several Best of the Year anthologies for 2017, as well as an essay in the Hugo-nominated anthology *Luminescent Threads: Connections to Octavia E. Butler*. Her work additionally appeared on the SFWA and Locus Recommended Reading Lists for 2017. She co-hosts the weekly writing podcast Write Pack Radio, runs Amherst Writers and Artists writing workshops, and, under the pen name Kaseka Nvita, writes queer romances. She currently lives in St. Louis, Missouri, with a beloved collection of fountain pens, inks, and notebooks, and never enough time to write—or read—all that she wants

Michael Kelly is the editor of *Shadows & Tall Trees*, and Series Editor of the

Year's Best Weird Fiction. His fiction has appeared in *Black Static, The Mammoth Book of Best New Horror, Weird Fiction Review,* and others. As editor he's been a finalist for the World Fantasy Award, and winner of the Shirley Jackson Award.

Joshua King is a writer and illustrator from the UK, who currently lives in London. He received his MFA in Creative Writing from Adelphi University, New York and has had short stories published in BlazeVOX journal and The Matador Review. His nonfiction has appeared in London's Litro magazine and Texas' Newfound Journal. As well as fiction, he also writes plays, which have been performed at various venues in London, and comics about monkeys and science. His writing usually centres around the isolation of rural life and the ways in which people's beliefs and deeply-held worldviews can lead them astray. It is his great pleasure to appear in the Year's Best Weird Fiction, Vol. 5.

Rebecca Kuder's stories and essays have appeared in *The Rumpus, Shadows And Tall Trees 7, Resurrection House XIII, Tiferet Journal, Lunch Ticket,* and elsewhere. Her story "The Only Flower That Matters" is forthcoming in The Book of Flowers, an anthology from Egaeus Press; "Rabbit, Cat, Girl" was included in Year's Best Weird Fiction Vol 3. For creative nonfiction, she received an Ohio Arts Council individual excellence award. Rebecca toils to put the inner critic in its place by leading creativity workshops and teaching creative writing at The Modern College of Design. She lives in Yellow Springs, Ohio, with her husband, the writer Robert Freeman Wexler, and their daughter.

Alison Littlewood's latest novel is *The Crow Garden,* a tale of obsession set amidst Victorian asylums and séance rooms. Her other novels include *The Hidden People, Path of Needles, The Unquiet House* and *A Cold Season,* which was selected for the Richard and Judy Book Club. Her short stories have been picked for several 'Year's Best' anthology series and have been gathered together in her collections *Quieter Paths* and *Five Feathered Tales.* She won the 2014 Shirley Jackson Award for Short Fiction. Alison says, "'The Entertainment Arrives' was written for an anthology celebrating the work of Ramsey Campbell, and I'd like to thank Ramsey for allowing me to use elements of the world he created in his story, 'The Entertainment.'" Alison lives with her partner Fergus in Yorkshire, England, in a house of creaking doors and crooked walls. You can visit her at www.alisonlittlewood.co.uk.

Ben Loory is the author of the collections *Stories for Nighttime and Some for the Day* and *Tales of Falling and Flying*, both from Penguin. His fables and tales have appeared in *The New Yorker, Weekly Reader's READ Magazine,* and *Fairy Tale Review*, been anthologized in *The New Voices of Fantasy* and *Best Bizarro Fiction of the Decade*, and been heard on *This American Life* and *Selected Shorts*. He is also the author of a picture book for children, *The Baseball Player and the Walrus*. Loory lives in Los Angeles and teaches short story writing at the UCLA Extension Writers' Program.

Carmen Maria Machado's debut short story collection, *Her Body and Other Parties*, was a finalist for the National Book Award, the Shirley Jackson Award, the Kirkus Prize, LA Times Book Prize Art Seidenbaum Award for First Fiction, the Dylan Thomas Prize, and the PEN/Robert W. Bingham Prize for Debut Fiction, and the winner of the Bard Fiction Prize, the Lambda Literary Award for Lesbian Fiction, and the National Book Critics Circle's John Leonard Prize. In 2018, the New York Times listed *Her Body and Other Parties* as a member of "The New Vanguard," one of "15 remarkable books by women that are shaping the way we read and write fiction in the 21st century." Her essays, fiction, and criticism have appeared in the *New Yorker*, the *New York Times, Granta, Tin House, VQR, McSweeney's Quarterly Concern, The Believer, Guernica, Best American Science Fiction & Fantasy*, and elsewhere. She is the Writer in Residence at the University of Pennsylvania and lives in Philadelphia with her wife.

Helen Marshall is a Senior Lecturer of Creative Writing and Publishing at Anglia Ruskin University in Cambridge, England. She is also the general director of the Centre for Science Fiction and Fantasy there. Her short stories have won the World Fantasy Award, the British Fantasy Award, and the Shirley Jackson Award. Her debut novel *The Migration* will be released by Random House Canada in February 2019.

Michael Mirolla describes his writing as a mix of magic realism, surrealism, speculative fiction and meta-fiction. Publications include three Bressani Prize winners: the novel *Berlin* (2010); the poetry collection *The House on 14th Avenue* (2014); and the short story collection, *Lessons in Relationship Dyads* (2016). Among his other publications: *The Ballad of Martin B*, a punk-inspired novella; three novels—*The Facility*, which features among other things a string of cloned Mussolinis; *The Giulio Metaphysics III*, a hybrid linked short stories-novel wherein a character named Giulio attempts to escape from his creator; and *Torp: The Landlord, The Husband, The Wife and The Lover,* a ménage-a-trois mystery set in 1970 Vancouver during the War Measures Act. 2017 saw the publication of the magic realist short story collection *The Photographer in Search of Death* (Exile Editions). The short story, "A Theory of Discontinuous Existence," was selected for *The Journey Prize Anthology*; and "The Sand Flea" was a Pushcart Prize nominee. Born in Italy, raised in Montreal, Michael lives in Oakville, Ontario. For more, visit his website: www.michaelmirolla.com

Ian Muneshwar is a Boston-based writer and teacher. He holds an MFA from North Carolina State University, and his fiction appears in venues such as *Clarkesworld, Strange Horizons, Liminal Stories, Gamut,* and *The Dark.* In his short fiction, Ian is interested in arthropods, queerbrown subjectivities, and the uncanny, among other things. You can find out more about his work at ianmuneshwar.com

David Peak is the author of the black metal horror novel *Corpsepaint* (Word Horde, 2018), as well as *Eyes in the Dust* (Dunhams Manor, 2016), *The Spectacle of the Void* (Schism, 2014), and *The River Through the Trees* (Blood Bound Books, 2013). His writing has been published in *Denver Quarterly, the Collagist, Electric Literature, 3:AM,* and *Black Sun Lit.* He lives in Chicago.

KL Pereira's debut short fiction collection, *'A Dream Between Two Rivers: Stories of Liminality,'* was published in 2017 by Cutlass Press. Her fiction, poetry, and nonfiction appear in Lit Hub, *LampLight, The Drum, Shimmer, Innsmouth Free Press, Mythic Delirium, Jabberwocky, Bitch,* and other publications. She's a member of the New England Horror Writers Association and has taught creative writing in high schools, libraries, domestic violence shelters, colleges and universities, and writing institutions throughout New England for over ten years. Find her online @_klpereira and klpereira.com.

Eric Schaller's debut collection of dark fiction, *Meet Me in the Middle of the Air,* was released in 2016 from Undertow Publications. His stories have appeared in various anthologies and magazines, including *The Year's Best Fantasy and Horror, Fantasy: Best of the Year, The Time Traveler's Almanac, Wilde Stories, Nightmare Magazine, Black Static,* and *The Dark.* He is a member of the Horror Writers Association and an editor, with Matthew Cheney, of the on-line magazine *The Revelator* revelatormagazine.com

Robert Shearman has written five short story collections, and between them they have won the World Fantasy Award, the Shirley Jackson Award, the Edge Hill Readers Prize, and three British Fantasy Awards. He began his career in the theatre, and was resident dramatist at the Northcott Theatre in Exeter, and regular writer for Alan Ayckbourn at the Stephen Joseph Theatre in Scarborough; his plays have won the Sunday Times Playwriting Award, the World Drama Trust Award, and the Guinness Award for Ingenuity in association with the Royal National Theatre. A regular writer for BBC Radio, his own interactive drama series The Chain Gang has won two Sony Awards. But he is probably best known for his work on Doctor Who, bringing back the Daleks for the BAFTA winning first series in an episode nominated for a Hugo Award. His latest book, *We All Hear Stories in the Dark* is to be released by PS Publishing next year.

Paul Tremblay has won the Bram Stoker, British Fantasy, and Massachusetts Book Awards and is the author of The Cabin at the End of the World, Disappearance at Devil's Rock, A Head Full of Ghosts, and the crime novels The Little Sleep and No Sleep Till Wonderland. He is currently a member of the board of directors for the Shirley Jackson Awards, and his essays and short fiction have appeared in the Los Angeles Times, Entertainment Weekly online, and numerous year's-best anthologies. He has a master's degree in mathematics and lives outside of Boston with his family.

Aron Wiesenfeld's artwork has been the subject of eight solo exhibitions in the U.S. and Europe, and has been a part of over 50 group shows. Among the publications his work has appeared are *Juxtapoz, Hi-Fructose, Art In America*, and *The Huffington Post*. His work has been in a number of museum shows, including The Long Beach Museum of Art, Bakersfield Museum of Art, and The Museum Casa Dell'Architettura in Italy. His paintings have been used for covers on dozens of books of poetry, including "The Other Sky," a collaborative book project with poet Bruce Bond. In 2014 a large monograph of his work titled "The Well" was published by IDW Press. He was recently named one of the top 100 figurative painters by Buzzfeed. Aron was born in 1972. He attended Cooper Union School of Art in New York, and Art Center College of Design in California. Four of his solo exhibitions have been at Arcadia Contemporary, and the gallery continues to represent his work.

Chavisa Woods is the author of three books of fiction, *Things to Do when*

You're Goth in the Country, The Albino Album, (both released by Seven Stories Press), and *Love Does Not Make Me Gentle or Kind* (Fly by Night Press/Autonomedia/Unbearables). Woods has been a Shirley Jackson Award nominee, and was the recipient of the Kathy Acker Award in Writing, the Cobalt Prize for Fiction, the Jerome Foundation Award for Emerging Authors (2009), and was a three-time finalist for the Lambda Literary Award for fiction. Her writing has appeared in *Tin House, Lit Hub, Electric Lit, The Evergreen Review, New York Quarterly, The Brooklyn Rail, Full Stop Magazine, Cleaver Magazine, Quaint,* and many others. Woods has appeared as a featured author at such notable venues as The Whitney Museum of American Art, City Lights Bookstore, Town Hall Seattle, The Brecht Forum, The Cervantes Institute, and St. Mark's Poetry Project.

Alligator Tree Graphics (www.alligatortreegraphics.com) is run by writer and designer Robert Freeman Wexler.

COPYRIGHT ACKNOWLEDGEMENTS

"The Convexity of Our Youth" by Kurt Fawver. First published in First published in *Looming Low*, Sam Cowan & Justin Steele, eds.

"The Rock Eater" by Ben Loory. First published in *Tales of Falling and Flying*.

"Corzo" by Brenna Gomez. First published in *Prairie Schooner Volume 91, Number 1, Spring 2017*.

"You Will Always Have Family: A Triptych" by Kathleen Kayembe. First published in *Nightmare Magazine #54*.

"Flotsam" by Daniel Carpenter. First published in *Tales from the Shadow Booth #1*, Dan Coxon, ed.

"The Possession" by Michael Mirolla. First published in *The Photographer in Search of Death*.

"Skins Smooth as Plantain, Hearts Soft as Mango" by Ian Muneshwar. First published in *The Dark #27*.

"The Unwish" by Claire Dean. First published in *The Unwish*.

"Worship Only What She Bleeds" by Kristi DeMeester. First published in *Everything That's Underneath*.

"House of Abjection" by David Peak. First published in *Nightscript III*, C.M. Muller, ed.

"The Way She is With Strangers" by Helen Marshall. First published in *Dark Cities*, Christopher Golden, ed.

"The Anteater" by Joshua King. First published in *The Matador Review*, Fall 2017.

"When Words Change the Molecular Composition of Water" by Jenni Fagan. First published in *Somesuch Stories*, 2017.

"The Entertainment Arrives" by Alison Littlewood. First published in *Darker Companions*, Scott David Aniolowski & Joseph S. Pulver Sr., eds.

"Take the Way Home That Leads Back to Sullivan Street" by Chavisa Woods. First published in *Things to Do When You're Goth in the Country*.

"Eight Bites" by Carmen Maria Machado. First published in *Gulf Coast #29.2*.

"Red Hood" by Eric Schaller. First published in *Nightmare Magazine #55*.

"Curb Day" by Rebecca Kuder. First published in *Shadows and Tall Trees, Vol. 7*, Michael Kelly, ed.

"The Narrow Escape of Zipper-Girl" by Adam-Troy Castro. First published in *Nightmare Magazine #57*.

"Disappearer" by K.L. Pereira. First published in *A Dream Between Two Rivers*.

"The Mouse Queen" by Camilla Grudova. First published in *The Doll's Alphabet*.

"The Second Door" by Brian Evenson. First published in *Looming Low*, Sam Cowan & Justin Steele, eds.

"Live Through This" by Nadia Bulkin. First published in *Looming Low*, Sam Cowan & Justin Steele, eds.

"Something About Birds" by Paul Tremblay. First published in *Black Feathers: Dark Avian Tales*, Ellen Datlow, ed.

CPSIA information can be obtained
at www.ICGtesting.com
Printed in the USA
BVHW03s1257161018
530325BV00001B/22/P